SOLOMON'S SEAL

"Whip-smart, gritty, and fascinating. Olivia Talbot is a badass, and a mother, I'd want on my side if the world went to hell. Skyla Dawn Cameron's deft characterization, complex plotting, and brutal action leaves the reader gasping for more."
—Lilith Saintcrow, *New York Times* Bestselling Author

"It's well written with a balanced blend of humor and adventure you can't deny is spellbinding."
—My World...in words and pages

DEMONS OF OBLIVION SERIES

"This not-to-be-missed release rocks from word one. Skyla Dawn Cameron writes as though she's been producing bestsellers for years."
—Bitten by Books

"Urban fantasy at its best with characters and a plot that makes it stand out from the rest of its genre."
—The Romance Reviews

"A dark and gorgeous heroine that will have you enthralled in moments."
—Bookmark Your Thoughts

"What a riot this book was! I felt like rediscovering what the genre of urban fantasy is about all over again."
—Nocturnal Book Reviews

"...fast, funny, and furious... The action and fight scenes were intense, the romance bittersweet, and it left me wanting more."

—The Romance Studio

RIVER WOLFE SERIES

"River is a powerful and new take on your typical young adult paranormal story and I absolutely loved it!"

—Bitten by Books

"...a fresh and unique take on the werewolf legend."

—Judy Bagshaw, author of *Kiss Me, Nate*

"...a terrific book, filled with unique and well-drawn characters, realistic dialogue, and a great deal of humor..."

—ParaNormal Romance Reviews

"This book is a permanent addition to my keeper shelf, and will be revisited many times in the years to come."

—Elaine Corvidae, author of *Tyrant Moon*

"...a story about love. Not just the happily-ever-after fairy tale kind, the real kind, the sort of love that takes two people and cements them together in relationships that are like lighthouses on rocky shores."

—Long and Short Reviews

SOLOMON'S
SEAL

A
LIVI TALBOT
NOVEL

Books by
Skyla Dawn Cameron

SOLOMON'S SEAL

A
LIVI TALBOT
NOVEL

SKYLA DAWN CAMERON

1st Edition: September 2016
eBook ISBN: 978-1-927966-16-7
Print ISBN: 978-1-927966-17-4

Published by Skyla Dawn Cameron
P.O. Box 1833
Campbellford ON
K0L 1L0

DEDICATION

———— ◆ ————

For the survivors.

"...and he had found in certain of his books, that whoso
should wear the seal ring of our lord
Solomon...Jinn and birds and beasts and all created things
would be bound to obey him."

—"The Queen of the Serpents"; *Arabian Nights*
translated by Sir Richard Burton

———— ♦ ————

Malo periculosam, libertatem quam quietam servitutem.
(I prefer liberty with danger to peace with slavery.)

1
WE ARE FAMILY

———◆———

THE MAN HANGING FROM HIS bound ankles over the cliff's edge hadn't been forthcoming with answers thus far.

I've always been a try again sort of girl when not first succeeding, so I decided to provide him with another opportunity. "I saw the tire tracks leading from the cave. Just tell me where Martin is taking my knife."

Sweat soaked my forehead, neck, and down my back, both from the early morning Arizona sun and the effort of keeping my quarry suspended over the bluff. My muscles burned but I maintained my hold on the rope coiled around my hands. He was maybe two hundred pounds and I wouldn't've been able to hold him without the rope wound over a large boulder behind me. Even with it braced, I was tiring.

If I was a six on the sweaty scale of one to ten, he was approaching eleven; moisture poured over his beet red face and soaked his dark hair. He twisted his head, grunting with the effort. Hard eyes glared up at me but he said nothing.

Sometimes a simple cock of one's brow while threatening a hired gun is enough to shake his tongue loose, but I wore dark sunglasses and figured he couldn't see my practiced I-will-let-you-die detachedness.

I sighed and made a show of uncoiling the rope from my hands. His eyes tracked the movement until I had the rope gripped tightly but not securely.

I paused. Waited.

Then I loosened my grip and let it slide.

He slipped an inch. Just an inch. When you're dangling by your ankles over a sixty-foot drop to dirt and rocks, however, an inch feels like quite a lot more.

I held tight again, bracing my feet in the dirt and leaning back; the rope went taut in my gloved hands and he jerked to a halt. He didn't shout, no, but let out a panicked yelp in a higher register.

Before I could prompt him again, the small cell phone in the padded pocket on my belt chirped a familiar tune—the theme from *The Last Unicorn*.

I sighed. "I can't hold you forever and I really should take that call."

"They've got a helicopter!" he sputtered, his mouth tight as if he hated himself for giving in. "Thirty miles west. Probably reached it already."

Hmm. Knowing my target, I strongly suspected I drove faster.

"Now let me up!"

I stepped closer to the edge and nudged the four feet of pooled rope over. It tumbled and rolled down his body. "How's your upper body strength?"

He snatched the rope and frowned. "Huh?"

I let go.

The mercenary yelped again and the rope skidded, spitting up sand, but he didn't go plummeting to his doom so he must have held on. The boulder it was wrapped around would hold, but it was up to him to get his ass up. I am, of course, not a coldblooded murderer, but I also didn't fancy being followed. He'd be tired by the time he pulled himself up. Too tired to pursue.

Still, I rushed for my cherry red Jeep waiting near the sand-dusted road, skipped the door, and hauled myself up through the open back and climbed into the driver's seat. My keys waited in the ignition; I gave them a twist, popped on my seatbelt, shifted into gear, and spun around to drive west.

Heat rose in waves from the dirt and barren land stretched on for miles in either direction. I didn't know precisely where my target went, but I'd probably see the helicopter rise in the bright blue sky if I neared it and they took off. I stomped down on the accelerator and flexed my hands on the steering wheel, wishing I could teleport or something.

I hadn't forgotten the call. Phone synched to the rental, I dialed up home.

"Hi, Mommy," said the little voice after one ring.

I smiled absently. "Hey, buttercup. Shouldn't you be in school?"

"Pru slept in. The school called."

I go away for one day and everything falls apart. "I'll talk to the school when I get home. She's okay?"

"Yeah, just tired. And she let me make my lunch."

Oh dear. "And did she also let you *clean up* after making your lunch?"

Emaleth sighed. "*Mom.*"

I was going to come home to peanut butter on the ceiling, I knew it. "There are few things as dangerous as you preparing your own meal." The Jeep hit a bump, jostling me around on the rocky terrain. Well ahead in the distance, light glinted off something shiny—vehicles, one of them containing the artifact I'd come to retrieve, if I was in luck. Luck obviously hadn't been with me that morning since they'd reached it first, but I would put up a fight. As always.

"What time are you coming home?"

I slid a USP Match from the holster on my left as I pushed the pedal to the floor. The ground was rough, Jeep's tires spitting stones and dirt, and wind rushed through the topless vehicle, so I raised my voice to answer her. "Not sure yet, sweetheart. I have a few more things to take care of."

There was little I could hear over the noise around my vehicle but the pouting silence of a child is unmistakable. "You're supposed to meet Miss Jennings today."

Right. My daughter's troll of a teacher who hated me. I greatly disliked the requisite parent/teacher meetings just after school started, since they involved dealing with people I wasn't allowed to dangle over cliffs to make my point. "I will. That's not until tonight and my flight is only four hours. I'll be there."

Muffled talking sounded in the background that I was unable to pick up. My gaze narrowed on the vehicles ahead. The wide, flat black Hummer had to be Martin's. The SUV more than likely housed some of his hired "help" who would be armed and see my Jeep coming.

I dropped the gun in my lap and powered down the window beside me. At least I was as adept shooting left-handed, although driving at the same time would cause...issues. More wind tore through, tossing my long braid of dark hair back over the seat. I went to great lengths to braid it tight so it stayed in place, but pieces fell and whipped against my face and sunglasses.

"Pru says the meeting is at 6:45," Emaleth informed me. "You should be there early."

I was in a different time zone and couldn't do the math at the moment, but didn't see how that would be a problem. "I haven't forgotten. It's written down in my day planner."

"You don't *have* a day planner."

"If I'm going to be late, I'll meet you and Prudence there, okay?"

"Don't be late," she warned in a tone that sounded more adult than six-year-old.

The side window of the SUV rolled down and a moment later I caught sight of an elbow, a hand, and what appeared to be an AR-15.

Wonderful.

"I won't be late," I promised as I raised my gun and stuck my arm out the window, prepared to return fire. "But I'm going to have to go now because I'm in traffic and about to say some nasty things you shouldn't hear."

Another woeful sigh. "You shouldn't say bad words, Mommy."

"No, darling, *you* shouldn't say bad words." *Nor should you chase down vehicles aiming automatic weapons at you.* I'd save that lesson for when she was older, though. "I have to go but I'll see you tonight."

"Are you bringing me back a present?"

The guy aiming the gun out the window was shouting something at me—presumably regarding slowing down or ceasing my pursuit. As if I either heard or cared. "*If* you clean up the kitchen, I might bring you something."

"'Kay. Love you, Mommy."

"Love you too, Em." I disconnected the call just as bullets tore through my windshield.

Motherfucker. I ducked, keeping my right hand on the wheel, and fired randomly until the other shots ceased. The glass cracked but didn't shatter, just impossible to see through. I figured at least Martin would have them shoot out my tires, not attempt to shoot out my *face*.

I'd have to be a bit more aggressive.

I twisted the volume knob on my dashboard so it blared high energy pop rock. Vocals cut over the wind, bass thrummed loudly to drown out all distractions so a backup plan could form. I tend to playlist my aggression; it helps.

I dropped the gun in my lap, grabbed the wheel with one hand and the stick with the other, and swung the Jeep off the road. The rough terrain knocked me around even in four wheel drive, jostling the weapon on my lap. In the rearview mirror, a cloud of dust puffed, covering the sky and anything I left behind me. Ahead, nothing but empty desert, some mountains, and a whole lot of rocks—no vehicles but the ones I pursued, and the road was pretty straight, too. Perfect. The Jeep held at one-twenty clicks as I sped past my target. Damned if I could guess what they were likely talking about in there, besides the fact that maybe I'd lost my fucking mind.

Pretty sure they won't be expecting this.

I went left and swung the Jeep in an arc, steering it back onto the road at a sharp angle. The seatbelt cut across me painfully as I jerked against it but there was no chance to think, to catch my breath; I kept my foot on the pedal as I switched into reverse.

The wide, intimidating Hummer blew through the cloud of dust, slowing almost imperceptibly as they realized what I was doing.

I grinned and unlatched my seatbelt.

Foot on the gas, right hand on the steering wheel and left on the gun, I rose in my seat so I could see past the cracked glass, over the top of the Jeep, and fired at the Hummer.

Wind whipped my braid around wildly, the Jeep careened. I wore fingerless gloves with good grips on them any time I was out the field and I kept the wheel clutched tight, easing it back and forth as needed. My focus was on the tires—with me moving, the Hummer moving, and the wind blasting, I was doubtful I'd hit, but damn if I wouldn't try.

The gun popped holes in the Hummer's grille; I hit the end of the mag, last casing flinging out and disappearing onto the road, just as the SUV sped up with the same jackass hanging out the window, firing at me again.

I dropped down, cast the gun into the passenger seat, and changed hands: left on the steering wheel, right withdrawing my second gun. It was seconds before the rifle was out—intimidating, yes, but impractical—and the guy slipped back in to reload.

Once more I rose, wind tearing and roaring around me as my vehicle flew backwards on the road. Just as I aimed, the Jeep hit a bump. My bullet went wide and I fought to regain control. Wind stole my breath and my chest ached, heart thudded hard, and I was developing a headache. Just another day on the job.

Money. You're doing this for money. Em deserves nice things.

Money. A good motivator.

Irritation prickled under my skin but I raised the gun again, letting the world around me fade as I focused on the tires. I moved the barrel to the right just slightly, narrowed my eyes, and squeezed the trigger.

I popped off half a dozen rounds in rapid succession; one hit the tire and the Hummer swerved wide. The SUV hung back to avoid a collision, both vehicles slowing.

The Jeep jerked suddenly, careening to the left. I cursed under my breath, dropped to sit again, and gathered my bearings. Checked the rearview; still nothing but mountains, boulders, and desert. No helicopter.

I glanced back at the road to see the SUV approaching, speeding past the Hummer, gunning for me.

Well. I'd pissed someone off.

I fought to keep control of the Jeep but couldn't push up the speed any further while driving backwards. The SUV's windows were dark-tinted but I could easily imagine someone in there on the phone with Martin, who no doubt cursed my name and said to get me off the road.

Any sane woman would call it quits, cut her losses. But my daughter was in private school and that doesn't come cheap—I wanted what I came for.

The mercenaries—sorry, as Martin would call them, "armed escorts"—approached and slammed into my Jeep. I abandoned my gun for a moment, grabbed the wheel with both hands, and struggled to keep on the road. The SUV slowed, then sped to gather momentum and slammed me again. I jerked forward. Held on.

Shit. Shit *shit*.

I don't enjoy being on the defensive.

The moment they backed off a bit, I grabbed the stick and swerved, spun in a hard left off the road; not expecting that, the SUV flew past me.

Me and Martin, then.

Once again I pushed the Jeep forward, straight for the Hummer that jostled along, the bare rim sparking on the road. I glided easily next to it, then swung to the left, slamming into the other vehicle, but the Hummer kept on the road. If I got it in the ditch, threatened everyone a whole lot, maybe—

I blinked and caught the SUV ahead, gleaming in the sun, a second before it collided with me.

It hit the front corner of the Jeep and the wheel spun out of my control. I braked, swerved, narrowly missed the Hummer. My shades were knocked off and the world went by in a whirl of bright blue, burnt orange, and yellow, then jerked to a halt when I struck a boulder about half the size of my vehicle. The airbag inflated, struck me in the chest. Metal crunched and screeched in a way that was almost physically painful to hear.

Son of a bitch.

The music cut out, engine died. Might be fixable, might not be. Irritation and anger wove around me, clutching me in a death grip—I was *not* giving up. Not so easily. I pushed down the deflating airbag, grabbed my loaded gun. The driver's door was pinned against the rock, so I hauled myself out the back and readied to aim.

Bullets clipped the side of my Jeep; I ducked down and hoped they were just trying to scare me because cars don't actually stop those things.

A vehicle door opened. I waited, tensed, gun in my grip. Loose hair fell over my eyes and the bright yellow sun beat down. My heart thudded hard but I breathed, slow and sure, calming my body down from its adrenaline high.

"I'm not giving you a ride back," Martin called.

"Not even if I promise to be good?" I returned.

More car doors—they were on the move, perhaps shifting into the SUV. Shit. I glanced under my vehicle and glimpsed feet shuffling.

"How about you give me the knife and I'll give you a finder's fee from my client," I said. "It'll pay far more than whatever museum hired you."

"It's not about the money, Liv. When are you going to get that?"

Easy for him to say—he didn't have to worry about paying bills or taking care of a little one. "I'm going to get it, even if I have to steal it from whomever you give it to."

"I'll recommend they tighten security, then." Car doors began to slam—I had one more shot to it.

I rose, gun pointed right on Martin's smiling face. His hair was my natural color of strawberry blond, though clipped close to his head, and he wore dark shades I envied because I had to squint against the sun with mine lost.

He held the plain stone knife I'd been after, ancient Navajo and used by Locust to cut the horns from monsters.

Whether it did that or not, I didn't know, but my private client wanted it nonetheless.

Martin managed to hold it both reverently and teasingly.

I tightened my finger on the trigger, part of me very much wanting to put a bullet in the forehead of that very smug face.

Then one of his "escorts" stepped around him and lobbed a concussion grenade at me.

Fuck! I spun and ran, kicking up dirt, bolting as far from the Jeep as I could. A moment later the explosion rang in my ears and metal flew as the Jeep burst apart. I ducked, covered my head, waiting as debris rained.

When I stood again, my Jeep was torn to hell and the other vehicles were gone. I fished the cell phone from the padded pocket in my belt, cursing under my breath a number of words that would have upset my daughter.

I did hate my brother sometimes.

2
INVITATION

———————◆———————

I MISSED THE PARENT/TEACHER meeting.

It was after eleven EST at night before I walked up the front steps to my house. We lived in a bungalow, and I could have rented a larger one—or nicer one—if I'd gone for a place with less property. But the house sat on a corner lot with tall fences around it, keeping out any view of neighbors with junk in their yards, and with room for Emaleth to play plus a big oak tree for her to climb. Granted, I was the one who did most of the climbing, but I figured she'd grow into it.

A light burned faintly toward the back of the house. Pru must have stayed up. At least there was no tapping of little feet as I closed the door—Em was asleep still.

Good thing, too, as I wasn't in the right headspace to face the poor kid.

I shucked off my desert combat boots in the corner, slipped off my backpack, holster, and custom belt to hang on the rack, and then padded down the creaky old hall on sore feet. I made a right into the dark kitchen, skipped the light and went for the refrigerator. My socked feet stepped down on something wet and I sighed.

Fucking fridge.

I blindly jerked several squares from the paper towel roll over the sink and tossed them where I'd been standing. The first few times, I thought the cat had peed out there just after we moved, upset with the change of scenery, but it didn't *smell* like cat piss. Then I figured out the shitty old fridge was leaking dirty water and the floor sat at such an angle that it all snaked to puddle in the middle of the kitchen.

Landlord had been insisting for two years now that nothing was wrong with it, and unless the fridge stopped working, he wasn't obligated to give me a new one. And for two years I'd been resisting the urge to flash my guns in his face.

I grabbed a glass of water, ibuprofen, and a cold pack, skirted where the paper towels soaked up the mess, and then made it the rest of the way to the living room before collapsing on the end of the couch.

Prudence Cortez—my best friend, roomie, and occasional babysitter—sat on the overstuffed chair-and-a-half, legs curled under her with a brown chenille blanket over her lap and a book in hand. She glanced up and smiled; her dark eyes were half-lidded and sleepy. I knew she didn't sleep a lot when I was gone, since I was usually doing something that could lead to a gruesome end, so I didn't bitch about her sleeping in and not getting my munchkin to school on time. For all I knew, Em stole her alarm clock, and Pru had enough going on—she could sleep in whenever she needed to without me caring.

Didn't change the fact that I silently cursed myself for not being there in the first place.

"It's Martin's fault," I said immediately as I pressed the cold pack to my elbow. It had seemed okay an hour ago, but then the swelling came back and I was hoping some ice would quiet the ache again.

She shook her head and set her book on the end table. "So you've said."

I'd already called and filled her in when I didn't think I'd make the meeting with Em's teacher, but I still felt defensive about it. "This is the second time he's done this."

"Third if you count the time he had customs waiting at the airport for you."

Right. I forgot about that. "Fratricide isn't illegal, is it?"

"You'd be convicted before opening arguments."

It was true. He was the altruist, the good guy, the one who hadn't been disinherited. Archaeology doctorate, top of his game. I was the ex-debutante party-girl, now single mother with no education, who stole supernatural artifacts for private clients. No question who won the Favorite Talbot Kid Award. "Did you get a line on who he gave the knife to?"

Pru yawned and brushed curls of black hair from her face, then stretched her arms over her head. "Not yet. Short list should be narrowed down by morning. You're really going after it?"

"I need the money. We need a new fridge plus Em's tuition doesn't pay itself."

"She's six. She doesn't need a private school."

We'd already had this conversation approximately seventy thousand times. "I totaled the Jeep, but that and the plane tickets were the only expenses. Grant will give me fifteen grand for the knife."

"Probably," she said. "That was fifteen grand for the first shot—if you draw attention to him stealing it back..."

"Yeah, yeah. But Grant likes me. I think." Truthfully, I'd never actually met Iluka Grant; he was some dealer in Australia I worked with sometimes, someone who hired out help if clients requested something found stateside. He'd hired me a few times now, so I was guessing he liked me well enough. "And if I make a fuss about losing my deposit on the rental, I'll be able to squeeze out more."

She shook her head. No sense arguing with me.

"How are you?" My question was weighted and I studied her, not trying to disguise it.

Pru knew it, too. "Fine. I skipped my nap yesterday."

"You know, if you have a bad day, and I'm not here——"

"I know, I know——"

"——the munchkin doesn't need to go to school."

"I'm fine," she insisted. "I got her to class, skipped the therapy pool, came home and took a nap, and got her from school again."

I bit my tongue. The last thing I would ever do was treat her like an invalid but I did worry about her pushing herself for Em's sake when I wasn't around to help. It required trust, I knew, but I could be a little mother hen-ish sometimes.

And that the Pulse four years ago managed to activate relics and powers and supernatural creatures of old but *didn't* do fuck all to bring about a cure for real world things such as multiple sclerosis pissed me off to no end. What's the point of living in a supernatural world when it didn't cure the lesions on her spinal cord and brain?

Prudence changed the subject, of course. "There's a package for you on the kitchen counter."

Huh. "Bomb?"

"Hasn't exploded yet, and why do you *always* ask that? Has anyone ever actually sent you a bomb?"

They hadn't but as daughter of a rich guy, my childhood had its share of worst case scenario discussions, usually kidnapping but occasionally miscellaneous topics like bombs. Apparently it traumatized my psyche. "Give it time."

"Delivery boy said it was for Olivia Talbot and that's it. You also received two phone calls. Richard Moss?"

I groaned and held my eyes shut for several seconds. "Tell him we're lesbians."

"I'm not doing that anymore."

Ugh, just 'cause it scared off a guy she liked *one* time. "Tell him...I died. From...a mail bomb."

"He was very polite."

Of course he was polite—that's how he finagled my phone number from someone in the first place. I looked at Pru and cocked a brow.

"Where'd you meet him?"

Uh... "A couple of months...remember that Inca necklace?"

"That you were trying to steal from the museum?" Pru's voice turned sharp with disapproval.

She was *not* happy about that job—museum thefts were frowned upon, in her opinion. I'd deemed it too difficult after I was arrested just casing the joint—my brother's work, of course, when he was visiting with the curator and saw me there—but Prudence still made her displeasure known. "Yeah, that one. I ran into him *before* I was surrounded by a dozen terribly handsome uniformed men with handcuffs. Just a patron. Took me twenty minutes to lose him and the bathroom trick didn't work."

"Persistent."

"Understatement. He's pushy, about six-four, wicked hot, and thinks me dating him is a foregone conclusion. You know how that normally turns out."

"Either you sleep with him or you punch him."

I nodded. "Sometimes both. I don't need this right now. Also, his name is Dick Moss. *Dick Moss.*"

"He said it was Richard—"

Clearly she wasn't listening to me. The ice pack crackled against my elbow as I leaned forward for emphasis. "Dick. Moss. It sounds like a venereal disease."

"You shouldn't judge someone by their name."

"Can I judge him for leaving flowers on my car? Twice?"

Her mouth opened. Closed. She frowned. "That's..."

"Something someone with the middle name 'McStalkerpants' would do. I'm *done* with his type, I told you. Then he tells me he's at the museum for a 'story' because he's in the newspaper business—uh, no, he *owns* the newspaper business. Well, blogging, but still."

"You mean—"

"Yeah. *That* Moss." No date in eight months, no *sex* in ten, and the first guy who seriously gets sniffing around me is set to inherit *The Stargazer*—tabloid extraordinaire with an online presence that specialized in making unsubstantiated rumors believed—and is incapable of understanding the word 'no'? Former celebutante karma, apparently.

Pru raised her hands. "You win. He must be avoided. Should I see about changing the number?"

I waved her off. "He probably didn't get the memo that I'm broke now, or doesn't realize what girls who did the pageant circuit grow up to be. I'll scare some sense into him."

"I leave it to you, then." She rose in her pink pajamas, left the blanket on the arm of the chair, and gathered her book. "See you tomorrow."

"I'll take Em to school," I called.

She mumbled something that I missed and disappeared down the dark hall to the bedrooms.

Though I spared a glance at the phone on the end table, I shuddered at the thought of messages waiting and instead leaned back on the couch to stare at the popcorn ceiling. The *water-damaged* popcorn ceiling. Landlord repaired the roof leak last spring but didn't do anything about the damage inside. "Put a coat of paint on it," he said, like a) it was *my* problem to fix in the first place, and b) my concern was cosmetic only.

The idea of holding him at gunpoint was getting more and more appealing.

Gooseflesh spread down my arm from the cold pack. I ached from head to toe and needed to take some painkillers, but the mere thought of moving had me exhausted. After digging my canteen and GPS from the destroyed Jeep that morning, I'd walked four miles to something vaguely resembling civilization, failed to track The Wonderful and Amazingly Good Dr. Martin Talbot down, then fought for hours just to get a car to take me into Phoenix. My feet were blistered, I had scrapes and bruises just about everywhere, and I was giving serious consideration to sleeping on the damn couch.

So I stared at the ceiling some more. I needed to finish this job and then quickly find another.

And there would be more—there were always more. For every person like me trying to cash in on what the Pulse brought, there were millions of people who denied anything happened at all. Like with anything else, there were the deniers, the believers, the haters, the stay-the-hell-out-of-its-way-ers, and the hunters who had a treasure trove of things to find. The important thing was to get a line on items—before do-gooders like my brother did—and sell to the highest bidder.

I'd never understand how there could be deniers. I remembered, still, the moment the Pulse happened—it was around seven-thirty in the evening, I was reading to a two-year-old Em after tucking her into bed in our shitty little apartment, and I *felt it*. Felt the rush of hot then cold swell in the air, the pinprick of electrical charge, the sparking colors flashing briefly in the air, the pressure that made my ears pop. I didn't know what it was then, tried to push it from my mind, but my gut knew it was *something*.

Something that, ultimately, had bought me a way out of my life back then, even if I didn't realize it at the time.

At last I reached over, cracked open the pill bottle, and swallowed three. I'd checked in with my client on the way home; Grant wasn't pleased, but he knew I wouldn't give up so didn't fire me. I'd get Em to school in the morning, see if Pru got any info on who Martin gave the knife to, and hit the job hard again by noon. It had been a few months since I'd broken into anyone's place; I was curious to know how rusty my skills were.

I couldn't actually sleep on the couch or I'd never get up without an alarm clock, so I dragged myself to my feet again, turned off the light, and padded through the black house. I backtracked to scoop up my backpack and my holster—the latter because I didn't like leaving firearms about for my daughter to run into—and headed down the hall. Prudence's door was closed, light off, and I figured she was asleep before she even got in there; both her disorder and her meds made her tired. My own bedroom door waited at the end of the corridor, open and dark. Em's door was open a crack, spilling a faint blue glow across the floor.

I hefted my backpack over my achy shoulder and continued toward the welcoming darkness of my bedroom.

A sniffle in the next room paused my steps. Then: "Mommy?"

I smiled, shook my head, and took two steps back to glance in her room.

She had a four-post bed with a white canopy and loads of pillows that seemed to swallow her whole. The dark spherical thing curled at the foot of the bed on the white comforter was her cat, the ever-diligent Giles.

I eased into the room without touching the light and crept to her bed. Giles glanced up once, green eyes flashing briefly, then dropped his head and descended into a throaty, contented purr.

"You're supposed to be asleep," I whispered as I perched on the edge of her bed. My eyes adjusted to the near darkness and her face took shape, pale against her dark, dark hair. Her favorite stuffed unicorn was clutched in her arms.

"You didn't come to the school tonight." Her tone was somewhere between disappointed and unsurprised, and it pinched my heart.

"I know. I had a problem with my Jeep and couldn't get to the airport on time."

"What happened to it?"

"Your Uncle Marty blew it up." I personally don't believe in lying to children when the truth will suffice.

Em gave a little *tsk* sound and probably would've followed it up with a plaintive, drawn out "Mom!" but was interrupted by a yawn.

"Time for you to sleep, little miss."

"Did you bring me back something?"

"Maybe." I had and it was in the knapsack slung over my shoulder, but I figured I should try to resemble a responsible parent by waiting. "You can have it after I have that progress meeting with your teacher."

She said nothing. That suggested I wasn't going to like what Miss Jennings had to say, but I wouldn't push it. No arguments before bed: it was One of the Rules.

"Sleep now. Present soon. I'll take you to school."

She clutched her unicorn tightly and rolled onto her side, facing the door as I rose. "Did you know *you* got a present?"

"That's what Pru said. Did you peek?"

Em shook her head, yawned again. "Can I see it tomorrow?"

"Sure." *Unless it's a bomb.* One upside of being poor was that she hadn't had to worry about abductions for ransom or bombs or anything, just basic good-touch/bad-touch discussions and "how to get away if someone grabs you in a mall". "Night, baby—love you."

"Love you too, M…" The rest faded into a long, noisy yawn, and I backed out of the room silently, easing the door mostly shut.

I paused in the hall. The right: my bedroom. Bed. King-sized, comfy. Clean sheets I'd leave bits of Arizona dust on because I was too tired to shower first. Thick pillows. Mmm.

Left: the kitchen. And the mysterious present.

I hung a left because I'm like a five-year-old when it comes to curiosity. Throw a red button with a sign over it proclaiming DIRE CONSEQUENCES IF PUSHED, and I'll damn well push it just to see if it's my definition of dire.

My eyes had fully adjusted to the dark house now, and as I approached the kitchen this time, I easily saw the long narrow box on the breakfast bar. A simple dark ribbon crossed it horizontally and it looked like a traditional flower box.

Hmm.

I approached, gripped the edge of the counter, and leaned down to listen. No tick-tock. Nothing odd. No card, either, which wasn't promising. I turned the light on over the stove and eased the ribbon off the box, then the lid. Tissue paper waited within, crinkling under my touch as I folded the layers back.

A single red rose lay within and a large piece of cardstock with artfully scalloped edges sat on top of it. Black cursive writing demanded a closer look, so I lifted it and read.

You're Invited to the Children's Hospital Gala Event at Kent House.

Interesting. I didn't normally receive invites to galas anymore, what with my lack of ability to pay the thousand dollar dinner fee. This one was slated for tomorrow evening—Wednesday. The address put it in the city, about an hour from the suburb where I lived.

I turned the card over to see elegant handwriting on the back, a custom note scribbled for yours truly.

I have great interest in hiring someone of your abilities to retrieve an item of importance. Your plate at the gala has been paid and you're on the list of attendees. Do come so we can discuss business.

The invitation itself wasn't addressed to me personally, but with a note like that on the back, it might as well have been.

I flipped it again and studied the front. Gold filigree around the edges. No RSVP information—apparently I was fully expected to be there at seven in the evening and dinner was at eight. No question about it.

Of course, *I* had questions—many of them. One was who wanted to hire me. Another, whether it would be worth my while.

Okay, mostly the second.

3
DADDY DEAREST

———◆———

I SLEPT IN AND GOT Em to the school just as the bell was ringing, so didn't have time to speak to her demon teacher. Pru still didn't have a line on who hired Martin to retrieve Locust's knife, but there were only so many museums he regularly worked for so I figured she'd have it narrowed down soon. Odds were he'd obey silly international laws and leave it within the country he found it, which would mean another hop across the border into the US for me.

In the meantime, I could either twiddle my thumbs or go to the charity gala. Prudence also gave me the rundown of main players going to the party—that she could find, at least—and of the names I vaguely recognized, no one stood out as private collectors of supernatural artifacts.

Going in blind and thinking on one's feet sadly went hand in hand, and often resulted in me colliding with walls.

I gathered Em from school right when the bell rang and took her with me to get ice cream and get my hair done. We both got a fresh trim, I had my roots touched up and had to endure her complaints that she wanted blue streaks, and I was the meanest mom *ever* for not permitting her to bleach her hair to accommodate it.

Mommy-daughter mani-pedis followed. Somewhere, in the back of my mind, supposedly there were memories of doing that with my own mother; back when he was speaking to me, my father claimed Mom took me to the salon with her when I was a little girl. But she'd left us when I was young, and of the memories I retained of her, that wasn't among them.

Em didn't get a new dress when I did, but was sure to not complain, as she was still angling for the souvenir I hadn't given her yet. As soon as we got home, she went straight to help Pru with dinner while I dressed and a rented limo picked me up half an hour before the gala.

Not that I could particularly afford limos and salon trips and new clothes, but the dress I'd return tomorrow after skillfully returning the price tag to it—I hated feeling cheap, but I wasn't going to wear it twice—and the limo was borrowed half price because the driver owed me a favor.

Kent House was someone's home, once upon a time—a manor converted into an art gallery in recent years, and an ideal spot for charity events. It was in the heart of New Bristol's "traditional" district, a sprawling mansion on almost no property. My ride couldn't park with so many vehicles on the road, but idled on the corner long enough for me to slip out. The driver had a real job to get to immediately afterward, and I would have to more than likely stay later than was customary to wait for him to pick me up off-shift.

Ah, the lifestyles of the formerly rich trying to mingle with the currently famous.

A handful of people walked ahead of me along the wrought-iron fence that surrounded the property. I did a mental check of each dress the women wore; nothing is worse than being seen in something everyone else is wearing, and it's especially a danger when shopping right off the rack. My gown was a rich shade of purple—in itself unique, as most women at these events went for black or something in a modest tone, unless they were looking for attention and then red was the choice. Strapless with a sweetheart bodice showing off the reason I mostly gave up dance come puberty, long flowing skirt

31

that made me feel quite girly and a total change from the shorts and pants I wore in the field. I wore a loose, gauzy white wrap over my shoulders—while my arms weren't quite Linda-Hamilton-in-*Terminator-2*-esque yet, I clearly had more definition than the average woman at one of these functions.

I carried a clutch with nothing important in it aside from a Taurus 605 .357 Magnum.

The mysterious invitation didn't say I couldn't be armed and while I wasn't a fan of the fact it kicked like a shotgun, it would only be needed on the rare chance I had to make a very loud, very permanent point, so I'd manage. Having a backup gun is just as important as picking the right shade of lipstick.

It felt like time traveling, walking up the wide steps to the ornate door held open by a man in a tux—like I'd stepped back half a dozen years and never left the life I used to have. The world I once knew opened up as I stepped inside: elegantly dressed people mingling in the grand foyer, large open doorways leading left and right to more rooms of quietly chatting socialites and millionaires. Music drifted in the air, definitely a live band and playing vaguely familiar classics from the forties somewhere within the manor.

Glittering lights shone from sconces and a crystal chandelier, striking champagne glasses and expensive jewelry. I did feel slightly naked with nothing around my neck, but then I'd sold nearly anything worth something that I didn't care about back when Em was born, and anything I *did* care about was locked up in a safe deposit box. My hair hung in wide, loose curls around my shoulders and covered my lack of earrings quite well, at least.

Immediately I snatched a class of champagne from a passing waiter and wandered about, pretending to eye the art on the walls while scoping out the guests. Whoever wanted to hire me had to at least know what I looked like—I supposed he'd come to me at some point. In the meantime, I'd see if I could identify likely candidates.

I made a right from the main foyer, scanning faces as I walked; when my gaze caught one in particular, I stopped abruptly, heels clacking loudly on the floor and drawing the attention of a grouping of people each twenty or thirty years my elder who looked on in distaste at my lack of grace. Still, I couldn't spare them a glance of apology.

A man had caught my attention—tall and broad, fine sandy hair just long enough that it brought to mind a surfer, cheekbones to die for, and a wide smile of perfect white teeth. His black suit looked like the others but the cufflinks, I imagined, were platinum, and his tie was a pale silver. He was in his thirties, the cliché of "ruggedly handsome", and the three women in his orbit suggested I wasn't the only one who thought so.

Richard Moss stood across the room.

Dick Moss. My heartrate kicked up a notch or three. The damn invitation—it had a rose. It *could* be him...couldn't it?

And maybe that's why he's been stalking me—he wants to hire me.

Strangely, that did not make me feel *any* better.

I backed up and turned, crossed the foyer again, and took the left hall out this time. I squeezed my clutch, wanting nothing more than to pull out my cell and contact Pru, but though it had been a lot of years since attending such a function, I was relatively certain they frowned upon texting. It would have to wait. I'd give the party half an hour of avoiding Moss—if no one else had approached me by then, I'd chalk it up to him and leave. Call a cab and make a spectacle of my exit, no doubt, but whatever.

I took a few sips of champagne that turned into the entire glass, deposited the empty cut crystal with others on the tray of a passing waiter, and grabbed another.

Music grew louder the deeper I went into the house and soon I saw the platform with the small orchestra set up. Too often there would just be string quartets and purely classical music at these events, but this one had a singer in a stunning silver gown crooning "Smoke Gets in Your Eyes." She managed to come across as authentic and not lounge singer, so I'd give the organizer props for that.

The room was dome-shaped with three walls and a ceiling entirely made of glass, as if it had once been the manor's conservatory. High above, hard pricks of starlight in a velvet sky and a nearly-full moon shone. All in all, it might've been rather romantic and glamorous, if I wasn't now the kind of woman mostly comfortable climbing cliffs and driving really fast cars.

Very good thing I avoided Mr. Moss. I did not need to be nostalgic and vulnerable around his type tonight.

Across the room, I caught the gaze of a man staring at me. Youngish—perhaps slightly older than me. Black hair, east Asian features, refined charisma coming off him in waves. He was the kind of man who could be a prince or a stripper and women would throw themselves at him regardless.

Probably gay.

If he was, however, he was studying me awfully closely. He raised his glass and cocked an eyebrow at me.

He could be my client. I'd prefer it over *Dick Moss*, but in that case I assumed he would've approached me by now. And he didn't. Since I wasn't there to ogle the pretties, I glanced away and moved in the opposite direction, sipping my drink, eyeing my companions—

And promptly saw my father.

Oh, this night officially *sucked*.

Regardless of a girl's age, something about the sight of a disapproving parent knocks her to about two inches high. Given that Oliver Talbot could take disapproving to its own art form, I felt even lower than that.

My heart sped, stomach turned. The ground could've given out below me and it would not've been a surprise. He stood with small group of men I didn't recognize, tall and proud and grayer around the edges from when I'd last seen him. Of my brother and me, I'm the one who looks like our father through and through. Oval face, brown eyes, straight nose and full lips. Certainly if I walked up to him right that moment, whoever he spoke to would immediately guess I was related whether they knew about me or not.

And that temptation was just too much to pass up.

A smile plastered on my face, I walked easily toward him; he glanced my way, his gaze barely flickering before returning to his companions then shooting back to me for a longer look as it just dawned on him who the woman approaching him was.

I should dig out my phone and take a picture.

He pointedly turned, giving me his back.

I wasn't daunted, but instead hung a left to squeeze between him and the elderly gentleman currently speaking.

"Hi, Daddy," I said brightly and took a sip of my champagne, batting my eyelashes innocently.

None of the, "Oh, this is your daughter, Oliver?" ensued, so they must've known our history; instead everyone stood there quietly, looking awkward.

It was entertainment that served as a balm to my many hurt feelings.

My father deigned a look at me; while I might resemble him, the high-and-mighty almost-sneer he gave me was all Martin.

"Quite the shindig. I think I saw the mayor over there—I should totally take a picture for Em." I looked at the man I'd interrupted. "Say, do you know where the little girl's room is? I've had, like, a *lot* to drink."

Dad's companions swiftly excused themselves. I couldn't imagine why.

My father's hand lashed out for my arm and dragged me back several steps to an empty corner. "*What* do you think you're doing here?"

I blinked up at him blankly. "I was invited."

"Bullshit."

"*Tsk tsk*. Such language, Daddy-Dearest." I tactfully disengaged him from my arm and went back to sipping my drink. "Do you really want to cause a scene?"

"*I* am not causing a scene. You have no business being here."

"I'm pretty sure you stopped being privy to my business the day you kicked me out of my home. Would you like to know how your granddaughter is doing?"

"I have no granddaughter."

It stung. Still. Years later and I felt it still, that harsh little prick of his words and the feel of them driving under my skin. Disown me for my wild child, slutty ways, fine. But for having a child out of wedlock who you then deny exists? Not cool. Not at all.

"Wow, Mom would be *so* proud of how you handled all this," I said.

And instead of responding, he turned to stalk away, disappearing into the next room.

That didn't seem fair—surely he should give me time to get in a few more jabs, making up for that comment about his granddaughter. Indeed, decidedly I wasn't quite done bothering my dear father that evening.

My focus narrowed on the direction he'd taken, something cold and calculating settling in my veins as I started to follow.

Fingers wrapped around my wrist, drawing me back. I tensed, about to react in a rather negative fashion, and hesitated initially by the remembrance that this wasn't the environment for a scrap—

And then by the sight of the man who stopped me.

4
CAT & MOUSE

———————◆———————

I BLINKED. TWICE. AND HE didn't release my wrist.

I had a much more focused view now of the stranger who had attempted to engage me with a smile from across the room. His hair was a short, unruly mass of glossy black, and his handsome face had a sculpted look, almost too perfect to be real. Perhaps Korean, and yet his eyes were a light, clear blue. Blue and predatory, like he'd already assessed me before going in for the kill, and in seconds he'd be at my throat.

Probably with teeth.

My peripheral vision picked up a simple black and white tux like the other gentlemen in the room, and he wore it like he belonged in it; I'd grown good over the years at discerning between those with money and those playing at having money. He was as comfortable in the tuxedo as any rich child practically born in one.

I continued to stare at him. "That's my wrist you seem to have."

He made a point of looking at my fingers coiled around the stem of my near-empty champagne glass. "So it is."

My skin prickled strangely and heart beat faster. "You should do something about that."

"Excellent idea." His fingers holding my wrist deftly shifted to snatch my champagne glass and drop it on the tray of a passing waiter, then gripped my hand, drawing me to him as his other palm came to rest low on my hip. At that precise moment, as if he'd timed it, a new song picked up, the songstress sinking into the opening of "I Only Have Eyes for You", and Mr. Tall, Dark, and In My Personal Space pulled me into a dance.

You have got to be kidding me.

He stood a few inches above my height in heels, and this near I had to tip my head back to look up at him. I had the distinct sense that he liked it that way.

And I kind of wanted to knee him in the balls.

Unfortunately, my body settled into dancing like second nature; my shoulders pulled back, neck elongated, and I followed his steps. He wasn't overly broad, no, but there was strength in the way he held me, coiled tight and reined in. Precise and deliberate. He moved with a feline grace—a cat playing with his meal.

"You know," I said as he swept me along, and at last I settled my hand—and the clutch gripped in it—on his shoulder, "I was rather looking forward to making a scene."

"My timing is impeccable."

"And an intrusion on mine."

His lips quirked in a cocky smile and not once had his stare left mine. "Perhaps I'm with security, tasked to keep scandals to a minimum."

"By dancing with potential threats?"

"Now that," he had us part for a moment and turned me once before returning me to his embrace, "was purely my decision."

"Lucky me."

"Indeed."

His hand was a heavy weight on my hip—a little too firm. Come to think of it, so was the grip on my hand. As if he expected me to dart away.

I had no clue where he'd get such an idea.

I still held his gaze because he hadn't looked away and I wasn't about to give in. "So do you have a name?"

"I have a few."

Oh, this was promising.

"Do you?"

"Just the one, actually."

Interestingly, he didn't ask it. Maybe he knew. Maybe he really *was* with security and knew exactly who Olivia Anne Talbot was and why he had to watch me for a scandal. While I liked my reputation proceeding me sometimes, I didn't like being at a disadvantage in the knowledge department.

My gauzy wrap slipped off my shoulders, pooling low in the hollow where my arms bent at the elbow. It left my skin exposed, vulnerable, and I suppressed a shiver.

The air around him was charged and tense, and I still hadn't eliminated the possibility of him trying to kill me if we weren't in a room surrounded by wealthy people who were scandalized by things such as drinking cheap wine. Murder would definitely be frowned upon, but I took comfort in the gun in my purse.

And at least he wasn't Dick Moss.

My skirt breezed around my legs as he forced me into another turn, and his slight grin grew into a full-fledged smile. "Used to leading, are you?"

"Used to practicing solo these days," I said mildly.

"I have trouble picturing you as lacking for partners."

"It's more an issue with finding one to keep up."

The song was blessedly ending, and as the singer belted out the last words of the final chorus—drawing out, "only have eyes," sensually—he turned us swiftly three times and dipped me low. His face came within inches of mine and my head was tilted back, exposing my throat in an unfortunately submissive manner.

It's an odd feeling as a woman being suspended in the air like that, a few feet from the floor, trusting one's partner not to drop her. My heart sped because I most certainly didn't trust this man.

"Let's test that some time," he said in a deep voice that settled right under my skin and gave me goose bumps.

He held me there as breathless seconds passed, then the tempo and music picked up again with the very end of the song, and he righted us. A brief nod—not deep, but enough to acknowledge me—and he turned to exit the room, moving fluidly as he wove around people.

Right. People. Gosh, there were quite a few of them and they all were looking at *me*.

Heat touched my cheeks. I pulled the wrap up over my shoulders again and casually turned to stare at the glass of the nearest wall like nothing happened.

"Olivia!"

I tensed at the voice booming my name, gaze darting around, but there was *nowhere* to hide anyway.

I turned toward approaching steps and attempted not to sigh. *Please don't let him be my client. Please.* "Dick."

Mr. Moss frowned, briefly, as he stopped in front of me. "Richard."

"Of course."

"Great to see you here." He offered me a sexy smile and his arm.

Oh no. Mr. Possibly-Security-Guy had me flustered and wound up, and Moss would certainly go for the kill with me too off my game to put up a fight. I took a subtle step back, angling myself so I was no longer quite facing him and definitely obvious I had no intention of taking his arm.

The appendage hung there a moment before it seemed to sink in that I wasn't taking it. He returned his arm to his side. "Well. I almost never see you at this kind of thing."

"No...you don't." I went to take a sip of my wine and realized the previous guy had taken it. And left.

There were too many guys for me to keep track of. I needed another drink.

Moss would simply *not* be daunted by my lack of desire to participate in conversation with him. "Did you get the flowers?"

I kept up the smile, hoping he didn't mean last night's rose was among them. "Yes."

"Both bouquets?"

My face is going to freeze like this. What the hell was wrong with me—why did I always stand around and put up with this sort of thing rather than *run away*? "Mm-hmm."

He waited, as if he expected me to explain why I hadn't responded to either, blinking those pretty dark eyes, and not revealing yet if he was indeed my client. "You know, I haven't been able to stop thinking about you since the museum."

He'd left before security arrested me—good thing, too, as I didn't trust my picture wouldn't've ended up on his blog in front of millions. "Well..." *Where is the wine? Why won't someone bring me wine!* "Lucky me."

Moss's sandy brows pulled together in confusion.

"Miss Talbot?"

I swung around immediately to see who the new intruder was. It wasn't my random dance partner this time, but an older man in a tux who brought to mind the wait staff; he held himself differently than the others, shoulders turned inward and head slightly bowed.

"I'm to bid you to join your patron this evening. He's ready for the meeting to commence."

I might have to go to church if prayers I haven't even formed yet are answered with such frequency.

My attention returned briefly to Moss, thankful he wasn't my client. "If you'll excuse me."

"Sure." He seemed about ready to reach for my hand in goodbye, so I abruptly turned to my savior. Ridiculously persistent—despite being pretty to look at, and probably a decent enough guy, it just would end so, so badly. Maybe I'd have to change my number after all.

The older man gestured for me to follow. I smiled politely, nodded, and let him lead me through a side exit and down another hall. I scoped the place out as I went, remembering the layout—force of habit. We passed the other guests, went down a dark corridor, and up a narrow flight of stairs I suspected had been servant ones when the house was a home. Perhaps I'd done enough to make my presence known, and the man who invited me wasn't interested in parading me up the proper staircase in front of the guests.

The second floor was quieter than the first, whether because it was out of bounds permanently or just for the evening, I didn't know. The lighting was poorer and we walked down a long hallway of closed doors. There was one at the very end and it didn't surprise me when my guide stopped in front of it, opened it for me, and bowed.

Nervous energy ran through me, though I moved with practiced calm and showed none of it. He'd ushered me to a conference room with a wall of windows at the far end. The other three walls were paneled in dark wood, the area rug Persian in autumn tones and undoubtedly expensive, and a long oval conference table waited in the center. I was offered a glass of wine by the man standing just inside the door, which I accepted and continued on into the room.

Facing the windows, with his back to me and hands knotted against his lower spine, stood the man I assumed had called me here. He was tall, shoulders thick and proud, hair a gleaming black combed smoothly back.

He glanced over his shoulder at me and offered a smile. "Please, have a seat, Miss Talbot. We'll get started shortly."

Nothing about him was familiar—I couldn't even say if he lived in the city. When I reached the table, the man from the door darted over to pull a chair out for me; I accepted it and sat more out of habit than desire to.

I studied my host as he rounded the table and made a gesture to the side door, which the doorman swiftly went to. He was perhaps my father's age, though strangely with no sign of gray around the edges. It was more something in his expression that made him seem old.

And powerful. There was no mistaking the aura of respect-me-or-else about him. The "else", I was certain, wouldn't be pleasant. My father was the CEO of Phoenix Enterprises, which owned half a dozen different companies, and he could be an utterly ruthless businessman—hell, he was the kind of guy who could hate his own daughter. If my host was that type, well, consider me on edge.

"I'm Moses Ashford," he said. "And I would like you to retrieve something for me."

"I gathered from your invitation."

He walked around the table slowly, dark gaze away from mine as he appeared to ponder something. A floor to ceiling cabinet waited off to the side, and he slid back one of the doors to reveal a large monitor. Seconds later the lights dimmed and the screen glowed.

A presentation. Wow. This potential client went all out.

The side door opened and figures stepped inside; I couldn't make them out well until they approached the table and neared the blue glow of the screen. The first was a large man with dark hair in a ponytail—sort of the quintessential Comic Book Guy, though he smiled shyly at me and gave off an air of kindness. His button down shirt and pressed pants were new, however not enough to get by downstairs; he must not have attended the party at all. He took a seat off to the side, shoulders hunched like an awkward sort of teddy bear.

Someone else stepped up to stand by the screen: a woman, thirtyish, petite with very dark skin, curly black hair closely cropped to her head, and glasses. She held a clipboard, which—when you're used to freelancing and doing your own thing, shooting randomly and bouldering and stuff—was utterly terrifying. Her skirt and jacket business suit was a simple beige but a smart pair of Louboutin pumps in red suggested the girl knew how to dress.

Still a third person stood off to the side and I couldn't make him out from where I sat with the lights so dim.

"Are you familiar with the Seal of Solomon?" Ashford asked, his eyes on me.

I took a sip of my wine. "Very vaguely—not much beyond the Wikipedia version."

Ashford nodded at the woman, and she lifted a controller and pointed it at the monitor. The screen flared to life with simple drawings of the Star of David and various other symbols, and some Hebrew writing I couldn't read.

"It was a signet ring which, according to legend, belonged to Sulaiman ibn Da'ud," he said. "King Solomon, the son of David as you know him." Another nod and the screen changed again, this time to show various drawn depictions of the ring. "Earliest versions say it was made of iron and brass. It had the true Name of God written upon it, was inlaid with four jewels, and is said to give the wearer the ability to control demons, genies, speak to animals, and had various other powers."

"Handy...for those nasty demon infestation problems that always seem to crop up."

Nothing, not even a smile.

"Or the Dog Whisperer?"

He pointedly ignored me.

Since I was pretty sure I didn't want to be fired from a job I hadn't even yet been given, I decided to be a team player. "It was primarily mentioned in *One Thousand and One Nights*, no?"

"Yes." His voice lightened a little, as if it pleased him to realize I wasn't a drooling idiot. "Legends are also mentioned in a handful of medieval grimoires from around the sixteenth century."

His assistant brought up images of old books I'd never read but seen on display various places. I honestly found occult texts painful to read and hoped my part in this expedition wouldn't involve combing them for evidence.

"No one knows precisely what it looks like—accounts varied—or where it is."

"Or if it existed," I pointed out. "King Solomon supposedly lived three thousand years ago if he even existed at all; if he wasn't real, the ring isn't." I mean, I hunted down supernatural stuff for a living, but *someone* had to say it.

"Let us say I wouldn't be calling this meeting if I wasn't quite certain of its existence," Ashford said.

"Touché." The Pulse, after all, activated all sorts of shit humans hadn't believed in, so anything was possible.

The next image was of some sort of modern-looking war medal, with the Star of David and a cross. "Do you recognize this?"

I shrugged. "Not all the elements combined, no."

"This is The Order of the Seal of Solomon, instituted by Emperor Yohannes IV in the nineteenth century. The kings of Ethiopia have claimed to be direct descendants of King Solomon—the Solomonic dynasty, if it did indeed exist, was no doubt broken a few times over, but it is a popular claim still heard today."

"You think the Seal might be there."

The medals faded into a map of southeast Ethiopia, and from there images of a cave system with several photos that he cycled through. "That is my theory. I have reasons for it I will not get into at this time; suffice to say I've spent some time since the Pulse tracking the Seal and this is where I continue to land."

I didn't recognize the caves, but they looked like any other—limestone carved by rivers over centuries. The lights flickered on again though the screen remained on with the vast cave photos. I blinked, adjusting to the light, and sipped my wine some more while I thought. "Why me?"

Ashford stood before the table, hands behind his back. "I have approached a handful of people in your line of work but have yet to find a good fit. Too many have a history of turning items over to local governments."

"Ah, yes, I don't think so. They rarely pay as well."

"There's also your particular...skill set." Lest I think he was referring to my ability to model swimwear and answer questions with "world peace", he tilted his head in the direction of the monitor where the images of caves remained, faded in the room's bright lights.

Nowadays treasure hunters like me seemed to come in two breeds: those with a flat out burglary background, and the outdoorsy types who got their hands dirty. I lacked a certain *je ne sais quoi* for slipping into a guarded fortress in a black catsuit, but send me outdoors where it was less about having a precise plan and with no rules to follow, and I was right at home.

Ashford continued, as if that answered any lingering questions about why he chose me. "I've assembled a team to go in. Dawson Fabrini," he nodded to Comic Book Guy, who gave me a simple little wave, "heads tech. Laurel James," he gestured to Clipboard Woman, who eyed me with distaste, "is my representative—my eyes and ears while you're out. You'll be in charge but she'll have my authority. Finally, there's Mr. Rolph."

The white man standing at the back of the room had one of those pornstaches, so thick and dark it hardly looked real. The top of his head was mostly bald, bringing to mind the idea that perhaps the hair fell from the top of his head and just landed on his upper lip. A tiny gold cross hung at his throat, light catching it and sending darts across the room. He watched me from behind thick glasses—those bottle type not popular for years—that interrupted my viewing, and evaluation, of him.

In summary, he kind of looked like he should be a serial killer named Kevin who lived someplace like the end of my street.

"He is familiar with the region you'll be visiting *and* legends surrounding Sulaiman ibn Da'ud. He'll be advising you from a scholar perspective."

When Ashford said nothing else, I glanced over my new "team" again before returning my gaze to his. "While I have no doubt of the qualifications of the people you've brought on board, if we're going caving, I'm going to need a party of cavers—preferably extremely experienced ones. A team no fewer than four, and preferably six."

He nodded as if he'd been expecting it. "You'll have people at your disposal there when the plane touches down. Hired help. Mr. Rolph and Ms. James will also accompany you inside; the former has experience caving, the latter has been taking classes and will be quick to adapt."

Right. Sure. Maybe I should sit her in front of *The Descent* before going in, and scare her into staying at the campsite. I didn't enjoy potentially dangerous activities with newbies on board.

"As for the matter of payment..."

I tried not to *noticeably* perk up, as there's nothing worse than looking desperate.

"You'll be paid five hundred thousand when the ring is in my possession."

I blinked.

He stared back at me and made no move to correct himself.

I swallowed a sudden lump in my throat. "Do I get an initial deposit? Good will gesture?" *So I know you plan to pay up?*

"Ten percent now, as well as most expenses paid during the trip. I'll cover airfare there and back, accommodations—which, you understand, will be camping at the site—as well as meals, all for the duration of the hunt. I will provide any *necessary* equipment, where necessity is defined by me."

That could bite my well-toned derriere later but offering me *that* much money suggested he was dead serious and I would want for very little during this excursion.

"I'll also have a contract drafted up, detailing my expectations and what you're agreeing to," he continued. "That way everything is clear."

There could be any number of reasons why he wanted me to sign a contract. One was so I couldn't take the ring and then try to sell it to the next highest bidder when I got it. Another was so he had legal recourse to come after me if something went bad, even though I was being sent to steal something and there was no way he'd take me to court.

That place down deep in my gut I'd developed and listened to over the years tightened and twisted, warning me this was a very, very bad idea.

But, quite frankly, I wanted some semblance of my old life back.

"Regardless of your decision, I do have a gift for you for meeting with me this evening." Ashford raised his hand and gestured over his shoulder; Laurel James moved immediately to retrieve something from behind the monitor, and handed it to him.

Ashford carried the flat, rectangular box over and set it on the tabletop in front of me. I glanced at him in question, but was only met by a tight smile pulling at the creases around his mouth.

I gently lifted the lid.

And tried not to look surprised, but it was incredibly difficult.

"So," Moses Ashford said, "do we have an agreement?"

———————— ◆ ————————

I SAT AT MY KITCHEN breakfast bar with just the lamp over the stove on, still in the dress I might keep after all.

Prudence leaned across from me, elbows on the counter, staring at the contents of the box. "Martin wouldn't have sold it to *him*, would he?"

I gently lifted Locust's knife from the red silk it rested on. It was heavy, the stone blade worn away. In fact, it barely looked like a knife any longer, but I had no doubt as to its authenticity. "Martin wouldn't sell it to anyone. Ashford made it clear, too, that he's not into the do-gooder type of employee. Maybe he pulled the customs trick on Martin. I can't say for sure, but he's handed it to me to turn into Grant for my payment, whether I take his job or not."

"*Are* you taking it?" Prudence was staring at me—I could all but feel it. She probably didn't have a good reaction to this adventure either.

"I...don't know. I said I'd let him know tomorrow."

Silence hung between us while I stared at Locust's knife some more.

"I know the money is good, but..." Pru sighed. "But we're doing okay. You don't *need* this paycheck."

Pru was tutoring on the side via her laptop and Skype, bringing in extra money, but I didn't want to rely on that and her disabilities check when things got rough.

"This seems like a bad idea," she continued. "He knows a lot about you, apparently, but I couldn't find anything on Moses Ashford when you texted the name earlier. Nothing at all—no one knows him and he's unlisted. No online paper trail. It's like he doesn't exist."

Worse and worse. So, fake name? Wouldn't be the first time. What I didn't believe to be fake, however, was his money, and certainly not the Navajo artifact sitting right in front of me. And it was that money that spoke to me, the possibility of being handed something that could change things for my family permanently. Seeing my dad again hung in the back of my mind, a painful reminder of what life used to be like.

I put the lid back on the box. "I'll get this to Grant in the morning after I get Em to school and deal with that troll teacher. Then figure out this Ashford thing. I have time to sleep on it."

If I sleep at all after tonight.

5
THE SHE-DEMON OF
NORWOOD SCHOOL FOR GIRLS

———— ◆ ————

I WALKED EMALETH UP THE steps of Norwood School. It was fifteen minutes before the first morning bell was to ring, which should give me just enough time to apologize to Miss Jennings without having to endure too long of a lecture. We passed the throngs of little girls, all dressed identically in burgundy and gold plaid skirts and burgundy blazers, though my daughter sported a new silver and turquoise cuff bracelet I'd picked up while stuck in Arizona. Of course I broke down and gave it to her that morning and couldn't wait another day; all it took was a look from those liquid brown eyes and a few bats of her long lashes, and I was putty.

Em waved at a few of the girls, noticeably with her bracelet on display. A showoff—couldn't *imagine* where she got that from. The mothers still doting over their daughters before retreating to their cars all gave me looks.

It was common enough in the twenty-first century for young woman to have children out of wedlock. It was *not* common for them to be disgraced minor celebrities who are still willing to send their daughters to expensive private schools.

I dressed to fit in with the rest of them, of course: plain black slacks, a charcoal gray wool coat, all as expensive as I could afford and only worn when I needed to Make An Appearance. My hair hung long and straight, whispering against my coat when I moved. I dyed it dark brown to look similar enough to Emaleth's thick brunette locks so that no one made remarks anymore about how she must take after her father. I generally had a sarcastic reply to such questions which tended to embarrass her; now I avoided them and pretended I wasn't naturally strawberry blonde.

We moved up the stone steps and through the double set of doors into the old school. The day we left behind us was gray and dull, air tinged with the scent of approaching rain, and inside wasn't much cheerier. Even the plaques with the school colors seemed drab somehow.

Em didn't say a word while we walked through the school. She likely knew I was tense and this was why I gave her the souvenir early: it bought her silence while Mommy Faced the Dreaded Beast.

Honestly, I'd been shot twice in the past few years, fractured my wrist, scraped off probably enough skin to cover another human, and barely managed to avoid being arrested at least a dozen times and *successfully* arrested twice. Send me in to face a disapproving first grade teacher? Even my toes were trembling.

Thankfully I wore expensive boots to mask it.

We made a right and I faced the door to room 109, my stomach in knots as if I were the six-year-old and meeting the principal instead. Miss Jennings was at her desk already, sitting prim and proper while she typed on a laptop. I gestured for Emaleth to wait outside the door and stepped into the room.

"Although the door is open, I believe it's customary to *knock*." Miss Jennings didn't look up from her work, fingers never missing a keystroke.

In my head, I always heard her with a British accent, but she was Canadian through. The part that killed me about the woman was that she couldn't have been much older than me: I was twenty-four, and I'd bet money she hadn't yet hit thirty. Hair was blonde and always in a French twist, stature petite. I shouldn't've been intimidated by her. I had two years of Krav Maga on top of a body that endured strict dance and even gymnastics training until I was a teen; I had taken down mercenaries in the field twice this woman's size. But no, I had to be pleasant and proper and not drop her head first out the window, so she freaked me out.

We were only on the first floor, though—it wasn't like she'd fall far.

"Should I go back out and knock and pretend like I didn't just walk in after seeing the large WELCOME sign on the door—which, I assume, means one is welcome to enter—or shall I file that tidbit away for next time?"

That caused Miss Eloise J. Jennings to stop typing and dignify me with a look.

My daughter was more than likely cringing in the hallway, or perhaps pulling out her iPod to drown out my embarrassing remarks.

I smiled pleasantly, took several more steps into the room, and draped myself on a student's desk in front of the teacher's. "I'm terribly sorry for missing the meeting Tuesday night. I was very busy working overtime. You know how it is, on your feet all night."

The staff at Norwood suspected I was a stripper. Admittedly, I did nothing to contradict this assumption.

Miss Jennings took off her glasses, folded them, and set them with precision on the desk beside her laptop. "You'll have to book another; there are things to discuss."

My smile didn't waver but a fresh dose of dread plummeted again in my gut. "Oh?"

"Emaleth is failing three of her classes."

Although Norwood's first semester started two weeks earlier than public school, that was still... *Ugh, I hate math.* "It's only been three and a half weeks."

"Precisely," she said curtly.

If Prudence was here, she'd be rattling off something about how first graders shouldn't be graded. Of course, she's a hippy who begged me to pick a Montessori school when I insisted on going private, citing her experience as a teacher—before her illness—as her expertise. "We'll work harder on her homework."

"Her homework isn't the problem, *Ms.* Talbot. The problem is her inability to focus on her assignments and her propensity to distract the other students."

"She's social. I'm sure she means no har—"

"It took *fifteen minutes* just yesterday to settle the class into working after lunch. Apparently she was telling stories about her mother"—the woman took on a slightly higher-pitched tone and I could all but see her using air quotes—"fighting a jaguar. *Last week.*"

"It wasn't so much a jaguar as a jaguar shaman." *And I got almost two grand for his staff. Score one for me.* "Jaguars are endangered—it would hardly be responsible of me to fight one. Also, it was two weeks ago."

Miss Jennings' eyes narrowed severely and a beat of silence passed in which I assume she was trying to set me on fire. She was a Pulse denier; I could fight said jaguar shaman on the desk in front of her and she'd insist the whole thing never happened. "Her constant lying is inappropriate behavior."

Outside in the hallway, shoes made the slightest scraping noise on the floor. Probably my poorly-focused, highly creative little angel ready to throw a fit over being called a liar. You can say anything else you like about that child, but never call into question her truthfulness. I suspected *Pinocchio* traumatized her or something when she was little.

"Let me speak plainly," she continued. "Your check on Monday *bounced.*"

I swallowed thickly, feeling my face drain of color and that sick sensation take up in my stomach again.

"Your child is in no way qualified for a scholarship. You will pay the amount owed to the school—with interest—by Friday, or you will take Emaleth elsewhere. Is this in any way unclear?"

For a single, beautiful moment, I imagined her dangling off the roof by her feet, begging me to let her up again. And this was why my smile to her was genuine. "Absolutely clear, Miss Jennings. Have a wonderful day."

I rose and walked with smooth, steady steps back outside the classroom, even though my heart beat wildly in my chest. I was to the door before the forceful push of her fingers on the keyboard resumed.

Fucking bitch. I am going to kill her. I am going to kill her. I am—

Em stood just outside the classroom door, leaning against the wall and peering up at me guiltily. I said nothing, just folded my hand over her shoulder and led her back toward the front of the building. It wasn't until we were out of the drab school environment and in the chill September air that I stopped her at last and knelt so I was eye level.

She clutched her bracelet and her eyes grew huge. "Are you gonna take it back?"

"No. It's yours."

"I didn't tell lies."

"I know. But most mommies don't fight jaguar shamans."

"When I grow up, *I'm* going to fight jaguar shamans," she insisted.

I was kind of hoping she'd aim for something safe like being an accountant, but that was a ways off. "Still. *Maybe* tone down those stories. Tell them Mommy's a dancer instead."

I am *such* a shit disturber.

"I'll try to pay more attention." Her dark eyes picked up a sheen, red edging them, and my heart broke a little more.

"Make a game of it," I said, clutching her shoulders and hoping it was comforting. "If you pay attention and pull up your grades, you win. If you don't, the She-Demon-Jennings wins. And we don't want her to win, do we?"

A smile fought her pouty lips. "No."

"That's my girl. Now, I am going to go deliver something that Uncle Marty stole from me the other day so I can pay my bills, and *you* will wait for the bell to ring so you can go in there and show off your bracelet while you work really hard. Gimme a hug."

Some kids didn't want to hug their parents at that age; mine remained blissfully unaware thus far that it was borderline uncool to be seen doing so, and happily threw her arms around my neck.

"Have a good day." I smoothed her hair and patted her back. "And don't tell your teacher I called her a She-Demon."

———— ◆ ————

"THEY'RE GOING TO KICK HER out." I paced in the kitchen and despite the fact that I'd just mopped the floor, water soaked my socks again and I was too flustered to worry about it.

Prudence sat at the breakfast bar, her energy calm and a sharp contrast to mine. "What about Grant—"

I stopped abruptly and spun to face her. "He waited until *after* I shipped it to text that he was 'less than impressed' with how things went in Arizona and the fucking cheap bastard—who covered the costs on the Jeep Martin blew up initially—decided to take that out of my pay. He gave me less than three thousand dollars. *Three thousand.* Less my fee to fly, even."

"I think you need to have a cup of tea and stop pacing."

"Fuck your fucking tea!" My lips pressed together and I took a deep breath, regretting the outburst. "Look, I know what you're going to say. You hate her school, you hate what I do for a living—"

"No, I don't—"

"But I have to give the school that for the rest of her September tuition and now there's nothing for October, and—"

"They offer biweekly. Give them fifteen hundred now, and that'll give you a few weeks to figure out it."

But we were less than three months from winter. Electricity costs doubled when it was time to put the heat on and I couldn't have my kid walking the house in a snowsuit all the time. Heat was more important than private school, I knew, but...

But I *hated* this.

I took a step and my heel landed again in the puddle of water from the fridge—I couldn't help it and gave into a frustrated scream, swung my foot out and kicked the cupboard.

All that did was shoot pain through my big toe straight up to my ankle and jarred the cheap cupboard door enough that it cracked, hinge coming loose.

"And now I have to fix the fucking cupboard."

Pru was still and silent for several minutes longer, then she slowly rose, rounded the breakfast bar and me, and went for the stove. "I'm making tea."

With a heavy sigh, I slumped down on a barstool and pulled my sock off. Chipped a toenail and it was blooming with a blue bruise, but I didn't think I'd broken anything. I swiped angry hot tears from my eyes.

Water rushed from the faucet as she filled the kettle. "We could take the door off completely and put a curtain over it."

"What the fuck are you talking about?"

She set the kettle on the stove and spun the dial. "The cupboard." Again she spun the dial. And again. And frowned.

Oh god. "What?"

"Probably just a fuse. Let me go look for one." She left me in the kitchen to go be the grownup and fix stuff while I sulked.

Maybe the stove was broken. Maybe everything was broken. I hated thinking about bills and tuition and new appliances and everything.

I tried very, very hard to be an adult—I'd had to, having a baby so young—but I was twenty-four and I'd jumped straight from living in a mansion with my daddy and my every need taken care of to having to figure out how to navigate the world like an adult woman and a mom when I couldn't remember what it was like to have a role model for either.

And I wanted a new house. Hell, I wanted my *own* house. I'd never lived in a place so small, not counting the previous three crappy apartments I had. First was in my third trimester with Em and I had to leave the friend's house I was staying at— I got the best place I could afford while rationing what remained in my bank account, which was a total shithole. Briefly I upgraded to a much nicer place while I lived with a guy, but there are certain things I won't sell my soul for and a nicer place to live was one of them. That was when Martin accidentally introduced me to the world of magic artifacts, a year after the Pulse happened, and got me sucked into a whole other world. I got an apartment slightly better than the first with Pru later before "upgrading" to this house, all funded with money from my private clients and her disability checks. So it could be worse, I knew—I'd *seen* worse firsthand, with ceilings about to cave in and flying roaches and radiators that shook like they were going to explode.

Still. Money meant freedom.

Freedom from stress and worry—we could live where we wanted and have no barriers, no more sacrifices. Money meant a new house. My bedroom growing up was the size of this damn bungalow. And it wasn't bad. Emaleth had a good life, if I did say so myself. She never went without.

But I wanted more for her. I wanted riding lessons and dance lessons and music lessons and the best clothes and the best toys and the best schools...I wanted a fund set up so she could go to any university she wanted one day and stay long enough to get a PhD or three. She deserved everything she could ever want.

And I had to find a way to give it to her.

Prudence returned with a box of fuses and fiddled with the ones on the stove until she stood and turned the dial again. This time the light came on and she grinned. "See? No problem." Silence followed as she stared at me just sitting there. "You're taking that other job, aren't you?"

I was. I had to. It was too much money to pass up—just the down payment alone for accepting the job made it a no-brainer. "I am. It's not just the tuition and the college fund I want for her—I could afford to *buy* a nice little house with that money, have a great down payment. A house of our own with a fixed ceiling and a new fridge."

While the water boiled, she leaned on the counter across from me "Did he give you more details?"

"Just that I'm to be at his private airport Saturday morning at six if I agree to this."

"Length of time?"

I sighed heavily. "Unknown." Which I hated. When possible, I tried to time things for a couple of days, a week at most. Once I was away for two weeks and I called damn near every day. "He said he 'strongly preferred' no more than seven days and that there'd be something in my contract to that effect. So we're going to Ethiopia and, given the task and likely location of the ring, my cell phone getting reception might be an issue."

"Denny called today while you were out."

56

Oh, hell. I dropped my face into my hands and groaned. Too many men. *Too many.*

"He wondered if he could have her for the weekend. It *might* be good timing."

Chase Denham aka Denny was my ex from several years ago. He thought he was Em's father. His mother thought he was Em's father. In fact, if I'd married him and just raised her as his, my own father wouldn't've disowned me.

And while he most certainly was *not* my daughter's father, no amount of convincing on my part would shake him from this belief—or the belief that he should have visitation rights. If he wasn't so earnest and so good with her, I'd've thrown the completed private DNA test at him years ago. For now, he was content with the delusion and I permitted him in our lives though I insisted he didn't belong there. Besides, Emaleth needed a decent male figure in her life. It wasn't like she even had a grandfather.

If I was gone for over a week, having him to take Em on weekends *would* work out well. Pru could handle my little girl, who was generally well-behaved, but I knew full time on Saturday and Sunday could be draining.

"What do you think?" I glanced up at Pru.

The thing about her is that she's pretty anyway—smooth skin, heart-shaped face, delicate features—but she has incredibly soulful eyes. Years ago we could go into a club and I, the decked out old money rich girl who was three years her junior, would pale in comparison to her in jeans and no makeup, boys lining up to buy her drinks with just one look in her eyes. There was life there. A spark of something honest and real that just drew people to her and gave her opinions that much more weight. Even I fell for it and never really questioned why.

"I think it would be good for the weekend," she said at last. "I'll check in with her. Let Chase pick her up Saturday morning, take her to school Monday, and I'll get her that night afterward."

It was a plan. "Can you keep digging for info about Ashford while I'm gone?"

"Absolutely. And Denny?"

"Yeah, I'll call him. It'll be good for her."

The kettle whistled and she moved again to get to mugs.

Weight was lifting from my shoulders, not completely but enough that I felt my head was above water finally. Nothing had changed, not really, in the past few minutes, but knowing I could take the job made a big difference, and having Pru here support was invaluable.

"You're my favorite, you know," I said.

She grinned over her shoulder. "I know. I'm pretty awesome."

I gave my face a final wipe and no tears followed, then I rose to retrieve the canister of tea bags from the pantry cupboard.

And some ibuprofen for my toe and temper.

6
SKIPPING CUSTOMS

———— ◆ ————

WHAT GEAR ASHFORD FELT I could bring of my own, I wasn't entirely sure, but I packed my usual caving fare—proper clothing, hiking boots, hard hat, flashlights, harness, rope, descender, ascender, and so on. Even if everything wasn't the newest, it was reliable. Plus I brought my guns and enough ammo to take down a god.

Better safe than crushed by a deity.

Saturday morning at twenty past five, I had the cab waiting out front packed with everything but my overnight bag of essentials. Prudence slept still, in theory, though I'd heard the floor creaking under her steps minutes ago, and knew she'd be up soon. I'd talk to her later and didn't need to now—no, my focus was on Emaleth.

That early in the morning, her room had a glow creeping around the blinds. With the canopy over her bed and mountain of pillows, she had the look of a sleeping princess—which surely was her intent when she chose that particular bed out of a catalogue. Her guardian Giles remained curled at her feet, not lifting even an eyelid to inspect me as I approached.

I wouldn't wake her, not this early. She'd be up at six as usual, begging to watch cartoons with her breakfast cereal instead of sleeping in like the rest of the world.

I'd call her later at Denny's. While I was on the plane, when we reached Africa. And Pru would check in on her too.

Still, my heart ached with a low, deep throbbing. Emotion welled and I blinked back sudden wetness in my eyes. I hated leaving her. Loathed it. I was a supernatural bounty hunter second; mother first. Always.

And with the payday coming up, maybe I could afford a nice vacation with her, if only to stay home for a month and do normal Mom Things, like go to a parent council meeting or volunteer on a fieldtrip or bring a platter of cupcakes for her class thereby making her teacher's head explode.

I smiled absently down at Em, then took a few steps back, not daring to lean down and kiss her cheek as it would wake her and I'd probably turn into a sobbing mess.

My overnight bag was a heavy weight on my shoulder as I padded silently down the narrow hall. By the front door sat my small pack I was never in the field without, and I slipped it on over my long-sleeved fitted black shirt. The gun harness and weapons were packed in my bag, and I'd decided against strolling to Ashford's airport with them directly on my person. Private flight, so I wasn't exactly sure how customs was being handled, but I was going for "intimidating" and not "threatening" with my host so it seemed best to keep them locked away.

I cracked open the front door, blinking against the damp air and bright light of the porch. The cab idled in the driveway and the driver waited in the front—so he was *not* the man standing off to the side staring at me.

I sighed, shook my head, and turned to lock up. "She's still asleep."

Chase Denham held a paper bag and grinned. "Brought breakfast for when she wakes up."

In an attempt to solidify his belief in being a parent, he'd given himself a full parental role: The Fun One. The one who brings fast food. The one who will let her eat a candy bar for breakfast. This package said Tim Hortons and I had no doubt it contained an assortment of donuts.

Little did he realize *I* fought jaguar shamans, therefore *I* would always be the coolest parent ever. At least until the teenage years.

I shifted my weight, fidgeting with the strap of my bag. "And you think you're going to sit around in my living room until she gets up?"

"I was excited to see her," he said with a shrug and offered a slight smile. His charm was still apparent, never mind that we hadn't been a couple in years—there was a reason why I dated him for eighteen months in the first place. His hair was dark brown and curly, like silk to the touch—he used better conditioner than I did anymore. Eyes were hazel, jaw strong and square, and he had a kindness to him that drew women like flies to honey infused with fly pheromones and really good hair. Former prime minister's son—that political charm was in his blood. But his personality backed up his looks: he'd do anything for Emaleth, anything for me.

But I still didn't love him.

The front door cracked open, Pru sticking her head out as she blinked sleepily. "He can wait inside, as long as he doesn't wake her yet."

Denny glanced back at me. Grinned and cocked his eyebrows.

I shook my head and rolled my eyes, hefting my bag again. "Whatever. I'll call later."

I made it down the front steps before he called, "Liv."

A glance over my shoulder showed the pair of them standing in the dim glow of the porch light, mood decidedly melancholy.

"Be careful," he said.

"I'm not the one with a six-year-old for the weekend," I said. "You are in far more danger than I am."

———◆———

ASHFORD HAD A PRIVATE PLANE—because of *course* he did— with Laurel James and Dawson Fabrini already on board. And

Mr. Rolph. It still kind of bothered me that he didn't have a first name, or at least not one I was permitted to know.

I had a passport, permits for everything I carried though as far as I knew Ethiopia still banned carrying weapons, so I had to trust Ashford's team had a plan for dealing with it. My main luggage had been taken from the taxi's trunk when I arrived, whisked away from view.

The small cabin interior was luxurious without being over the top. Seats were plush and white, like La-Z-Boy recliners, single file on either side and some facing one another with a table between. At the back, a curved couch sat by a mini fridge, opposite a television screen.

I dropped to sit opposite Dawson. Laurel sent a pointed look at my overnight bag beside my seat and before I could reach for it, Mr. Rolph immediately scooped it up, giving me an indecipherable glance as he walked past. His gaze was steady and somewhat unsettling since he remained so silent, but I preferred disapproving to "planning to serial kill everyone...probably with Laurel's okay".

"Always stow things in the overhead compartment." Dawson indicated above our heads with a shy grin. He had dimples on either cheek when he smiled and I warmed to him immediately; he was absolutely adorable, though I declined to say that aloud as my experience said thirty-something men didn't particularly care for that adjective.

I raised an eyebrow at his laptop open on the table between us. "Except for expensive electronic equipment?"

His large hands grasped the laptop and gave it a tug, showing it stuck in place. "It's locked down."

I hadn't relished the picture of it barreling toward me if the plane crashed, so that was good to know. I angled out of my backpack's straps and dropped the pack on my knee as I leaned back in the comfortable seat. A soft pillow was nestled against the small of my back.

I *loved* private planes.

"Have you been on many flights with him?" I asked, lifting my chin in the direction Rolph had gone. Seemed more causal than, *How long have you known our weird—and absent—host? Or at least his henchman.*

"Only the flight from Texas a few weeks ago. I was hired just for this trip."

Curiouser and curiouser. At least I could maybe bond with the fellow newbie.

Apparently I had been the last to arrive; within minutes, the engine started. Safety belts were discreetly tucked to the sides of our comfortable seats, and I immediately latched mine together. Dawson took a bit more time, using an extender to cross the belt over his midsection. His hands gripped the armrests and he tipped his head back.

"Nervous flyer?" I asked.

He heaved a loud sigh. "I don't really *like* being thousands of feet in the air. Gravity is my greatest nemesis."

God help me, I wanted to cross the table and hug him—my maternal instincts are their own force to be reckoned with. "I understand—my issues are with being underwater. Scale down a thousand foot drop in a cave? Great. Scuba diving? No, dear god. But flying is actually a very safe form of travel. I mean, so long as we don't pass the Bermuda Triangle, now that the Pulse has probably activated it."

"Are we passing it to get to Africa?" His tone crept up higher at the end.

"I imagine the pilot has taken that into consideration."

The plane rumbled and my stomach gave a nervous turn as we moved through space and lifted off. Dawson still stared at the ceiling like we might land again faster if he didn't look away.

"Of course, there was this time I was flying back from London—in coach, unfortunately—and I'd retrieved this medieval grimoire supposedly with a demonic entity bound within the text. It escaped midflight—not certain why, but perhaps it occurred when leaving the protective confines of the area that had housed it for so long. The creature was telekinetic and started tossing around beverage carts and disrupting services to the point the pilot lost control of the plane and we began plummeting toward the ocean."

Dawson gulped almost audibly, tension working through his arms and his knuckles going white as he continued to grip the armrests. "So this story isn't, um, really helping me, Ms. Talbot..."

"My point being that you'll notice *I* am in fact alive and well, telling you this tale now."

At last his dark gaze shifted down to meet mine. "Did you crash horribly into the ocean but swim for safety? 'Cause I can't swim very well."

I waved off his concern. "Of course not. There was a teenage amateur shaman on the flight. We had the entity bound once more in the grimoire within ten minutes of it escaping. And I'm not at present traveling with anything—grimoire or otherwise—containing demonic entities, so we're perfectly safe. And if not"—I patted the pack in my lap—"I'm armed."

His shoulders relaxed slightly and his grin widened, cheeks dimpling again. "Thanks."

"Livi," I said.

"Livi," he repeated, thankfully. I'd have no more of that 'Ms. Talbot'—it made me feel old in the way even being the parent of a six-year-old doesn't.

Laurel had been ignoring us thus far and continued to, but I noticed when she unlatched her belt and I did the same. She had a tablet in her hands, scrolling through something—perhaps documents related to our trip or perhaps a game. But then she looked too boring to play games. I'd have to get the lowdown from Dawson later.

He'd removed his seatbelt as well now that we were safely in the air, and reached for the bottle of water to his left. I peered out the window between us; the sun had risen sleepily, casting orange and pink through thick clouds. Emaleth would be up by now and probably watching cartoons, eating donuts with Denny while Prudence puttered around the kitchen to put away last night's dishes.

I wished I was home.

"So tell me what sorts of equipment you'll be manning," I said, shifting my attention and smile his way.

His hazel eyes lit like I'd said the magic words. "Well, cameras and communication equipment while you're in the cave, to start with. And there's no telling how you'll have to get the Seal out, so I have some basics for digging while maintaining the existing structure of the cavity."

Cave *digging*. Oh joy of joys. I tried to think back to my contract regarding hazard pay.

My cell phone buzzed within my bag and I retrieved it. I expected Emaleth or perhaps Pru.

I glanced at the number and sighed, then answered the call. "Hello, Martin."

"You found my knife after all," he said, voice laced with what I suspected was false amusement.

"*My* knife," I corrected. "You might have to start admitting I have better resources than you do, brother-dearest."

"I don't know about that. Guess who is at the airport waiting for their flight to Ethiopia for the Seal of Solomon?"

Son of a bitch. I smiled sweetly though he couldn't see it. "Guess who's getting there before you?"

Silence on the other end. "I heard your flight was tomorrow."

I sighed dramatically for his benefit, snapped a photo of the plane's window, and then sent it to him. Just as I pressed the phone to my ear again, I heard him cursing. "And how many layovers are you expecting?" I asked innocently.

"Getting there first doesn't guarantee you'll find it first. I think you technically touched down in Arizona before I did."

"And yet I still ended up with *my* knife."

"Best of luck, Liv."

"Enjoy customs, Martin." I ended the call and shoved the phone in my pack once more, chewing the inside of my mouth as my stomach turned.

This wouldn't be good. It couldn't be a coincidence he was being turned onto the Seal *now*, of all times, right when I was. Ashford had competition, apparently, which meant *I* had competition, and while of course I could steal it from whatever museum Martin might hand it to—should he succeed over me—that was not an eventuality I was looking forward to. Ashford didn't strike me as the type to forgive me for it and it was my outdoors skill set he wanted for this mission. If a theft was needed, he might seek help elsewhere and withdraw my paycheck.

"Is there a problem?" Laurel spoke up in a cool voice, drawing my attention her way.

"Yes," I said mildly. "I just *have to* know where you got your shoes."

Her dark eyes narrowed. She put on a headset and moments later the dull thrum of music entered the cabin. I tended to be difficult with people who had already decided they didn't like me and she definitely went in that column.

"*Is* there a problem?" Dawson said softly, thick brows raised.

When isn't there? "Nothing I can't handle."

———————— ◆ ————————

WE LANDED OUTSIDE OF GOBA, in the Bale Zone. The flight was fourteen hours, roughly, and the time was seven hours ahead of home, so I was thrown for a loop trying to do the math. My phone told me it was eight in the evening my time and that made it three the next morning in Ethiopia.

It hurt my brain just thinking about it.

Before rising from my once-comfortable-and-now-horrible-because-I-was-sick-of-it seat, I called Emaleth at Denny's. She *loved* his penthouse and not just because it didn't have a water-damaged ceiling or crappy leaky fridge. No, he had a wall aquarium of tropical fish and let her stay up until midnight eating cake and watching movies. Of course, she tried to assure me she was getting ready for bed and it was an apple she was chewing while talking, but a mother knows the sound of cake in her daughter's mouth.

Next I checked with Pru, who of course was fine and had already talked to Em once that night. I set my nervous energy aside and promised to check in with them again as soon as possible.

I stretched, my body cracking and aching with each movement; I'd paced the cabin a few times during the flight, but then it started to annoy Laurel. Then I'd done it a few more times before sitting back down for a nap. None of it had been enough to keep my muscles from tiring and I looked forward to being outside again.

Laurel and Mr. Rolph went ahead of us outside while Dawson and I gathered our overnight bags. I took in my first breath of fresh air as I neared the open door at the end of the cabin. The night outside was black with brittle yellow light spilling out from the plane. I worked my way down the steps and dusty ground met my feet as I glanced around. I'd expected us to land in Addis Ababa, it being the capital and where most flights stopped, but Ashford clearly didn't play by the rules. We were on a long stretch of grassless land—perhaps an old airport landing strip.

At least we are definitely ahead of Martin.

I stepped away from the stairs so Dawson could descend, shouldering my bag and picking through the darkness. A Jeep without its top waited twenty feet to the right, with a dark paint job—only the occasional gleam of metal let me identify it easily.

Mr. Rolph swept past us, back up the stairs. Laurel had her cell phone to her ear as she paced, I assumed keeping Ashford abreast of our situation. Her expensive-looking—Jimmy Choo, by my guess—pumps were already dusty, a pale brown settling over the black. A business suit with a pencil skirt was probably not her best wardrobe choice.

And she's going caving with us. I can't wait!

Dawson pulled out his cell phone as well, shining blue over his face, and let his overnight bag thump at his feet. Like me, he wore a long-sleeved shirt and jeans, and he even had a bomber jacket overtop, so seemed prepared for the chilly evening temperatures.

"Man, I have a really, really bad feeling we're going to have to camp right away." He sighed and shoved the phone in his pocket, hunching his shoulders—which I barely came up to. He glanced down at me. "I was kinda hoping for a hotel with room service. I'd kill for a cheeseburger."

I was pretty wired on coffee at this point and didn't think dumping food on my stomach would be a good idea, though I wouldn't say no to French fries. "I don't think we're going to find a McDonalds."

"We're totally not in Kansas anymore, Toto."

"I don't think I've been in Kansas for a good long while now, Dorothy."

"Hey, did you ever wonder if Toto got euthanized after the happy ending when she got back for biting the neighbor?"

"They really did leave it up in the air in that movie, didn't they?"

Mr. Rolph returned, dragging our main luggage down the stairs. A figure walked from the Jeep—a tall man with closely cropped blond hair moving into the dim light. He was in his thirties, dressed in fatigues, and had the hard look of hired muscle. I'd tangled with hired muscle a lot over the years—I could tell in moments with someone, from the deliberate steps to the cautious awareness in their eyes. This guy looked at Laurel for direction.

She gestured to the heaps of trunks and suitcases. "All of these in the trailer. The plane departs in fifteen minutes and we need to be on the road and gone by then."

Our nameless driver nodded his understanding and gave Dawson and me barely a passing glance before heaving two of our bags up and heading back to the Jeep.

Dawson leaned over to speak to me in a low voice. "So he's really friendly."

"Let me tell you," I whispered back, "I am *so* glad I have someone to snark with here."

"I know. I kinda hope you don't get eaten by flesh-eating, subterranean cave-dwellers. If you do, the return trip is going to *suck*."

———— ◆ ————

WE'D BEEN ON THE ROAD for several minutes before the plane took off again; Dawson, Laurel and I sat in the back of the Jeep, all watching the craft depart into the night sky. This left us with little to see by, save for the headlights at the front and lights at the back, which shone over the small trailer housing our luggage and equipment. The road was rough and narrow, dirt flying and rocks rumbling under the tires. To either side, tall grasses stretched on into the darkness.

I was contemplating another nap when the Jeep halted, and our driver got out. Dawson and I sat up straight, glancing around. No sign of a hotel or a McDonalds—despite it being the first night, we were definitely camping out. The air was crisp and fresh, far from the desert most people pictured Ethiopia as being.

"The Kadhim cave system's a kilometer out," our hired muscle said, his voice drawn out with a Southern accent—Tennessee or Alabama was my guess. Normally I found that kind of thing sexy but he continued to make me uncomfortable. He moved around the vehicle to the trailer, intent on our bags. "I'll lead you just after dawn."

Giving us like three hours of sleep. Good times. "So do you have a name?" I asked.

He paused with both hands on two separate bags, icy glare on me. "Tucker."

"Hello, Tucker." I smiled sweetly. "Nice to meet you."

He grunted at me in response and hefted the bags out. After collecting four of them, he started off into the darkness.

"Don't antagonize the mercenary," Dawson whispered.

"On the contrary," I grasped my overnight bag and slipped it onto my shoulder, "as they're motivated by money, it's much harder to piss them off. Unless you stop paying them."

He shouldered his bag as well, both Laurel and Mr. Rolph picked up theirs, and the group of us started off after Tucker. There was more left in the trailer and I assumed Tucker would be heading back for it. I quickly saw why he hadn't simply brought the Jeep—wherever camp was, it was well off the road. The ground was uneven, tall grass swishing and cutting against my legs and the bottom of my bag. The glow from the idling Jeep didn't extend far and the night above was clouded over. Even without a flashlight, our guide seemed to know our path.

Bugs chirped and whispered, birds chittered, and I shuddered to think what else might be lurking nearby. Wild animals were lovely—from a distance. I was not fond of getting up close and personal with them.

Eventually the flickering glow of a fire showed in the distance, highlighting large rectangular structures. Several minutes later we reached the camp in a good-sized clearing.

It was a far larger set up than I'd anticipated; we were "roughing it", sure, but not in tiny tents on the ground. These were large and a glance past open canvas flaps where a lantern lit one revealed suitable cots beneath mosquito netting.

One woman sat at the fire, though with large logs on either side of her and the closed tent flaps, I assumed there were more people resting. She wore dark fatigues like Tucker and firelight caught flecks of gold in her shoulder-length red hair. I put her around forty, maybe, but I was notoriously bad at judging ages

"Any trouble?" Tucker asked.

New Merc shook her head, chewing whatever her late night dinner was. "Nope," she managed around a mouthful of food.

Tucker tossed the bags inside the open tent and looked back at me pointedly. "Dawn."

"I haven't forgotten," I said.

He shook his head, muttering under his breath, and went to sit next to his friend. Mr. Rolph stayed with them as well, waving us ahead. Dawson and I followed Laurel inside and I released the tent flap once we were all in.

"They are *Ashford's* hires, right?" I glanced at Laurel as I tucked my bag beneath the bed at the far end.

She eased herself onto the end of her cot and pulled off her heels to rub her feet. "Whose else would they be?"

Not answering my question. "I make it a point to know who works for whom. Just checking."

"They're our escorts." She yawned and definitely *must* have been tired if she was talking with me.

Or the ring's *escorts, I'm sure.*

"They know the terrain," she continued. "They'll be taking us tomorrow."

"You get stuck with Tucker," Dawson said with a grin.

I stuck my tongue out at him.

7
THE CAVE

———— ◆ ————

I WAS UP BEFORE THE others, barely getting in a catnap before the sun rose. A cave interior could vary greatly, so I dressed in layers. My standard underclothes—shorts that were the equivalent to boxer-briefs as I didn't want panties riding up and a fitted tank top with a built-in sports bra—then an insulated caving undersuit and coveralls. Elbow pads and knee pads underneath the coveralls. Double pairs of socks—wetsocks over wool—and hiking boots. I loaded up my pack with rolled up garbage bags, batteries and matches in a Ziploc bag, extra flashlights, glowsticks, and a travel first aid kit that included my package of antimalarials.

Also my custom holster, magazines, and boxes of ammo in another sealed extra-large Ziploc with guns. Despite what I'd told Dawson, I didn't entirely trust Tucker. Or Mr. Rolph for that matter. My equipment all went into a separate, larger pack—without knowing what the others had, at least I knew I had enough to take care of myself.

Sun was a pink glow in the distance as I rubbed sleep out of my eyes. The scent of spices filled the air; on a table by the tent across the clearing sat a spread of shredded bread and some kind of dip or butter. It smelled divine but I skipped it and first went to fill both of my canteens with water from the large drum parked to the side.

Around the now-cool fire pit sat Curtis—mouth full again, this time with breakfast—along with two others I didn't recognize. Both were men, who nodded in my direction. Middle-aged, one lean and Caucasian with a twisty mouth, who I suspected was another merc. Given the hired muscle adding up, this trip was feeling less like an adventure and more like Ashford expected us to be attacked. This one gave me a once over, that mouth twisted again, and he went back to his food.

The other man with the two mercs was tall and slim, African—Ethiopian?—with a generous smile. His gaze lingered on mine, politer than the others had been, and I suspected that whatever he brought to our caving party, it wasn't guns. These new additions were also dressed in coveralls and boots, so I assumed they were going with us.

"Brandon and Moti," Curtis said without looking up from her breakfast, her voice curt. She shoveled in another mouthful. She was built, with biceps showing below her T-shirt sleeves that put mine to shame, and apparently required a lot of calories to keep them like that.

I nodded at both of them as well just as Dawson stepped out. His sleepy gaze moved in the direction of one of the tents; I followed it to see Tucker standing there.

"To the tech table, Fabrini," he called.

Dawson trundled to the table under a canopy set up between two tents, avoiding Tucker's gaze and short ponytail swinging after him.

Eventually Laurel turned up as well, looking exhausted and muttering something about needing coffee. She'd dressed in crisp casual caving gear and I strongly suspected her boots weren't remotely broken in. Mr. Rolph was the last and he came from around the tents, ready to go. Where he'd been, I couldn't say, and he studied all of us with a level gaze.

"Energy bars in the crate by the water drum," he announced. "Stock up and see Mr. Fabrini for your equipment."

Laurel shifted and I all but expected a subtle groan from her, though she remained professional. I took the cue and stuffed my bag with a variety of energy bars—there were freeze-dried packages of other foods there, but I wasn't sure if we were taking the right equipment to cook it, so left them be—and snatched some of the warm breakfast laid out, and then headed to Dawson's table before the others.

More sun crept over mountains in the distance. Pink and orange light scattered over the table as Dawson pulled out equipment. His laptop was already open and on.

"Here." I set the food down next to him.

"You should probably eat something since you're going to be in a cave without good food and stuff."

I shook my head. "Energy bars are fine. I don't like anything heavy in my system."

"Easier to move around?"

"There's no ladies' room down there."

"Ah." He pushed a small sealed box toward me. "Okay, your goodies. Cave radio. Cutting edge technology tweaked by yours truly."

I popped open the yellow plastic box to see knobs and dials, and some cables wound into the lid.

"Purpose is twofold. One, to communicate with us. You open it, put in the cables—color coded—and you'll see a keyboard on the back for sending short texts. The signal will be going through a lot of rock but it'll come through. You can also flip a beacon that will tell us your location if there's trouble."

"By 'us' you mean Curtis, since it looked like she's staying here."

"Um...I'm sure there'll be a rescue mission."

At least for the ring.

"Standard walkie-talkies, in case they're useful down there." Dawson handed one to me, which I tucked into a holder on my belt. "Also, a camera for you." The next piece of equipment was a speck of a thing with no wires.

"Ashford?"

Dawson nodded as I lifted the tiny cam and glanced over it. "He wants a record. There's about three days of recording time, battery should last a week. I'd turn it off while sleeping or, like, peeing and stuff. I think he wants to see the location where you find the Seal."

"He knows we'll be *in a cave,* right? Where something like this will be scratched, banged, and water damaged?"

"It's waterproof, if that helps."

Nothing is ever waterproof, just water *resistant.* I sighed and looked for a spot to pin it to. The collar of my coveralls was a possibility, until the first time it was banged loose. A plastic piece folded out from the camera and I suspected I could coil it on my ear. *Which won't be at* all *distracting.*

"Finally," he popped open a foam-padded box and withdrew a headlamp for my helmet, "these. Top of the line. Has sensors that detect how much light is needed and adapts accordingly. Double the usual battery life and I'm sending along an extra—batteries are rechargeable."

I lifted the sleek headlamp, quite certain I was in love at last. "I don't want to know how much this cost, do I?"

"I was allowed a very generous equipment budget."

I glanced over my shoulder to see everyone else busy, a good distance from us, and leaned forward, resting my elbows on the table. My voice dropped lower. "So what's the story on everyone?"

"I, um..." His gaze darted over my shoulder. "I don't really—"

"C'mon, Dawson. You're telling me you're our super tech guy, in charge of communication, and you haven't googled who you're working with?"

He sighed and gave his chin a little lift; I took the hint and rounded the table to crouch next to him. His fingers slid over the laptop mouse pad and tapped, opening a folder. The first file he showed me was labeled with Laurel's full name. "Laurel James is all over. The real deal—detailed online portfolio, job history, et cetera. Did you look her up?"

I nodded. "My friend did as soon as I had names. Nothing about her raised any red flags."

"Same here." He had photos, links to websites, cached social networking profiles, and more files than I could glance over. "From what I've pieced together, she's worked for Ashford for a year or so now. According to LinkedIn, her previous job titles have been things like 'Personal Assistant to the CEO', 'Organizational Management'—her specialties are an attention to detail and, pardon my French, but getting shit done."

And wearing great shoes. "Outdoors experience?"

"None. This is...an odd kind of thing for her to be sent to, based strictly on what I've read."

Interesting. "Mr. Rolph?"

"Nothing. You?"

I shook my head. "But we had little to go on."

"He's a ghost, at least under that surname and no one has ever spoken his first. I did find *this*, though." He showed me a single photograph with a group of men standing in front of a building in a city—a professional photo, the glass of the background skyscraper gleaming white and a very blue sky above. There were eight men and one on the far right was Mr. Rolph—the thick mustache, thin hair, and bottle glasses.

"Name?" I asked.

"Only three of those guys had names on the photo. The other ones I've identified—some investment business from about five years ago, no longer around."

"Has anyone said what his job is for Ashford? Beyond 'scholar'?"

"I *think* he was hired specifically to work with you on this mission like I was. But otherwise no idea and can't find anything else."

This did not ease my worries at all. "You know, I couldn't find records of Moses Ashford either."

"Offline resources said he's a prominent collector of relics."

That I have never heard of? Seemed unlikely unless he was outside North America, but if that was the case, why meet me at Kent House in the city? "Where's he from?"

"Supposedly New Bristol—I've found a lot of property deeds in his name, though they took some digging to find."

Also odd, as I thought I knew everyone in the city's community related to my line of work, but maybe I'd been out of the loop living in the suburbs. "That's all?"

"Nothing...shady that I've turned up."

"Which doesn't mean that there isn't anything, just that *you* haven't found anything?"

"Right."

"Our mercs?"

Sure enough, he had files on them too—the two guys and the chick with the guns. "They did a tour ten years ago in Afghanistan. All three abandoned the army and are just muscle for hire now. Came here from..." He clicked the mouse and drew up some screenshots of online articles. "...Venezuela. Where they turned a couple of FANB posts into craters, as you can see."

I could and I stifled a shudder at seeing the destruction; the Venezuelan military likely wasn't happy about *that*. "So that's what you were looking up at last night."

"Couldn't sleep right away, so yeah."

"Moti?"

"No idea but haven't had a chance to dig yet. Local, maybe? Sorry."

I supposed that would have to do. I plucked my cell phone from where I'd stuffed it in my pocket and set it in front of him.

Dawson glanced up, thick brows furrowing. "Um—"

"On here, you'll find the number for Prudence Cortez. If something happens, you call her. She's my best friend and she's taking care of my daughter."

He grasped the phone in his big hands, turning it over as he gazed down at it. "I didn't know you had a kid."

"That didn't show up on my Google results?"

A blush bloomed on his cheeks. "Well. Okay, it did, but I didn't go looking for details about your family."

"She's six. And there's a clause in my contract that specifies she's paid a sum from Ashford in the event of my demise before I obtain the ring. Do remind him of that." I collected my tech and turned to go.

"Carlotta Ann-Marie Fabrini," he spoke up.

I glanced over my shoulder at him.

He worried at his bottom lip. "Two Pines Nursing Home, in Austin. My grandma. I...I take jobs like this to help her."

I nodded in understanding. "Deal."

Hopefully it won't come to that.

———— ◆ ————

THE MOUTH OF KADHIM CAVE yawned before us in the now-bright light of day

In a word, it was stunning. I'd been caving, mostly in North America, but there were few places that could compare to this beauty. Limestone had been cut away over centuries by water, etching the walls in curves. Ankle-deep water ran along the center and widened outside the cave into a pond. It was startlingly blue, reflecting the sky above.

I made a point to switch on Ashford's cam that Dawson had me equipped with to scan the area and take it all in, before switching it off again to conserve power and recording time. I had a digital camera of my own—tiny and tough for trips like this—which I pulled out of a padded pocket in my gear belt so I could take a few photos too. It might give Em more to tease her classmates with.

Curtis had been made to stay back at camp. I wasn't sure why but perhaps Ashford felt it best to have someone guarding Dawson and the rest of the equipment. Brandon, Moti, and Mr. Rolph all carried rope bags and equipment, including drills and bolts for when rigging was needed. My own equipment bags were heavy on my back; the rule was a third of your body weight in a backpack, but I knew within half a day I'd be questioning the logic of it. I insisted on some of my krabs and hooks, too, and they hung on my belt to jangle at my hips while I walked. Laurel came up beside me, seeming tiny in her large hard hat and caving clothes, particularly petite without her high heels. She gazed at the expansive entrance, lips parted, but when she noticed me watching her she scowled and looked at her feet.

Tucker pushed between all of us. His caving clothes were all camo-green, and I figured a gun was definitely stowed in his backpack. On his right hip sat a walkie-talkie, on the left a bowie knife.

"There are three entrances," Mr. Rolph said. "About four to five kilometers have been mapped from each one." He unfolded a large map on special thick paper and we gathered around to look. There were details about the entrances and then a huge space of nothing representing the center. The thing looked hand drawn and the accompanying survey didn't resemble the standard ones I'd seen most cavers use.

"Locally made?" I asked.

He nodded. "I've never been in the place but I came here last week to piece together information from residents in a village on the other side of the Shebelle River."

I checked the scale and compared it to what had been mapped. If that was almost five kilometers from each entrance, it would put the size at... "How big *is* this thing?"

"Twenty-six kilometers long, approximately."

Jesus. "Vertically?"

"Currently unknown."

"And we're headed into no man's land in the center?"

"Yes."

I eyed the water again, not liking this. "Diving going to be necessary?"

"Too much for you, beauty queen?" Brandon called over his shoulder with a grin.

Well. Apparently I'd been googled ahead of time by someone besides Dawson. Some people were so judgmental about things pregnant, disowned teenage girls will do to pay the bills.

"Perhaps," Mr. Rolph answered my query and nodded as he folded the map again and slid it in his pack. He removed his glasses and rubbed spots from the lenses with his sleeve. "We have equipment for short dives on us."

Oh god. Do. Not. Want. I forced a smile and tried not to stress about it. I could make it through sumps—*had* made it through sumps—and despite my aversion to it, I was trained in scuba diving and had done cave dives before. I just really, really preferred not to. I didn't see anyone carrying rebreathers, nor had I been briefed on special equipment usage, so hopefully this meant the chances were fairly slim that we'd run into deep water.

Further, I didn't particularly want to know *why* no one had mapped that center part, though I was starting to think we'd be better off bombing everything and then sifting through the rubble.

Mr. Rolph glanced at me and smiled. "Nothing in the geography indicates water runs deep here."

He must've sensed my discomfort and I appreciated his reassurance. Without the glasses, he seemed much less standoffish, and I regretted my previous snap judgment regarding him. "Thanks."

Tucker moved ahead; Mr. Rolph seemed to know the area best but if the muscle wanted to jump in first, so be it. I walked a few steps behind him. Ashford had led me to believe *I* would be leading this expedition, but perhaps the others would ease back once we were underground and my own expertise came to light.

With the mouth of the cave so wide, sunlight permeated fairly deep at first. We kept to the side, single file, to avoid the water as much as possible. Water resistant clothes are all well and good, but wet fabric is heavier, colder, and it's something to avoid. Dank smells drifted up, of what, I didn't know, but hoped to grow used to it soon. After making a left, when the cave narrowed considerably, darkness mouthed us and three of us flipped on our helmet lights—not all, to conserve energy—and I turned on my camera. White beams bobbed as we walked, cutting this way and that.

Caves are alive. Not sentient-alive—though sometimes I wondered—but they have internal systems like living things do and they breathe. Depending on the size of the cave, it can be a small sigh or whimper, or a great, heaving roar with winds that can knock you off your feet. Kadhim opened with a long steady breath, promising deep, narrow depths within.

A giddy thrill went through me, for a moment drowning out any worry. In these cases, danger was always balanced out by sheer beauty and wonder that was the locale before me. Though I enjoyed the idea of time off after this paycheck to look after my daughter, places like this would always call me back again, along with the adrenaline exploring them provided.

When the water snaked off to the side and we had a bit more room, I fell back into step with Mr. Rolph. "So, scholar?"

"Not officially, but working in that capacity," he said with a wry smile.

"Out of curiosity, do you know if we are looking for a ring randomly on the ground, or is there something I've not been told yet?"

"Manmade room somewhere near the middle." His gaze remained focused straight ahead, not glancing to me once. "Allegedly."

Ten kilometers horizontally to the center, then. Not *that* bad. Maybe. But I said nothing and tried to ignore the twisting in my gut.

———— ◆ ————

ONE OF THE THINGS NO amount of preparation will help you with in caving is how the complete darkness messes with your sense of time.

Jetlag had already set my brain behind so the kilometers passed on foot—and via rebelays—alternated between feeling like both hours and minutes. There was little conversation between any of us, which didn't bother me; the only person I thought I might talk to was Moti, who had a friendly, easy energy about him. Unfortunately, the odd time he spoke to Mr. Rolph, it wasn't in a language I was familiar with. I'd learned a handful of Amharic phrases for travel but I didn't think it was what he spoke, and my knowledge wouldn't translate into an actual conversation, either. I mostly held my tongue and wished for music—I had a caving playlist that would've brightened my mood considerably.

Brandon and Tucker stuck close to one another, body language confirming Dawson's implication of familiarity; the former didn't have the Southern drawl so I nixed the possibility of brothers, but perhaps only by blood. As Dawson said, they'd worked together in difficult situations and once upon a time in the military, and that bond could be as close as a familial one. Both eyed me frequently and exchanged glances—it was the, "We've heard rumors she's an ex-rich girl—what's she doing here?" look. My reputation, as usual, proceeded me. It typically took having to accomplish some dangerous task for people to believe I knew what I was doing. There was a reason I most frequently worked alone when I could.

Tucker gestured for us rest when we reached an open pocket of the cave. Mr. Rolph immediately pulled out the map to confer with him and I caught the words, "about to hit a lead" before their voices dropped too low for me to hear. So that would mean we'd gone roughly the five kilometers if not slightly farther, with no man's land ahead.

Lovely.

Moti hummed cheerily, something that sounded like a pop song but not one I knew. Laurel was silent, still completely out of her element. When we reached a place to stop for a bit, she sat first and leaned against the limestone wall, head tipped back and eyes closed. Tension hovered around her, prickling the air as if she might go off on anyone who got too close. At least she wasn't wearing heels she could've stabbed me with.

I eased myself onto the cave floor, only noticing just how sore I was when I sat. I slipped off my packs and pulled out an energy bar. It had been, what, maybe four hours or so since we left? Five? Six or seven? There had been several awkward passages and some slow going that took a while to pass, so I couldn't say for sure. With the time zone difference, Em might still be asleep, it being Sunday morning. I could all but picture her sprawled on Denny's living floor surrounded by a pillow fort, plate of chocolate cake crumbs to the side, TV on the menu for some Disney movie she'd fallen asleep during. Denny would be passed out as well but on the couch, sleeping with his mouth open and snoring horribly.

I blinked and shoved the thought away, focusing on opening the wrapper of my energy bar. Odds were that we'd have to camp out in the cave over a few nights and there was no sense stressing about my daughter in the meantime when I couldn't reach her.

I took a long drink from my canteen next. It only held so much but I had a backup in my pack, and we had tablets for purifying flowing water we might find.

Everyone took turns heading just outside the cavern into an alcove to squat and do their business in a makeshift pit dug in a sandier spot we found. One of the rare occasions I disliked being a girl was during such an act, though thankfully there were items that made outside urination much easier. Brandon was the last to take his turn and I didn't particularly *want* to think about the smell back there given how his lips got even twitchier, but such is the luck of drawing the proverbial short straw. Though I couldn't speak for the others, I chose to keep my camera off for this act.

While the others packed up, I moved toward the opening at the end of the room, supposedly the path we'd be taking. The air was damp to breathe but we'd climbed a recent incline and there was very little water to encounter now even if I still felt it everywhere. The cave walls often stretched up, up, dozens of meters high to a ceiling barely visible with my headlamp. City skyscrapers are one thing, but nothing ever made me feel quite as small the way nature does.

The light on my helmet cast a strip of white over more limestone walls and rough ground. I tilted my head, glancing deeper where the light faded at the back. Some more tight squeezes to go.

I pulled my compass out of my pocket. "North, right?" I called.

"Yes," Mr. Rolph returned.

Then this was definitely the path. The others were gathering at my back but no one pushed past me, so I headed into the unknown area first, hoping like hell Rolph was mapping the route so we could find our way back; rigging remained where we'd been climbing but, turned around after a few days of being down here, getting back could be confusing The slight sound of scratches on the wall came as a relief initially until I thought about it and glanced back. "Isn't that a rather big no-no?"

He stood next to a white arrow, pale against the limestone, and dusted his hands off on his coveralls. "These caves aren't a big tourist spot like Sof Omar. Safety over cave integrity on this trip."

Interesting. Not something I'd argue with.

I moved forward, glancing around. The space was narrow but tall, walls rising at least twenty feet over my head. I twisted around so I could squeeze past the narrowest part, keeping my head turned and watching where I was stepping. Mr. Rolph followed after me with Tucker after him—Tucker was the largest, after all, so with new things to encounter, it was best to have him in the center in case he got stuck and needed help. I cursed my chest—as usual—and sucked in a breath as I got past the narrowest spot. My braid caught on limestone, tugging at my scalp, and helmet echoed on the rock it hit, but I made it through and took a deep breath as I stepped into a new area.

Another cavern opened up, cool air brushing my face. I called to the others and minutes later Mr. Rolph joined me.

This cavern branched off in three directions. "Suggestions?"

Mr. Rolph had a lighter and went to the opening on the far left to measure the air flow. I held back and looked at the other two openings, finding both looked pretty much the—

Something caught my eye.

The others were piling into the cavern with grumbles and curses, so I left them to slip through the middle archway, frowning and staring at something pale on the ground. The lamp on my helmet compensated and brightened to fill the larger space.

"Ms. Talbot," Rolph called, but I waved him off, still focused on whatever it was on the ground. I moved close and fell into a crouch, peering at the thing wedged between two boulders. White, stripped down and smooth.

Bone.

"We're waiting," Laurel snapped.

Better take a seat, then. I ground my teeth in irritation, but focused on my find instead of her grating tone.

I grasped the end of the bone and wiggled it free. The weight of people behind me pressed down, so I raised it for them to see as I stood.

Tucker barely gave it a passing glance. "Plenty of animals come down here to die." He turned to Mr. Rolph. "Which way?"

"It's down this path," he replied, but hadn't taken his gaze off the bone. I figured, like me, he had at the very least noticed we hadn't encountered a single sign of so much as a bat or bug during the last several hours. I also assumed he *wasn't* a serial killer but had taken some anatomy classes and knew we were looking at a human femur bone.

One that had been gnawed upon.

8
NOT ALONE IN THE DARK

———— ◆ ————

LITTLE ELSE WAS SAID AMONG my companions as we moved on but a chill had settled deep in my bones and I couldn't shake it, no matter the exhilarating fun of our activities. These were not men—or men-plus-a-woman—to take my instinct seriously, I suspected. "Female's intuition" still got batted around like nonsense among many in this line of work, so I saw no cause to speak up.

Yet.

Still, Dawson's joke of flesh-eating, subterranean cave-dwellers remained in my head.

Besides the utter darkness, the silence worked on my nerves, stretching them taut until I was jittery, as if I'd had five shots of espresso and Red Bull for breakfast. I moved ahead of the group once again, leading the party while Mr. Rolph marked our path, and the unfamiliarity between everyone left me extra tense.

You can hallucinate in caves. There's a partial sensory deprivation quality to being down there, and it is easy to believe you hear or see something that isn't real. I kept my focus, shifting my head and blinking often to give my eyes a rest, listened. I caught the occasional drip—water, somewhere, steadily tapping. Steps and scrapes sounded behind me, my companions moving. Any muttered curses were amplified by the cave acoustics. All normal sounds, thankfully—I'd never forgive myself if *I* was the one to be compromised on this mission.

We reached a dead end with a hole in the wall about halfway up—one that would require some maneuvering for the broad-shouldered men in our party. Mr. Rolph moved past me, presumably to check the air flow, though there were no other exits in the area so obviously it was the place to try.

"It's this way," he confirmed and looked at me, awaiting direction.

Right, I was officially in charge, then. I turned to the others. "Single file. Laurel, you're the only newbie here, yes?"

She glared at me so harshly I half-expected one of those grimoire poltergeists to pop out of her head. "New to caving. *Not* to keeping an eye on things, so keep in mind that I'll be the one delivering your paycheck later."

She had to know my camera was on; perhaps Ashford wouldn't care, then, that she was being a snarky bitch. My jaw ticked but I ignored the jab and tried to keep my voice calm— and not condescending. "Move up front and go after me." There was no sense getting her claustrophobic and I preferred the experienced Mr. Rolph to bring up the rear.

I dropped my pack and gear bag behind me, grabbed a glowstick, and went first. I rose onto my toes, took a breath, heaved myself up and through; my headlamp caught the narrow, uneven tunnel around me. There was just enough space for me and my helmet, which I happily left on.

The hole went for maybe nine feet or so and then disappeared into darkness. I squeezed, shifted. Panic naturally rose, though I breathed through it and kept calm. I'd been through worse. I couldn't *recall* worse at the moment, but certainly I had at some point. I wiggled, snake-like, along the few feet until I reached the end where darkness yawned. My light only crossed so far—it must've been another massive room. A grunt left my lips echoing in the enclosed space.

I came nearer to the end and grasped the edge, hauling myself forward. Looked down.

Nothing.

My heart thumped hard and I fought down the panic clawing at my throat as I glanced around. I couldn't see the other end of the room, nor anything past the sheer drop below—my headlamp sensed the difference and brightened; though I *thought* I saw the bottom, my eyes were tired and the weight of hours in darkness could have left them unreliable. A glance up put me a dozen feet from the ceiling of the cave, however—my headlamp shone over stalactites. There had to be a bottom.

I cracked the glowstick, illuminating bright green, and tossed it down. It twirled and fell, landing maybe ninety to one hundred feet below. A breath of relief left my lips—not *that* bad, then.

I scrambled back until my feet hit the other edge and I slipped out, brushed stray hair from my face and back into my helmet. "There's a drop, several stories. I need a lot of rope, bolts, and a drill."

Brandon dug through his equipment bag while I gathered some supplies from mine, like my harness which I immediately slipped on. I was the one to drill the bolt and set up the rigging outside the hole because of course I trusted no one but myself— sometimes I was such a control freak, I thought it a miracle I let anyone else help raise my daughter. I cast the rope through the hole and with Tucker's assistance went back through feet-first, on my belly and dragging my packs after me.

I felt with my toes until I got near the edge, then kicked the remaining rope down. It was awkward as hell but I managed to slip down, gripping the rope and climbing backward with my feet scraping the cave wall. When I was at the end of the small tunnel, I gave the rope a tug, found the rigging secure, so let myself go over the edge.

Despite the fact that I was hanging a bazillion feet in the air, I felt remarkably better being out of that awkward crawlspace. I slung my packs over my shoulder and began the descent, gazing around in wonder at the massive cavern. It was the largest we'd been in thus far, and the cave seemed to swell with pride, fresh air whistling around me. The glowstick still shone green below, promising solid ground was in reach.

My feet touched down at last and I slipped off of the rope and out of my harness. "I'm here!" I called. Laurel would be next and I hoped like hell she'd had decent training ahead of time.

I left the glowstick as-is and cast my headlamp around, taking in the walls. It looked like another typical cavern, though several times the size of any of the others we'd been in and definitely *not* the manmade one with the ring. Walls were rough limestone, asymmetrical. I swung around, glancing at the floor next, and when I spotted something white, my stomach plummeted again.

Finding human bones in this excursion really wasn't inspiring my confidence.

Yelps and squeals sounded above me; Laurel was slipping through the hole and I could all but imagine her white-knuckled grip on the rope as she descended. I paused my look for creepy things to toss a few encouraging words her way and watch she was doing everything right.

She grunted as her feet touched down, brown eyes huge and dark skin sweat-soaked. Her hands shook so I helped get her out of the harness and off the rope. She said no words of thanks but plucked the helmet off at the end of her journey and rubbed at her forehead, leaning forward and panting. "I am not enjoying this trip."

I had plenty of snarky comments but held onto them for the time being. "It'll get better."

The heat from traveling was starting to get to me as well. I took off my hard hat first, tucked my harness in my pack, and then slipped my coveralls down to hang at my waist, over my belt. I shone the headlamp in my hand over at the pile of white I'd spotted earlier and started over there to take a look.

"What is that?" Laurel asked as she followed.

I wasn't entirely sure she'd want to know, but given Ashford wanted eyes and ears with us...

Even without picking them up, I could tell the bones were human. How long they'd been there, I couldn't say, but were definitely stripped right down to nothing and I saw no sign of clothing. I toed the pile, which was scrambled and not laid out how a skeleton is in the movies, and spotted a skull.

"Oh my god," Laurel whispered beside me, fear unraveling her voice. "Could someone have fallen from where we came through? Is that what...?"

They could have. One would have to lay out the bones to check for breaks to indicate a fall, though I'd seen no sign of other caving equipment. But *something* had disrupted the pile and I saw nothing on the skull to suggest an obvious head injury. The bones did, however, look gnawed upon.

I said nothing because there wasn't a point. We didn't know precisely what might be in the cave—or at least I didn't suspect most of my party knew, and I couldn't yet ask—and since it wasn't obviously attacking us at the moment, it didn't need to be their focus.

I took Laurel's shoulder and steered her back to the hanging rope, then set her helmet back on her head. "Keep several feet back—rocks can become dislodged and fall. Watch whoever is coming down for signs of trouble. I'm going to take a look around."

Laurel stepped away from me with irritation but nodded and crossed her arms under her breasts, gazing up at the rock face. The light from her headlamp barely touched the feet of whoever was slipping through the hole above.

I inched along, my steps slow and cautious. I'd feel better with my guns, but they were still sealed away in Ziploc bags in my pack. Instead I reached for the easily accessible large combat knife sheathed in the pocket of my pack. My headlamp, from the helmet gripped in my other hand, shone white back and forth over the rock walls and jutting stalagmites.

I listened, picking through the sounds around me. Laurel's breathing was loud still, noisy through her nose as if it was plugged. Maybe allergies. Her steps shifted nervously, pebbles and dirt scraping under the soles of her boots. Beyond, more boot treads skimmed rocks, someone else from our party descending. The descender squeaked. Voices echoed in the distance, perhaps someone else moving through the short tunnel to squeeze through the hole—

There. Sand whispering. *Click click click*, ticking over stone.

Prickles rolled down my spine and my throat went dry. I backed up, swinging my head—and headlamp in hand—from side to side, fingers tensing around the handle of the knife.

It darted suddenly, swiftly, streaking in an instant and disappearing in the darkness far to my right. I'd had little more than a flash to take in but one thing was for sure...

It was big.

My lips parted to shout when it dashed forward, great, gaping mouth open and hissing. The creature was long and sleek, maybe fifteen or more feet from nose to tail. Body of a large, thick snake but with four legs jutting from its sides, some evolutionary link in between creatures far bigger than something like that should be. It scampered forward, kicking up dirt, charging at me with a long forked tongue flicking.

I dodged, dropped, rolled. Its tail whipped past me, cutting through the dirt—I did *not* want to be hit with that thing.

Laurel screamed, babbling something, but I didn't hear—I was already on my feet, bracing. I'd tossed aside the helmet and now it threw white over the dirt, fading off into blackness. I had but a small area of light to maneuver in—too far in any direction and I risked ending up in the dark.

"Quiet!" I called and Laurel squeaked to silence, just her occasional whimper and the creaking of someone descending on the rope breaking the quiet. I glanced back and forth, hand tense on the knife's hilt, hair cutting over my face, the top of my coveralls folded over my belt rustling at my sides.

A second before I saw it, I heard it rushing at me again, scampering over the rocks and dirt. This time when I dove to the side, it anticipated, braking suddenly to turn. I couldn't move fast enough and its tail snapped out, hitting me in the gut and knocking me off my feet. I flew back, slammed *hard* into the ground, gasping for breath. I blinked dirt from my eyes and winced as I struggled to rise—my arm hurt from the landing, ribs stung from being struck. Now dread sank in my stomach as I found myself with darkness at my back, Laurel, my helmet and the glowstick far ahead.

And no sign of the creature.

I stepped forward cautiously, glancing around in a rush, wincing as I breathed in and pain zigzagged through my chest. I squeezed the knife handle.

Should've pulled out a gun, I knew it.

Light was bouncing high up—Tucker had stopped his descent, holding the rope with one hand and pulling out a gun with the other. "What the hell was that?" he shouted, voice echoing off the walls.

Well, at least I could assume he *hadn't* been prepared for any potential monsters in the cave. Small comfort that he didn't know and simply hadn't warned me.

I parted my lips to answer before movement flashed again in my peripheral vision. The snake-thing rushed forward. It barreled toward me, that pronged tongue firing out, black eyes on mine—

Shots fired, Tucker shooting from his spot suspended in the air.

The creature halted, hissed. Its eyes widened but a sheen of white covered them—I suspected the thing was blind. A bullet pinged its rough hide, perhaps what would've been a headshot if it wasn't already running toward our resident merc.

Shit.

I dove, reached for the tail—missed it by inches, landed on my stomach in the dirt. The thing leapt for the wall, slithering madly, Tucker firing again and again. It clung to the wall, climbing, the clicking of nails punctuated by the firing of bullets. Voices shouted, echoing, probably from the rest of our party trying to figure out what was going on.

Then something cracked.

The creature dove from a stalactite to the wall just above the hole and rock snapped, buckled. My helmet was gone—I was dimly aware of where I'd left it due to the light from its headlamp ahead—but I shouted warning of the collapse just as I dropped to a crouch and covered my head. Someone screamed, a male voice bellowed, rocks tumbled. I glanced up through my arms—it was too dark to see the hole, which worried me, as a glimpse of light from our collected companions gathered there should've been visible. I stood warily, dust and pebbles rolling off my back and arms. Laurel was on her hands and knees, choking several yards away; Tucker groaned, tangled in rope and pinned in a mess of rocks, his headlamp bobbing light around the dark cavern as he shook with a cough.

The room was so, so black, the patch of light I stood in seeming smaller than before. I tensed, gaze darting around. *It* was here, still. Breathing. Waiting.

It moved.

Slithering from the darkness, mouth parted in a hiss, it spilled blood from holes in its torso as it went. I took a breath, held still. It raced closer, closer—twenty feet, fifteen, twelve...

I ran.

Toward it.

Dirt gave and kicked up under my feet, pebbles flying. Its mouth opened wide, fangs sharp and glistening.

Two feet away from it, I pushed forward on my right foot and leapt, high, flying, feet kicking, its mouth snapping and missing me by inches. My foot stepped down on its snout, pressing its mouth closed, then I jumped again.

I twisted as I landed on its back, both hands on the hilt of the knife. Weapon raised, I plunged it down, down, even as the creature kept moving and threatened to topple me over. The blade sank into its skull, just behind the eyes, biting down deep and through bone. For a moment, the creature thrashed, knocking from side to side violently, but I gripped the damn knife and pinched my knees against its sides like riding a bucking horse, holding on with everything I had in me.

The monster stilled.

9

FRACTURES

———◦◆◦———

I HEAVED A GREAT BREATH, still tense and holding on, legs splayed over the beast like I was riding a pony. Hair was in my eyes, sweat dripped down my brow.

It didn't move.

Shaking, blinking dust from my watery eyes, I got one knee under me and braced against the creature. The knife, I gave a twist and blood oozed out, striking my fingers and then slinking down the dark, scaly head. Satisfied—mostly—that I'd put it down for good, I yanked the knife out, got onto my feet, staggered as I climbed off the thing but righted myself. My blade dripped blood and I was too anxious to clean it, half expecting the creature to jump up again and eat me.

It lay there, still, eyes closed, brain bleeding. I got a long look at it, from the reptilian head to the snake-ish body. Its thick tail was so long, it disappeared into darkness.

"Well. That was fun." I sighed, shook blood from my gloves and fingertips, and reached painfully for my helmet; my breaths were labored but I'd had a broken rib before and this wasn't near as bad. Maybe slightly bruised. I shone the lamp up at the wall where the hole had been, reaching my arm up to extend the light's reach—it was caved in now. I decided not to think about what shape our companions were in. Instead I moved for Laurel, who leaned against the limestone wall. She met my eyes and nodded in answer to my unasked question— she was okay, then.

Now to see about Tucker, who was half sitting up, thrusting away large rocks. His gun was dusty and cast to the side, slide open and indicting he'd run out of ammo—not like it had done him much good. These creatures would need either massive bullets to put them down or headshots.

And there would be more of them; I was sure of it.

I knelt and started pushing rubble off our mercenary. His right hand was bloody even through the dust, mangled and twisted at an odd angle. "You'll need to set that."

"Saw it." He grunted, pulled himself onto his knees. I reached for him but he jerked away, cold glare settling on me.

Okay, if he wanted to fix his broken bones himself, he was welcome to.

Instead of dealing with that right away, he pulled out his walkie-talkie, cradling his right hand in his lap and holding the device with his left. "Brandon? Come in."

The signal could rarely go through rock. Good for short distances but that was all—not through the cave-in, apparently.

I scanned the ground for my small pack and couldn't find it—I had a sneaking suspicion the creature might lay on it. Stifling a groan of displeasure, I went to it, pressed my foot to the beast and gave it a push.

It barely budged.

Goddamn it.

Steps hit the ground behind me, not Tucker because I still heard him cursing over the radio. Laurel came to my side, seeming so frightfully tiny in her gear. "What is it?"

"I haven't the slightest," I said with a sigh. The thing was three feet wide—perhaps I could glimpse *part* of my bag and ascertain which part of the beast needed to be moved. "Tell me, as the official eyes and ears of Mr. Ashford, are we having fun yet, Laurel?"

She said nothing, just watched me do my circle. At last I glimpsed the bright yellow strap of my pack peeking out between one of the hind legs and the part of the body that led to the tail. Basically, its big snaky ass. I dropped to my knees, coiled the strap around one hand, and pushed at the creature with the other until my pack came loose. I believed most of the items in it were safe from being flattened, but I'd find out in a moment.

Tucker cursed and tossed his walkie-talkie, the device thumping and skidding in the dirt. He gave us his back next and shouted a string of expletives I could scarce identify in a particularly thick southern drawl, presumably as he realigned whatever he'd broken in his hand.

I shuddered and tried not to think on it too much.

I left the beast, enjoying the idea of distance from it even though it was dead, and kicked through rubble until I located the glowstick. I found a spot to sit and set both the stick and my helmet down to give me light. My side ached as I lowered myself to the floor, and I unzipped the front of my undersuit to better feel my ribs. No, nothing broken, just tender. The more breaths I took, the less it hurt—I was in better shape than Tucker.

Next, I went through my pack. The first aid kit—which was stocked a little more thoroughly than a typical one from a drugstore—I held out to Laurel.

She glanced at the box, brow furrowing, and refused to take it. "I'm not—"

"You are used to being in control things and giving the orders—I get that. *I* am used to dealing in an actual life or death emergency, so you're going to buck up, swallow your pride, and listen to me for a damn second. There are a couple of small splints in with my first aid supplies. Tucker will tell you how to help him with it." *If he needs the help.* Honestly, I'd've done it, but men could be babies about such things and refuse assistance. I'd let her fight with him.

Laurel took the kit and went to Tucker, where he still cursed up a storm.

For the following task, I switched off the camera wrapped around my ear and dug out the small box Dawson had given me, which thankfully held up quite well. I popped it open, pulled out the parts, and peered at the small pictorial instructions printed on the interior. Seemed simple enough, so I went to work plugging the wires in and unfolded the keyboard. A light told me it was on.

Please let this work.

I took a deep breath and began. There was no fanciness, no worrying about complicated punctuation—the tiny keyboard was even more simplified from a cell phone's.

I typed: CAVE-IN. 6 OR 7 KM IN. 3 OF US OK. OTHERS UNKNOWN.

I sent that and paused, looked at Tucker. His face was beet red and Laurel, tying his pinky and ring fingers in a splint, was muttering under her breath—yeah, *that* seemed to be going well. "Supplies?"

He glanced at me. "What we were carrying."

Wonderful.

SUPPLIES LIMITED. WILL NEED HELP.

I paused again. Waited.

About a minute later, words blinked on the LED screen in green. GO IT. WIL SEND PEPLE.

Hmm, some letters went missing in the transmission—he'd warned getting messages through rock would still be tough. I hoped he got everything I sent and that he wouldn't think I was joking when I added more.

NOT ALONE DOWN HERE. ANIMALS. FAST. VIOLENT. RESCUE NEEDS TO BE PREPARED.

Dawson returned with another. CANNIBALS?

I snickered and sighed. It felt good to laugh for a moment. REPTILIAN. VERY VERY BIG.

Another two minutes passed. ASFORD SAYS KEEP GOING.

Of course he does.

"Right, we'll try not to die down here, then," I muttered.

BE CAREFL, Dawson typed next.

WILL DO.

AND TURNN ON YOUR IGNAL.

Oh yes, that would be handy. I managed to locate it in the box and a red light flickered—supposedly they'd be able to find us above ground with that and track us as we moved. He'd said they had digging equipment, after all.

I sighed. SEE YOU SOON.

I disabled the other pieces and folded them back in the little box, then slipped it in my pack. My canteen was scuffed up; I pulled it out and took a long drink. "We need to keep moving."

"So is someone coming?" Laurel asked as she approached.

A bitter smile twisted my lips. "Dawson says so. The boss man says we're to keep going."

"But..." She looked back at Tucker and then the collapsed tunnel. Her eyes were wide and frightened and I did feel bad for her, as she couldn't have been prepared for *this*. "I read before the trip—we're supposed to stay put."

"Well, Ashford apparently didn't write the literature you were reading." I pulled out my gun harness, guns, and loaded extra mags into my pack's pockets for easy access. Thus far, the temperature was cool but not cold and I had a feeling I was going to need to fight—I wasn't being caught off guard again—so I stripped out of my coveralls and set about getting my hip gun harness on without disrupting my belt of caving gear. I'd feel better in shorts but my undersuit would protect me from scrapes for now. "Tucker?"

"I'm good." There was the click of weaponry moving, him reloading his gun. I was sure it was difficult, but he had enough movement in his remaining fingers to reload, which was useful.

I rolled up my coveralls and stuffed them in my pack, loaded my guns in place, brushed hair from my brow and stuck my hardhat back on. Backpack and gear bag slung over my shoulder, knife cleaned on the dead creature's body and stuffed away, and glowstick in hand, I nodded. "Let's get moving then."

———— ◆ ————

WE FOUND A PATH IN the back corner of the room and a lit match of Tucker's suggested there was air flow, so we kept going. Laurel said nothing, walking in the middle of our tiny group as we moved from room to room, tunnel after tunnel, climbing and descending as needed. She was the only one of us unarmed and, I suspected, the only one who took Pilates rather than any kind of self-defense training. Not like I believed some weekend martial arts were going to do much against those creatures, but at least there was some self-preservation and preparedness taught. Laurel would probably freeze up and there's nothing quite like having to protect yourself *and* someone else to increase the odds of mistakes and certain death. Tucker periodically tried the walkie-talkie and came up with nothing. I walked with my hands loose at my sides, ready to grip my guns, with the small camera on to record our trip.

And trying very hard not to worry.

We were without anyone who knew the caves—never mind that the map was useless because no one had ever been this deep before. Every cave was a bit different, and I had at least felt Mr. Rolph knew the area and would have instincts for us to trust.

I wondered if Em was awake yet.

The next passage went narrow again, forcing even me to duck to squeeze through it. Laurel managed okay but Tucker had a hell of a time, angling his hand so he wouldn't hit it and his shoulders so he wouldn't get stuck. My empathy for him wasn't where it would be for someone more pleasant; I'm on the cusp of Scorpio and Sagittarius, and not known for my forgiving nature.

I took a breath and stretched my neck when we were in a more open space again. "So would anyone like to speak up regarding the pest we ran into before?" I glanced back at them both and no one answered. "Because I'm starting to suspect armed mercenaries weren't hired solely to escort me and the ring back to Mr. Ashford."

Laurel still said nothing but Tucker caught my eye with his dark, hard gaze.

"He didn't tell you what to expect, did he?" I asked.

Tucker pushed past me, trudging rather ungracefully through the current room we traveled. "I assumed competition."

Competition.

Martin.

I immediately stopped and knelt in the dirt, dragging my backpack around so I could rifle through the pockets.

"What are you..." Laurel began. When I neither moved nor answered, she went after Tucker, calling for him to hold on for a moment.

The device from Dawson popped open and I swiftly hooked the wires up again. When it was ready, I hammered out my message on the keyboard.

CALL MARTIN TALBOT ON MY PHONE. TELL HIM TO AVOID THE CAVE. SERIOUS DANGER. NOT KIDDING. I'M TRAPPED DOWN HERE. PLEASE TRY TO CONVINCE HIM. TELL HIM ANYTHING YOU HAVE TO.

It seemed a long shot. Martin and I were far too competitive and had been since childhood—the curse of siblings even when not close in age. Had he sent *me* that message, I probably would've laughed and ignored him, but it was worth a shot.

WIL DO. Dawson returned after a moment.

I breathed again, willing down my nervousness, and folded the kit back up. It was the best I could do for him. I could've warned with "enormous murderous cave-dwelling reptilians" but then "giant stone lemurs" didn't work the one time I tried it. Dawson, of course, might go that route anyway. Either way, I hoped Martin was at least cautious.

I rose and started toward where the others waited impatiently, my backpack angled in front of me so I could zip the device back inside and big backpack of gear thumping against my spine. "Just touching base with Dawson—"

Stone cracked, a thundering noise echoing all around us. Immediately I looked around, glancing about for the source, and dust rolled down on me. Nails clicked on rock; it wasn't merely a cave-in.

Another creature dove at me, my peripheral vision catching it as it rushed from the darkness. My right hand went for my gun, wrapping around the grip, drawing it from its holster.

Before I could shoot, Tucker did; the creature hissed, turned. The tail struck my hip, whipping me into the dirt. I spit out a mouthful of sand though grit remained against my tongue, and crawled onto my knees, discarding the pack and radio kit in favor of a second gun.

More stone cracked, drowning out the sound of Laurel screaming. I glanced up just as a chunk of limestone hurled toward me; I rolled, narrowly missing it, and scrambled to my feet. Movement caught my attention, something crawling up the wall.

There was a second—

Oh shit, no, there's a third.

10
WET

———— ◆ ————

ONE WAS BAD.

Two...not great, but at least we were armed.

Three?

I don't think so. I re-holstered left gun again and screamed, "Run!"

I didn't see the others, didn't even bother looking because the cavern was full of dust and noise and bobbing lights and chunks of limestone falling—I had to trust, had to believe they were running too. If they weren't, there was fuck all I'd be able to do for them anyway.

My headlamp caught the lump of my primary pack on the ground; I scooped the strap up as I ran by, firing randomly every time I saw a definitely-not-human shape come near me. There might've been more than one exit in the cavern but I didn't know, didn't care, bolting instead for the nearest one I saw.

It was narrow, barely a crack in the wall, and I turned as I neared it to squeeze through. Ahead of me light moved, someone having already made it in and shifting to give me room to follow. Rock scraped against my shoulders, my pack, my helmet, as I moved deeper.

A whimper to my left drew my attention to the room we'd just exited, and I glanced back to see Laurel squeezing in after me, shuffling and twisting in a panic to make it away from the creatures pursuing us.

"Get down!" My voice echoed, bouncing back at me, and Laurel dropped just as I raised my gun at the reptilian thing pursuing. I squeezed the trigger once, twice, three times in rapid succession but nothing slowed the creature down; it slammed into the wall headfirst, fighting to break through the crack.

I held my breath, my heart a jackhammer pulse in my throat, and kept my gun raised.

It reared up and shot forward again, once more striking the crevice we'd slipped through, but not making it in after us.

I scrambled back, holstered my gun again, and tugged Laurel with me. My pounding heart didn't let up, terror racing through my veins not easing. Boot treads scraped the ground, limestone cut into me with every movement, but at least it couldn't pursue—

It slammed again into the wall where we were, trying to break through, and rock cracked above. Dust shot down, swirling in the light from our headlamps.

"Keep moving!" I shouted, wiggling to make it through the cramped space. I saw little but the limestone in front of me and blinked against the rising dust. Laurel coughed beside me and something hard thumped my head, cracking on the plastic helmet.

Please don't let us be stuck in a cave-in. Please, deities I don't believe in, please.

I shifted forward as swiftly as I could, the sound of breaking rock echoing around the confined space and filling my ears. The lessons played in my head—of breathing deep, not panicking, and keeping a level head—but the cave situation was swiftly turning into something that would leave me very susceptible to acting irrationally. My lungs ached and hot air bounced back against my dusty face; feet moved on instinct, feeling around, and I prayed the space wouldn't get too tight to squeeze through.

My right foot stepped down a good six inches lower than the ground had been and I pitched to the side, sudden chill air rushing over me before I met water.

I landed hard on my padded right elbow and forearm, a heavy breath pushing past my lips in a grunt. Water soaked through half of my undersuit and iced my skin. I coughed, air scraping my dry throat, and struggled onto my knees just as Laurel landed in the water beside me.

I glanced up to take in the space; another wide, dark cavern, this one with a curved floor and several inches of water at the deepest point where we sat. The light from my headlamp bounced on the glassy surface around me, catching ripples as the members of my party and I moved to gather our bearings. The walls were pale and wet, gleaming with trickling water—flowstone.

While Laurel pulled herself onto her hands and knees, coughing still, I trudged through the water to peer at the crevice we'd gone through. Light hit fallen rocks at the end, keeping the things chasing us at bay but preventing us from turning back.

And from retrieving my cave radio with its help signal still blaring.

Wonderful.

"Please tell me someone else has one of those radio things Dawson prepared—"

A shriek caught my attention and I spun, right hand automatically going for the gun at my hip and the gear latched onto my belt rattling. But it wasn't some fucked up creature from beyond attacking.

No, it was Tucker.

He was perched on Laurel's stomach, straddling her. Right hand still useless in the splint, he had his left locked onto the loose fabric of her coveralls at her throat and he thrust her into the cold water, holding her as she thrashed. Bubbles surfaced, water splashed; fabric strained against his shoulders and arms as he held her tight.

"Tucker!" I shouted.

He jerked her up again, ignoring me. "Start talkin'."

Water poured from her helmet, slid from her face, and she blinked up at him, terrified, saying nothing, gasping in great gulps of air.

Again he pushed her down, water cutting off a choked cry.

And I had very little doubt he would in fact drown her if he didn't get whatever answer he wanted. I latched onto my gun and drew it out, aiming the barrel at his temple. I was a few feet away—far enough that I'd see him move if he tried to flick it away, giving me time to fire, and near enough that he didn't have a hope in hell of dodging.

Tucker yanked Laurel from the water again and held her there as she choked and cried, his eyes shifting to look at the gun but not me.

"We are down three people," I said in a low voice, "down supplies, and we're being hunted. If you want to be useless on this mission, I will happily leave you to find your own way, but for the time being, *let her go.*"

"Down three because we didn't know what we'd run into," he said darkly. "She knows something."

My grip tightened on the gun. "Probably. And drowning her won't get you the answer, especially if you're as skilled a medium as you've been an escort thus far."

He let Laurel go and she dropped with a splash, kicking up water as she scrambled away from him. Tucker turned and rose in one smooth movement; I took two quick steps back to add space between us and lifted the barrel to his forehead.

"9mm?" His voice was monotone, not quite threatening but edging there. "How many of those do you think it'll take to put me down before I disarm you? 'Specially since you didn't reload."

Fucking macho idiot. "What I lack in stopping power, I make up for in accuracy. There's one in the chamber and placing it in your brain will be enough for to slow you down for a little while. Quality shots over quantity, which you'd know about me if you looked beyond some beauty pageant bikini shots on YouTube. You want to know how this ends? Hint: it involves holes in your forehead."

Getting in a pissing match with this man was probably not one of my better ideas but I had major issues with backing down or playing nice. I might get a knife in my back over it later—time would tell.

But it was in his best interest to *not* test my rather exceptional aim.

Tucker gestured to Laurel, who was well across the cavern now, without looking in her direction. "She starts talking."

I shrugged, then holstered my gun as a show of good faith. "Fair enough."

We both turned to Laurel, our headlamps crossing over her, and I turned off my camera for this.

Ashford's "eyes and ears" was crouched up against the limestone, spine curled and knees pulled up. If she'd had a weapon, I was sure she'd've drawn it; instead she huddled there, a speck of fear in the overwhelming dark room.

"I didn't know," she whispered, voice jagged-edged like it would either break or cut us at any second. "I *didn't know* what was down here, exactly..."

Dread sank, a lead ball rolling in my gut. "But Ashford did."

She straightened and wiped at her eyes, then slipped off her helmet. Water dripped from her short black curls and she blinked as it rolled into her eyes. "You're not the first."

I swallowed a lump in my throat. "Excuse me?"

"He sent people. Before. Just mercenaries. Two times so far, that I know of. None of them made it back. Th-then there was another team of specialists—archeologists, experts. Scholars. They didn't either."

Motherfucker. MotherFUCKER. I thrust at my rising anger but it did no fucking good. My fingers twitched, wanting to grasp the gun and unload a few dozen rounds into the ceiling. It would cause a cave-in but I might feel a bit better.

"He sent me because he *said*," she spat the word bitterly, as if she didn't believe it anymore, "I'd carry his authority and ensure things were done right."

Well, Dawson claimed her specialty was getting shit done.

"Your boss have a reason for the last minute change up with my team?" Tucker asked.

I glanced at him. "What do you mean?"

He didn't turn away from Laurel and his left hand flexed, probably considering reaching for his gun. "Curtis was supposed to be down here, then Rolph showed up this morning with that black guy instead. Said he had orders to come with us."

Laurel shrugged. "I don't know where Moti came from or why Curtis didn't come down here too."

And no one had told me any of this while Ashford had me under the impression I was more or less running things. So we had someone whose function no one knew replacing someone who might've been a bit more helpful down here, and no one knew why.

"He's local?" I suggested. "Maybe *he* was the one who would've known what was down here?"

"Doesn't explain why Curtis was made to stay," Tucker said.

No, it didn't, and I was liking this less and less the more I thought about it. She wasn't about to be a one woman rescue team.

Laurel's haunted dark eyes met mine. "Mr. Ashford wanted experts for this trip. Mr. Rolph came highly recommended—he's even worked supercaves before—but my boss wanted someone who was more of a bounty hunter. I researched several people in your line of work and offered him suggestions. People like you who...who do this sort of thing, who specialize in it. I thought..."

You thought I was somehow magical and could do this without the facts. "So we were sent in unprepared?"

"We didn't know what—"

"But you knew *something.*"

Her voice pitched higher, as if she grasped for some sense of control she normally had. "We didn't know why the other teams didn't come back, but I was sent because he thought I could guarantee things were done right this time. It's either success or our *lives.* I am in the same position as both of you." She struggled to rise, water dripping from her coveralls that had to be quite cold and heavy by now. "We need to find the ring and hope....*someone* comes for us."

She was right on that. "I repeat my earlier inquiry: does someone else have a cave radio?"

Laurel nodded and she pulled off her pack to check. Tucker stalked through the water toward the tunnel at the other end of the room, headlamp tracking over the walls as he went.

"Anything else you want to reveal while we're out of earshot?" I asked in a low voice.

She finished turning on the radio's alert, then met my gaze. "The mercenaries get us here and help, Mr. Rolph advises you, and you get the ring. That was the plan I was hired to oversee. I really didn't know what was down here."

I did believe that—few people would be stupid enough to put themselves in this position with prior knowledge of what they'd face. "Did Mr. Rolph?" He definitely had to be hiding something.

"I...don't *believe* so."

That'll have to do. I nodded in Tucker's direction. "Let's go."

11
SUMP

———— ◆ ————

EXHAUSTION DOESN'T MERELY CREEP UP when you're on little sleep, little food, walking constantly, and fighting hellish creatures from beyond. No, it slams into you full force, dropping weight into your body until you think you're going to fall rather than stay on your feet a moment longer. When we found a dry cave room with a crevice we could fit into but the reptilian creatures couldn't, and only one other exit to watch, we sat to take a break. I'd been conserving water but now I was parched and allowed myself several long drinks from my canteen between eating an energy bar. Whoever had the small cooking supplies and freeze-dried crap food must've been in the other group, as we only had the basics to survive on.

That break turned into us taking turns napping, with two standing watch while the other slept. It lengthened the time we had to stay there, I knew; it would've been easier for one to stand watch while two napped, and two watch while one did, but though we didn't say it, the elephant in the room pointed to Tucker as the one to be nervous of. Laurel didn't like me but I didn't think she'd up and leave me, and I didn't suspect she believed I'd leave her to be alligator food.

When everyone woke again after little more than fitful catnaps, we all took a moment to eat and drink again. Tucker had the added task of doing everything only with his left hand, from unscrewing the cap on his canteen to unwrapping his food. I, of course, offered no assistance, and he didn't ask. He kept his peace in the far corner of the cavern we all shared, a dozen feet from the exit and crouched to lean against the wall.

I was about a meter from Laurel, who sat in her still-damp coveralls. She'd stripped off her gloves and blew on her hands in between eating and drinking.

I eyed her after polishing off my food, catching the continuing quiver in her hands and occasional twitch of her shoulders. "Why are you still shaking?"

She cut me one of her death looks—I was quite used to them now. "We landed in that water several hours ago. Remember?"

Vividly. "Please tell me you wore a water resistant undersuit."

Another scowl, rendered ineffectual by chattering teeth. "Just a T-shirt and sweat pants."

I resisted the urge to make a snarky remark as I suspected she was entirely serious. "Cotton?"

"They're my favorite—"

No wonder she was freezing. I stowed my empty wrapper in the pocket of my pack then rifled through for my rolled up coveralls. "These will be big on you, but warmer than wet clothes."

She stared at my offered help for a moment, brows furrowing.

"Cotton is useless when wet—I learned that the hard way my first time out. Get out of those things, put these on, roll up the cuffs, and then we can get moving."

At last Laurel accepted the assistance, warily wrapping her fingers around the corner of rolled up fabric, then met my eyes with a nod of thanks.

I rose and strolled across the cave, my back to her so she could change in peace. Tucker stepped away likewise, whether out or propriety or simply a desire to move, I couldn't say, but he slipped through the crevice to exit the room, headlamp bobbing over stone.

I stood several feet from the archway, thinking. The enormity of the task before us seemed to unfurl more with every passing moment until it stretched before me, daunting in its impossibility. Three people, surviving long enough in these caves, hunting a tiny ring? With giant iguana-snakes traipsing about, ready to feed on us? In what world did Ashford think we were going to succeed?

And what of Em?

I couldn't do the math anymore telling me what time—or what day it was—for her, and the app that would calculate it for me was on my cell back with Dawson and I was so used to having the phone that I'd stopped wearing a watch. I might have to send him a message at some point to give to her and Pru. And the stark realness of that possibility had tremors working through me, shaking me to my marrow, and panic clawing up my chest.

I might have to say goodbye to my daughter.

Laurel's steps were heavy on the dirt behind me, boots dragging from her likely exhaustion. "Ms. Talbot."

I looked back over my shoulder at her with a sigh. "Yes, Ms. James?"

Her eyes were shadowed under her helmet but still wide, grave and worried. I saw no sign of her wet underclothes but her coveralls hung over her pack, swinging down by her knees. My coveralls she was wearing might've fit at least one and a half if not two of her, but she'd rolled the sleeves and pants legs up as I'd suggested so nothing dragged.

Her lips parted but it was another ten seconds before she spoke. "I haven't taken you seriously, despite having reviewed your file."

I cocked a brow. "I've noticed."

"But I'm not sure I'd be alive if you hadn't been with me and Tucker when cut off from the others."

Another fair assessment. "Probably not."

"I just wanted to say...for my part in things, I'm sorry."

She was a woman who had trouble admitting this, I guessed—I knew because I had the same malady and immediately recognized it in another. It is difficult to apologize. It is difficult to admit you were or have done wrong, as it requires an alternation of one's entire world view.

But sorry did nothing for me. Not a single thing. It didn't change things, didn't mend things, didn't bring me any comfort. It didn't make me any more likely to return to my daughter. But I nodded because she meant it, though I wouldn't offer her any kind of forgiveness.

"I accept that. And in return, I expect that *when*"—*not if, but WHEN*—"we leave this place, you personally will see to it that I am compensated according to my contract. And, should I *not* leave this place, *you* will do so and ensure Ashford upholds his end of the bargain and sees that my daughter and her guardian are given my pay. Is that clear?"

Laurel nodded once then her chin lifted solemnly. "Absolutely."

"No more surprises," I warned.

"None."

At least she and *I* were on common ground now. I had no such hope for our mercenary, however. "And you know nothing more that would help me find the Seal?"

She shook her head. "Not my area. Mr. Rolph was supposed to...handle that."

Fair enough. "Let's keep moving."

Tucker awaited us by the exit, and the light from my headlamp speared past him to reveal it actually was a long, narrow tunnel

Oh, this looks promising. "Did you check how deep that goes?"

Tucker took a few steps back and turned to me, his frown deep enough to be a full blown glower. "A bit. It's deep. Narrows to the point of crawlin', but I can't see another way through. Couldn't see how far it goes."

Once again, we had a slight dilemma: common logic dictated me or Laurel going first with Tucker in the middle, as the largest person can get stuck and might need help on either end. But then I felt much safer with the smaller, unarmed one of us three in the middle. "Will you take up the rear?"

He hesitated, but perhaps he liked the idea of the resident cave guardians having to get through two of us to get to him, because he nodded. "Fine."

Laurel moved without me asking her to, falling into step behind me as I passed Tucker and stepped into the tunnel. Stones crunched against dirt under the heavy treads of my boots and limestone banged my helmet as the walls seemed to close in. The deeper I went, the lower I had to crouch, until I was on my hands and knees, crawling. Dust was thick as I moved, the air stale, and a few times behind me, Laurel gave a small cough. Each sound echoed, bouncing back at me. The air grew stuffier, losing its chill.

As the decline we crawled along deepened, dirt shifted to rock, and from there my headlamp caught water. Soon I was wrist-deep in it, cold seeping through my gloves to ice my skin as I sloshed about. My knees soaked next and with the nicks already in my undersuit, I knew I'd feel it soon. Laurel would be hit doubly hard with even her borrowed clothes getting wet, but at least my coveralls would dry faster for her. Not far from the beginnings of water, a mini waterfall cut through the tunnel, a sheet of it running from a slat above. I crawled through it, wetting the rest of me, and continued on.

A good twenty feet or so along and fresh air whispered in, drifting over my face and chilling my nose. It was welcome and I moved faster. Trickling water warred with—and won over—the sound of limestone scraping on my gear and the puddle beneath me shifted. I glanced up as best as I could in the cramped space. My headlamp hit blackness, much as it had earlier before we were first trapped. *Please don't let this be another drop, please don't let this be another drop...*

I had no room to maneuver to retrieve a glowstick, so instead I inched along until my fingers wrapped around the wet end of the pitch, and leaned over to look.

It wasn't far this time, thank god; trying to crawl backwards was not going to be in the cards for us. Drop was less than seven or eight feet with water rolling down the rocks, so I shifted in the mouth of the tunnel until I could stick my head and upper body out. I arched my spine, limestone tearing at my backpack, and gripped the sides of the tunnel opening while I got my feet under me. With a deep breath, I edged forward and plunged down.

My feet struck the pond, splash echoing loudly, and sank into the water. I went down three feet before hitting the bottom. Shock jolted up my calves to my knees and thighs, twining with all the exhaustion in my muscles and the sudden breath I sucked in hurt my ribs, but I was otherwise fine. I trudged through the water and glanced around as curses and squeaks sounded behind me, coming from Laurel.

There was no reprieve from the water in this cavern—it covered the entire floor, up to my knees in some places and my thighs in others. The walls were curved and etched with lines carved by a river at some point, mostly pale calcite and going up at least sixty feet. I saw no sign of the creatures sharing the cave with us, which didn't mean they weren't *here*, of course, but just that they hadn't arrived *yet*.

Some basic species information would've been nice, like whether or not they could swim, and I wouldn't pretend to be some expert able to determine based on appearance if one might be hiding in the water around me. *Happy thoughts.*

As I moved deeper, my headlamp caught on the walls again. I paused, gaze narrowed, and sloshed through more water to take a closer look at an odd shape drawn on the wall. The limestone was deeply lined and grooved, yes, but this was different—lines cutting across the grain, deep and precise.

The symbol was the Star of David with two crosses, remarkably similar—though not exact—to the Order of the Seal of Solomon.

Bingo.

The others splashed in the water behind me, Laurel moving nearer and Tucker grumbling under his breath after jumping. I ensured my camera was on and moved closer so my headlamp could shine directly on the wall's marking.

"Is that...?" Laurel started.

"Seems to be." Any rising elation I felt, I shoved back down again. This didn't necessarily mean *anything*.

Except that apparently people where down here long enough to carve it and not be eaten.

I swung around with my light, checking for another way out, and wandered along while the others did the same. No more markings that I could see—no exit for that matter either. *But there has to be—how would someone carve that and get out? Climb the way we came? Surely not—*

"Ms. Talbot," Laurel called.

I glanced back at her—she remained where the symbol was carved. "Yes?"

She cast her flashlight downward, shining over the water where it met the wall. "This dips down—I think there's a passageway."

Motherfucker. Tucker and I joined her and I eyed the opening. She was right—the water did dip down, and the arching hole was more than big enough to fit through. A sump. Sometimes they merely dipped down then up again; other times they went on and on, and into some tight places.

"What the hell?" Tucker asked.

"It's a sump—a spot where water gathers in caves like this. And the symbol must mean we're meant to go through it." I imagined my companions were no more thrilled than I was. "Does anyone have diving equipment?" Of course I'd ask, but I'd seen the contents of their packs earlier when we took a break, so knew the answer.

"Mr. Rolph had the basic scuba gear," Laurel said.

Of course he did. Maybe it would end up being a short path. Maybe not. I'd have to check, even though I had no idea what was on the other side.

Or precisely how far would we have to go without air.

This was such a bad idea. *So bad.* But I removed my guns and magazines, sealed them away in my pack, and pulled out a glowstick and some rope, the latter of which I planned to bolt just outside the tunnel.

"You're not really going to—"

I interrupted Laurel with a look. "Are either of you going first?"

Silence.

Pussies. "Then yes, yes I am."

"You could get stuck," she warned.

Don't remind me. I ended up skipping the bolt and instead pulled out a spring-loaded cam, tied the rope to the end, and found a crevice to wedge it into. "I'm going to run the rope through so you have a diving line to follow." I wrapped the rope around my belt a few times and tied it until I was sure I wouldn't lose it and then crouched in the chilly water to eye the passage. "Be careful about following me."

"And we gonna know if you're dead?" Tucker asked.

"Well, if the line goes slack after a few minutes, you can count on it." I could hold my breath for ninety seconds to two minutes comfortably, depending on how panicked I got, which was a danger as I didn't like the water. "Hopefully there'll be spots to stop and breathe, or this attempt might be pretty short. I'll jerk the rope when I get to the other side so you know you can follow." I looked at Laurel, as she was the one I figured would need the help. "The water's going to be cold but feel the tunnel above you for air pockets where you can steal a breath from. Okay?"

She stared at the spot in the water I was about to swim through and vaguely nodded.

"In the meantime, you'll pray for the best—and, Tucker, that your linebacker shoulders are going to fit through here." My heart hammered, terror real and palpable around me, as I eased down onto my stomach. I cracked the glowstick in my right hand and stripped the glove off my left; my fingers were cold but not numb yet, and hopefully I *would* feel air pockets.

Bad idea, bad idea... I took a huge breath and dropped down, shifting immediately through the hole.

I blinked as I moved, eyes adjusting to the water, and slithered forward. Bubbles drifted around me, highlighted by the green glowstick. I couldn't see much at all—and cursed myself for not bringing goggles just in case—so I relied on my hands, feeling along the walls, and pushed my feet against the ground to urge me along.

Of all the things I had to do in my line of work, this was my least favorite. Disorienting and dangerous. Silt stirred around me, worsening visibility. My lungs burned and unlike on the surface I couldn't merely breathe through my rising panic this time.

My free, bare hand left the icy water and touched dry air above; I immediately twisted and lifted my head, fingers fumbling to ensure my face was lined up right. My nose and mouth surfaced and I took a deep breath. Then another. I held there for thirty seconds total, just breathing, desperately not wanting to move again though I knew I had to.

Another deep breath and I submerged, turned again, and moved forward. My helmet banged the limestone and I ducked further, feeling still with my free hand.

I squeezed past a particularly tight spot, wiggling until my backpack popped free, and rushed ahead, pushing along. Still I felt above me but the sump seemed to be tipping down again and there was no break, no precious inches of air to steal. I needed to breathe again. Soon. Every time panic rose, I fought it, thrusting it back all but physically, but I needed breath, needed air, needed—

The space around me widened. I reached up, driving my hand through water until cool air iced my fingertips. My head surfaced and I sucked in a huge breath, gulping chilled cave air down until I was gasping and hiccupping. I blinked against water falling in my eyes, struggling to focus.

Then hands grasped my upper arms and hauled me to me feet.

12
REUNION

———————◆———————

MY REACTION WAS IMMEDIATE; I twisted to dislodge myself, arm shooting out with the heel of my hand poised to strike my opponent.

A man grabbed my wrist midair. "Calm the fuck down."

I blinked. Stared. It did nothing to slow my jackhammering pulse. Water irritated my eyes, drip drip dripping from my hairline, but I couldn't think to command my arms to move. The voice was vaguely familiar and I focused at last on Brandon, of all people, his lips oddly grimacing in irritation and exhaustion, rough dark stubble prickling his jaw. My gaze shifted over his shoulder to where Mr. Rolph stood.

They were alive. And they found us.

Relief was put on hold while I continued to gulp down air and stare in shock. "Where's Moti?"

"He went back to camp." Brandon let my wrist go and my arm dropped bonelessly to my side. "Where the fuck's Tucker?"

I gestured over my shoulder. "With Laurel in the room I just left." *Speaking of...* I fumbled with numb hands, my bare one swollen with cold and fingers useless as I plucked at the rope tied to my belt. When I had it free, I sloshed for one of the stalagmites outside the sump and wrapped the diving line around it, and tugged the rope so they'd know I made it.

Since I wasn't eager to stand around in the water waiting for them, I trudged forward. This cavern was much like the last but water only covered about half of it, and I pulled myself onto dry limestone then eased to a sitting position against a wall. My braid was soaked and splashed fat drops of water on the ground as I twisted it like a rag, the sound echoing. I glanced up, briefly, as if expecting some creature to descend on us from the noise, but it never happened.

"If they're not coming, you're more than welcome to tell them I made it through safely," I called to Brandon. "Maybe try pulling on the rope in Morse code?"

He gave me a glare and went to inspect the sump.

Mr. Rolph knelt two feet in front of me. His coveralls were filthy and soaked up to his knees, helmet dusty. So was his pornstache, which must've been irritating. Warm brown eyes met mine, this close more readable despite the thick glasses than they had been at a distance. "We spoke to Dawson—he said you were attacked."

"Oh yes."

"Are you sure—"

"Not hallucinating." *Though I wish I was.* "Was there...nothing at all in your research of the area that indicated precisely *what* would be guarding these caves?"

I watched him, my exhausted brain tracking and trying to interpret the hesitation as his mouth opened but no words came out.

"Mr. Rolph?"

"This cave is named after a holy man, Ms. Talbot, and it's sacred to local Oromo people and Islam adherents. People stay clear. I heard no rumors of what might prowl it."

"The bone we found didn't ring any warning bells?"

"It rang many. But after the Pulse, anything could be down here."

My gaze snagged the gold chain at his neck; while I couldn't see it, I remembered the cross hanging there the night Ashford gathered us at Kent House initially. I was raised in an atheist

117

family and might not put much stock in religious symbols, but in a world where the supernatural was real, I understood people who did. And I honestly believed he didn't lie about not knowing what we were going to encounter down here.

"If you didn't run into anything," I said, "perhaps they don't frequent this part of the cave. Here's hoping I don't have to introduce you. How *did* you get around the cave-in?"

Mr. Rolph stood and gazed over the water where Brandon was helping Laurel through as she sputtered and choked. "We went back the way we came and then took another entrance."

If they had time to do that, we had to've done a hell of a lot of walking and climbing. "How long have we been down here?"

"Three days."

Holy shit. My circadian rhythm was *way* off because it didn't feel like that at all. "Have you seen any symbols on the walls?"

He gestured over his shoulder; squinting, I could barely make out the marks, but they were there across the room.

"So we're going in the right direction?"

"I believe so. We were about to head through that tunnel when Brandon heard you. Any injuries?"

"Tucker broke his hand. He set it himself, so I can't speak as to the quality of his work. Do you have training?"

He nodded. "Beyond first aid, yes."

"You might want a look at it."

Tucker was climbing out of the water just then and Mr. Rolph rose to see him. Maybe he'd get that hand taken care of after all.

I retrieved my guns while the others drained water from their clothes, reorganized my pack and checked my equipment, had another drink from my canteen, and rose. I ached straight into my bones but the only solution was to get moving again or I'd seize up and be stuck. There was still a ring to find and giant snake-lizards to avoid. The odd groan and grumble sounded behind me. Honestly, if *they* wanted to sit around and wait to be eaten, they were quite welcome to.

There were multiple paths into the room; I found another symbol like the previous one and followed the passage beside it. The others fell into step behind me, silent but for the odd low-voiced whispering I couldn't make out between the two mercenaries. Perhaps Tucker was filling Brandon in on everything Laurel had said.

A narrow path led out of the water and up a slight incline, fallen rocks here and there for us to climb over. Dust scraped under my boots and I was sure I left a trail of water behind me like breadcrumbs through the forest. No other noise but that from my companions moving sounded.

"Mr. Rolph," I called. "Did Dawson happen to have any messages for me?"

"This isn't a fucking answering service, beauty queen," Brandon snapped.

There seemed a very good chance I was going to stab him and leave him for reptile food.

"He said to tell you Martin thought you were very funny," Mr. Rolph spoke up.

But of course. Hopefully we could find the ring, get out, let him know it was futile, and—

Something crunched underfoot. I paused and glanced down, shifting my boot tread back. White peaked through the dirt, a weathered and bleached bone. Perhaps a rib. Probably human.

My right hand eased to the gun on my hip and pulled it from its holster.

The others grew quiet behind me, all silent but for the rustle of clothing. Whether or not they saw the bone, I wasn't certain, but surely by this point if I showed a desire for caution, they had to figure there was a reason. Tense stillness wrapped around me, clutching my shoulders with cold, clammy fingers.

We hit a partial cave-in, chunks of rock in our path. I glanced up to see darkness above, no sign of more rocks ready to tumble. Still, I remained silent and careful as I navigated the fallen boulders, squeezing through a particularly tight passage. One by one they followed me until we were walking a relatively flat surface once again.

The tunnel curved, pale limestone cutting over the bend. My clothes still dripped water and the wet lump of my braid shifted over my back, irritating me. I raised my gun and slowed my steps, eyes picking through the poor light as I rounded the corner.

No creatures. Yet. But the tunnel opened into another room, white narrow shapes I *could* identify—but didn't want to—scattered across the floor.

And there was definitely more than the remains of a couple of mercenary parties.

Some bones were old and gray, a brittleness to them, while others were white and gleaming. Not all were human, I didn't think. I shone my light over the room; parts of the walls were regular limestone but changed toward the back into what almost looked like a type of brick, as if someone had been building on to make it like a room before abandoning the task.

A room or a tomb. I was leaning toward the latter.

Many of the bones were confined to the corners and scattered haphazardly, pieces everywhere. Either they were shifted by these creatures over the years, or they tore their victims limb from limb. I couldn't decide if I was glad they didn't swallow them whole like a snake.

"Shit," someone cursed behind me.

I moved faster, wanting distance between me and the people making the noise. This room had multiple exits besides the one we came from; the first was off to the side, a natural archway in the wall like we'd come through. Another was barely a crevice and I doubted even Laurel could squeeze far through it. The other was opposite me and I walked to the center of the cavern, bones and skulls rising on either side of me, toward the bricked far wall with a manmade arch. Above the doorway was another Seal—this had to be the right direction.

No comment on whether I thought that was a good thing or not.

My face and hairline had dried but now it was sweat beading across my brow, rolling into my eyes, and cold terror worked its way through my veins. My clothes were still sopping wet, dripping as I went, but at least were otherwise silent. Dirt slid beneath my boots I crept through the main doorway and around corners as the passage snaked left and right, tension climbing up to grip my shoulders and squeeze me until I could scarcely draw in a breath.

At the end of the tunnel, I peered around the final dark corner.

Dozens of them.

My headlamp crossed back and forth over the bodies. I lost count, staring, eyes widening, my hand holding the gun dropping because my weapon suddenly seemed far too heavy to keep raised. My lips parted in an unreleased gasp of horror.

The same reptilian snake creatures as we'd seen before lined the floor, stretched out and sleeping. Long tails, thick bodies. Those horrible snake-like heads.

My gaze traveled to the other side of the room, a good sixty feet or so. Another doorway arched, this one with a seal above it too, and all the walls were the same limestone finished brick-look.

Someone had, once upon a time, built this room. And possibly populated it with these creatures to keep out people like me.

There was no way past them. Even with my vague memories from taking gymnastics for a while as a kid...I could be a fucking Olympic gold winner and *still* not make it through there—the spaces between the creatures were too wide to reach with a step and I couldn't jump and land with such precession.

I backed up, bumped into Tucker, and bit back a curse. He and the others crowded, staring on, until they backed up one by one and we got out of there as silently as possible.

Only when I was once again in the safety of the other room did I let out a breath at last. Fingers shaking, I holstered my gun. Took another breath. Exhaled. None of it was helping. Jaguar shamans? Great. Demonic entities in books? Bring the fuckers on.

But no way in *hell* was I setting foot in that room without a flamethrower.

"There must be another way around," I said. "We passed another door."

Mr. Rolph said nothing.

I pressed. "Help me out here."

His gaze trailed the entrance to the winding path that led to the creatures. "It looked...official. In my opinion. The entire way through the cave, *nothing* has looked like this." He indicated the designed archway, the brick-look of the limestone walls.

He was right. Official. Like the closer we got to the Seal, the more formal looking the cave became, as if we'd run into some sort of temple to it deep in the bowels of Kadhim.

Shit.

"We *could* look for another entrance," Mr. Rolph said in a low voice. "Even go back out and around to another passage into the cave? Surely there's something."

The expression Tucker and Brandon gave me suggested they didn't like that option very well. "We'll find another room guarded like this, right?" Tucker asked, eyeing Rolph.

The older man hesitated for a moment before nodding. "It's a safe bet that they're here to guard the Seal. The closer we get to the target, the more of them we'll find."

Plus god knew how many others were scurrying around in the meantime. "Anyone happen to bring some way to nuke them? Because, really, how in the *fuck* are we supposed to get through there? Are you going to jump in and tackle them, Crocodile Hunter style? Hmm?"

Brandon lips twisted in something vaguely resembling a smile, calmly raised his gun, and pointed it at my chest. Five feet away, I wasn't going to disarm him, and my heart thumped sickly at the large barrel on me.

"Let's be reasonable," Mr. Rolph said.

Tucker lifted his weapon as well but pointed at Laurel. She squeaked in response, eyes growing huge and meeting mine. He couldn't grab her with his broken hand—she could run and dodge—but I wasn't outrunning Brandon.

"We're gettin' the ring," Tucker said in a cold voice, "so that we can leave. You're the expert. Get yer ass in there and *do it.*"

Shit. And I had no doubt that if I went for my gun right then, they'd shoot me and make Mr. Rolph go. Granted, the gunfire would wake the beasts in the next room but I suspected they weren't thinking that far ahead.

Or maybe they did, because Tucker didn't even blink when his friend pulled a gun on me. Maybe they'd been discussing more than just what they'd missed while separated.

Goddamn it. Okay, I just had to think. I was a problem solver. It's what I *did*. Pregnant at seventeen, disowned and left penniless? I solved the problem. Need a better education for my daughter? I solved the problem. On a job and stuck in a cave with a gun to me, forced to go through a room full of mythical monstrous creatures who would kill me?

I will solve this motherfucking problem. There is no sense wasting time on something you can't control. You do what you can, adapt and keep moving, and when circumstances change, you seize things for your advantage.

And my advantage would come yet—I was determined.

I set my jaw and turned back toward the archway. Crossing the space on foot...not an option. No way. But I crept forward, back through the tunnel, hoping to come up with some plan of attack—even if it was to hide in the damn corner, throw a rock at the entrance, and send the creatures after the rest of my party. I'd lose Mr. Rolph and Laurel, yes, but sacrifices had to be made.

Brandon kept close enough that he could shoot me with ease and I still couldn't pull a gun on him or disarm him. I grit my teeth and focused instead on the room once I reached it again. Even knowing what I'd see this time, panic still clawed through my veins as my headlamp trailed over the sleeping bodies.

*I can't do this. Can*not. I had a little kid at home, waiting for me.

And I couldn't get myself shot, either.

I gave myself a mental shake and tried to regain my focus. *Think. Plan. Problem solve. I can do this.* The creatures, I still suspected, were blind. So I had to make very little noise...and if I stepped on one...

My gaze traveled to the ceiling.

When I backed up and gestured at Brandon, he stepped backward through the tunnel slowly, gun still trained on me, and we returned to the adjoining room.

"Empty your packs," I said, eyeing each of them in turn, "and let me see what equipment you have." And I set about working out of my sopping wet undersuit so I was cold but dry.

Dripping would be a bad thing considering what I had in mind.

———————◆———————

TEN MINUTES LATER, MR. ROLPH—eyes dark and worried, pornstache twitching—helped hoist me up in the entrance to the reptilian lair.

I bit savagely at my lip, keeping in any noise that might escape as I balanced precariously on his back. He held steady, to his credit. The chilled cave air rolled gooseflesh up and down my bare legs, and fine hairs rose on my arms. I had boots, shorts, and my tank top on, plus the knee and elbow pads, and a pair of spare, *dry* gloves—that was it besides my belt, climbing harness, and guns in holsters. All the water I could wring out of my hair was gone and I hope to hell it kept for a while.

Spring-loaded climbing cams were tucked in various spots on my belt and even in my damn bra—I didn't want them jangling at my hips but I needed as many as I could carry. I slipped the first one out from between my boobs and lodged it in a ceiling crevice, carefully releasing the device until it locked in place. From there, I hooked my harness on so I could hang.

When I was successfully suspended from the ceiling, I released a shuddering breath and gave the signal. Mr. Rolph backed off and I was dangling several feet in the air. For an instant I made the mistake of glancing down and seeing what awaited me throughout the room.

This was a much better plan when I wasn't thinking about them.

I looked away, took a deep breath, and then fed the rope I had loosely wrapped around my waist through the new anchor in the ceiling. Brandon had the other end and I was putting tremendous faith in him to hold it. When the rope was in place, hooked once again onto my harness, I eased out another cam. I reached, stretching my arm as far as I could go, until I squeezed the cam into the nearest crevice and hooked another strap of my harness on. Two straps on two cams at all times except for when I was moving to hook onto another—it was the only way to move. Once secure, I unhooked my other strap from the first anchor and let myself hang over the second. I breathed. Shifted. Tried not to look down past my dangling feet at the floor.

Little by little. You can do this. Or you'll be shot.

Bleeding out might be more fun than being eaten, however.

Though I thrust her back, Emaleth flashed in my mind and I ached for her, wondering what time it was, what she was doing, if she worried—

You're not "Mom" here. You're a badass mofo artifact hunter swinging from the ceiling over monsters and you cannot be soft.

I eased to the next spot as silently as I could and already my arms were sore, tired from the climbing thus far and the exhaustion settling on me. The cams creaked and squeaked softly, hopefully only *seeming* loud to me because I was so close, and bits of dust drifted down. Sweat dripped in my eyes; I swiped it with the back of my hand, swallowed dryly, got the rope fed through, and reached for the next crevice. The process was painstakingly slow, my arms shaking by the time I was almost half of the way there. Tremors rocked my muscles, burning. I slowed for a moment and breathed, trying to work some feeling back in my arms.

The rope above me jerked; I cast an irritated glare back to Brandon. I saw little of his face, the lip of the helmet shadowing his eyes where the headlamp's light hit it, but made out his impatient gesture.

So not only was I forced to cross the room alone, but I couldn't take a break. I definitely had to ensure Laurel survived as I expected a rather lengthy speech for Ashford about this in which she'd probably have these two mercenaries killed.

But that was not today and I couldn't entertain fantasies any longer. I pulled out another cam, reached over, and wedged it in place. I shifted my harness and the rope over, biting back a grunt of frustration as I unlatched one of my straps to lock onto the other—

The cam slipped.

I fell.

13
INTO THE NEST

———◆———

IF BRANDON JERKED ON THE rope to draw me up again, he failed. My feet hit the ground first then I slipped, landing hard on my right side. My leg was bent over a tail, elbow propped against the ground to hold me up. My left hand darted out to press against the limestone floor and I glanced around.

Don't. Move.

The light from my headlamp moved over the sleeping creatures, dark green-gray skin and diamond scale patterns. I held my breath, my throat closing to the size of a pinhole, heart hammering painfully hard against my ribcage, and waited there. I'd fallen nearly in the center of the room and I lifted my head, looking over the bodies, but not finding anywhere easy to step to.

Shit. SHIT.

I swallowed thickly and began to turn, careful not to knock the tail by my legs, and got my toes under me, readied to rise. Trembling fought to overtake me so I fell back on yoga, lining up breaths with my movements. *Exhale*—I rolled onto my stomach with both hands flat on the floor. *Inhale*—I lifted my head.

And stared at blinking white eyes set in a huge snake-head inches away.

It drew in a breath, slit-nostrils flaring. Then another. Its muscles tensed and I froze, like my body iced over and I couldn't've moved if I wanted to.

And I did want to. A *lot*.

Don't move, don't breathe, don't move... It might go back asleep. It might—

Its mouth opened and fangs shone, glistening wetly as it hissed. Hot, putrid breath struck me in the face and its tongue darted out, licking the air and coming dangerously close to my cheek.

I rolled, got onto my feet, but it was too late—the other creatures were rousing, tails flicking, nails scratching, shifting and ready to attack. I wasted no time and ran, leaping over one, avoiding a tail, running in the opposite direction as I'd been going because there were at least thirty of these fuckers and no *way* was I heading any deeper into the cave alone. We could head back to the sump and—

Pain pinched my gut and I lurched to the side—something caught the rope attached to my harness. I slammed hard onto my hands and knees and twisted, fought, yanking at straps until I had the harness worked down to my thighs, over my guns. When a beast leapt for me, I rolled, tangling my legs in the rope and harness but at least missing its clawed front feet. Teeth veered toward me, fangs as thick as my daughter's wrist.

So many things coming at me, my brain shut off and body took over; I was untangled, on my feet, dodging without thinking and running without hesitation. When training kicks in, it's all muscle memory, ducking and avoiding hits in a way that bordered on preternatural instincts. The doorway was my goal, where my companions no longer stood—beyond that, I'd figure *something* out, just so long as I was away from the nest I'd fallen in.

A creature swung in front me, cementing itself between me and the door out. I thrust aside any idea of grabbing my guns and just ran—*step, step, dodge, duck, step*. When the obstacle in my path charged, I veered left and vaulted in the air. Right foot stepped down, touched its head to snap its mouth shut and give me extra height as I kicked off. Left foot hit the crumbling bricked wall beside me and I ran, two feet, three, moving in an arc, flying through the air, speed and momentum the only thing keeping gravity from taking hold. I narrowly missed the beasts charging me and near the end of the wall I jumped, landed both feet on the floor, and kept running even as impact shocks jolted my legs.

Through the tunnel of knife-edged turns. Around the corner. My boot treads slammed limestone, crunched dirt, stones, and bone remnants. The ground thrummed under me, all those creatures at my heels. My right hand locked on my gun as I screamed a warning to the others, then I reached back and fired blindly. Limestone spat chunks and dust as bullets made impact.

The others were scattered in the next room, the men all with guns and poor Laurel pressed back against the far wall in a pile of bones. The lights from their helmets bounced jarringly. My own helmet irritated me and I jerked at the strap with my free hand, casting it to the side so I could see and maneuver better.

"The other room! The water!"

We started in that direction but it was too late; Tucker in the lead was hit head-on, one of the beasts colliding with him. I skidded to a halt, swung away from its thrashing tail. My heart thumped hard and painful, pulse throbbing in my neck, and any exhaustion I'd felt dissipated under the flood of adrenaline. My left hand procured a grip on the knife sheathed at my belt, fingers tightening as I drew it out and slashed the snout of the nearest creature.

A wail of a cry snapped my attention to the right where blood flew and a hunk of flesh was torn from Brandon's thigh. He fired at the creature frantically when another latched onto his arm, severing it just below the elbow.

I ran for the one that bit his leg, leapt on its back and buried the blade of my knife in its head. Brandon hit the ground, shuddering and bleeding profusely. The one who had a chunk of his arm spit the offending limb out and its tongue flicked towards me, bloody spittle flying.

I scrambled back, firing until the last brass flew and the open slide reminded me to hurry the fuck up and reload. My feet darted back until I hit the pile of bones, which cracked and slid under the soles of my boots. I fumbled, reloading as quickly as I could, while the beast lumbered toward me.

Bone gave under my left heel and I went down, striking the crumbling limestone brick before landing flat on my ass. Pain jolted through me and I yelped, abandoned reloading my right gun, and threw my knife at its head. The blade slashed over its eye but the throw was too wide, too weak; the weapon clattered on the ground. It was enough of a distraction, though, for me to reach for my left gun and fire. One bullet. Two. Three. Each ripped into its skull, its shoulder, taking chunks of flesh, but the 9mm bullets barely slowed it. I kicked at the bones, drawing my legs up—if this fucking thing was going to eat me, it would do it headfirst as I was *not* limping out of this goddamn cave. Terror gripped me as I reached the end of my other magazine and nothing had slowed it—

Fresh shots fired, blasting through the space in rapid succession, spraying blood across the floor. The creature before me turned to the right just as I did.

Figures in black—at least half a dozen of them—dotted the room with automatic weaponry in hand. Fifteen feet away stood one, the AR-15—with a light and scope—raised with the stock against his shoulder. The creature turned, charged, bleeding profusely and still pissed the fuck off, but the man didn't move or flinch; when he reached the end of the magazine, he signaled over his shoulder and someone else took over, cutting through the creature until it slumped forward.

A blast rocked the ground, dust spitting up across the room. I braced and waited for rock to fall, the sound of a concussion grenade unmistakable, but it never came. Another figure came through the manmade arched doorway, limestone dust whirling around him, and he didn't seem the least bit worried about the creatures following.

I glanced around. Brandon was bleeding and gasping in pain to my left; to my right Tucker was limping, arm holding the gun wavering. Laurel was in the corner whimpering, being helped to her feet by one of the men in black tactical gear, and Mr. Rolph stood alone, staring at the carnage and frowning.

A magazine snapping into place in the AR-15 drew my attention and I glanced up, back to the guy who'd drawn the creature's focus from me. The flashlights and headlamps on various people in the room brought a glow to the cavern, highlighting a familiar face.

My dance partner from the gala, Mr. Cat and Mouse himself, stared down at me, his lips quirking into a grin. "If this is you playing solo, I think you might want a partner after all."

14
RESCUE

———◆———

HE STARTED TOWARD ME—WHETHER to help me rise or not, I didn't know.

Or care.

I glanced down, got my feet under me, pressed my back to the wall, and stood stiffly. Still nothing broken but oh god, how I ached. I avoided his gaze for a moment while I reloaded my guns, prickling irritation rising. *Why* I was irritated, I couldn't say, but something about him bothered me and I had a horrible suspicion he was another bounty hunter. Maybe Ashford hired two of us. Maybe—

"We've got too many injuries," Mr. Rolph said in a low voice. I glanced up again to see me forgotten, the head of the other team turned to face Mr. Rolph who stood near him. "And I don't think it's wise to split up—we should retreat."

Our guest nodded. "I know. We drilled through to a vertical pitch not far from here—easier than taking the long way around. We can come back more prepared in the morning."

"They're dead!" Laurel spoke up, her voice fraying as swiftly as her sanity seemed to be. "Jesus, West, can't a bunch of you just go and get what you came for *now* and—"

"The trouble there, is..." As if on cue, nails scraped on rock in the distance, and fresh fear rolled down my spine. But while those around me froze, he didn't, instead grinning wider as he met *my* gaze. "These were just the babies and you've woken Momma."

Son of a bitch.

He gestured at his team to see to Brandon first, and they looped a tourniquet around the injured merc's thigh to stop the bleeding and bound his remaining wounds, though he still seeped blood. Two of them lifted him and started for a plain, unadorned archway off to the side. Tucker followed, silent and seething, while Laurel swiftly moved at his heels, eager to get out.

The leader watched as his remaining men followed before starting after them.

I blinked. Was I the only one still wondering what was going on? "And who the fuck are you?"

"I'm the rescue team, Talbot." He threw a look over his shoulder, unsmiling, intense, and chilling me through. Whoever the hell he was, he radiated power that had my inner alarms shrilling. "You're welcome."

Something about this man brought out the urge to shoot him in the back of the head, but I grit my teeth, scooped up my fallen helmet and clipped it on my belt, and followed next to Mr. Rolph.

"That's Dale West," he said in a low voice. "Mr. Ashford's right hand."

His 'right hand'? *Perhaps I'm with security, tasked to keep scandals to a minimum.* Security indeed. If Ashford had this guy, why the hell did he have to hire *me* and some shitty mercenaries for?

Precisely what 'right hand' entailed, I had no idea...or if I wanted to know. But both Laurel and Mr. Rolph seemed to know him; Laurel, I could understand as she worked for Ashford, but Rolph was supposed to be new on this mission like me.

Questions would have to come later—for now, I just wanted to get out of the goddamn caves.

Around the next corner I recognized Moti, whose gaze was on the ground as he gestured at one of the dead creatures. West walked straight past him but Moti kept up, ranting up a storm in his native language, and while I couldn't particularly follow it, I figured it could be translated as: "OMGWTFBBQ THOSE ARE MONSTERS WTF??"

Approximately.

West tossed a few words in reply, then continued on. Moti stopped, staring wide-eyed, whatever West had said apparently not being the answer he wanted. Instead of following immediately, he turned to Mr. Rolph, where several more words were exchanged, before Moti took off after the others again.

"I really should've learned the local dialects," I said in a low voice.

"Oromo," Mr. Rolph replied. "The gist is that he isn't pleased as no one signed him up for demon monsters."

"Well, we all have that in common."

His lips twisted in a wry smile, but he said nothing.

Mr. Rolph and I kept up with our patrons. I glanced back frequently, checking over my shoulder but seeing nothing pursuing. Still, relief never came, never eased the tension in my shoulders or the flood of adrenaline in my veins. I held my tongue as we trekked back the way the other men had came—down a limestone hall, around a few bends, in an awkward spot we had to crouch to wiggle through, and the up the odd slope with the assistance of ropes already rigged up. Travel was painstakingly slow moving not just a severely injured man, but with Tucker as well who could only navigate ropes with one hand. Exhaustion gripped my original team as well, as we'd been down here longer, which made for a slow trek back through the cave.

It might've been half an hour or so later when we reached a massive, rounded cavern with vaulted ceiling. Mr. Rolph mumbled something about recognizing it, though he stared upward with a frown. The space was black around the edges; above, white light shone through a long vertical pitch with a single rope hanging through—a lifeline promising safety. It seemed far too late for daylight but I'd been underground for what felt like a week so I had no idea of the time.

The members of my "team" mostly no longer had proper harnesses, including me. One of West's men went up first, while two others set about strapping Brandon down to the travel stretcher retrieved from a bag. His periodical moans and whimpers confirmed he lived, though how much longer, I couldn't say.

A second rope rolled down and the team tied the gurney to the end so they could hoist him up. Those two men followed and next went Mr. Rolph, then Tucker with his broken hand dangling uselessly at his side.

West went next, but paused at the bottom of the rope, predatory gaze scanning the area. His eyes moved to mine. "Keep up."

"To quote my six-year-old, *duh*, Mr. West."

He held my gaze past the point of comfort before reaching for the rope, swinging his gun strap over his shoulder, and climbing up after the others. He moved swiftly and with ease, the black clothes doing nothing to disguise the muscles working in his arms—he didn't even bother with a harness. His job for Ashford likely involved punching people, by the look of it. Laurel still fought with her harness, so once his feet disappeared, I went after him.

The light brought a measure of comfort, even if part of my brain didn't want to believe it. It was white and crisp, bright enough I had to blink after hours of dimness and tip my head down to avoid the strain. Once I dangled in the air and reached the actual pitch, I braced my feet on the rock on either side of me as I went, glad for my gloves holding the rope so I didn't damage any more of my flesh. I heard Laurel grunting in frustration below me but she made it, hauling herself in the harness up the rope. Her borrowed coveralls were all but dry now, though where her own stuff had gone, I didn't know. Regardless, I didn't think she'd come back with us on the second trip.

I can't believe I am either. But then I needed to get paid and I did, grudgingly, feel that much more secure with others there, even if I didn't trust their leader. At least on the next excursion, we'd know what to expect.

I had another six feet before the top and shadows played overhead, faces I couldn't make out periodically peering down at me.

The man still waiting at the bottom screamed.

I froze, as did Laurel beneath me. The rope I clung to swayed, anchor above creaking under our combined weight; I braced either foot on the walls around me to hold still and looked down, tried to glance past her. The passage was roughly four feet wide, and I angled myself to the side so I could see. Light traveled past our figures to hit the floor—there was no sign of the guy, but something dark streaked over the rock.

They found us.

"Move!" West barked before I could, and I set aside my irritation to start climbing again.

A squeal of fear and the clicking of nails on limestone drew my attention again—it was another of the reptilian-snake things, this one having made its way into the pitch we followed, half slithering, half crawling its way up toward us.

And it was bigger.

Limestone chunks fell under its feet as it lumbered forward and the mouth that opened to hiss—god, that mouth could swallow a linebacker whole, maybe without even unhinging its jaw first. The pitch was barely wide enough to accommodate its girth and I could no longer see anything below, like the ground had opened up and a lizard from hell appeared to devour us.

These were just the babies and you've woken Momma.

Wonderful.

Laurel scrambled but she wasn't fast enough, fumbling to get herself up. A frantic cry left her parted lips—it would catch her and she knew it.

Goddamn it...

"Talbot," West warned as I stopped climbing.

I continued looking down at Laurel. "Stop and lean back," I ordered her.

She glanced up, still moving. "What!"

"Talbot." West's voice was edged in irritation.

"I'm busy." My focus remained on Laurel, despite him grating on my nerves. "Brace your shoulders against the walls and make yourself *flat*, goddamn it, or I'll leave you here."

She didn't argue and the rope shifted with her movement.

"Talbot!" West shouted above me, making it extremely difficult to concentrate. "Fucking hell, get up—"

But I ignored him.

Both hands on the rope, I couldn't shoot. Take one hand off the rope and I just had one to support my weight—and I was tired. Too tired.

When Laurel was as flat as she could make herself, I took a deep breath and let go.

I plunged down, struggling to keep my body straight even as my shoulder clipped the rough limestone. Plummeting, I had no time to hear the shouts above me or glimpse Laurel's expression as I flew past her; feet held flat rather than pointed, and my braid whipped above my head.

The soles of my boots collided with the snout of the creature below and the impact jarred my stance. I careened to the side as I fell, scraping my bare flesh and knocking my skull against stone.

The pair of us—beast and I—fell, it under me and cushioning my fall as we landed. My helmet, still dangling from my belt, cracked on the ground and the light went out. I rolled onto my knees, drawing my guns, and fired, both barrels aimed at its head. I had eighteen rounds in each gun; that might be enough to cause some serious brain damage if I kept both trained between his eyes. Or I might fail—perhaps trying to kill things without a playlist was messing with my mind and I wasn't thinking clearly.

I had no time to ponder it—the creature was coming at me and I scrambled up and back, firing at it, feet skimming across the floor. The pitch blackness of the rest of the cavern didn't bode well for the possibility of more of them in there, but I forced myself not to think on it, to focus on the one I *could* see. Because if there were more, they'd eat me soon and there was nothing to be done about it.

Blood flew as the creature ran, crimson spraying across the floor, and its mouth was open wide, strong jaws ready to snap my bones. Its horrid nails clicked and scratched, and I swore I'd hear that noise every time I tried to sleep from then on.

My left foot stepped back, struck something, and even as I tried to right myself I went down. I landed hard on my ass, falling back onto my thankfully-padded elbows, legs slightly raised over what had tripped me—it was the body of the guy killed before he could follow Laurel. Dead eyes were open and stared at the ceiling and his head was partially removed, hanging from stringy bits with a flash of a white spine.

I looked up again and the beast was gone.

Dread rose and clawed down my back. My throat went dry, swallowing doing no good to ease the terror from it. I squeezed my guns and silently crept to my feet, gaze shooting around the space, listening for anything that might indicate where it went. Dirt scraped against limestone under my thick boot treads, echoing in the silence.

Three seconds later, it collided with me from behind.

The guns left my grasp as I hit the ground, sliding across the limestone away as the hulking mass of several hundred pounds knocked me. My chin slammed against the floor, blood blooming across my tongue from my lip. I twisted, struggled, reached for the knife at my belt and realized it had been left behind when we were attacked previously.

Fangs angled dangerously near my head and I dodged, banged my temple against the rough scale of its skin, but its incisors sank down into the dirt just inches away. I wiggled, shifting under the creature, pulling myself down away from its mouth, hoping to escape past its lower body.

A foot sank down on my left thigh and I howled in pain, its weight grinding my bones together mercilessly. I punched, fought—nothing moved it, nothing drew it off of me, but I felt its body twist, likely to attack. Pain was spiking through my thigh, burning with agony, and claws dug in to prick my skin until something wet and hot slithered down my leg. I tipped my head back, looked for my guns, couldn't see a damn fucking thing—

The creature over me grunted as something crashed into it and tipped it to the side, slamming it into the ground hard enough that rock vibrated against my back. As it rolled, I scrambled, not looking back or worrying about who attacked; my gaze scanned the ground until it settled on my guns, one four feet away, the other seven steps to the left.

Blood seeped from my leg, messing with my traction as it coated the ground. I tried to walk but failed, scrambling up and forward instead, pushing on until I latched onto my first gun and then the second. I stood, spun, swinging the weapons around, trying to point in every direction at once, but there was no sign of the creature or what hit it.

The rope swayed silently in the pool of white light in the center of the room and I eased in that direction, swinging around after every cautious step in case something followed. Hot pain zigzagged up and down my thigh but my leg successfully held my weight. No voices called down to me, and I hadn't a clue if Laurel made it up there or not—at least I didn't see her body.

The direct light from above struck me as I stepped under the pitch. Fresh chunks of limestone and dust crunched and ground under my boots. My gaze gave the room another sweep.

Steps thundered and a hiss sounded; I did a one-eighty, swinging to fire at the reptilian lunging for me. It hit the light, gaping mouth stretching wide, tongue whipping out. I darted back, preparing for it to tackle me again, when it gave a hiss and was hauled back into the darkness.

Something howled and screamed across the cavern, and though I narrowed my eyes, I couldn't make anything out. My grip tightened on the guns, fingers twitching and wanting to squeeze the triggers. Red cut across the ground from the darkness, blood arcing and splattering.

A growl sounded, rolling straight into my bones, and my entire body tensed. Footfalls padded on limestone, slow, steady. My breath held, pulse throbbing in my temples, and I kept the barrels of my Match pistols raised.

The edge of a paw hit the circle of light first, stepping from the shadows—a massive paw, white but for streaks of blood across the fur. My gaze traveled up, up, as it continued out of the dark and the head came into view. It was enormous, white fur framed with black stripes, ears twitching as if listening, predatory eyes watching me.

A goddamn tiger.
Great.

15

EYE OF THE TIGER

———— • ◆ • ————

THE DISTANCE BETWEEN THE TIGER and me did nothing to diminish its size, shoulders at least putting it as high as my waist. No other sound permeated space, just its steps and my own fearful panting.

I shifted, my feet feeling their way backward as I couldn't pull my eyes from the new beast to look where I was going. My guns lowered, coming close together to deliver a double headshot.

The tiger stalked forward more boldly, pushing me to retreat faster.

My fingers tightened on the triggers.

The light covered half its body now and it suddenly slumped, a partial step all it managed before collapsing. Moments later blood trickled from its side, snaking over the limestone; whatever happened in that tussle, it resulted in Momma Reptilian gone, yes, but the tiger injured. Its breathing was labored and despite another attempt to drag itself forward, it thumped on the ground.

"Ms. Talbot?" Laurel's voice echoed down, falling into a squeak at the end.

I kept my guns aimed on the tiger but glanced back at the rope. I could be up and out in an instant.

My gaze returned to the big cat, meeting its eyes that drifted heavily closed for a moment before struggling open again.

Blue eyes.

Very, very blue.

I took a deep breath then lowered my guns inch by inch, bracing in case it was baiting me—no matter how illogical it seemed. When the tiger didn't move, I eased my weapons into their holsters.

My thigh bled still but even as adrenaline wore off, I could still put weight on it—nothing broken. I eyed the pitch again, then the weakening tiger that had come to my rescue.

"Ms. Talbot?" Laurel whispered.

I sighed. "Do they have another stretcher?"

Silence followed, punctuated a moment later by feet scraping on stone above, as if she had to see the others for confirmation. "No."

Damn it. "Harnesses, then? Belts?"

A few minutes later, a pile of thick nylon and leather struck the ground beneath the pitch.

I slipped off my own belt and gun harness, stuffed the guns, extra mags, and other items in my pack until I could barely get the zipper closed, then carted everything over to the big cat. I tensed as I knelt next to it, waiting for a swipe or an incisor in my jugular, but it never came. Instead the tiger watched me, heaving great breaths that shook its torso. The gashes on its side weren't just red with blood but white with something bubbling—maybe the reptile fangs were more snakish and poisonous after all.

It might be foolish to take it with me—might be one of the stupidest things I'd ever done. But I believed strongly in trusting my instincts, and if I left it—*him*—down here, I knew I'd probably regret it.

I took the mess of harnesses, untwisting them and then attaching clips, fashioning them into something that could hopefully hold however many hundreds of pounds the tiger was.

His eyes had drifted closed by the time I was working his hulking body into the contraption though he continued breathing and wheezing. It fell to me to grasp the nylon cutting over his torso and haul the creature several feet toward the pitch, and after a few minutes, it was clearly not happening.

I let out a frustrated sigh and looked back into the light. "Would you be a dear and throw down more rope?"

———————— ♦ ————————

THE INITIAL PITCH WAS LIT by floodlights, not daylight. Not far from the first one was a second, and above it, the crisp night air filled my lungs. It wasn't until I had both feet on the earth that I let myself breathe and accept I was safe.

From monsters, at least.

I was left with Laurel and another man I didn't recognize from West's team—black fatigues, olive complexion with a long crooked nose and dark, deep-set eyes. I wasn't given a name and didn't ask for one. Neither he nor Laurel commented on the fact that I dragged a huge tiger out of the cavern with me, which raised more than a few red flags since tigers aren't native to the continent nor am I prone to carting one around in my spare time, but I said nothing. The other team members had gone ahead with Brandon, including Mr. Rolph, Tucker, and Moti, and it was another ten minutes before Curtis returned with the Jeep for the rest of us.

She swung the roofless Jeep around, spitting up stones and dirt under the spinning tires, and threw on the brakes. Lights shone and the vehicle hummed while it idled with the keys in the ignition and she hopped out. Her confident steps halted three feet from the tiger, where she gaped at it. "What the fuck?"

"It's my new pet," I said with a sweet smile. "I'm thinking of calling him Buttons."

Blue eyes flickered open to glare at me and a growl rumbled in the tiger's throat.

I strongly suspected he would behave himself, though, and gestured at Curtis and the other man with us. "Do give me a hand, would you?"

We lifted the bazillion pound cat into the back of the Jeep, then all climbed in. Mr. No Name and Laurel rode in the back with it, while I took the passenger seat. Curtis didn't speak during the trip, her red brows pulled into a tight frown and shoulders hunched—I imagined she was concerned about her coworkers. Or perhaps her own well-being if she was sent down next.

The Jeep parked a ways from camp again, leaving the three of us—Laurel didn't help—to cart the tiger on foot. The mere thought of moving had my body aching but I hauled myself up and out of the vehicle, wincing with every step. Though bleeding had ceased in my leg, it started anew.

The harnesses I'd put together couldn't've been comfortable but we had no other way of carrying the thing, so the three of us each grabbed at an angle and lifted. There was a gap of darkness between the Jeep and the camp, over a hill thick with underbrush and tall weeds. Dry plants scraped at my bare legs and arms, and I sincerely hoped the scent of blood didn't draw anything particularly nasty our way.

Firelight glowing around large rectangular tents promised a sanctuary, and I almost sank to my knees in gratitude upon reaching it. I hadn't time, however; Mr. Rolph stepped out as we approached, his hands raised with water on them glinting in the light, sleeves rolled up as if he'd just washed and waited for them to air dry. His gaze narrowed, expression unreadable.

"Do you also moonlight as a vet?" I asked innocently.

Our charge let out a throaty growl and twisted; the three of us dropped him on instinct. The beast fought to his feet, makeshift harness dangling. Fresh blood and something foamy-white oozed from his side but he lumbered on for a newer tent at the far end of the camp. Mr. Rolph didn't say a word, retrieved a large white case with a red first aid cross emblazoned on the side from the tent he'd left, and followed the tiger.

Answers wouldn't be given any time soon, apparently. I went straight for the water drum, refilled one of my canteens, and downed about half of it before filling it to the brim again.

Dawson padded over, eyeing the direction Mr. Rolph had gone. "What happened?"

I stood after turning off the spout, my back spasming. All my wounds flared to life and I groaned as I tried to shake them off. I clasped the cam still hanging from my ear and handed it to him. "It's all there. I hope our employer enjoys."

He glanced down at the camera in his big palm for a moment, then followed as I limped toward the fire. "Do you need help?"

I sure as hell hoped not—wounds I couldn't treat myself tended to be debilitating ones. I eased to sit on the bench near the fire while he did the same, and peeled back the leg of my shorts until it was rolled high up on my thigh. A gash ran diagonally across my skin but it wasn't as deep as I thought—didn't require stitches. Plus there was *far* too much stubble on my legs—I really needed to shave.

"No, I'll live, but I thank you." I dumped water from my canteen over the wound, hissing as it made contact and pushed the blood away. The first aid kit was still in my pack, and I retrieved the box to dig out antiseptic. "Where is everyone?"

"Your guys were being patched up. Brandon looks bad."

We couldn't've been too near a hospital, either; perhaps they didn't expect him to last the night so didn't bother taking him. "The newbs?"

"Patrolling."

"Moti?"

"Uh, not anymore. He ranted in at Mr. Rolph for about ten minutes straight, who said something back, and then just took off."

Smart man. I swiped at the wound until it was clean, then wrapped it in gauze.

"So, um, is the tiger a ring? Was this some kind of trick question?"

My gaze narrowed on the other tent, where the flap was closed and I had no idea what was going on beyond. "The tiger is something else entirely. But I appreciate that you're thinking outside the box." I returned any remaining items to my kit and snapped the lid again.

I hurt. I was exhausted. I needed a shower, which we didn't have access to. Probably more medical attention in case I had a concussion. And a very, very long chat with Ashford.

I rubbed at my eyes and yawned. "What day is it?"

"Uh...here or stateside?"

"Either. Both."

He looked at his watch. "Wednesday night in Texas. Thursday morning here."

This time zone thing was all kinds of messed up, but we'd been under ground for far too many days. "You can get an internet connection here?"

"Yeah...I've kinda got it boosted."

"Would it be possible to use your laptop in a bit to speak to my daughter? There's my phone but I'd like to see her a bit better."

"Of course. I can do it right now—"

I waved him off and rose unsteadily. "First, I need to change. Then..." My gaze trailed to the tent with the cat. "I need to have a conversation with someone."

16
BUTTONS

———◆———

I STRIPPED OUT OF MY torn and bloody clothes, wiped myself down with a towel soaked in canteen water, patched up the odd cut that needed it, then slipped on black yoga pants and another tank top.

I let my braid out, shaking it into wavy kinks. My fingers touched grease near the roots—I had some waterless shampoo in one of my bags, and I'd have to give it a thorough cleaning that night before it drove me mad. I slipped on a fleece coat with pockets next, where I stowed a reloaded gun. The weapon harness was still otherwise engaged, so this would have to do.

My feet were achy and blistered so I changed my socks and slipped on running shoes, letting my boots sit and dry out. Standing up after sitting on the end of the cot for a few minutes was just about the most difficult thing I'd done all day, including facing off against giant reptilian snake things, but I got my ass moving again, though stiffly.

Adrenaline had completely left me by this point and I felt everything anew: the aches and pains in my body, the chill night atmosphere, the pinch against my sore scalp as wind tossed my hair. The camp was silent, no sign of the patrolling team if they'd remained near. Dawson waved at me from his tech table and I waved back—I'd head over shortly to check in on Em and Prudence.

But first I strode for the tent Mr. Rolph had disappeared into. I wasn't sure if he remained, but I paused at the closed flap and called, "Knock knock."

Steps rustled inside and a moment later the flap opened, Mr. Rolph meeting me. Sweat beaded on his forehead, dripping into his dark eyes behind thick glasses once again. His sleeves were still rolled up and he wore latex gloves coated in blood.

My heart beat harder even as I tried to smile sweetly. "How's the patient?"

He glanced over his shoulder and from within a voice called, "It's fine."

Mr. Rolph sighed, stripped off his gloves, and shook his head. "You're not going to listen to a word I said, are you?"

"Nope."

Muttering under his breath, the resident medic left without a word to me and I slipped through the fabric doorway as he did.

Dale West was stretched out on a cot, a sheet up to his waist and chest bare above. A wound in his side was covered in gauze; he had other cuts and bruises but none as bad as what I assumed was under the bandage. Flesh was pulled tight over defined muscle, unnaturally pale except for inky black veins snaking through his skin around the large bandage—definitely venom after all. Bloody towels and a dish of pink-tinged water sat on the floor beside the bed.

Very blue eyes met mine, arresting despite the exhaustion edging them; his gaze pressed on me until I was nearly stepping out of the tent, ready to hightail it into the night.

He had my heartrate kicking up with just one look, exuding a sense of authority that sneaks up on a person, sliding behind you until it's wrapped around your throat. I took a breath and moved for the tangle of harnesses and belts on the small table next to the cot, a lantern in the middle casting light on what was a total mess. West watched me like a predator on prey, unwavering and patient even as I avoided his gaze—his was a heavy look near palpable in the atmosphere. I unhooked nylon and leather pieces bit by bit to keep my trembling hands busy, weaving straps through the mess until I had part of my gun harness loose, and pointedly disregarded him.

West shifted, moving in my peripheral vision to a sitting position and he leaned against his hands stretched behind him. "Buttons?"

A faint smile curved my lips but I still didn't look at him. "Because of your adorable little button nose."

Silence. "I don't have a button nose."

"Not as a human, no, but you do as a cat." At last my harness was properly detangled as was my belt, and I deposited the rest on the table. My gaze hit his. "And I prefer the pussy version, by the way."

He smiled, exposing his teeth, and I didn't take it as a friendly gesture. "You're welcome."

I cocked a brow in question.

"For saving your life. Again. You might need to work on that whole gratitude thing."

"Maybe you ought to as well, considering I dragged you out of the cave and took you with us."

"Which wouldn't have been needed if you just climbed the goddamn rope like I told you to."

"And leave Laurel there? To be eaten?"

West shrugged.

Irritation heated my blood, and both the gun harness and my belt creaked in my grip as I squeezed them. "You're an asshole."

"I prefer pragmatist."

"So what made me worthy of not being reptile food?"

He sat up straighter, the lantern to the side cutting light artfully over his sculpted chest. "One, they're not reptiles. *Drakones Aithiopes.*"

"Which is...a fancy word for lizard demons?"

"'Serpents of Ethiopia', but a *dragon*-serpent to be specific. What you saw down there pales in comparison to the full grown ones."

I swallowed a thick lump in my throat but tried to keep my voice calm. "That last one wasn't the mother?"

"The adults reach over one hundred feet long."

Holy shit. I couldn't even contemplate where something that fucking huge even resided in the cave system—and I definitely didn't want to run into her.

"Two, you're needed. I'd ask you not do anything else stupid so no one has to risk their neck to bring you back in one piece. I can survive the *drakon* venom. Humans can't."

"So *I'm* needed, but Laurel's expendable?"

"That's why she's here."

"She's supposed to be representing Mr. Ashford." *Or so she said.*

"She managed to misplace some paperwork last month that caused him to lose a major land deal and substantial amount of money."

"So she can prove herself here but if she dies, no big loss?"

"Exactly."

Jesus. "You're not just an asshole, but your employer is a motherfucking asshole himself."

He wasn't fazed, still half-smiling at me. "Also, that's *your* employer now as well, Olivia."

My face flushed—he was right, I was a hypocrite. But I still wouldn't back down. "If I'm down there with a team, *no one* is expendable to me." I couldn't keep up the high and mighty act for long, however, so I amended. "Except maybe Tucker and Brandon. Also, you."

"What's your problem with the mercs?" He frowned, black brows pulling tight, as if I'd thrown him off kilter for the first time that night.

"They pulled guns on us and forced me to try to cross a nest of those *drakones.* Alone. Where I was almost eaten. It seriously put the entire mission at risk. That was about twenty minutes before you made your grand entrance, by the way. Since you're cozy with Mr. Rolph, I'm sure he can confirm."

"Do you have evidence other than your word?" he asked as he shifted, twisting so his legs hung over the edge of the cot. He grasped the mattress, breathing deeply as he began to rise though his expression remained neutral despite whatever pain he was in.

"Video record which I just gave to——" My gaze darted up to stare at the tent ceiling as he rose and the sheet slipped away.

Buttons was very, very naked.

"To whom?" he prompted innocently.

I swore the bastard was grinning. "To Dawson. It's a mite cold out there, though, so I'd maybe consider pants if I were you."

West moved closer, every hair on my body suddenly standing on end. Even nudity didn't bring out vulnerability in him; he towered over me, intimidating and owning the entire space of the tent which was growing far too warm for my liking.

I breathed in stuffy air and scented a whiff of sterile hospital supplies slightly edged out by the male musk of sweat.

He was inches from me and gooseflesh rolled across my skin under my jacket. "Interested in the ceiling fabric or is there something I don't see up there?"

My lips pursed, clamping together to keep from grinning. "Very fine quality. High thread count to keep out bugs. I approve."

"I'm sure the makers will be thrilled to know you've spent so much time studying their work."

So he wanted to be like that, did he? I turned my gaze again to meet his eyes. His irises were a cool cobalt blue and they paled to ice, seeming to flash in challenge, and I kept his stare even as heat suffused my cheeks.

Before either of us could speak, the tent flap opened abruptly, the shape of Mr. Rolph taking up some of the doorway. A rush of cool night air drifted in, icing the sweat that had started to dampen my skin and cooling away the heat in my cheeks. Rolph didn't move, didn't speak, staring and likely wondering what the hell was going on.

West remained unfazed.

I gazed down pointedly then looked back up at him again, raising a brow. "Like I said, it's a little cold out there, Buttons. You might want pants."

Before anything more could be said, I ducked out of the tent and past Mr. Rolph, who gave me a quizzical look. Squabbling with Ashford's right hand was not my best use of time, so I put on a smile, nodded at Mr. Rolph, and swept away from the pair of them. The tent flap swung back into place behind me, eliminating the shadow I cast on the ground in front of me, and the low rumble of arguing voices followed. I heard something about bed rest due to the injury and that was all as I swiftly paced away.

Laurel was on her way from the tech table and I felt a flash of sympathy for her. No wonder she seemed so frazzled down there, and her words had extra weight now. *It's either success or our lives. I am in the same position as both of you.*

Indeed, she was.

She headed straight for me, despite looking exhausted, and slowed as our paths intersected. "Mr. Rolph and I have checked in with Mr. Ashford, and he wants to speak with you."

I glanced over her shoulder at the tech table. *Wonderful.* "Do we still have a job or is West supposed to take over?"

"Mr. Rolph and I...discussed it and decided not to mention the trouble we've had."

"Dawson touched base with Ashford and West is *here*, though—he must know already?"

"I don't know, he didn't mention West. But, my advice?" She tilted her head to the side and gave me a look that suggested I accept it.

"Sure."

"Assure him everything is going fine. Minor setback to regroup but we'll have the Seal shortly. Believe me..." She hugged her arms and shivered. "You don't want to be disposable to him."

We all truly were on the same side now. I nodded. "Okay. He's not talking to the mercs, is he?"

"I don't think he even knows their names. This rests on us. Or at least you."

God, I couldn't wait to get home. "You get some rest," I said as I started past her.

"That's the plan. Goodnight, Ms. Talbot."

Poor Laurel. She'd definitely quit after this.

Dawson held back from the tech table as I approached and gestured at the laptop. I nodded my understanding and rounded the table to take the chair waiting in front of the screen. The Ethiopian wilderness was at my back but I was close enough to the fire that I didn't worry. Too much. After all, apparently there were giant serpent dragons out there somewhere.

Moses Ashford waited on the screen, visible from the shoulders up and in a dark suit. Late night back in North America but he didn't look like the sort of man to ever relax. He nodded. "Ms. Talbot."

I forced a smile. "Mr. Ashford."

He let a pregnant pause pass. "I hadn't expected to see you before you completed your objective."

Oh god, he reminded me of my father. I stuffed down the urge to be a snarky bratty bitch. "Likewise. But we were separated underground and lost some of our equipment, and needed to regroup. We're hitting the cave again at dawn."

Another moment of silence. "I don't think I need to remind you that I don't like delays."

My stomach tightened and I rubbed at the back of my neck. "Oh, believe me, I want to get home too. We're very close—no more delays." If I wasn't running on physical exhaustion, I could probably fake it better; as it was, I worried my tone was too light, too casual. But I couldn't think of another way to reassure him that everything was okay.

Because nothing is.

He continued watching me, his expression unchanging. "You'll recall your contract specified you are to be on the plane with the Seal seven days after you landed."

I struggled to calm my suddenly thumping heart. "Yes..."

"I'll deduct one hundred thousand from your fee for every day you're late."

Shit. Shit shit shit. My lips parted to argue, tired brain trying to remember my contract and how he could be wrong, but I had nothing. I'd read the papers front to back and scrawled my name right there, agreeing with his "strongly preferred" seven days from landing to departure for my five hundred thousand. "That sounds fair. We arrived Sunday morning—we'll be gone, Seal in hand, by Saturday at the latest."

"I'll see you when you return, then."

I kept up my smile. "Looking forward to it."

Mr. Ashford nodded, not breaking his steady stare, and the screen abruptly went black.

I let out a heavy breath, my shoulders sagging as tension left. Two minutes of him breathing down my neck and my temples had started to throb.

Like I needed something else to worry about.

17
DON'T TELL MISS JENNINGS

———————◆———————

DAWSON HOVERED A FEW FEET away and I waved at him to join me, then leaned my elbows on the table, tipping my head down and rubbing my temples.

"So we're pretending everything's great and there isn't a couple badly injured mercs and a tiger running around?"

"Yep."

"Okay, then." He came to stand next to me and I looked up to see him gazing in the direction of the tent. "Who was the naked dude?"

"Dale West. Works for Ashford."

"Oh...hell."

I just could not take any more bad news tonight. "Hmm?"

His dark eyes were locked on the tent, though no one had emerged yet, and he pressed his large palms on the tabletop beside me to lean in and speak in a low voice. "He is *bad* news. Bad. Really bad."

"So not good, then?"

He gave me a look that suggested for once he wasn't amused with my smart mouth. "That's Ashford's right hand."

Second time of the night I'd heard that and I was liking the sounds of it less and less. My stomach twisted. "Meaning?"

"He does..." Dawson heaved a breath, his gaze skirting mine, and he brushed a lock of dark brown hair behind his ear. "Bad stuff."

"Ashford's dirty work? Shred tax documents?"

"No, I mean...the bad stuff. If someone was gonna break your kneecaps, it would be *that* guy."

"You make it sound like Ashford's a mobster."

"Well, it sounds like this West guy is an enforcer, so maybe he sorta is."

We both looked again at the tent that housed the injured man. Tiger. Man-tiger. Whatever. Chills danced up my spine, possibilities hanging in the air and not a single one I liked. Was he here to help us, double cross us, or punish us if we failed?

"Here." He tapped the keyboard in front of me and thumbed the mouse until he had a virtual corkboard up filled with audio files and notes, more detailed than what I'd seen before.

I took over from there and clicked the first recording. When a voice burst on, Dawson hit the volume a few times so it dropped lower. I leaned forward to listen.

"*No, you're shitting me...*" I vaguely recognized the voice, frowned, but kept listening. "*Not West.*"

"*That's who's on his way.*" That was a female voice, though rough around the edges.

"*If the boss man sent him, we're dead. He's the motherfucking enforcer. Cleans up and he makes loose ends disappear. Jesus, we're fucking dead. So dead.*"

"*Calm the fuck down,*" she said. "*All I heard is that he's on his way. Doesn't mean—*"

"*Means we can sure as shit forget about getting paid—*"

"*Keep your goddamn head on you!*"

"*Didn't you hear?*" The man was damn near hysterical. "*C'mon, you heard. Everyone heard. You're lucky if all he does is put a bullet in your head. Bachman's crew? Remember them? Did some private security work for Ashford two years back. They're not working anymore—know why?*"

"*Brandon—*"

"*Do. You. Know. Why? Because Bachman tried to steal something from the old man's vault. And now every one of the dudes on his team are* missing their hands."

"*Calm the fuck dow—*"

"*I fucking met Salvador. No hands. Hacked off, not even. Said if he tried to cross Ashford again, 'The sins of the father would be visited on the son.' You get that? They'd go after his fucking kid—*"

"*Nothing is gonna happen if you just do your motherfucking job. You make sure that dumb cunt gets the ring or whatever the fuck he wants and we deliver her, then be on our way.*"

The call abruptly ended and I looked at Dawson.

"Curtis," he said in a low voice. "Brandon called when they got out after the cave-in and went around. I'd already heard from West—he's who answered when I called Ashford, and said the boss wanted you guys to keep going and that he would head here to get you out."

"You record everyone's calls?"

His smile went sheepish and even in the lowlight I caught a blush darkening his cheeks. "Um...just the mercenaries when I don't trust them."

"Good thinking."

He minimized the window and straightened. "They're scared of him. And they kill people sometimes for a living, so..."

So we should be scared as well. Perhaps I made a very, very bad mistake back there when I pulled that cat out with us.

"Never guessed," Dawson's gaze trailed to the tent again, "that the right hand was a tiger."

"Kinda makes you wonder if he bit the hands off."

He made a face and shuddered. "Aw, Livi."

I rolled my eyes—really, I *couldn't* be the only one thinking it.

"I didn't think...the Pulse could make people tigers. Have you heard of that? I mean," he continued before I could respond, "were there a bunch of people *before* who just had tiger genes that got activated? Or what?"

"Talismans, spells—different things like that make it possible." I was, of course, pulling that idea out of my rear; I had no particular clue what West was or how it came about that he could turn into a tiger, but I suspected the usual rules didn't apply to the man. The only shamans I'd ever heard of who could shapeshift did so at great magical cost and it required an extensive ritual beforehand—which I didn't think he had time to do tonight before jumping in after me.

Then there were the *drakones* in the caves. Had they somehow always been there, guarding an inactive Seal? Or did they pop up four years ago when the Pulse happened?

Normally I kept my head down and didn't think too hard about it. At the end of the day, I didn't care about all this stuff. Magic. Dragons. The power of the artifacts I stole.

I just cared about my little girl and what I could give her.

"You're taking this too well," Dawson said.

"Well, I was almost eaten a few times during the past few days." I rubbed at my eyes. I needed sleep, badly, but had to talk to my daughter first. "Thanks for the heads-up. I'll keep an eye on him."

Dawson nodded and stepped back. "I'll give you space to call home."

"Thank you." I offered him a smile of gratitude, though it was weary, and waited until he'd moved across the camp for the water drum before heading back to Skype. I logged in and rang up home. Pru usually kept the program on when I was away, just in case I was able to get in a call, and I drummed my nails nervously on the desk while I waited.

The call picked up and the video wavered, freezing for a moment on Pru's face. Her dark hair was bound up in a messy ponytail and she wore her pajama top—it must've been near seven or eight her time. After a brief stutter, the video returned to normal. She leaned closer to the screen—the tiny window in the corner representing me was almost black so I turned up the brightness and gamma, hoping she'd see me better.

"We were getting worried." Her voice came through as she leaned back, and a moment later her lips moved. The video was choppy but emotion welled in me—there was our tiny office space in the corner of the living room where the computer sat, big chair back looming behind my best friend, and in the background a bookshelf lined wall with uneven rows of book spines and knickknacks.

Home.

Broken appliances, damaged building, rough neighborhood, shitty landlord, but still: home.

I blinked; it was too dark for her to see me get weepy, but I didn't want to risk it. "Sorry. Complications."

There was a delay, her focusing on the screen as she listened, then she nodded. "Are you okay?"

For the time being. I forced a smile and the poor quality of the video told me she probably wouldn't notice the difference. "Yes, I'm fine."

"Did you find the Seal?"

I groaned. "Let's not talk about it. Have you heard anything from Martin?"

"No..."

"He's after it too."

Pru shook her head and gave a dramatic sigh that didn't lose any of its seriousness with the millisecond time delay. "You two are terrible."

"Can you look into who hired him?"

"I can try." She reached across the screen, her arm cutting over the lamp to the side, and returned with a pad of paper and pen where she jotted down my request. Most days her memory was still good but part of her disorder affected cognitive function and there remained the chance that if she didn't have a note, she might not remember. "Got it. Is he already there?"

"I imagine so." *And hope not.* Even if his flight was delayed, or had transfers, or he got stuck in customs, surely he'd be at the caves by now. Yes, we competed and threw grenades at one another, but at the end of the day, he was my brother.

"Anything else while I'm at it?"

Oh, many, many things, and top of the list was Buttons. But there seemed too good a chance someone would hear that request so instead I shook my head. "Not at the moment."

"Richard Moss called. Again."

I groaned.

"He wants to take you out for dinner. I said you're in Africa and probably contracted malaria so you aren't available for a while."

"Good woman. Where's my Buttercup?"

Prudence raised her hand and pointed a manicured nail-tipped finger downward.

Hiding under the desk. *Not* a good sign. "Does no one else want to come talk to me?"

We waited but Em didn't speak up or move.

Prudence made a show of looking around the room. "No one I can see."

"Hmm." I drew the word out dramatically and spoke a touch louder. "I'm sure there was someone else. How about Giles? Does he want to see me?"

"I think he's taking a nap."

"Oh, well." I gave a loud, dramatic yawn. "I guess I'll be going."

"That's probably best," Pru agreed. "Hopefully you can call back in a few days."

"Probably a few *weeks* at the earliest—"

Very slowly a head of dark brown hair crept up from behind the desk off to the corner of the screen and Emaleth's big owl eyes peered at me. She paused there, fingers clasping the edge of the desk.

My heart seized, emotion clawing at my chest. I bit at my bottom lip for a moment until I was certain I could speak without shattering my calm. "Hello there, little miss. Glad you could join us."

Not taking her eyes from the screen, she shifted sideways until she was in front of Pru, who lifted her to sit on her lap. "Hi, Mommy."

"Why were you hiding under the desk?"

Her shoulders deflated and she looked away.

"She was suspended," Pru informed me when it seemed my daughter wouldn't.

I blinked, my voice pitching to a shrill level. "She *what?*"

"She apparently punched another girl and the school has a zero tolerance policy."

Oh my god. My jaw nearly twitched. I kept blinking. "I'm sorry, but *what?*"

Prudence gave Em a little nudge but she didn't speak up. "She broke her nose."

This couldn't be happening. My six-year-old *couldn't* be starting yard brawls in private school in the first goddamn grade. "Please tell me I died in that cave and this is some kind of hell or purgatory."

"I didn't hit her that hard!" Em burst out, her face going red and tears spilling down her cheeks.

But I would not be swayed by some crying. "You shouldn't be hitting anyone at all."

"I didn't! But then she yelled and I hit her and she was bleeding and—"

I clamped down my lips while she spoke, counted to ten, then cut her off. "What is it you think justified assaulting this classmate?"

Em sat back in Pru's arms, growing quiet.

My patience had long run out that day. "Emaleth Marta Anne Talbot, *what* was going through your head?"

"She was making fun of me," she whispered in a small voice the mic barely picked up.

"You're going to have to do better than that."

"I didn't like what she was *saying*!"

I resisted the urge to bang my forehead against the tabletop. "And what, pray tell, was she saying, darling?"

"Kaitlin said that Annabelle's *mom* was saying stuff about you and Dad...dy..." She froze as she caught herself.

My blood pressure wasn't getting any lower.

I peeled my fingers back from where they gripped the table's edge, not even realizing I'd grasped it. Counting to ten wasn't helping, so I opted for twenty before giving up all together.

I unclenched my jaw with effort just to force out words. "We need to have a long talk when I get home. Epically long. One that will continue probably until I'm too old to physically keep you in the room while I lecture. Let me give you a taste: First, you don't hit people. I don't care what the hell they say to you, Emaleth, even if it's about me. Second, Denny is not your father. If this fact is difficult to remember, I'm sure no longer going for visits will go a long way to help. Are we at all unclear about any of this?"

She said nothing. Neither did Pru, who was very much the anti-disciplinarian, but she knew enough not to say a single hippy word about it when it came to my parenting.

My breaths heaved and I hadn't realized exactly how tense I'd become until I got it all out. I didn't speak again until I'd centered myself and was certain I could talk without losing my temper. "I was nearly killed tonight." Emmy's eyes grew huge and I almost regretted it, but continued on before I could pause to worry. "And I have to go back into a very dangerous situation again in the morning. I do not need to be worried about what you're doing while I'm gone. How long are you suspended for?"

Em still stared at me, so it was Pru who spoke up after clearing her throat. "Three days."

Sounded fair. "Emaleth, you're grounded for the rest of the month. You do homework and chores. No video games, no TV. Absolutely *no* visits to Denny's house. No friends over. Am I understood?"

She nodded.

"Now is there anything else you'd like to share with me before bed?"

Em bit at her lip, still staring at me. "I miss you, Mommy."

Little vixen—knew immediately how to melt my heart. I ached for her, for home, and my voice softened. "I miss you too, baby."

Her body relaxed, slumping against Prudence, and she rubbed at her eyes while Pru combed back her hair soothingly. "When can you come home?"

I hated making promises I couldn't keep. "A few more days."

"You got hurt?"

"No, I'm fine. I'm over the worst of it." *Lies lies lies.* I couldn't stand the taste of them. It would make her feel better, though. "And I think it's almost your bedtime."

"Um…"

"Yes, dear?"

"There's a naked man behind you."

Oh, for the love of— I sighed. "West, please tell me you have pants on."

"Of course," his deep voice came behind me.

I looked at Pru and cocked my brow.

"He does," she said.

"Thank god for small favors. Now, *you*," I pointed to Em, "to bed. Brush your teeth."

Em rolled her eyes, apparently forgetting my ire moments ago. "Yes, Mom."

"Properly."

"I know."

"For thirty seconds each side."

"I know!"

She was going to be so much fun as a teenager. I glanced at Pru next. "Get any homework from her teacher tomorrow, please, and see that she completes it as well as extra chores."

"Yes, sir." Prudence smiled sweetly.

They were lucky they were on another continent. "I will endeavor to survive my talk now with my naked friend as well as any dragons I encounter tomorrow."

Em's eyes went wide. "*Dragons?*"

I held up a finger to stop her. "Don't tell Miss Jennings. Not the dragon bit, nor about the naked man. Got it?"

She solemnly nodded and I didn't believe her for a second.

"G'night, baby—I love you."

"I love you too." She waved, as did Pru. My finger hovered for a moment on the mouse, heart aching, before I gave in and disconnected the call.

With a near physical force, I pushed away thoughts of home—my house, my family, my place in the world—and locked it away, because it couldn't come back with me here. I couldn't let it follow me when I was trying to work, to survive, to—in some cases—kill. There, I was "Mom"; here, I was Olivia Talbot, retriever of supernatural artifacts and willing to make a payday at all costs. The more the worlds threatened to connect, the greater a liability I might end up being.

I shivered in the cold night air, my body chilled after sitting far from the fire. My eyes burned but deep breaths and blinking eased the ache, any tears I felt retreating to be locked in a box while I went back to work.

"Now." I pushed my chair back and stood from the desk, steeling myself before facing West. "What did you want?"

He gestured over his shoulder, his expression impassive. "A walk and a conversation."

Just in case, I took a moment to slip on my holster, snapping straps into place over my yoga pant-clad thighs and hips, and then slipped my gun into place on my right. I left the belt on Dawson's table for retrieval later and nodded. "Lead the way."

18
GETTING TO KNOW MR. WEST

——————◆——————

WEST DIDN'T LIE ABOUT THE fact he was wearing pants, a fact which I was quite grateful for.

He did skip the shirt, however, whether because the cold didn't bother him or because it made some sort of sense I didn't understand to keep the bandaged wound exposed to the elements. He'd forgone shoes as well, stepping evenly across the rough ground as if it was nothing—stalking, one could say, like a cat. He led me from the camp into the darkness; the firelight remained to my left, and he walked in utter blackness to my right with nothing visible beyond.

I kept aware of the gun at my side, my fingers flexing every few moments in case I needed to reach for it. My left thigh stung as a reminder I shouldn't get in any scrapes with him, even if instinct cautioned me it might be necessary.

West broke the silence a dozen yards from camp. "I wasn't aware we'd graduated from acquaintances to friends."

"I think it's more frenimies at this point."

"Ah."

"Better than nemeses," I offered.

"There is that. So was that your girlfriend?"

I kept my poker face rather than snicker; if he was trying to be scandalous, he was a little late as it wasn't like I hadn't heard that before.

"Or, I'm sorry, is it 'life partner'?" he continued before I could.

"Just because I'm not interested in your penis doesn't make me a lesbian."

"Never suggested such a thing. Was curious if she's single is all."

"You're not her type." I wouldn't dare chance a look at him but could all but picture his feral grin in the dark at my remark.

"Why's that?"

"She's over the bad boy phase. We both are."

"I don't think I qualify as a boy."

"Bad *man*, then."

"That sounds extremely sordid."

"I rather think so as well."

Curiosity hung on my lips, many things I wanted to ask but then I didn't want to expose my thoughts. I'd rather ask *around* him than him directly, since I figured any head-on collision wouldn't end well. I'd heard stories of the odd shapeshifter before but they weren't particularly common post-Pulse—he really didn't strike me as a shaman. Perhaps Pru might be able to unearth some info for me later, or Dawson might stumble across something.

Wind stirred my hair, caressed my head and pushed my eyes closed, reminding me how much I would rather be sleeping on an uncomfortable cot again at some point tonight than be walking out here with him. "Is there a particular reason you're subjecting me to your presence?"

"You're not one to let questions lie. You have the opportunity to ask them *now* so you're not distracting me with them tomorrow back in Kadhim."

That answered one, then: he was sticking around—despite the injury—to help end this. Despite the assurance that I was for some reason not expendable, I did not find his involvement terribly promising. "If you had the tools to dig another entrance into the cave, why couldn't we have done that to begin with?"

"Your flight didn't stop in Addis Ababa or any airport in the country."

"I noticed."

He allowed a beat of silence to pass, whether to rethink what he was to reveal or draw the tension between us taut, I didn't know. "Ashford has special permission to be here. He's owed favors by a few members of parliament and decided to cash in for this trip." West raised one of his large hands to count on his fingers, and for a moment the massive paw of the tiger stepping out of darkness an hour ago flashed in my head. "One, he may use that old airstrip for travel. Your pilot was flying under certain banners so your landing wasn't questioned. Two, if he didn't draw any attention to himself, the understanding is basically that they will look the other way."

"Including stealing what amounts to a national and maybe religious relic?"

He dropped his hand at his side again. "That wouldn't be part of the bargain, no. Also not included is altering any landmarks, like—"

"Drilling through a sacred cave named after some holy man. Gotcha." Which raised the question of what made me the non-expendable one, worth sending a team in after in a way that broke one of those very rules, but I held my tongue on that for a moment. "Two-parter: any other conditions, and what's the penalty for breaking that last one?"

"His business in the country must conclude within the week."

Bloody hell. Hence the contract and him springing it on me that he'd be cutting a hundred grand a day beyond it—the guy knew money would speak to me more than anything else.

"If it doesn't," West continued, "or if he did something to expose his presence here...he has friends in high places but they'll cover their own asses. That might mean Ashford or any of his associates are thrown in jail. It might also mean he or his people are simply forced to leave and barred from reentry."

Pieces were beginning to arrange themselves in my brain but I had a few spots left to fill. "The others who went before me but were never heard from again?"

Silence. Tension crept around him, simmering in the air, and when more than the usual amount of time passed without an answer, I shifted my gaze his way, fingers flicking absently toward the butt of my gun.

The corner of his lips curved upward but his steady gaze remained locked ahead of us. "Do you shoot if you don't like my answer?"

"Perhaps only if I don't receive one. Will you cut off my hands if I try to?"

His lips twitched again, whether to broaden his smile or grimace, I didn't know. "Is someone telling you stories?"

"People talk. You're not denying anything."

"I have no intention to. Working for Ashford isn't a job anyone should take lightly."

"Or...*you cut off their hands.*"

West sighed and shook his head. "Once. Just once and it's all anyone can talk about."

I can't imagine why. I made no move to relax my hand, still itching to grab the gun. "Are you planning to answer my question?"

"The other teams of mercenaries," he continued immediately, not even asking me to repeat it as if the hand-cutting discussion had bought him enough time to formulate an answer acceptable to give me, "were hired here, on the ground. The most recent time, he had mercs take scholars—experts in their fields of study—into the cave. Ashford tried for subtle and avoided cashing in favors, and they didn't make it out of the caves alive."

I almost asked if perhaps they simply escaped with the ring, but that would be foolish—we both knew what was down there and how anyone unprepared would fair. "So this is his last shot."

"Hire well, call in favors, get in and get out."

And I'm not expendable because they can't go back to the drawing board with this. All or nothing, and Ashford had made it clear he wouldn't accept the latter option. I wasn't a scholarly expert but perhaps he preferred someone without ethics who would retrieve the ring, no questions asked.

I was missing *something* here, but damned if I could figure out what it was—for now, I'd have to take everyone at face-value, with caution. At least nothing West said so far suggested he intended to cut off our hands and threaten our children, but I wasn't about to trust him.

"Next."

This twenty questions game was getting on my nerves. "Is it bigger than a breadbox?"

"Depends on the temperature."

I tried to suck back a laugh and just ended up choking, air catching in my throat. "You win. I concede."

"I wasn't aware this was a contest."

We'd turned back toward the camp at some point and now the fire grew larger the nearer we got; the air warmed, wrapping comforting fingers around my shoulders and drawing me closer. "Oh, I suspect, Mr. West, that you are *always* competing."

"That's assuming there's ever any competition."

I shook my head and avoided his gaze as I stepped past him for my tent. "Goodnight, Buttons."

Just as I pushed open the tent flap, he called me back. "Olivia."

I glanced over my shoulder.

Firelight cut dark orange over him, the color violent and sinister. "You mentioned a recording."

"Check Dawson's tech table—I'm sure if you ask politely, he'll let you watch it on his laptop." I slipped inside the tent and let the tent flap close behind me.

———— • ◆ • ————

SLEEP WAS FITFUL AND UNPLEASANT; I'd thought exhaustion would take me into the depths of unconsciousness but instead monsters loomed in the corners of my brain, chasing me and sinking fangs through my body while I tried to rest.

It wasn't the headache blooming in my temples nor the pangs of hunger that woke me at last; it was the bark of testosterone-laced voices shouting in the distance.

My eyes blinked open to a pale white canopy of mosquito netting near my face. Muscles ached as I turned onto my back, brain struggling to wake even as my body moved. I stifled a yawn and drew myself up, looking around. The other cots were empty, Laurel and Dawson both missing.

I'd slept in the clothes I'd changed into the night before so I was decent as I kicked off the sheets and swung my feet to touch the dirt ground. I hadn't time to pause long enough to rub sleep from my eyes when the shouting drew my attention again and I launched forward, batting away the mosquito netting and stumbling across the tent. Sand skidded under my bare, sleep-numb feet, my hair bound in a loose ponytail swishing across my back and shoulders. Chill morning air met me, icing the skin my tank top left exposed, and I blinked against the daylight, eyes adjusting to take stock of the camp.

A handful of figures stood outside the tent on the other side of the fire pit from mine—a tent I struggled and failed, with my sleep-deprived brain, to remember who had been occupying. I recognized Laurel and Dawson hanging back, one on either side of the tent and both looking at me as I stalked forward.

"What the hell is going on?" I didn't wait for an answer, instead jerking open the tent flap even as Laurel started to argue.

The tent must've been the mercenaries'—Brandon, wounded but still alive, lay on a cot to the side. His left arm was a stump now, tied and bandaged just below the elbow; the gauze was soaked dark red, almost black with blood. His pants were cut over the right leg and his thigh tied off as well, but veins ran black under his skin, whatever venom the *drakones* carried doing its work. His flesh was soaked with sweat, sheet over the mattress beneath him dark with it as well, and his skin had gone scarily pale.

I had no love for the mercenary with the situation he'd put me in the night before, but the sight of his poisoning made me flinch in empathy—numerous times, I'd been close enough to those fangs to be bitten, and I could all but feel the creature on me last night as I fought to avoid its mouth. Pain flashed in my thigh again where its nails had dug in.

I blinked and took in everything else; the space was full to capacity. Mr. Rolph stood near the cot, angling himself between people with his arms out and hands splayed in a supplicating gesture. To the right was Tucker, face so red his hair was pure white in contrast, and Curtis at his side pointing a gun past Mr.

Rolph; to the left was West at the end of the cot, deadly calm, head tilted down and eyes glowing blue under black brows.

He also had a SIG Combat pistol.

Aimed at Brandon.

The air in the tent was thick and tense, stinking of blood and antiseptic, and the sick-sweet scent of approaching death. I braced, reaching for my hip to realize I wasn't armed, and glanced between them all again as my heart beat hard. Brandon's head thrashed to the side, unfocused eyes blinking in the low light. Whether he knew the gun was on him or not, I wasn't sure.

I dropped my voice as I repeated my previous inquiry. "What the hell is going on?"

No one spoke for seconds that stretched into a full minute.

It was Tucker, to my surprise, who broke the silence. "He came in here about to shoot Brandon."

A flash of movement caught my eye, Curtis tightening her fingers on the Glock in her hands, muscles in her arms going taut.

I swallowed dryly. "Okay—"

"See," West interrupted smoothly, not taking his focus from the near-incapacitated man on the cot instead of worrying about the very real, pissed off threat holding a gun on him, "there's this rule Ashford has, which includes not threatening his employees and putting a job at risk. Instead, Mr. Kelso here made a reckless decision that resulted not only in his current predicament, but me being down a team member, and we had to collapse the nest room to ensure we could leave without being followed, which was our path through the cave. I'm not in a very good mood about that."

He was just so fucking calm, a chill rolled through me and my feet fought to inch backward. His gaze was as steady as the gun in his hand and I had absolutely no doubt he could shoot everyone in the tent and not blink an eye.

"Put your fucking gun *down*," Curtis warned, her voice like sandpaper scratching the tense air around us.

Rolph shifted uneasily, his dark eyes tracking back and forth between the people on either side of him. "Let's all keep calm—"

"We're not keeping calm while he's threatening to shoot one of our own," Tucker spat.

I strongly suspected he wasn't threatening so much as about to demonstrate. "Okay, Brandon sucks over what he did, but he's also about to die of *drakon* poisoning so this seems kinda pointless."

"There's a lesson to be learned here," West said simply.

Despite the fact he was about to put out of his misery the person who damn near got me killed—which would've left my kid motherless—a sick feeling wormed in my gut at the idea of things going down the way it appeared they were about to. "A lesson he can't appreciate, what with being dead and all. Now, he's dying. I'm going to guess here and say there's no antivenin. You want to let someone put a bullet in his head and end it now out of mercy, I'm on board with that. But he's beyond revenge or warnings being useful at this point, don't you think?"

"Not a lesson for him. But I would like Mr. Tucker and Ms. McKay to pay very close attention right now as I'm going to say this exactly once." His voice was as dark as the shadows in the tent, and just as deadly, perhaps, as the weapon in his hand. "They are here as backup. The chain of command from now on starts and ends with me. They are not to threaten anyone nor make decisions. If I *suspect* one of them is about to step out of line, he or she gets a bullet in their skull. If one of them succeeds in stepping out of line, both will be wishing for a bullet though I assure everyone present I'm adept at making pain last indefinitely."

More silence and I was at a loss of what to say, my stomach churning and clenching, ready to evict its contents if I'd actually eaten anything recently. My gaze darted from person to person, watching the realization sink in.

They weren't saving their friend from this.

Curtis straightened her arms, jaw set and eyes narrowing. "We protect our own and you aren't killing him."

"Think, McKay. Think about what you've been told. Do you *really* want to test my reflexes at the moment?"

The mercenary didn't move but for her square jaw working, teeth grinding. No one dared breathe but Brandon, who flinched and gasped with pain, still unable to focus on anyone.

"Put down the gun and step out," West warned.

Ten seconds passed. Twenty. Thirty. My arms grew tired just thinking of how long they'd all been standing like that, holding firearms.

A full ninety seconds later, Curtis turned and stalked from the tent, jarring my arm as she pushed passed me. The fabric flap snapped in her wake before settling again.

My chest ached, like I still couldn't breathe as I looked back at the nearly-dead man on the cot.

"Look," I bit out, "*I* am the one he fucked with. I get ending his suffering, but surely there's a better way—"

"Step outside, Ms. Talbot." He pronounced my name carefully, nearly monotone, and still didn't take his gaze from Brandon.

Blood drained from my face and I went lightheaded, like my legs might give out and drop me on my ass. "West—"

His voice turned colder. "*Leave*, Olivia."

My gaze darted again to Brandon. Before I could speak again, Mr. Rolph was crowding my space, urging me to step back. My spine hit the tent flap and it gave, my bare feet stumbling on the dirt as I ended up outside. I stared, still, as the flap closed again, a tangle of emotion twisting in me— something horrified and sick even if part of me thought the mercenaries were getting what was coming to them. Still, I would've fired them, perhaps, not kept them around with threats—no, *promises*—of violence.

But you're not the enforcer for a very wealthy—and apparently very dangerous—man, now are you?

Even worse, I was starting to wonder if Ashford truly *was* the dangerous one.

I swallowed, my throat parched and aching, and blinked against the rising sun. Laurel stepped away from the tent, avoiding my gaze, and Dawson's face had gone sickly pallid as he approached me.

"He stayed up all night watching the video."

I blinked again, shaking myself from my reverie, and met his eyes. "I'm sorry?"

"The recording from the cave—yours. He sat up reviewing it all night I think—was there this morning still. Got to the end fifteen minutes ago, picked up a gun from his tent, and went in there and everyone started shouting."

Jesus. I shivered and turned, unable to even look in the direction anymore, feeling ill like I'd failed—somehow—in leaving Brandon to his fate in there. I started walking back to my tent.

I hadn't taken more than three steps when a single gunshot cracked the peaceful air.

19
RETURN TO KADHIM

———•◆•———

THE ATMOSPHERE AROUND CAMP WAS solemn and silent.

I cleaned my hair with waterless shampoo, dressed for the caves, then restocked my bag and sheathed my backup knife at my belt. I didn't feel like eating but forced myself to consume some fruit and an energy bar, and downed a lot of water. Dawson had a new cave radio for me, but I knew this time that if we had to call for help, it wouldn't do any good. I took my phone from him once more and tried to call Martin but it went straight to voicemail; I left my cell again with Dawson, the heavy sense of *just in case* weighing on me.

Laurel wasn't coming. I didn't argue or even ask when I saw her sitting by Dawson's table, making herself useful typing up something on his laptop. Glasses were perched on the bridge of her nose but couldn't hide the hollows under her cheeks. She gave me a brief nod when she saw me, then went back to work.

It would *not* surprise me if she happened to be typing her letter of resignation already.

While the others were preparing their gear in silence, I saw Mr. Rolph head for the Jeep first, his large backpack slung over his shoulder. I latched onto my backpack and jogged after him, putting distance between West, his team, the mercs, and myself for a few moments of conversation.

Mr. Rolph's steps slowed for me to catch up when we were a ways from the camp.

"Now that we know the creatures are *Drakones Aithiopes*, I'd wondered if you'd recovered anything else regarding them that might be of use?"

He shook his head. "Mentioned only vaguely in Greek texts from about two thousand years ago, when they allegedly existed above ground. They're capable of eating elephants and are among the longest-lived animals."

I didn't think he referred to parrots or sea turtles. "They existed pre-Pulse?"

"Could've."

When he offered nothing more, I pressed. "They can't be just four years old."

"There are...*some* things that basically went dormant, activated during the Pulse. They tend to be referred to as Pulse-born. Shamans you would've encountered are like that—the Pulse woke genes that makes them capable of certain things now."

"But the *drakones* can't be...snakes or something with dormant genes that turned them into dragons?"

He shrugged, and wasn't looking at me, which I found no comfort in. "It's a possibility. I don't know the how or the why. It's a new world, Ms. Talbot."

That was true. Much like stepping into a rainforest and discovering a hundred brand-new different species, post-Pulse there was so much to seek and document and understand.

After this trip, though, I was looking forward to limiting my discovery to what dust bunnies were hiding under my sofa cushions.

"Is that what West is, then?" I asked, remembering Dawson had supposed something similar last night. "Pulse-born?"

"West is something else entirely."

I waited, but he didn't continue, and honestly the thought of pressing for more information regarding Ashford's enforcer just did not appeal to me at all, so I said nothing. If he wasn't Pulse-born...what the hell did that even make him?

Mr. Rolph sighed after a few more minutes of walking in silence. "That was an ugly thing you had to witness this morning, and I'm sorry for it."

I clasped the strap of my bag and hunched my shoulders as we walked. "I probably seem silly, caring that much about someone who drew a gun on us and was only going to die anyway."

"It's unexpected," he conceded, still staring straight ahead. We neared the Jeep and both eased our packs into the back. He leaned against the hood, watching and waiting for my explanation.

"My very first job was three years ago." I avoided his steady gaze and looked for a moment instead at the rising sun on the horizon. "My brother was searching for this sword in southern Scotland. One of my friends from school had married into the family who owned the land the sword was allegedly hidden on and Martin—my brother—offered me a modest sum just to worm my way in as her friend and get his team permission to search the location."

"*Dyrnwyn*," he said, and I met his gaze immediately. "Or 'White-Hilt.' I've read your file. You were the one who found it, too."

I nodded and came to lean on the side of the Jeep next to him, staring over the field at the others moving in the distance toward us. "Yeah. Bitten by the treasure hunting bug first time out. But what's probably not in my file is how we had someone on the team who double crossed us and I nearly lost that sword. Another team member died. And there was constant fighting and bickering, and all it took was that one job to teach me something."

"What's that?"

"Not to sound cliché, but there is no 'I' in 'team', Mr. Rolph. Things fell apart for us because we weren't working together. I may not *like* the people I have to work with sometimes and more than once I considered shooting Brandon myself. But the only way anyone comes out of jobs like these alive is if we have one another's backs. That is why no one gets left behind and why I have a problem with West deciding to shoot an unarmed man as a lesson for others."

Silence stretched and I sensed my companion readying a reply I might not like.

"West," he began at last, "has the same goal. But he reaches it by making examples and insisting people follow the chain of command."

Which now begins and ends with him. I clearly saw him now, the other team members flanking him as they walked toward us, and I avoided his stare as, even fifty yards away, I felt it weighing on me. "Am I now obsolete in this mission?"

"To the contrary," Mr. Rolph said. "This is still your show."

"Even with a cat prancing around on stage?" I dropped my voice some, as I had little doubt West's unique abilities included better-than-human hearing.

Mr. Rolph's mouth fought a grin. "He'll mark his territory and back down when he's sure everyone's sufficiently scared of him."

"I should've brought catnip."

The closer the others came, the more restless I was, chest tightening with anxiety.

"He'll have your back," Mr. Rolph spoke up after a few minutes.

I glanced at him but his gaze was focused on West, still walking toward us. He seemed awfully familiar with West, which was odd as I was under the impression Mr. Rolph didn't know Ashford prior to being hired for this excursion. "Do you?"

"Do I...?"

"Have my back."

He gave me a sideways look and a faint smile. "Absolutely."

Call me crazy, but I believed him.

———•◆•———

TUCKER WAS STILL COMING WITH us, for some reason, despite the broken hand which he had properly set now, along with Curtis. Three of West's remaining team members were there, as well as Buttons himself. He was dressed head to toe in his black tactical gear with a knapsack slung over one shoulder. He handed me a new helmet, which I accepted without a word, avoiding his eyes.

The fact that he'd killed a man in cold blood that morning would *not* leave my mind, despite Mr. Rolph's assurances.

Eight people did not fit in the Jeep all that well. One of West's men drove, West in the passenger seat, and the other six of us crammed into the back, Curtis and myself tucked on the floor. The Jeep jostled me and items in my bag dug into my back for the duration of the trip; they pulled to a stop near the spot where we'd climbed out of previously.

In daylight, I saw the digging equipment off to the side under a camo tarp held down by rocks; floodlights on tripods were aimed at the hole, hooked to a small generator, though turned off. I climbed from the back of the Jeep and stretched my legs, still aching all over. The more I moved, the sooner I'd hopefully stop feeling like someone had scooped out my muscles, dumped sand in my limbs, then sewed them shut again.

I paced while I waited for the others to unload and check their gear, nervous energy running through me. We were, at least, very near the pitch we'd come out of. It wouldn't take long to get back to where we'd left. They'd collapsed the room with the *drakones*, yes, but perhaps there would be another somewhere nearby. Either that or we'd be hauling around a whole lot of rocks.

I didn't help West and Mr. Rolph set up new ropes to lower us below. While they did that, I slipped on a new harness I'd been provided with, over my gun harness which I would *not* be going without now. My guns were reloaded and ready, fresh mags and one in the chamber, back up ammo sealed in my pack. It was an awkward set up over my spare coveralls, but those and the shorts/tank top combo were all I had with my undersuit scraped up to the point of uselessness.

Once they had things ready, West directed Tucker and a man from his own team—the one who had remained with us the previous night—to stay behind with the Jeep. The injured merc and other man were to escort us out no matter the circumstances. Worry crept over me—even more, that is—and I strongly suspected West thought this was going to end with us running for our lives. It wasn't expected to be another three or four day trip; we were going down and getting that ring before the Ethiopian government figured out what we were doing, otherwise leaving would be quite difficult.

West went below first, then Mr. Rolph. I followed them, Curtis coming after me then two more men whose names I hadn't yet picked up. It wasn't the sort of group for friendly introductions but both looked late thirties or early forties. One was African American and built like a linebacker, head shaved bald and with a square jaw you could punch and probably break your hand on. The other walked slightly behind him and was like a size-down version—a Caucasian guy who brought to mind a bulldog, short and broad and he had a small nose and jowly cheeks. At this point, I didn't need to know anything about them to trust that if they were with West, at least they would have my back. Until he got the ring, maybe.

Blackness wrapped around us at the bottom of the first pitch and already I missed the light of day. If I ever wanted to go caving for pleasure again after this, I'd be surprised.

Air was stale and vaguely moist, and it took several breaths to grow accustomed to it as we walked. Equipment waited fifty feet east of the surface pitch where the second drop was; just glancing into it had my stomach in knots, remembering the creature climbing up. A mess of limestone chunks and dust still waited at the bottom and if I looked closely, I could glimpse trails of blood from West's wounds. If the venom or injury still bothered him, he hadn't shown it yet that morning.

I went first this time and dropped down another level in silence, just the squeaking of the descender on the ropes breaking the quiet. The corpses—both of the dead merc and the *drakon*—remained as faint shapes in the darkness. I turned on my helmet's lamp as I stepped away from the rope and shone it around the space. "Anyone know where we're going?"

West touched down behind me and stepped silently to my side, his headlamp on as well. He gestured ahead. "We need to work our way back around there. There has to be other paths to the room."

179

"And if there isn't?" I chanced a look up at him; his helmet shadowed his face but the light on mine cut brightness over his blue eyes.

"You can be the one to let Ashford know you couldn't find his artifact."

I grimaced. "Point taken."

He didn't glance back at the others descending but started forward for a small archway opposite the one we'd left in the night before and I followed. While I might not trust his company, it was that or wait for Curtis.

West walked like he owned the cave, shoulders back and steps confident. I wouldn't say I cowered, per se, but I definitely let him take the lead. If we were going to be eaten, I was fine with him being the appetizer. But the silence bothered me, so I cleared my throat. "You seem to know your way around a cave."

He crossed a cavern ahead of me, barely glancing around for danger—perhaps his preternatural Buttons-senses picked up things I couldn't. "The point of the questions last night was so that you wouldn't distract me today."

"Just wondering why Ashford hired me instead of sending you."

The others made the slightest noise behind us, working their way along. West paused for a moment to glance at four possible exits, then went for the farthest one left—it was in the opposite direction of where he said we should be going, but he seemed so damn sure of himself, I didn't argue. The exit was a narrow tunnel and we had to turn to squeeze through. Limestone pulled at my braid and cracked on my helmet as I stepped sideways, my boot treads scratching the ground. I glanced back the way we came and vaguely saw lights; the others hadn't quite caught up but West made no move to wait for them so I didn't either. Wind whistled through this space, and whatever breaths the cave had offered previously, now it was closer to showing what it was truly capable of as a forceful breeze blew past me.

Water rushed in the distance, white noise that seemed to echo in the narrow space, and god I prayed we wouldn't run into another sump. I might forfeit my pay—and possibly my hands—just to avoid that.

West slipped free of the narrow tunnel ahead of me. Darkness opened ahead and he stepped down, the top of his helmet bobbing as he climbed. "You weren't supposed to be hired at all."

I stopped at the end of the passage. "Excuse me?"

He offered his hand but I was still staring, dumbfounded. With a shake of his head, he stepped forward and grasped my wrist, giving me a tug. My feet slipped on the damp rock and his grip moved to my elbow, guiding me down as I regained my bearings.

This was a room of floor to ceiling columns, each roughly two feet in diameter and organic, made over time as ceiling stalactites and floor stalagmites merged. They dwarfed us as we moved downward, and the sound of rushing water intensified.

"My hire recommendation apparently wasn't seen as enough for this trip."

Hmm... "Mr. Rolph?"

West said nothing.

"Or Moti?"

That got me a look.

I elaborated. "There was some talk that he was put on the team rather unexpectedly. And he seems to know both you and Mr. Rolph."

"He's gone now. Don't worry about it."

Thank you for the non-answer, douchebag. "Laurel said she was told to put together files on potential hires and I was high on the list." So perhaps Ashford didn't trust his judgment? *Something* was going on here, but I didn't expect West to be forthcoming with the details. Whatever he was, he *wasn't* on my side of this. "Perhaps Ashford thought two cavers were better than one?"

"Perhaps."

I followed a few steps behind as we navigated boulders and neared the rushing water. "I still think, given your Buttons-form, you would've been more useful here than any of us."

We paused beyond a grouping of stalagmites and cluster of columns where a narrow, foaming stream ran. It wasn't wide, maybe six to eight feet at most, but the flow was strong enough that, if we hit a deep spot, I thought we'd easily be swept away if trying to wade through. Water struck jutting rocks in its path, splashing and spraying a fine mist in the air, and snaked into darkness ahead. I wasn't sure if we'd have to cross it or not, but West was spending a fair amount of time studying it.

"I have...other duties," he said at last, returning to the previous conversation, and he sounded as though he chose his words with care. "And couldn't be sent."

"But you could be sent to rescue us?"

He began following the stream, keeping two feet from the edge and studying the landscape as we moved. While he said nothing, it was enough for pieces to slide into place.

"Ashford doesn't know."

West still didn't speak until we'd gone several more feet and glanced over a precipice where the stream turned into a waterfall, rolling down a dozen feet into a large, aquamarine pool below. The pool itself, while lovely, wasn't particularly remarkable; what *was*, however, was its shape.

The water formed distinctly into a six-pointed star.

At least we're going in the right direction. The others carried the equipment, and we'd need them to set up ropes to descend; while jumping several feet into the pool might not be too bad, there was no way to climb up it afterward.

I paced a few steps away and rubbed at my tired eyes.

West remained near the precipice, studying the area. "My employer doesn't like to be troubled with problems," he continued at last. "He expects results. I intercepted any messages pertaining to this mission and dealt accordingly."

"Lucky us."

He spun to face me, crowding my space; I took a step back and hit a column, and his hands came out to strike the limestone on either side of my shoulders. His expression was serious and cold, stare holding my eyes. The ice in his irises flashed, for a moment looking more beast than man, and I tensed head to toe.

"Yes, lucky for you," West said carefully. "I admit no one knew what you would encounter here and perhaps the backup you were sent with should've been more thoroughly vetted, and you have done the best you could do with what you were given, but none of that changes the fact that you would be dead right now if I hadn't intercepted Fabrini's call for help, broken Ashford's agreement with government officials and dug our way in to find you, and saved your life. Sarcasm isn't needed nor is it becoming of you, Ms. Talbot."

I started to snark back but shut my mouth, pressing my lips together. He was right. And the glint of warning in his eyes certainly helped to hold my tongue. I swallowed uncomfortably, disliking both his proximity and the fact he had me trapped, and kept my voice low and even. "You're right and I'm sorry. Thank you for what you've done so far, and for not sending me back home without an opportunity to retrieve the ring and my paycheck."

My fingers twitched into fists and I held my breathing steady as he scrutinized me.

"You're not scared of me." Not a question. A statement.

"No."

"Even knowing what I am."

Whether he referred to the big cat or being Ashford's enforcer, I didn't know. "I'm raising a six-year-old. You'll have to do a lot better than turn into a tiger or shoot people to scare me. Don't mistake that for trust, however."

The steps of the others grew near but he hadn't moved, hadn't even offered a half-smile. Still I resisted going for my guns, both because I didn't want to provoke him and I didn't want to see the reflexes he alluded to earlier.

West eased back at last, dropping his arms to his sides and standing straight. "Any more questions, or can we get on with this?"

I didn't leave my spot against the lumpy column. "Planning for any more macho displays of aggression and intimidation?"

West seemed to consider this, tilting his head to the side. "One or two, maybe. I don't so much plan as wait for a need for it."

This mission just could not end fast enough.

"West?" Mr. Rolph called, probing.

West held my gaze a few moments longer, then turned and nodded at our companion. "We need a—"

Tension rippled through him as he turned; one hand came out to grip my shoulder and push me down, the other flicked a knife from his belt. My back scraped against the stone and my knees ached as I was forced into a crouch just as cracking stone thundered through the cave.

My hands locked onto my guns and yanked them from their holsters, and I blinked against the rising dust, trying to make out what caused the disturbance even as a sinking feeling told me the answer to that. West was gone, disappearing into the pale limestone mist, the light from my helmet unable to track his movements.

Something cut through the dust over me and I dove to the side just as a tail struck the column where I'd been crouched. Rock crumbled and I scrambled back, getting my feet under me, raising my guns. I glimpsed the tail again and pointed the barrels downward, firing, bullets spitting through dust and arcing blood across the ground as they met their target. Rocks rolled and crunched under my feet as I ran forward; I holstered my guns again and went for the combat knife, popping the thumb break and sliding it from its sheath. The *drakon* thrashed, hissing and kicking up dirt. Another gun fired and I hoped whoever was doing the shooting could see better than me—dust was settling but not near fast enough.

I dove onto the creature's back, knife raised, slipping back as it tried to whip me to the side. My right heel dug into the scaly flesh at the base of its tail and I pushed myself forward. The knife's blade sank into its shoulder—not far enough. I clutched the handle with both hands and hauled myself up, digging my knees into its sides. My heart beat hard and if I'd had time I would've ripped off the stupid helmet that was tight on my sweat-soaked head. I wrenched the knife out and sank it forward again, this time hitting just behind its brain.

The *drakon* turned and thrashed again, throwing the both of us to the side. We twisted, tumbled, and for a terrifying moment I felt it, along my back: the hard edge of stone and nothingness beyond.

I had but seconds to fearfully try to scramble back when it was too late and we tipped over the precipice.

20
MY BROTHER'S KEEPER

———— ◆ ————

THE WORLD WENT BY IN a rush as we fell. My body slapped the water below, a deafening crack that sounded as bad as it felt when I hit. The injured *drakon* was over me, pushing me deeper into the water. Silt rose, blooming upward and destroying all visibility. I kicked at the bloody beast over me, jerked my knife from its head, and struggled away from it, flapping my arms madly and scrambling upward.

My face broke the surface and I drew in a breath of cold cave air, water streaking from my helmet. The pond rippled. A dark, thick tail flicked up as the creature twisted. I swam back, choking on water, until I hit the edge of the pool. Elbows braced on the rock, I lifted myself up, scrambling away as the *drakon* dove after me. Dark crimson snaked through pool behind it as it swam.

Hands grasped my upper arms and jerked me to my feet; I glanced back to see Mr. Rolph there and beyond him a swinging rope.

The *drakon* drew itself from the water, bleeding profusely but still going. My fingers flexed around the handle of the knife I still carried as the beast clambered toward us.

A chunk of limestone three times the size of my head sailed through the air and struck the creature, cracking its skull and painting bright red across the wet, rocky terrain on either side of it. It slumped under the hunk of stone.

I choked out a breath and wiped uselessly at my brow, glancing around. My gaze shot upward to see West standing on the edge of the precipice, dusting off his hands. Again I looked at the hunk of rock, still intact by the *drakon's* bloody head. I couldn't fathom how much it weighed but I made a mental note to remember West could lift damn near anything.

While the other team members worked their way down the rope, West leapt off the edge and landed with ease on the ground an inch from the pool. He stared at the unmoving *drakon* for a moment. "You're bleeding."

Though I scanned the others, I found no one else hurt and hadn't a clue who he meant—not until Mr. Rolph stepped closer to me, eyeing my head where I felt something dripping. I nodded when he reached for me and let him remove the helmet. I felt around the left side of my face and my fingers came away with blood staining my gloves.

"It's not bad," Mr. Rolph said, switching my helmet to sit under his arm while he took my elbow and led me toward a spot back from the pool.

I sat without being asked to and set down the knife while he rifled through his pack for a first aid kit, and pulled out my guns. I'd need to change the mags to some dry ones, dry the slides and the magazine holds.

"We can't keep stopping," West said. He looked at Curtis then tallest of his guys. "McKay, Thomas, we go ahead, clear out what we can and draw them off when possible." His gaze met mine. "Don't be long. Quiet, quick. Get the Seal."

Before I could respond, he gestured for the others to follow and sprinted for the exit with Curtis and the member of his team, Thomas, at his heels, leaving the cavern silent and pressing extra weight on my shoulders.

Mr. Rolph attended to my scrape while the third member of our remaining party paced around the fallen *drakon*, and I wondered if I was the only one disappointed that they seemed quite comfortable around water after all.

"I am so tired of caves," I said with a sigh.

Mr. Rolph had thoroughly dried off the side of my face and firmly affixed a bandage to my wound. "I've been in worse."

"Oh?"

"Chevé."

I blew a breath out between my lips in a low whistle. Chevé—in Mexico—was the deepest cave in North America, if I recalled correctly. "How's this one compare?"

His pornstache wiggled like a caterpillar as he smiled wryly, and then he snapped closed the lid of his first aid kit. "Much smaller."

I could barely even fathom it, actually.

A glance at the new guy showed him still pacing, so I took my time moving my guns from their holsters and ejecting the wet magazines, lowering my voice to speak. "You've known West awhile."

"I have." Rolph avoided my eyes, stowing the kit back in his bag.

I'd need to tread carefully with this one, but thus far he was the only person who seemed the most familiar with the man. "Despite his display this morning—or maybe because of it—I have some concern I'm going to be double-crossed. Quite frankly, I don't trust Buttons, but thus far you have been reasonable to deal with, and I have seen your reactions each time someone gets waving a gun around: you try to diffuse violence. And West, even if he hasn't acted upon your advice, I suspect at least listens. He recommended you to Ashford for this mission initially and you know him better than any of us."

Mr. Rolph zipped up his pack and sighed. "I met him in Seoul when he was fifteen, after he defected."

My blood iced over at that word. "Defected?"

He met my eyes. "From the north."

Shit. A fifteen-year-old kid from North Korea? I knew little about the country but that he'd have to physically escape somehow—people didn't just *leave*. "So it's bad."

SKYLA DAWN CAMERON

"He escaped a labor camp, Ms. Talbot."

Motherfucker. I rubbed at my eyes. "Jesus. They can do that?"

"No, they can't. But he did."

"So. Yeah, bad."

"He does his best given how he was raised, but he doesn't see the world as you or I do. And I'm not telling you any more than that, so I hope it paints enough of a picture for you."

Oh, it did. I glanced away and focused on my guns again. Whatever I had seen or experienced in life paled in comparison to anything West did—no wonder he seemed to have issues.

Steps crunched pebbles and dirt as the new guy continued walking around. I looked up at him and raised my voice. "So do you have a name?"

It was the bulldog guy. He plucked off his helmet and swiped the dust off his face, then returned it to his head of buzzed light brown hair. "Cal Pulaski."

"Well, Mr. Pulaski, I had some troubles with the last men sent to help me—do I need to worry about you forcing me at gunpoint over a nest of *drakones*?"

The man paled. "Oh fuck no. West would torture me."

Interesting that he didn't say "kill me"—couldn't've been an exaggeration, then. "Good to know." I looked at Mr. Rolph next. "Think we're close?"

"I *hope* we're close," he said.

"Good enough for me—let's finish up and keep going."

———— • ◆ • ————

ECHOES OF SHOUTS AND SCUFFLES plagued us as we made our way through the cave, following carved marks that indicated we were on the right path. Occasionally the bloody aftermath of *drakones* corpses met us—only two that I'd see, both much smaller beasts, but tunnels led off the main path and there could've been more. Movement was easier, however, without the constant threat of beasts after us. They must've enjoyed trailing the tiger more than humans.

We passed another room that looked manmade—no sign of the Seal, and thank *fuck* there was no nest—which continued into a tunnel. The tunnel then widened until it could fit two lanes of traffic easily; the ceiling rose higher and higher, dwarfing us, and darkness yawned ahead. Abruptly the large passage sloped downward, so deep my headlamp didn't pierce the darkness.

And we found rigging already set up.

I looked down the slope where ropes disappeared into darkness and didn't see the bottom, so I pulled out a glowstick, cracked it, and tossed it down. It hit the rock and rolled, twisted, spinning down a hundred feet until it splashed in water at the bottom and disappeared.

Great. A huge, gaping diagonal pitch into water and god knows what else.

I eyed the rig. "Would West and the others really get far enough ahead of us to put this together *and* be down there already?"

Mr. Rolph came to my side, gazing down the slope. "Not in my opinion—I think they branched off at the last fork chasing something." He met my gaze when I looked at him quizzically. "Tracks in the dirt."

"But someone came down here recently?"

"Yes."

Realization was slow at first, dawning for a moment before crashing hard, gripping my shoulders with tension and speeding my heart's beat.

Martin.

"Let's move." I already had my harness and descender clipped to the rope, and stepped off the rock, the rope rigged up taut and holding my weight. My feet left the ground and I gripped the rope with my gloved hands and eased myself down. Mr. Rolph and Pulaski followed.

The air chilled the farther down I went; I breathed in the dank, wet smell of mold and decay, choked on it, and kept going. Something dripped in the distance, a steady, irritating noise that I blocked out as best I could. The sloping tunnel didn't narrow, still wider than a highway—enough for a couple of buses to drive through.

Or a whole lot of drakones.

I dangled over the water at the bottom for a moment; extending my legs let my feet touch the water and inches from there I hit solid rock. I unhooked my harness again and slipped out of it as Mr. Rolph joined me. He cast his flashlight ahead, hitting more limestone and the huge black mouth of the cavern beyond.

No sign of Martin.

Worry tightened my throat and sped my steps as I walked from the pool, up an incline, and deeper into the cavern. Sibling rivalry aside, he was my brother—I couldn't bear the thought of anything happening to him. He had to live another day so that I could laud my finding the Seal over him.

I glanced around, my headlamp dragging over the walls immediately around me but not penetrating the darkness at the end—the cavern was the size of a stadium easily. Pulaski reached the bottom behind us, and I left Rolph with him as I headed into the chamber to explore. My steps were soft and deliberate, boot treads gripping the ground, and my knees were slightly bent as I readied for anything. An uncomfortable chill had settled in my bones and gooseflesh spread down my neck. My stomach twisted, a sense of foreboding pushing hard on me.

Whatever was down here, it wouldn't be good.

The walls around me branched off into darkness. My right hand moved toward my gun, resting on the butt, ready to draw it.

Fingers latched on my left wrist and yanked.

I spun, hand raised to strike, when my headlamp struck a familiar face.

I froze and Martin did the same. His brown eyes were wide, face smeared with dirt and something darker, possibly blood. He pressed a finger to his lips and let my wrist go slowly; I nodded and went with him when he took a few steps back.

My brother wore a helmet but his lamp was off, coveralls were stained in dirt and grime, and a large handkerchief was tied about his neck to be easily pulled over his face as needed. He didn't have a gun that I could see—rarely carried and wouldn't in a cave like this, which certainly explained why he was so ashen. We moved back from the large cavern, running into Mr. Rolph and Pulaski. An additional man I didn't recognize joined us, also with his light off and sticking close to Martin.

"My team is dead," Martin said in a low voice. "We're all that's left."

"Is the Seal in here?" I asked.

"In theory, yes, but," he leaned in close, "it's *not* the only thing." His gaze lifted over my shoulder.

I looked as well and couldn't see anything—nothing in the cavern but more rock. My lamp scanned the ground, catching massive boulders—

Wait. That isn't rock.

I left my companions and took three steps forward, eyes probing the shapes in the dim light.

Not a rock: the knuckle of a long clawed toe.

I looked up, up, the shape taking form—it was another *drakon*, all right, but bigger. Much, much bigger.

West said the adults could reach over one hundred feet long—he wasn't kidding. What I could see of her looked like something out of a dinosaur replica museum: she was a great, hulking beast of leathery skin, larger than any creature on land and, quite possibly, the sea. It was a gentle mercy she slept, eyes that were no doubt sightless closed and body curled.

I stepped back with caution, staring at the creature though it didn't move. The cavern was enormous to support such a thing—in fact I had no idea how deep this cave went underground—and the ring could be anywhere.

"Well," I said softly as I stood with the others, back from the mouth of the cave, all of us staring at Momma Drakon. "Guess you should've listened to me."

Martin's gaze flickered my way. "He told me *giant lizards*, Liv. You really thought I was going to buy that?"

"It was worth a try."

"We scouted around the cave. Symbols something like the Order of the Seal of Solomon's are carved all over so it has to be the right place—this was a temple at some point—but I can't figure out where the ring is."

"I would guess the other side of the cave," Mr. Rolph spoke up.

I sighed. "Of course. Any other creatures in here you've seen, besides the *drakon*?"

Martin shook his head. "Not even the smaller ones—haven't seen one of them since we got down here."

I will put that under the "good news" column. "I wonder why."

"She eats her young."

I didn't turn in the direction of West's voice but continued to watch the sleeping dragon ahead. "Being a single mother will do that to you. Did only you make it back?"

West moved to stand next to me. "The other two are waiting at the top in case they're needed to clear the path out."

I wasn't entirely certain I liked everyone separated but I didn't argue. "She eats them, you say?"

"They're cannibals. It's how they've survived down here so long."

Oh, Dawson was going to *love* stories about this—especially as I didn't think "so long" referred to just four years since the Pulse. "Any more tidbits?"

"I imagine she's blind as well."

So we could keep our lights on, at least. "Okay, let's split up—you go left, scouting, while Mr. Rolph and I go right." When West didn't argue, I continued. "Mr. Pulaski?" I didn't wait for a response. "Please keep a gun on my brother and ensure he doesn't follow me *or* get hurt."

"Liv," Martin started.

I cast a grin at him over my shoulder. "*My* ring, Martin. You get to watch your baby sister win the prize this time."

I stepped forward with caution, my stomach twisting despite my bravado. I kept the *drakon* in my peripheral vision as I glanced around at my surroundings. The ground was broken stone tile, large squares cracked and smashed—centuries old, at least. I stepped with care, feeling the ground before lifting my foot again, careful not to crunch stones under my boots though my footfalls echoed anyway. A breath in through my nose filled my lungs with damp cave air, and I tried to steady myself with each inhalation. Wasn't doing much good—of everything I'd encountered in a few years on this "job", I'd never seen anything quite so...big as the thing currently to my left.

I kept to the perimeter of the cavern but the mother *drakon* took up most of the space. The odd bone gleamed white in the darkness; I figured she ate her prey whole normally, but perhaps a few were from kills that invaded her territory rather than a meal. A recent kill was entirely human, slumped to the side, the wall above him cracked and streaked with blood. The *drakon* tail had to be like being hit by a bus, enough to kill on impact rather than bruise some ribs like when the baby hit me days earlier— the guy must've been part of Martin's team, and given the blood loss, I didn't check to see if he was still breathing. A machete was in the dirt a foot from his outstretched hand, not a speck on it—probably didn't get a single hit in before being killed.

Still nothing indicated the location of the Seal—no light shining on a pedestal like in an Indiana Jones movie, no ancient writing on the walls with a cryptic message I wouldn't've been able to decipher anyway. Rarely had I felt so far out of my league, despair hovering on the edge around me.

Movement caught my attention; I froze, turned. Held my breath.

And stared into a blinking, white eye the size of a platter. Terror iced through my veins as she drew in a breath through slit nostrils, scenting me from six feet away.

Momma *Drakon* was awake, and as she opened her mouth and hissed, she made it clear she knew we were here.

21
DRAKON RISING

———————— ◆ ————————

I BACKED UP AS HER tongue darted out and sliced through the air. The ground rumbled under my feet as the *drakon* shifted and rose. Her tail whipped behind her and someone shouted.

Shit. I had to *not* get hit by that thing.

She breathed in again and moved forward with more speed than a creature that size should be capable of, her head the size of an SUV coming dangerously close to me. I scrambled back, ducked. My heel slipped on loose rock and I fell back, thumping hard on my elbows even through the padding I had strapped on. I blinked and my headlamp caught her foot coming down, straight for me; rolling, turning, limestone crunched under me as I moved and she missed me by inches. Her foot thundered down, claws scratching stone. I scrambled away, kicking until I got my feet under me.

My heart hammered as I kept running, twisting from side to side, scanning the massive cavern. Ideally I wanted to get the Seal and get out but I hadn't a fucking clue where it was in the first place, and a leisurely look for it wasn't on the menu for us now.

Hisses. Stomping. The *crack* of smashed stone. Chaotic din rose around me as my companions shouted and I couldn't make their words out, not past the pound of my pulse in my ears. If finding the Seal and running was out of the question, there seemed two choices: run away and hope it goes back to sleep so we could come back, preferably without being eaten by the babies, or...

We had to kill it.

Someone else must've had the same thought as gunfire ripped through the cavern, echoing. Fangs glistening with saliva shone in the shaky light from multiple headlamps—fangs the size of a small person.

And those fangs were headed right for where Martin and Pulaski stood near the entrance.

Pulaski raised a gun and fired but Martin had nothing except a multi-purpose knife he pulled from the sheath at his belt, which wasn't going to do him any good. I slipped out both my guns and squeezed the triggers repeatedly, aiming for the head, but though they ripped through her flesh, she barely seemed to notice. Her tail swung toward me and I dove forward, hitting the ground an instant before she would've smacked me, so close the underside brushed my helmet and blew a breeze over my face.

Just as the tail was past me I was on my feet, running and holstering my guns. This wasn't working—she dripped blood but wasn't slowing. A fatal wound would put her down and not much else.

I didn't let the plan fully form in my head because it was just too insane to contemplate, even for me; I simply acted, racing around the dragon for the others as I angled my backpack around so I could rifle through it. I yanked out a plastic parka that was rolled up and gave it a shake, snapping it into place as I cast my backpack aside. The pack thumped at my feet, was left behind and temporarily forgotten as I struggled into the waterproof plastic. My hands worked automatically, pulling back the helmet to slip the parka's hood over my head, then back the hardhat went again, strapped under my chin. With the hood pulled down, most of me was covered except my lower face.

The others had scattered and I made Martin my target; as the *drakon* went after Pulaski, I met my brother and gestured for the scarf around his neck.

"Give!"

He frowned but didn't argue for once in our goddamned lives and pulled the handkerchief. I tied it around my lower face, old west style, and rounded the cavern again. My headlamp caught the dead guy and his machete, and my brain promptly went on autopilot, as if giving up on talking me out of this.

I grabbed the machete and scanned the massive cavern; between the darkness of its sheer size and poor lighting, and the prehistoric looking beast taking up most of it, I couldn't see much of anything.

"West!" I trusted he could hear my shout as foolish as it may be.

Movement caught my attention, West diving out of the way of the *drakon's* tail and landing in a crouch like a cat. He met my gaze.

"Distraction!" I said.

He barely nodded and was stripping off his shirt as fine white hair sprouted from his flesh. I nearly halted to watch with an awkward fascination, stripes rising as bone shifted, man turning to beast, but I hadn't the time.

The plastic parka crackled as I moved and the handkerchief over my face was musty, trapping my warm breath and bouncing it back at me. My grip tightened on the machete's handle and I rocked on the balls of my feet, waiting. West bounded past, a streak of white in the darkness, leaping with grace over the *drakon's* hind foot and darting under the body. A moment later he was on the creature's back, clinging with claws dug in deep while the beast thrashed.

One more piece needed to be in place. I glanced at Mr. Rolph and he met my eyes; perhaps he knew what I was about to say but I spoke it aloud anyway. "I need a boost!"

He jogged over, darting to the side as the *drakon* stomped, her attention still on West clawing across her spine. Rolph dropped to one knee, facing the creature, and waited.

I took a deep breath and didn't remember taking another after that as I ran forward. A foot sank into the ground near me, long nails chipped with age and spitting up dirt beneath them. I ducked under the creature's body, limestone crunching under my boots, and I ran past the underside of her neck, past Rolph several feet away, and then spinning and stepping back to gaze up. West darted along her spine and the tail flicked dangerously, cracking stone walls—I hoped the others had the sense to hide.

I ran, pushing my legs until they ached, not allowing even a moment of hesitation despite knowing how Mr. Rolph was about to hurt. I hit his lower back and he held; next foot landed on his shoulder.

Her head whipped my way just as I barely caught my bearings, jaw open to release a horrific, angry cry.

I pushed off Mr. Rolph and leapt.

My free hand latched onto her fang, pushed me forward, and I landed on the soft surface of the dragon's tongue. My knees sank and slipped, the creature shaking her head and throwing me off balance. Darkness closed around me, my headlamp adjusting to illuminate pink, wet flesh. A dank smell rose from bad teeth and the darkness that faded into her throat and beyond.

Shit shit shit... Even a playlist wouldn't make me feel better being in a *Drakon* Momma's mouth.

Her head shook and I latched onto the teeth, nearly losing the machete as she tried to knock me loose. I scrambled, feet kicking wetly at the tongue as I struggled up. She lurched, jostling me. Slick wetness coated my parka, plastic crackling. I reached blindly, grasped something smooth and long—a fang. Foul air was thick and hot, making it hard to breathe with the scarf over my face.

I glanced upward. *Now or she swallows you whole...*

I stood tall; my foot slipped. Again, I righted myself—it was akin to being in a closet during an earthquake, the tiny world I was stuck in shaking back and forth. I squealed like a damn girl, unable to even form a curse. The tongue beneath my feet moved, rolling as if to swallow me. My grip tightened on the machete.

I didn't count to three, didn't plan, just folded my other hand on the machete as well. Before I could lose my balance, both feet flew out to brace against the *drakon's* gums, practically throwing me into the splits, and I thrust the weapon upward, in a very awkward He-Man pose.

Blade bit through cartilage. Blood splattered and I bowed my head as it poured down. A deafening shriek worked up the vocal cords behind me, blasting my ears. Even as the mouth shook, I hung on, straining my arms to keep the weapon in my target. I gave it a twist, blade cutting through meat, screaming from the effort.

More fluid and hunks of flesh fell. Light not my own pierced my eyes—she'd opened her mouth.

I left the machete behind, kicked off her gums and trudged forward. Landing was gonna hurt but no more than being swallowed whole by a hopefully-dying beast.

My foot sank down behind her teeth and I pushed off, but my boot caught. I pitched forward, blinking as the ground rose before me, scrambling to free my foot before she chomped down. As her head twisted, gravity took hold and I was rushing forward, limestone and dirt greeting me with a hard landing. Blood and saliva splat with a loud, wet noise as I crashed on the ground.

No sooner had I hit when I was up, running, dripping dragon bodily fluid. I hit the wall with bloody palms out, panting, chest heaving, feet still itching to run before I realized stone blocked my way. I turned, blinking against the darkness to scan the cavern.

The ground thundered as the *drakon* fell.

She slumped forward, bleeding heavily from her mouth, eyes closed. A heaving breath blew out and she stilled.

The cave went silent.

22
THE SEAL OF SOLOMON

———◆———

I EASED OFF THE WALL, my weary gaze on the dead dragon.

My feet were still slow to respond and arms ached as I struggled out of the helmet and the plastic parka. I left them in a heap behind me, then plucked off my gloves and finally the handkerchief.

Martin rounded the *drakon*, eyes wide and somewhat horrified. "You jumped in its mouth."

I cast the ruined gloves on the ground and my helmet on top. "Yes."

"You *jumped* in its *mouth*, Olivia."

Besides our differing philosophies, this was *precisely* why we didn't work as a team. I thrust the blood-soaked handkerchief at him as I walked by in search of my backpack.

"Its *mouth*."

"I apologize for not sending a postcard while I was there."

"And...that guy turned into a tiger?"

"Yes, he does that sometimes."

West himself stepped around the dead creature, furless and quite naked. I gave a wet, racking cough but considering I was nearly eaten by a mythological monster, I was feeling fairly okay.

Hands gripped me, freezing me in place, and tilted my head up; I looked into West's eyes, still bright blue despite the poor lighting.

"I'm quite all—"

But he had my head tilted and peeled back my eyelids one by one. "You were the mouth of something venomous."

"Hence the parka."

That didn't sway him, however, as he wrenched my head into the light and peered in my eyes again. "Did at any point—"

"Just blood when I stabbed her." I clenched my hands into fists as struggling would likely do me no good. "Again, I covered myself up to prevent venom from getting in any sensitive places. I'm fine."

"Any itching?"

"No, I'm *fine*."

"Burning or pain?"

"Oh, there's pain, but it's in my *ass* in the form of *you*." I paused. "That came out closer to a sex thing now that I say it out loud as you manhandle me while naked, but I assure you I mean you're irritating me more than any venom could."

West muttered something and let me go; I blinked a few times and tried to regain my wits. My arms ached and I rolled my shoulders a few times as I walked. My coveralls were wet and crusted with blood, making it awkward to move, so I stripped out of them. This left me in shorts and a tank top. Chill cavern air touched my bare skin but I felt better able to breathe and move. I found my bag, took out my spare gloves to wear, then slipped the strap over my shoulder.

"I suggest hurrying," Mr. Rolph said as he came up beside me. "In case the small ones realize their mother is dead."

"Quite right." I glanced around and found Pulaski alive and well. "Oh, Mr. Pulaski, you remember my instructions regarding my brother?"

Light flashing on his gun as he withdrew it was my answer. *Good man.*

"Liv," Martin started but I shook my head.

"Still my ring, Martin."

"Liv!"

That was his Warning Voice. The one that said something was up. We used it, he and I, as children when we inevitably got into shit and he knew a reprimand was coming before I did.

I always listen to that voice.

I approached and went with him as he led me away from the others. He tilted his head down and lowered his voice. "Who hired you?"

"Who hired *you*?"

He stood straighter, giving me that big brother look.

Which did absolutely nothing to intimidate me. "I'm condescending to listen to you when I should be sending you on your way—you need to make it work my while."

"How about who *tried* to hire me?"

Son of a bitch. Son of a BITCH. I kept a straight face. "Moses Ashford."

Martin nodded. "And given the number of laws this is in violation of—"

"Spare me the altruistic spiel—I can recite it by heart now."

He leaned closer still, not answering my cocky grin with a roll of his eyes or any of his usual joking responses. "I came here to get it first. You don't know what you're dealing with."

I braced my hands on my hips, trying to look comfortable though my sore arms just wanted to dangle uselessly at my sides. "So tell me?"

Martin said nothing. The chilled cave air was starting to get to me and if he was going to pull the "just trust me" card, he thought me stupider than ever.

"Nice try. See you on the next hunt."

"Liv—"

I ignored him and swiftly returned to the others, rubbing my bare forearms for warmth as I went. Any sweat from the earlier excursion was iced dry and I needed to get warm.

West had a pair of pants on at last and carted a shirt and boots with him but the rest of his gear was gone. He pulled out a watch from his pocket and green LED light flashed as he checked the time before returning it. "Your brother probably left a vehicle near whatever path they took in here—I'll see he and the remaining member of his team are taken to the surface immediately."

That made my life *infinitely* easier—if West could be trusted. "Alive?"

He paused and cast an unreadable look at me. "Excuse me?"

"My brother is not to be harmed, Mr. West."

His eyes narrowed. "And I'm not to be here, Olivia—killing Dr. Martin Talbot of all people would certainly draw more attention than I'd like to my presence."

It was better than a shallow promise of his word. I nodded. "Okay. See you later."

"Probably not, as I intend to see your brother off to Addis Ababa and then I'm heading home."

I blinked. "Oh."

His smile turned cocky. "I'll miss you too, of course."

Bastard. "I wish you all the best at keeping your pants on in future endeavors, Mr. West."

Before moving, he fished something else from the pocket of his black pants and tossed it at me; I caught the tiny camera I'd worn while in the cave the past few days.

"Turn it on once I'm gone," he said.

Right. And I supposed he'd edited himself out of any footage from when he'd rescued us. I tucked it around my ear again. "Got it."

"Liv," Martin called as he was thrust by gunpoint in the direction of the exit.

"I'll call you about Thanksgiving next month—give my best to William."

Whatever reply he had for me was lost as they left the cavern.

I turned on the cam and started my long trek across the massive chamber, fumbling around my belt for where the walkie-talkie was tucked. It had survived the trauma of the *drakon's* mouth, lights flashing as I turned it on. I waved it at Mr. Rolph so he could raise his own, and spoke into the crackling receiver. "Any idea what we're looking for? Over."

Mr. Rolph took the right side of the cavern. "Any part of the cave that looks like manmade alterations are intact. The Seal's symbol would be prominent. Over."

I'd left my helmet behind me so pulled out a flashlight to shine around the space instead. The light didn't reach far and we had a *lot* of combing to do.

The path around the dragon's body was long and I stepped over chunks of limestone she'd dislodged. We should've had a larger team and proper equipment—we could've set up actual lights been able to find something better. Mr. Rolph and I could spend a week down here ourselves and not find a thing if this was meant to be an archeological dig.

The floor in some places looked like the remnants of tile still—it stretched all across the chamber. A temple of some sort, once—Martin might've known more. Or he at least would've brought someone who would know—perhaps I should've kept him around. It didn't surprise me Ashford tried to hire him first before discovering Martin didn't have a single mercenary bone in his body. Apparently all those genes went to me.

The flashlight hit a spot of darkness thirty feet ahead as I continued forward. I wedged it under my arm and reached instead for a glowstick; I gave the stick a crack and tossed it. Green light illuminated a set of crumbling steps.

I lifted the walkie-talkie again. "I found something. Over." I didn't look but assumed Mr. Rolph was on his way over, so slipped the walkie-talkie back snugly in its belt loop, reached for a gun, and cautiously stepped down the stairs.

The narrow walls were carved with the odd symbol of the Seal. Hair rose on the back of my neck and icy chills rolled down my spine; this lower space was silent and unthreatening but I didn't like it. I paused and cracked another glowstick to throw to the end of the hall.

This time green shone over a low pedestal.

It stood perhaps a foot and a half off the ground and was more a raised block than anything ornate. Spots for torches waited on either side of me, what had once illuminated the space having long burned out. The room at the end of the hall around it was small and dark, no extra doorways. The ceiling was low and I kept my head slightly bowed.

The center of the pedestal had a layer of dust so thick it appeared nothing was there. I drew closer still and stooped, shining my light directly over it until the beams caught a bump in the sand.

My breath ceased, pulse pounded. The room was eerily silent, no sign of trouble, so I holstered my gun. My fingertips trembled as I reached and brushed the sand away. I touched the bump and it shifted, casting dust to the side and my light shone on brass.

The Seal of Solomon.

I lifted the ring gingerly, gaze darting around as if I expected something to jump me at any second, but only silence met me. Again I looked at the ring and turned it over, blew the dust off the face of it. The Star of David met my gaze and curved Greek letters, symbols I didn't recognize in the spaces around it. The true name of God, allegedly. Four jewels were inlaid and the band was thick.

The power to control demons was quite literally in my hands.

In theory, of course. While blind skepticism bothered me as much as blind faith, a healthy dose of it was always good, in my opinion. The existence of one type of supernatural thing did not validate the existence of *everything*. I'd yet to meet a demon, therefore could not assume this ring actually controlled something that might not be real.

For the briefest of moments, I considered slipping the ring on, but the twist of dread in my gut was too great; instead I pulled a small black satchel from my pack and tucked it in there, then stuffed the whole thing down my shirt and into my sports bra. My bag could be lost at some point and things fall out of pockets; cleavage tends to be safest. At least mine is.

I turned and startled at the sight of Mr. Rolph directly in front of me, my heart speeding at the jolt of adrenaline in my veins.

His gaze passed me to the room at my back. "The Seal was here?"

"Yes, I have it safe."

He scanned my hands. "You're not wearing it, are you?"

"No...would that be bad?"

"Potentially."

I waited, holding my breath, that sense of foreboding still bothering me as I watched him warily. There was no relief to his expression, nothing I could make out beyond the helmet sitting low on his brow and thick glasses obscuring his eyes. We stood in a centuries-old tomb-like room and he could quite easily kill me, take the ring, and I'd never be heard from again—no matter how kind he'd seemed earlier, the truth was that I didn't actually know the man at all.

But Mr. Rolph nodded and turned, giving me his back in an obvious sign of trust. "We'd best hurry."

"Agreed." I trudged after him, eyes fighting to sweep around the tomb again before heading forward, still expecting something to pop out at us. A cave-in, some ancient security system, anything but easily walking from the tomb. But the ring was snug between my boobs, no hand of King Solomon himself about to strike us for that blasphemy. "When will the plane be ready?" I asked as we headed up the steps.

"It'll take us a few hours to get out of here but West has probably already put in a call. Tomorrow morning is my guess. The same airstrip where we were dropped off."

I'd be home in another day and a half, then. I resisted the urge to do a little dance—it could wait until our return to camp.

The air was less stale than below as we emerged into the cavern, dead Momma Dragon where we'd left her. Sticky blood coated the ground around her, reflecting green and white from tossed glowsticks and our flashlights. For a moment I paused to slip on my climbing harness and get it secure for the return trip. I needed to get my helmet on and then we could head for the surface—hopefully Curtis and Thomas had cleared any trouble waiting for us. My steps were rushed as we left the tomb behind, footfalls echoing in the large chamber. But as a prickle ran the length of my spine, my gaze was drawn upward.

Where the ceiling seemed to be *moving*.

I froze, confusion bleeding away under the terror icing me in place; I cast the flashlight up where the light couldn't even skim the ceiling, but white eyes shone in the darkness—at least a dozen of them, these ones smaller than the first we'd encountered. Younger, perhaps, and feeling bold now that their mother was gone.

"Run!" I barely had the word out before I was racing ahead, Mr. Rolph at my heels. Boot treads slammed against the limestone, skidded on dust and sand. My long braid whipped at my back, slapping my backpack that thudded against my spine. Though my right hand reached for the butt of my gun, I didn't pull it out, not wanting to waste the time shooting when it likely wouldn't deter the creatures at all. With their mother dead, they had nothing to fear and no reason to stop chasing us.

I hadn't time to find my helmet, just ran for the green glowstick highlighting the mouth of the cave and where the ground dipped into water before angling to a steep slope upward. I didn't bother attaching my harness to the rig, just pushed my legs faster, pumping hard, and splashed through the water before taking a leap and grasping the rope. It gave slightly under my grip but held and I scrambled up. My feet scraped on wet rock, and while I ran on an adrenaline high, it would die eventually and the burn in my arms might slow me—I had to haul ass, fast.

Mr. Rolph was right behind me, the sounds of him scrambling on stone and the bounce of the rope also in my grip echoing my movements. And just beyond us still was the scrape of nails on limestone and hiss of small serpent-dragons.

The slope ran up another eighty feet that felt even farther away as I struggled upward—it might as well have been miles. Wet, mud-slicked rock slid under my boots and even with the gloves the rope strained my hands. Seventy-five feet. Seventy. We had to make it—*had* to.

Sixty feet to go and I was aching, strength waning, when a sudden grunt of pain behind me caught my attention.

I glanced back; Mr. Rolph was slipping, arms outstretched and grasping the rope, his legs dangling. A tear in his coveralls leaked blood as he kicked at a *drakon* at his heels.

With a sinking feeling, I realized he'd been bitten.

"Keep going!" he shouted, struggling up as more of the beasts closed in.

I twisted, fumbled at my harness, got myself latched on just barely before slipping out a gun and firing at the creatures around us. These ones were smaller—still agile and fast, but shy as bullets struck, and the handful following held back, watching me warily. At the bottom, more approached, creeping up the walls of the sloping tunnel.

Mr. Rolph slipped, his feet losing purchase on the ground as he slid, hands scrambling to hold the ropes. I backed up in a hurry, holstered the gun, and snatched the sleeve of his coveralls, struggling to pull a man who weighed more than me up and onto his feet.

Sweat slicked his reddened face as he grimaced. "I was bitten."

"You'll be fine—just hold on." He wouldn't. Not with what I'd seen of that venom, not if he was human like all of us except for West, but I wasn't leaving him behind. I managed to get a hold of his sleeve and yanked.

Fabric tore but I didn't let go, not as my muscles burned, not as my voice broke into cries with the strain. He latched onto the rope but held my gaze, resolved in a way that had panic clawing up my throat.

The *drakones* rushed around us again now that my gun was down, growing bolder by the second. One leapt for me; I dodged and as it hit the slope beside me, I drew out a gun and put three bullets in its head.

Another landed on Mr. Rolph.

He slipped again and shouted as fangs sank into his shoulder. Fresh blood ran from the wound, spurting and fading into the dark mud on the slope. I shot the creature on his back but it was far too late.

"You have to climb!" I cried, as futile as it was.

But eyes behind bottle glasses met mine. "Trust West."

"We'll get you help—"

"Whatever West says, do it—"

Mr. Rolph slipped and the blackness below swallowed him whole.

23
CROSSED

———•◆•———

I GAZED FOR A MOMENT longer down the slope, still somewhat in denial—he'd been there one second and gone the next, his headlamp going out as he spun and hit the bottom. But I hadn't time to process; the fierce, hissing *drakones* babies were closing in.

And it was terribly dark now, just a faint glow coming from high above.

I scrambled, the gun back at my hip—I had to be running low on bullets anyway—and climbed. Each step forward was more of a lunge, hands crossing at the rope and pulling as hard as I could. A noise of frustration left my throat as the sound of creatures echoed around me.

The rope spun and I angled to the side as a *drakon* leapt and body slammed me. Its teeth missed, just barely, and I wished I'd've pulled the machete from their mother's mouth. I eased to the side, pulled out my left gun, and fired a few rounds until the creature hesitated, giving me moments to climb farther.

Five feet from the top and faces peered down—Curtis and Thomas—who both looked past me, their headlamps illuminating the huge tunnel. Seconds later their guns were out and bullets tore through the space. I kept my head down, my focus on the rope, even as lead sped past me to strike the reptilian bodies on either side. My arms were ready to give out as I reached the top and Thomas latched onto my elbow, steadying me as I stood.

"Pulaski?" I asked as I unhooked my harness from the rope.

"With West escorting the others out," Thomas said, his voice deep and booming. "Rolph?"

I shook my head and he glanced away, cursing.

"Do you have the fucking Seal?" Curtis shouted over fire from her own weapon.

I bit back a comment and started jogging from the tunnel. "Yes, let's *move*."

Both were at my heels and what else might be joining us, I didn't want to know.

———————— ♦ ————————

I'D PULLED OUT MY FLASHLIGHT to join the headlamps of my companions and we worked our way back through the cave the way we came, even as scratches over stone echoed behind us. I remembered the path but kept an eye on our tracks in the dirt, watched for landmarks we'd followed previously any time we weren't near the rigging left behind. I had no helmet and had to watch each time I ducked, protect my skull with my arms, and tried not to think of my headlamp still casting light over the floor in that massive chamber as the last of Mr. Rolph's body was torn into.

Trust West.

An odd last request that sent an uncomfortable chill through me.

At last the floodlights shining through that first deep pitch met my gaze. Thomas ran past me, skipped attaching his harness, and leapt for the rope; he climbed it with speed and agility I couldn't even hope for, like the top student in gym glass who demonstrated just *how the fuck it was done*. As his feet disappeared into the hole in the ceiling, I grabbed the rope and followed. My arms felt on fire and screamed at me, and if they worked for me tomorrow I'd consider it a goddamn miracle, but still I climbed. The sounds of creatures behind us had since faded but I moved fast, unwilling to chance them catching up.

Thomas grasped my arm and helped pull me up the final foot and to my feet on the edge of the hole, and he had my gratitude for it.

I massaged my arms as I stepped out of the way for Curtis to rise as well and rounded the floodlights. Hair irritated my eyes and I brushed it back. "He said the plane would be able to get us at dawn?"

"Tomorrow morning, then," Thomas said, and we started in the direction of the hole that would lead to the surface. "It's early evening. Is West coming back?"

"He says no."

Thomas said nothing—he came with West, so perhaps that made him uncomfortable. Still, I trusted he'd see us onto the plane with the ring, rather than risk his employer's wrath.

We trekked back though tunnels, up a small incline, and then came to the hole that would lead above. I blinked against the light of a late day shining through the pitch, welcoming if not painful to my eyes. My pulse was once again returning to normal, adrenaline seeping away, and hauling myself up that rope was incredibly unappealing.

But I had the Seal and I never had to come back to this motherfucking place again. I nearly wept with relief. Once again Thomas went first, and as I followed, it was his steady hand that got me standing on solid ground. Fresh air met me and I sucked in a breath. My eyes watered and I blinked against the light.

As my vision adjusted, I recognized the hard stare of Tucker on me; he leaned against stacked equipment crates by the floodlights, his arms crossed at his chest.

My flesh prickled beneath my clothes, irrational foreboding rising as Curtis climbed out after me.

"Got the Seal?" Tucker asked in his thick southern drawl.

"Yes," Curtis answered behind me.

For a moment it registered that they had me surrounded, then my gaze flickered to the ground behind the crates, the open palm of a lifeless hand barely visible.

West's other team member—

I hadn't time to reach for a weapon when Tucker's gun was out and it cracked through the air. Thomas went down at my side and I froze as the barrel landed on me.

"Hands up, beauty queen," Tucker said calmly.

I swallowed a lump in my throat. I could draw quickly but not fast enough, so I raised my hands, fingers splayed.

Curtis moved behind me and jerked the guns from the holsters at my hips, then pitched my weapons into the distance where I'd have little hope of finding them quickly. A few more steps put her behind me, too far to physically attack her, and Tucker was out of range as well.

I waited.

A wind kicked up as both my opponents studied me, fluttering my hair. They could shoot me easily, dump my body in the hole an inch to the right, and no one would be wiser.

In fact, I strongly suspected Tucker was thinking the very same thing as he asked, "Where's the Seal?"

"I have it. This is over, you don't need to—"

The barrel of the gun never wavered. "Where's West?"

I didn't reply.

Curtis shifted, moving into my peripheral vision with a gun trained on me. "Gone, she said. Took another exit out with the others. Already heading home, *she said.*"

Fuck.

"It would be easier if you hand over the Seal instead of making us search your body afterward," Tucker said, eyes on me and unblinking. "But it's your choice."

Oh yeah, choice. As if I had one.

I shifted, testing them, and they both tensed. Ready for me, apparently. I sighed and slowly moved my right hand toward my chest. "It's in my shirt."

A chilly grin touched Tucker's lips and my stomach threatened to heave what little contents it housed, but he made no move toward me.

I slipped my fingers down the front of my shirt, past to my shelf bra and dipped into my cleavage until I felt the satchel containing the ring. I plucked it out and raised my hand so they could see.

Tucker remained steady. "Hand it to me. Slow."

Nearly every instinct warned me not to hand them the ring—it was my only leverage, the only thing I had that would keep me alive. But I strongly suspected I could swallow the thing and they'd simply carve it out of my body. What happened to Brandon was my fault, clearly in their minds, and I wasn't getting out of this one alive.

The only thing greater than my desire for a paycheck is survival.

I started to hand the satchel to Tucker before I whipped my arm back and threw it.

The black bag sailed through the air, over Tucker's head, and both his eyes and Curtis' followed it; Curtis shouted something, Tucker snarled, dirt kicking up under their feet and guns wavering.

I took a short step to the side and plummeted down the pitch.

Two feet into darkness and I grasped the rope; my arms jerked straight, joints screaming as my weight tugged on them. Gunfire sounded above and I loosened my grip on the rope until I was sliding downward, my gloves barely protecting my palms from the burn as I rapidly descended. Bullets spit through the air and fire lashed my forearm, blood spraying in my peripheral vision.

The moment my feet touched down, my knees buckled and I crumpled. I scrambled back before more bullets could hit, got my feet under me, and stumbled into the darkness behind me. The rope swayed a few moments longer before stopping, and gunfire ceased.

I waited, holding my breath and shaking, but no one followed. I wasn't naive enough to think they'd leave the pitch, however.

I sucked in a few breaths and stepped back, not even daring to look at my arm where burning pain coursed through me. Blood was slippery, heavy, coating my flesh and soaking through my gloves. When I found the floodlight-illuminated second pitch, I attached my harness and slid down, with only the use of my left arm, and paused at the bottom to gather my bearings.

My bearings were fucking up and gone for the rest of the day, though, just one panicky thought after the other.

Fuck. FUCK.

They took my fucking Seal. They took my fucking *guns.*

Fuck.

I detached the harness and slipped my bag off my shoulder to retrieve the first aid kit, trying not to look at how much blood I was gushing. The 9mm bullet had grazed my right forearm, taking with it a chunk of flesh. Pink and red meat met my gaze and bile rose, though I choked it down. A three and a half inch gash was carved out of my skin, at least a quarter inch deep if not more—I needed stitches, but none were in my inventory. There was little I could do but bite the inside of my mouth to stifle a cry, disinfect the wound, and bind the fucker up. Six hours. Maybe more but I'd be pushing my luck. Without stitches soon, I'd need the wound excised and everything done by a medical professional.

No gun and more *drakones* in here. Now they might smell blood.

There were other exits, yes, but I hadn't a map. Or a helmet. Or much in the way of gear. I eased my backpack on, and eyed the various exits, shining my flashlight around.

The spear of light caught on a flash of blue near the archway to my far left.

I stepped closer, tired eyes narrowing, until I recognized the mark, or at least what made it: chalk. An arrow pointed through that door.

A sad smile formed on my lips.

Thank you, Mr. Rolph.

24
BACK TO CAMP

— ◆ —

IN ADDITION TO THE CHALK marks Mr. Rolph had left, signaling the path he and Brandon had taken to reach us days earlier, I found an HK MP5K fitted with a tactical flashlight and four extra magazines with the man of West's who had been killed the day before. Not *with* him, per se, but near his rotting corpse. I slipped the weapon's strap over my shoulder, stowed away the magazines, and carted it with me through the caves.

By the time I emerged from the cave exit, night had fully fallen and I only had one magazine left.

A black sky hung above with pinpricks of stars that did little to light the area around me and the air chilled my sweat-slicked skin immediately. I crept out on blistered, aching feet and glanced around cautiously. No sign anyone had been stationed there to greet me with a bullet but my flashlight was tucked away and I had my finger on the submachine gun's trigger just in case.

After a break for water, I set my compass on a large boulder and cast a penlight over it, aligning myself. I'd walked—and climbed—a few kilometers in the cave, though time was saved with the chalk markers to follow and climbing rigs already set up. Camp was a ways off but not impossible to reach.

And I'd reach it. I'd reach it and get my motherfucking Seal, deliver it to Ashford myself, get my goddamn paycheck, and let West know about the mutiny he'd left in his absence. I'd argued for Brandon's life, yes, but I was not going to object this time to the remaining mercs having their hands bitten off as punishment.

I just needed to find them before the plane came at dawn.

———— ◆ ————

I SAT CROUCHED IN THE darkness at the base of a small hill about fifty meters from camp.

The orange glow of a strong fire highlighted the tents and flickered in the night breeze. Tucker and Curtis took turns walking the perimeter of the camp, never venturing out as far as I waited. I'd seen no sign of Pulaski—perhaps, if he'd returned, they'd killed him like Thomas.

Dawson sat alone at his tech table and there was no sign of Laurel.

I slipped the cave radio from my knapsack, *very* glad Dawson had given me one, opened it and moved the wires in place while guided by the faint glow of my penlight pinched between my lips—shielded as best as I could with my bag, of course. I'd popped some ibuprofen but it barely took the edge off the ache in my arm. I needed medical attention of some kind but we were miles and miles from a city and I couldn't risk leaving without my quarry.

I typed a message with care to Dawson—one handed, so it took a while. I'M OK. DO NOT ALERT THE MERCS.

And I waited.

A moment later he shifted in his seat, head tilting as if to check the position of the others, then his fingers hammered on the keyboard. THINGS DIDN'T GO WELL.

No, they sure as fuck didn't. CAN YOU GET THE SEAL? ARE U INSANE?

I stifled a sigh. WHERE IS IT?

TUCKER'S TENT.

215

Oh joy of joys. On the bright side, Tucker wasn't currently *in* his tent. I just had to get close enough to obtain the ring.

PLAN? he asked.

One was forming but he probably wouldn't like it. Hell, *I* didn't like it. IS LAUREL OK?

A pause. Then: WONT LEAVE HER TENT. SCARED.

I'll bet. I KNOW WHERE THE JEEP IS. CAN YOU BE READY AND MAKE SURE LAUREL IS TOO?

YES, he returned without hesitation.

GOOD. DO IT.

He waited until about five minutes had passed, then made a show of yawning as he packed up his laptop. He spoke quietly to Curtis for a moment, then scurried for the tent I'd shared with him and Laurel.

I gathered the cave radio again, ensured everything was secure in my bag, and rose to a crouch, then crept around the camp until I faced the tent where he and Laurel waited. There was no easy way in without being seen; I left my bag and gun behind but pulled a knife out, waited for the mercs to be out of sight, and slipped forward silently, scampering for the tent. I angled my knife along the seam swiftly—the cut was a soft buzz in the otherwise quiet night, but glances to either side of me revealed no one had caught me. Once I had a decent slice in it, I slipped inside.

The tent interior was lit by a single lantern, casting tired yellow over the taupe canvas. Laurel sat on her cot and her eyes grew huge, but I lifted my finger and pressed it to my lips.

"Told you so," Dawson said in a low voice. He sat on the cot opposite her, two packed bags at his feet. My own luggage was nowhere to be seen—perhaps the mercs had moved or gotten rid it.

I slipped a single set of car keys from the pocket in my belt and handed them to him while keeping crouched low to the ground and out of the light. "Spare ones from the Jeep. You're both ready to go?"

He nodded. Laurel still looked like her brain hadn't yet caught up to what she was seeing. "But surely someone's going to come back for us," she started.

"West left. Mr. Rolph is dead. They shot Thomas and another of West's team. They were about to kill me. I imagine they're planning to deliver the ring to Ashford themselves with you two in tow, but I'm not taking any chances." Once more I turned to Dawson. "I need you to slip out," I whispered, "and fill your canteen, and come right back to tell me what the positions of the others are. Do you have my cell phone still?"

He nodded and slipped it from his laptop bag.

"Add your number. How's reception been?"

"Not...too horrible." He thumbed in the number and handed it to me. "Hit or miss."

Good enough. I stowed the phone in a padded pouch on my belt. "I'll text you when the coast is clear. Come out the way I came in, run straight, and I'll meet you back a ways from the camp and show you where the Jeep is."

"Uh, Liv, I'm not gonna crawl through that hole." His face flushed and immediately I felt bad, so I handed him my knife.

"Make it bigger, right along the seam like I did, and do it quickly—by the time they notice, we'll be long gone—and turn down the light, like you two are going to sleep."

He nodded, set the knife on the cot, took a deep breath and rose. I waited while he slipped out to fill his canteen and turned to Laurel.

"You're on board? No freaking out?"

She blinked, as if coming back to herself, and her dark eyes narrowed. "Am I on board with ditching those motherfuckers and heading home? Oh, hell yeah."

Good woman. She leaned down and checked the pockets on her overnight bag. Whatever else we'd brought would have to stay—can't be stealthy with bags of designer clothes.

Dawson returned, careful to ensure the tent flap was closed behind him, and tied his canteen strap to his bag. "They're talking over by the tech table."

Which was perfect, at least for me to slip out—I nearly asked them to follow immediately but then rushing would put us at risk. "Cell phone ready."

He nodded. His eyes were wide and worried—I hated putting them both in this situation, but then I hadn't. Some pissed off mercs had. I couldn't feel like shit about this—not until we were somewhere safe where I could stress-eat for a while.

I took a breath and crawled for the gap in the tent flap, dirt giving gently under my boots, then darted forward. I ran crouched low, slipped into the tall grass, grabbed my pack and gun as I ran by and didn't stop until I was cloaked in darkness away from the camp. I gave it a few minutes, watching Curtis and Tucker do their rounds, then sent a text to Dawson.

The light in their tent dimmed. If I squinted, I could catch the makeshift tent flap quivering in the darkness and two figures emerge. I held my breath, frozen head to toe waiting, not relaxing until they were stepping through the tall grass and nearing me. Their steps hurried the farther they went and I stood silently as to not startle them, gesturing for them to follow.

When the glow of camp was distant behind us, I flicked on my penlight, which was enough to light the immediate ground but I didn't think Curtis or Tucker would see, not past the hills and dips of the wilderness we traversed.

"The road is this way," I said in a low voice as we walked. Laurel kept so close she was nearly stepping on my feet, while Dawson cast a few wary glances over his shoulder but maintained half a foot distance from me. I aimed the penlight ahead and after a few more minutes of walking, it glinted off of the Jeep. I threw my pack and the submachine gun in the back. "Get in and wait for me."

Dawson halted beside the Jeep, handed me my knife, and his thick brows pulled into a frown in the low light. "You're not coming?"

"I will, after I get what I came for."

"Are you nuts—"

"If we don't come back with that ring, what do you think Ashford's going to do? Send us on our merry way? Or have us take a walk on West's wild side?"

"She's right," Laurel said, and she snatched the keys from Dawson's hand. She was a dwarf next to him but stood tall, shoulders squared, and nodded in my direction. "Do you know where we're going? Even without the Jeep, they could make it to the rendezvous point before the plane gets here in the morning."

And we could be ambushed by people carrying guns and a willingness to use them.

"We're near Goba—find a nearby hotel. There are the mountain ranges around here and the caves, so there must be somewhere tourists go. I'll be back in a few minutes—be ready to haul ass."

Laurel got in the driver's seat while Dawson stowed their bags in the back and pulled out his cell phone. I didn't waste time with a goodbye but instead jogged back for the tents. Risky and foolish, perhaps—I should just run, I should try to get more resources and track the Seal down later. But people had died. People had been *killed* over this. I wasn't going to be another casualty, not at the hands of rogue mercenaries, and certainly not at Ashford's right *paw*.

The camp was in sight and I rounded it, keeping from the light. Tall, dry grass brushed my legs, and I was glad as usual for my kneepads—at least I had no scrapes there to irritate. My arm throbbed, still.

I stopped and dropped to a crouch in the darkness, facing Tucker's tent. The merc himself continued his trek around the camp and I waited breathlessly in the darkness, making myself as small as I could, as he passed ten meters ahead in my line of vision. His eyes flickered over the darkness, passing where I lay in wait, and kept going.

Maybe I should've brought the gun but it was awkward to use with one hand, and slung over my shoulder I risked catching it on something. Had the gun been a sniper rifle, I might've taken both of them out, but I wasn't a good enough shot from a distance with one, and it would be bad enough alerting one while I shot the other; missing my target would have both of them on me in seconds. No, this was all stealth. Had to be.

I pulled my knife from its sheath, waited for Tucker to move out of sight, then I darted forward. The blade slipped easily into the tent's canvas, slid down the seam, and cut a hole long enough for me to slip through.

The tent interior was dark and silent. I returned the knife, pulled out the penlight, and cast it over the space. Where the hell would he put the Seal?

With the penlight held between my teeth, I scanned the tent and my eyes snagged on the dark shape of luggage beside one of the cots—seemed a likely place to put it. I crawled forward, my poor kneepads dragging through the dirt. Firelight danced gently in the crack between the tent and the ground and shadows cast every time someone walked in front of it.

Please don't find me, please don't find me... I didn't fancy being shot in the back. But their footfalls were steady, nothing to suggest I would soon be bothered.

I fumbled around the bag, checking the pockets first. Two multi-purpose knives, magazines for their guns. An inner pocket was zippered, and there I found a compass, a map. Passport. Stack of *birr* that I briefly considered pocketing—

There. My fingers settled on the small black bag and pulled it out.

I turned and started to rise, ready to go, when my penlight struck Tucker standing in the tent doorway, grinning coldly at me.

"I wondered when you'd show up."

25
INEVITABLE

———◆———

SILENCE STRETCHED BETWEEN US AS I tensed from head to toe, still in a half-crouch.

Tucker's gun was pointed at me. And I was still unarmed. Three feet separated us, not enough for me to make much use of the space for running.

So I talked. "This isn't the ring."

"Nope. Just knew you had to come back."

"You know West will probably bite your hands off."

"Won't know or find us. Did you send the others to the Jeep? Curtis is on her way now."

Well, news for her: I'd had the forethought to move the Jeep to the other side of the camp—Curtis would be going in the opposite direction and it was a pity I wouldn't see the surprise on her face.

If he hadn't shot me yet, maybe he had a reason—maybe he'd hesitate. My gaze flickered to the back of the tent where the hole was for an instant before I darted.

I scampered forward, banging my shoulder on the metal cot, scrambling for my exit when fire speared my scalp; he had my braid and jerked me back. A scream I couldn't stop left my lips and I turned, ready to fight back, when his boot struck my side. Pain flared hotly against my ribs and I grunted, barely had time to recover before his boot came at me again. I was on my side and curled, protecting my stomach, free arm coming up over my head. His boot struck my kidney and I howled again.

I hated being defensive and when he grasped my braid again, I lashed out, the knife in my belt finding its way into my hand. The blade scraped across his arm, splattering blood along the tent wall. I ached, gasped for breath, and got myself moving; I launched myself into him, knocking him off balance, and he lost his grip on my hair. Staggering to my feet, half-crouched still, I slashed with the knife again and it hit his thigh this time, cutting deep. A backhanded swipe hit my face, snapping my head to the side and briefly white played over my vision. I stumbled back. Something warm and wet slipped down my cheek.

I saw it, then: the Seal. He wore it.

Mr. Rolph suggested it would be bad to do so but I sensed nothing off about Tucker, no magic hovering in the air or additional threat beyond the steady, challenging glare of his eyes. Maybe he didn't know how to use it. Maybe it didn't have any real power after all. Regardless, right now I was still more concerned about the gun tucked at his hip which he could reach for again at any time.

The world narrowed to a hard point, seeming to slow as my brain sped. He stopped being a man and started being parts; he was stronger with more training, more experience, at least as a whole. But as parts, I could handle him. Thumbs, hands. Eyes to claw, throat to strike. Vulnerable groin, targetable kneecaps.

And that broken hand, wrapped up and kept straight by a splint.

He'd holstered the gun while grabbing my braid previously; now he yanked it out again with his good hand, arching it toward me, the barrel a dark, bottomless hole pointing toward my forehead.

I knocked his arm back with my forearm just as the gun went off, gunfire echoing in my ear far too close. When he swung it back toward me I grabbed for it, giving it a sharp push to redirect to the side; my knee rose to his groin as a follow up, then I gave the gun another twist. Bone cracked, the index finger of his good hand caught in the trigger guard an easy casualty. The gun slipped and I kicked it away.

Great move and at least I was rid of the weapon, but a bit of pain meant nothing to a guy like that; this wouldn't end until I put him down with something more permanent.

Tucker came at me again with a roar. I ducked, flipped the knife handle so the blade was in a defensive position against my forearm, and slashed again, cutting his wrist and biting deep into the meat of his palm. His ankle slipped behind mine and jerked, but if I was falling, I was determined to take the fucker with me. My free hand locked onto his broken one and I jerked him to the ground with me, angling him so he landed on his injury. The splint snapped and he screamed, his howl of pain rivaling the one I gave earlier.

The knife clattered beside me but I wouldn't need it for this. Both of us on the ground, exhaustion only kept at bay by the adrenaline in my system, I twisted and locked onto him, scissoring his torso and right arm tight between my legs and grasping his left wrist. Soon he was grunting, red-faced, and immobile. I wrenched his arm until he couldn't move without breaking it.

Though not stronger than him, certain positions have their advantages.

His left index finger was bent at an odd angle and a bright, ugly red as it swelled thickly. The ring glinted in my line of sight on his pinky finger just as Curtis shouted in the distance—she must've heard the shot. I couldn't let go of Tucker's arm to grab my quarry so I tilted my head forward, wrapped my lips around his finger, got my teeth on the ring, and dragged it off.

I couldn't hold him for long, my strength waning; I gave his arm a wrench and a pop sounded, jerking it out of the joint. Tucker screamed, no doubt alerting Curtis to our exact location. I took a breath and *moved*, releasing him from the scissor-lock and scrambling up. As he tried to rise, left arm dangling uselessly in the muddy blood on the ground, I gave his kidney a brutal kick and he slumped back down, puffing up dirt.

The knife, back in its sheath. The ring, down my shirt. And the gun, recovered from the ground and in my left hand as I darted again for the back of the tent, this time without him following.

I tore into the cool night, straight from the tent and into the blackness beyond. Steps thrashed through the tall grass far to my right but I didn't turn, didn't look, just plowed ahead. The ground was uneven and my penlight was gone; I stumbled, nearly twisted my ankle, but wouldn't give in and slow my pace.

Blue light from the face of a cell phone shone ahead, vaguely showing the interior of the Jeep. I crashed onto the road and Laurel yelped, Dawson jumped.

"Drive!" I shouted as I climbed in the back, and set down the pistol for the MP5K.

As the engine whined and groaned to a start, bullets cut through the night—Curtis had found us. I couldn't see, had nowhere to aim, but pointed the gun into the darkness and squeezed the trigger, spraying bullets randomly over the field to give us cover as the Jeep moved.

Tires spit up dirt and rocks and I jerked forward, jostled around as Laurel peeled away. I dropped the gun, crouched, and waited, but Curtis didn't return fire—either I'd hit her or we were out of sight. Laurel kept the headlights off and I doubted we were on the road anymore as the Jeep careened back and forth.

Agony hit my body at once and I sagged forward, breathing heavily. "I think you can put on the headlights now."

It was three more minutes before she did and she only drove faster once she could see where she was going.

I got myself onto my knees and turned around, and hunched between the seats to look over Dawson's shoulder. "Where are we going?"

"Wabe Shebelle Hotel," he said. "A few more kilometers. Nice enough place. Also pretty much the *only* place."

"Should we be keeping a low profile?" Laurel asked, not taking her eyes from the road.

"And do we have money?" I asked.

Dawson sighed. "Look...they have showers. *Hot* water."

Oh forget that—I'd sell my fucking body right then for a hot shower. My poor, bleeding, bruised body. Goddamn, I *hurt*.

I turned again and leaned against the back of Dawson's seat, cradling my arm, wind whipping my hair around and a headache starting in my temples. The ride was rough but it beat walking so I closed my eyes and tried to relax for the duration of the trip to Wabe Shebelle Hotel.

26
CHOICES

———— ◆ ————

THE HOTEL WAS SITUATED IN a park and the front of the building looked clean and welcoming. Laurel had a rather large stack of *birr* in her bag—prepared for any eventuality, perhaps—and she and Dawson headed into the hotel first to book us three rooms. He came back out to get the bags, give me my key, and lead me to where we were staying, so I could avoid any of the hotel staff seeing me directly given the state I was in.

I didn't actually get to see how bad I looked until I was situated in my tiny room, with its cheery yellow walls and tiled floor, and a double bed that under normal circumstances might have been forgettable but looked like absolute heaven after the shit I'd been through in almost a week. I skipped everything and went straight for a hot shower in the closet-sized bathroom. Dawson had promised me a chance to check in with Pru and Em, and I intended to take him up on that offer...just as soon as I stopped looking like I'd been chewed up and spit out by a dragon.

I painfully stripped out of every last piece of grimy clothing. Peeling off my socks left wet, black marks on the bathroom tile—although I was certain housekeeping was efficient, I sort of felt obligated to clean up before we left in the morning after this. My feet were blistered and bloody in the odd place, ankles had imprints from my socks and boots. Scrapes ran up and down my legs. Purple bruises bloomed, some going black, up and down my torso. My lip was split, side of my face dark blue, the cut Mr. Rolph had patched up was bleeding through the gauze, and my scalp ached as I let loose my braid.

My arm was a whole other matter.

I carefully unwound the blood-soaked gauze. It stung with every movement—goddamn, it looked bad. A hospital was still out of the question, probably. At least I hadn't passed out from blood loss.

Always looking on the bright side, that's me.

The moment I stepped in the hot corner shower, however, the sight of my arm left my memory. Water beat down, soaking my hair, loosening grime. A glance down and the water swirling at my feet was a mix of black and red. I had no shampoo but the soap was serviceable and I scrubbed at my roots until they felt cleaner if not clean*ish*. Soon my stomach was growling—I'd been told on my way in that they had twenty-four hour room service and I intended to beg some *birr* from Laurel to obtain it.

And maybe some gin.

I toweled off after what still felt like too soon, rewrapped my arm in the remaining gauze from my first aid kit until I could figure out who I'd get to stitch it up, and worked the largest tangles from my hair. Wrapped in a towel, I realized after a glance at my ruined clothes on the floor that I would also need to beg pants or something from someone.

The Seal couldn't be left anywhere; I fished a length of string from one of the pockets of my bag and threaded it through the ring, tied the ends, and slipped it over my head. The Seal disappeared between my cleavage beneath the towel and I suspected that whenever King Solomon was, he was likely rolling over in his grave.

I left the bathroom, ready to set off to borrow favors from Dawson and Laurel; I trekked through my room, past my boots to the side and West on my bed, and continued for the suite door.

And stopped as realization hit me.

"So much for not seeing you again, Mr. West," I said first before glancing back over my shoulder.

He sat as if he belonged there, long legs hanging over the side of the mattress and palms slightly behind him, propping him up. The tactical gear was gone; he wore black jeans and a dark brown coat with a white button down beneath it, casual as can be. His lips formed a canary-eating cat's grin like he knew no other expression. A white toolbox sat on the bed next to him.

West clearly wasn't going anywhere so I sighed and walked back into the room. "What?"

"Ran into trouble?"

"Yes, it seems Ashford's hired guns didn't entirely appreciate your threats and decided to take it out on me. Did that not occur to you?"

"I actually can't remember the last time one warning wasn't sufficiently believable."

"Well, maybe you're slipping, Buttons."

He glanced over me again. "You look like hell."

I blinked at him. "Thanks ever so much."

"Hungry?"

Just as he said it, the whiff of something delicious tickled my nose and I glanced around until I saw the covered dish on the nightstand. "You brought me food?" I started over but he leaned across the bed to grab it and set it next to him. So I'd have to endure his company to eat: I wouldn't object with the twisting my stomach was doing. I was fucking *sick* of energy bars.

I took a seat on the other side of the dish, the bed sinking beneath me in a way that left me longing to stretch out and drift into unconsciousness. The scent of spices held me in place, however, and I lifted the lid to find a plate of flatbreads and some sort of stew.

"*Injera* and *wat*," he said. "Not much else on the menu here."

"No objections." I already had a piece of spongy bread in hand and dipped it in the stew. No idea what I was eating but it was savory and delicious and I strongly suspected I'd be licking the plate clean in a most unladylike fashion quite soon. "And when did you join the hotel wait staff?"

"I was waiting at the Bole International Airport, ticket in hand, when I decided to check in with Thomas and he let me know what direction things had gone in."

I nearly choked on my bread and it wasn't until I swallowed water from the bottle he offered me that I could speak again. "Thomas is alive?"

He nodded. "And downstairs—he and Pulaski are under my orders not to let you from their sight. Again."

"Tucker shot him. Point blank. I saw it."

"He is..." West barely searched for the word—I strongly suspected he had no intention of telling me how the man could survive a bullet like that. "Resourceful."

"But *he got shot.*"

"And it was extremely painful." Apparently he wasn't going to explain further. His gaze settled on my arm and he held out his hand.

I was in rough shape and wouldn't argue; I extended my arm and let him peel off the fresh gauze.

"This looks horrible," was his assessment.

"You have such a way of making a girl feel special." Of course, I was busy stuffing my face and didn't take it personally. "I need sutures."

"I know. How long since it happened?"

"Over six hours. I've kept it disinfected."

"Your own kit?"

"Bathroom."

He rose, reached into his jacket pocket, and tossed a small red case onto the bed beside me; I couldn't read the writing in white across the front, but thumbed open the flap to find it was an emergency suture kit.

Handy.

West stripped off his jacket, left it on the bed, and started toward the bathroom. "I checked in with Dawson on my way back—he said it looked pretty bad."

At least I was losing the "beauty queen" reputation.

I eyed the white toolbox while he washed his hands. For all I knew, it contained explosives with which to blow up the hotel and me after he obtained the Seal. The hunk of brass itself was warm against my skin and he hadn't glanced at the string holding it once—perhaps he didn't notice.

Or perhaps he more than noticed and was doing that thing some guys did by purposely not looking at my cleavage. Usually they thought it earned them brownie points by not being obvious.

I finished another piece of bread in time for him to move the plate upon his return and sit next to me again but closer this time, knee angled toward me and brushing mine. Though he reached for my arm and I didn't fight it when he grasped my wrist, hairs rose on the back of my neck; it was easy to look at his hands and see claws, the strength of a beast apparent in his every movement. Unlike some women, I don't like my men dangerous and "about to rip my head off" was not a quality I looked for in anyone doing emergency surgery on my person. But while I held my breath and watched him closely, West didn't seem to notice.

He pulled out a bottle of saline water and a syringe. "It needs to be irrigated."

Oh, bloody hell. "Sure. Why not."

He was much more thorough washing out the wound with saline water than I'd been when cleaning it and I hissed, eyes squeezed shut with hot tears pushing against my lashes as it felt like he set me on fire.

"This is going to hurt more if you flinch," he warned as he removed the tools from the kit. "And I couldn't get any lidocaine."

"Did you bring me something to drink?"

West reached beside the bed and pulled up a bottle of...something.

I couldn't read the label but took it anyway, cracked open the lid, and breathed in. "Gin. You read my mind." A sip revealed it wasn't the best gin I'd had in my life but in a few moments I knew I wouldn't care.

The room was quiet but for the rattling of pipes as someone used the shower in the other suite. Occasionally the lights flickered but held for the most part; I was glad of it as the last thing I wanted was to be left in the dark with someone I thought might tear my throat out, especially while he was stitching my skin closed. The water in my damp hair dripped down my spine and I suppressed a shiver—poorly—as it worked over my skin. I avoided his eyes, looking longingly at the plate of remaining food that I couldn't reach, and instead filled the void with alcohol.

When the needle pierced my arm and *pulled*, I was glad I had the drink. Intense pain, perhaps worse than actually being shot, blasted up my arm. My eyes watered and I swallowed more gin, fire rolling down my throat to my belly. To my credit, I did *not* flinch, but I didn't look either.

"You haven't asked about Mr. Rolph," I said in a low voice and bit back a yelp as he tied the first stitch tight in the middle of the wound.

Though I chanced a glance at West's eyes at last, he didn't meet my gaze but instead kept his focus on his work. "You haven't asked about your brother."

Worry lodged a lump in my throat even if I thought it was unfounded. I took another pull of gin. "Is he safe?"

"On a plane for home." Several minutes more passed in silence, just liquidly sloshing around in the rapidly emptying bottle I cradled. With so little in my stomach, the alcohol was hitting quickly; soon remaining upright would be a challenge, so I tried to slow. When West finished the painstakingly long process of stitching to the ends of either wound, he bandaged me up again. "Did Damien go quickly?"

Guilt throbbed hotly against my breastbone; I hadn't even known his first name. "Yes. *Drakones...*"

"Right."

Silence thickened. "He was a friend of yours."

The quiet seemed almost loud before he answered. "A colleague."

Which didn't mean he wasn't a friend. "I didn't mean it as a question. He said he's known you since you were fifteen."

"Oh." West busied himself with putting things back in the kit.

I was drunk so I pushed. "Since you defected. From North Korea."

He snapped the kit's lid closed, the sound harsh and echoing. "Colleague and *mentor*, then."

That didn't make any sense, in my opinion; Mr. Rolph didn't seem at all involved with Ashford, nor did he seem the enforcer type, but I hadn't a clue how to tactfully ask that and I'd probably run out of goodwill during this line of questioning, which was also why I didn't ask about the labor camp. "Did he have a family?"

West rose with the first aid kit and returned it to the bathroom, ignoring me. Warm air still wafted gently from the bathroom and I shivered again. It wasn't until he left that I realized I'd started to relax somewhat in his presence without realizing it. I cradled my bandaged arm in my lap, dragging my fingertip over the comfortably snug gauze, then lifted the gin again and took a sip.

"A wife," he said at last as he sat again. "Though they separated last year."

Of course she would still likely mourn him, no matter the terms they were now on. Such a waste, all for the thing currently nestled between my breasts.

"Their daughter died a few years back," he continued without my prompting as he ran his thumb over the lock on the toolbox. "Neuroblastoma."

Hence the eventual split, of course. I tried and failed to quell the sick feeling in my gut. "How old was she?"

"Five."

Jesus. I shook my head, put the lid on the gin bottle, and twisted my hands together as they threatened to tremble. Pain spiked up my right arm, dulled only a little by the alcohol and ibuprofen still in my system. "My daughter turned six last month. I can't imagine. Will you have to deliver the news to his wife?"

"Have to, no; choose to, yes."

"I'm sorry."

West said nothing but reached for me instead. I froze, my focus on his hand as it neared my throat. The tip of his finger slid under the string at my neck and plucked it up, drawing out the ring hanging from the bottom.

Trust West, Damien Rolph had said.

232

I couldn't think of anything more dangerous, including tangling with full-sized *drakon*.

He wrapped the string around his fingers and dragged his hand down until he grasped the ring. For a moment his gaze focused on the face of it with the symbols I didn't understand and the tiny gems, then he wrenched the string in opposite directions, snapping it in half swiftly without so much as a tug on my neck. String drifted to the bedspread between us while he held the ring between his thumb and forefinger. The brass glinted in the low light, sparking yellow over his cool blue eyes.

My hair was wet and heavy, hanging down my spine and probably dripping on the bed, and the fact that I sat in a towel was bleeding away any confidence, despite the gin. I crossed my arms over my stomach and waited with my eyebrow cocked in question. "We can't still take the plane back, can we?"

"They've likely reported the location to the local authorities in Addis Ababa, just to get back at you. Too risky. You'll go through Bole Airport."

"Um..." I waited while he turned the ring over, studying it. "Did you retrieve my passport?"

"I have another." He barely lifted his chin to gesture over his shoulder and I followed the look—there was a crisp black knapsack propped against the wall, new and full of something.

"That was quick."

"I guessed you might need it when Thomas said you'd been double crossed and it took about four hours to put together. There are also plane tickets and extra *birr*."

"Clothes?"

His gaze dragged over me purposely. "Unfortunately, yes."

That was a relief, at least, and I was too tired to reprimand him for the sexual harassment. I grinned, plucked the bottle from between my knees, and opened it once more to take a swig.

He eyed the bottle as I drank. "You're not going to have a lot of time to sleep off a hangover. Might want to slow down."

"Yeah, probably. You know, my grandma always said gin is a panty-dropper."

West cocked a brow suggestively.

Damn it, do not *flirt with the psycho!* "I guess it's good I'm not wearing any."

Bad Olivia.

He didn't take the bait, though, and I was grateful for it as I suspected he'd win this competition yet again. "I brought you a pack of those, too."

I bit back a comment about being in love, but I so desperately wanted fresh underwear, it was hard not to. "I lost my guns too."

"Didn't bring you any of those."

"I really liked them. It was not cheap to get matching ones."

"Very sorry for your loss."

"How about a box to take the Seal home in?"

West reached across me and plucked my left hand from my side, then slid the ring onto my middle finger. I held in a breath, waiting, but nothing happened.

"Mr. Rolph"—I said the name without thinking and the memory of him descending into darkness was a sharp pinch in my head—"said it wasn't a good idea to wear it."

"Just don't try to use it and you'll be fine."

I stared down at the ring. "Use it?"

"You'll be able to tell if you are."

The brass was warm yet unsettling, like it didn't belong there and somehow knew it. He dropped my hand on my lap and popped open the toolbox. I glanced inside to see an assortment of glues, plastic boxes of items I couldn't identify, and small tools.

"Thomas," plastic cracked as he opened one of the small boxes, "was quite the cat burglar before he worked for me. A big fan of the 'in plain sight' theory of moving pieces." He retrieved a small round charm that was flat on one side; as he balanced it on the face of the Seal, I realized it was a mood ring part.

"You're going to turn this into tacky costume jewelry?"

My answer was a faint grin and the retrieval of glue from the toolbox. "It doesn't look like much more at the moment anyway. Not the finer tastes you're used to, of course."

Had my hand not been otherwise engaged, I might've smacked him. "I haven't experienced the finer things in a long while, thank you. Though I have a lovely macaroni noodle bracelet that is the prize of my current collection."

"Yes, your own 'defection' is quite the tale, as I understand it." He ran two lines of glue on the ring face and pressed the piece on top, hand gripping mine and finger and thumb pressing the ring in place.

"It wasn't so much as a defection on my part as it was a banishment on my father's." A fact which I'd never quite forgiven myself for. I *wanted* to be the strong one—the one who stormed off, determined to carve her own way. But it didn't happen like that and I'd never forget precisely how weak I was. Hell, even now, I wanted nothing more than my daddy to come and fix things, if I was being entirely honest with myself. Which I hated to do.

I tried not to think about it and instead focused on West, attempting a weak grin. "You knew who I was at Kent House and who I was speaking to."

"And that your encounters with Oliver Talbot normally end up in the tabloids, yes." He hadn't released my hand yet, still pressing the ring pieces in place, and I looked away. "Not that I blame you, if all those rumors are true."

They were. Not the more scandalous ones, but the basics. "Dropped the bomb that I was knocked up, keeping the poor fatherless thing, and he could do nothing to sway me." My voice went monotone despite the happy gin in my system, and I longed to pull my hand away and curl up in bed forever. No matter the almost seven years that had passed, nor how many times it was dredged up, it never grew any easier. I suspected it never would.

I got pregnant at my own debutante ball, just before I turned eighteen. Blackout drunk like so many other nights, only this time I found out I'd gotten pregnant. It was bound to happen sometime to a party girl, but still hit me hard back then.

When my dad found out, you'd think I had killed someone. "So Daddy said he was going to work for the rest of the day and if I wasn't gone when he returned, he'd have me removed from my own home for trespassing."

"And this is prior to you using guns to solve your problems."

"Yes. Instead I wasted several hours crying in my room while listening to 'Fake Plastic Trees' on repeat, having quite the pity party, before my friend picked me up and I left with what I could carry. He got rid of everything else I owned. So no, things don't exactly go well when I run into my daddy. And this must sound horribly trite compared to..." I shrugged and heat rushed to my cheeks. *A labor camp, Liv. Probably akin to hell.* "Well. Just about everything. Poor little rich girl."

"While its panty-dropping qualities are in question, the gin's a tongue-loosener."

I chuckled. "There is that."

Seconds stretched on before he released me, gently dropping my hand back to my knee before pulling something else from the kit—a thin brass strip peeled off waxed paper, the underside tacky. This he wrapped around the ring, finishing it so it looked like the fake gem was set in it. "Back to the ring..."

"Yes. *Please.*"

His eyes met mine. "It'll come apart with no damage—use nail polish remover."

"That's it?"

"That's it."

When he was done, I extended my arm and splayed my fingers. The low light caught the gaudy dark stone and despite it looking like a mood ring, nothing changed color. "That is..." Exhausted, giddy laughter rolled up my throat and past my lips—I couldn't stop it, couldn't choke it back, and all my bruises ached anew but I didn't care.

West shook his head. "That's insulting."

I waved my hand and the ugly ring on it idly. "No, I'm just..." I sighed, dropped my hand again. "Tired."

"Your flight doesn't depart until midnight tomorrow but it's a five hour drive from here to Addis Ababa, and you need to be there early."

Midnight? "Am I losing a day, then? Ashford said if I was late, he'd deduct from my pay."

"Late leaving on his plane because that's when his favors run out. You should be fine."

Should be. Right.

"You can rest on the plane."

And I no doubt would. I gazed at the ring again. Delivery, paycheck, then I could go home. I was definitely taking a month off after this. And vetting future assignments a bit more closely. Or maybe I'd go back to being a waitress or something.

The bed shifted as West slipped on his jacket and dragged the toolbox to his side. "I'm heading out right now—I won't be there if you get in trouble again."

I looked up sharply, mouth open to snap, but found him grinning. "And are you sure Curtis and Tucker won't be waiting for me? Since thus far they've been the ones to cause the problems, do I need to worry about them?"

"No." Silence.

"I'm not even going to ask."

"That's probably best."

I'll bet. He likely meant they were about to be dead or dead already.

And I wasn't going to cry about it.

West stood but didn't leave, instead taking just a few steps and turning to lean against the wall four feet away opposite the bed.

"So I suppose a, 'See you later' is out of the question?" I asked.

"I don't know about that."

"Really?"

"Really. I thought we should go dancing."

When he didn't laugh, I blinked. "I'm not going out with you."

"Since you're so starved for partners—"

I shook my head. "Not happening, West."

He eyed me. "It's the tiger thing, isn't it."

"It's the bad man thing we previously discussed."

"Well, I'll see you when you give me the Seal then."

"When I what now?"

The smile disappeared, seriousness pulling his lips straight, steady gaze locked on me. "You can't give Ashford the ring."

"Um, he pays me. He pays *you.* How can I not give it to him?"

"Take it home and wait for me to contact you."

Trust West. Mr. Rolph's last words. I thrust the echo of them away, however, along with the chill wrapping around me. "What the hell is going on?"

"You don't need to know that—"

"Don't tell me what I need. I *need* to get the hell home to my kid and get my money and forget all about this—"

He took a sharp breath and I recognized that expression—it was the one I used when counting to ten to avoid exploding at someone. "Just hold onto the ring until I pick it up. That's it. This is important."

"If it's so important, why don't you take it now and be done with it?" I extended my arm in a dare, flashing the ring in his direction. Truthfully, I was so goddamn tired I might not have objected at all if he stole the stupid thing right then.

"It's not safe for me to take it and I have elsewhere to be right now. Just get out of the country with it, take it home, and I'll come to you when I'm able."

"Um, you don't think Ashford is going to want it the moment I step off the goddamn plane?"

He shrugged. "Stall."

Stall. Right.

My hands settled in my lap, I gave the Seal of Solomon another long look, liking it less and less the more I stared at it. "And I'm not supposed to say you were here."

"Right."

"And if I don't help you double cross your boss?" I gazed up at him, hoping to catch some sort of reaction—something to tell me what I was dealing with. I understood West if he was a ruthless right hand willing to kill me to get what he wanted; I understood a man who threatened, who made it clear what side he was on.

I didn't understand this steady cool gaze, this expression that was guarded yet serious, this casual stance as he leaned against the wall, about as far removed from a deadly enforcer as could be.

So I pressed. "If I do my job and hand this over to Ashford immediately? What then?"

West still didn't move, didn't flinch, didn't even blink. "Then I'll be very disappointed, Olivia. But it's your choice."

27
CUSTOMS

———— ◆ ————

THE CLOTHES WEREN'T MY SIZE. There was a sports bra in the bag of stuff from West that was serviceable, a T-shirt that was a bit too big and jeans that were too snug. For the evening, I opted for stretchy black yoga pants. The labels were all in Amharic—probably from a tourist shop around the airport grabbed in a rush. No complaints from me, as the promised package of clean cotton underwear was welcome.

I padded for Dawson's room down the hall, unsteady on my feet given my date with the bottle of gin, and the Seal still heavy on my finger as I was afraid to set it down. He called me in after I knocked on his door. Laurel sat in there as well, both of them at his laptop set up on a table against the wall.

"West was there?" Dawson asked.

"Yes, patched me up proper." I perched on the chair he vacated for me while he sat on the edge of the bed. During the time after West left and while I changed, I'd been debating what to tell the others. Both worked for Ashford, Laurel regularly. There seemed too good a chance they'd warn him, so I kept my mouth shut. "How's the connection here?"

"Bit better than camp," Dawson said. He glanced at the ring but didn't comment. "Do you need us to go or—"

"I'll just be a few minutes. It's late my time."

"West gave me the tickets, so we're good to go in the morning." Laurel rose and yawned, rubbing at her eyes.

"Bright and early," I replied as I clicked on Skype.

The door had just closed behind me when Pru answered the call. My dimly lit office space flared into view and I unclenched my hands, relaxation rolling down my shoulders at the sight of her and home.

"I was getting worried," she said.

"Safe and sound, no troubles." I'd fill her in later. "I should be home...I don't know. Math hurts my brain. Flight departs our time tomorrow at midnight..."

"We'll land Sunday morning in North America," Dawson spoke up softly.

Either he looked it up earlier or ran the numbers in his head. If it was the latter, I got a headache just contemplating it. "There you have it."

"Will you need a ride from the airport?"

I was, in theory, supposed to head straight from there to Ashford, but West wanted me home instead. So I had no fucking clue. "Probably not."

"Em's already in bed—"

I rather desperately wanted to see her, especially after not being certain I would. My gunshot wound seemed to heat at the thought, reminding me how close I'd come to not ever getting home. But it would be more pressure on Pru to get her back to sleep again, possibly risking a cranky six-year-old come morning. "Don't wake her. Tell her I'll be home probably after breakfast tomorrow." If I did what West asked, that is. If I didn't and went straight to Ashford, it would be later still. Goddamn, I *hated* this internal debate.

Perhaps that would be a believable reason for stalling, though. Long flight, head home first. Nothing in my contract spelled out a need to meet Ashford with the Seal immediately.

And why in the hell am I actually *considering listening to West?* I had no answer for that one so I stopped dwelling on it.

"See you soonish," I said.

Pru nodded. "Take care."

I disconnected the call and leaned my elbows on the tabletop, massaging my temples.

"So...your girlfriend's hot."

I grinned and glanced at Dawson. "She is. Also not my girlfriend. Single, though."

He blushed. "Alas, I have to go back to Texas."

"You must keep in touch."

"Of course."

I reached into the pocket of my track pants and pulled out the tiny camera I'd retrieved from my backpack. Backtracking through the cave, I'd turned it off and mostly forgotten about it. But Ashford being Ashford likely wanted it, so I handed it to Dawson. "Will Ashford be able to tell if you edit the video?"

He turned the camera over in his large hand, then set it on the nightstand. "Not if *I* do it."

It was risky even asking him but I hadn't remembered to give West a heads-up about it. "Mr. Rolph's last words are on there—he mentioned West. And apparently he isn't supposed to be here."

Dawson nodded. "Got it. Won't be a problem."

At least one thing wouldn't be; I still had a bunch of my own to deal with.

I had to rise, had to go back to my room and crash for fewer hours than I'd like before getting up and attempting to smuggle a religious artifact past country borders with a forged passport, but my body protested the movement and I remained for a few minutes more. "Dawson, do you trust West?"

"More than Tucker."

"Touché." At last I rose, my limbs heavy and muscles sore. "How about Mr. Rolph? Did you trust him?"

"For a guy I knew absolutely nothing about, could find no record of—"

"Yeah, yeah, I get it, never mind—"

"Yeah. I mean, he wasn't that bad. I liked him. Mr. Rolph...it's just too bad he's dead. Yeah, I'd trust him."

If Rolph could be trusted, all that really meant was that *he* believed in West, not that West was worth trust by default. But it added more weight to the scale in his favor and I'd begun to regret even considering it.

———— ◆ ————

I HAD NEVER TRAVELED WITH a forged passport before but figured the best course of action would be to act as though it was a real one. While the bag of clothes and suture kit might've been a rush job, my documentation didn't seem to be as, despite the scrutinizing, I was cleared through Bole International Airport customs with no trouble, though received a few confused looks over my beat-up exterior. My explanation that I'd been mugged apparently was believable.

The Seal, too, didn't pick up any extra attention, and the glue held despite my worry when it was inspected. Still, I slept fitfully during the fourteen hour flight, my hands folded in my lap, clutching my small backpack and protecting the ring just in case. West hadn't sprung for first class so we were stuck in coach, but my body was too exhausted to care about the accommodations. I dozed next to Dawson and Laurel sat ahead of us. None of us spoke, not about what we saw in the caves, what the mercs had done, nor anything else. Dawson had all the recorded evidence still for our employer and part of me wanted to request a copy, if only for my records, yet part of me wanted to shove it all to the back of my mind.

Occasionally I glimpsed Thomas and Pulaski; I gave them each a nod when I did, but they acted like they didn't know who I was. Perhaps under orders to merely watch me but not engage, or perhaps the fact that I looked like someone tossed me in a wood chipper meant they didn't want to be seen with me. Regardless, Thomas was quite alive and well, which was nice to see, and if it meant no one else would come close to messing with me until I was home, I accepted their presence.

After we landed in New Bristol, I exited the plane with trepidation. I had no luggage beyond my small pack and prepared to deal with any questions. A history of diva behavior had its uses in that it was an easy role to slip in and out of now, and I had prepared to rant and rave about missing luggage and poor service on my way through customs if questioned.

The woman barely glanced up at me as I walked up to the counter. "Passport."

I handed it to her and set down my bag to be searched.

"Anything to declare?"

I plastered on my best smile. "Just that it's great to be back in Canada." It worked every time.

"What a lovely ring you have."

I iced over at the sound of a familiar voice behind me. *No. Please no. Noooooo...*

I glanced back to see Martin standing between a customs agent and a security guard. His grin was wide and easy, despite the dark circles under his eyes. He stayed where he was as the two agents walked toward me. In the middle of the airport there was nowhere to run, no real way to object. Dawson and Laurel were already through customs and though I looked around, I saw no sign of Thomas or Pulaski coming to my rescue.

I plucked the ring from my finger and handed it to the customs agent while the guard cuffed me. Someone in the lineup behind me stuck their camera phone out and snapped a pic.

"*Vive la révolution!*" I called, because I generally embraced making a spectacle of myself when possible. Martin shook his head, took my bag, and led me and the agents past the other passengers and toward the security offices.

———— ♦ ————

MY BROTHER STOOD IN FRONT of me, his hands knotted behind his back, brows pulled into a tight frown that was nearly comical. "Where's the ring, Liv?"

I leaned back in my chair, drumming my fingers on the chrome tabletop. My wrists were bound still but in front of me this time and I smiled as sweetly as I could. I had already spent four hours being held without interrogation and I wasn't about to rush to answer him. "The ring? You took it. I think there's another in my bag that I got for Em if you—"

He tossed the cheap, gift shop mood ring on the table. It bounced twice, spun, then came to a halt in front of me. "Not that. The Seal of Solomon, which you lifted from Kadhim Cave and crossed country borders with, in violation of several international laws and treaties. I know you have it."

"I have no idea what you're talking about."

His palms thumped down, jarring the table, and he leaned downward until he was eye level with me. "You wouldn't have left without the Seal."

"That's assuming there was one and the cave wasn't cleared out by looters years ago."

"I know you and you would still be in the damn place looking. Where the hell is it?"

This was beyond professional curiosity now, clearly; Martin *never* played Bad Cop like this and his expression left me wary, more jokes dying on my lips. Instead I said nothing and simply waited.

"This is off the record. Help me find it and I'll see that you get let out of here. Just tell me what you did with the ring."

"I haven't the foggiest idea."

Martin cursed under his breath, stood straight, and passed the length of the interview room. He paused by the mirror, staring at his own reflection or whoever watched from the other side of the glass. "They know your passport was a forgery."

I blinked innocently back at him. "It is?"

He met my gaze in the mirror. "Fourteen years under the Criminal Code, Liv."

Even as my heartrate sped, I kept up my act. "I had no idea. How do you think that happened? Could someone have replaced my real one? I'll of course cooperate with the authorities to find whoever—"

I didn't get to finish as he exited the room and slammed the door behind him.

Pru would be wondering where the hell I was. Em, too. The clock on the wall said it was afternoon and no one had offered me a phone call.

"Can I get a cup of coffee?" I called to the empty room but received no response.

———— ◆ ————

THE DOOR OPENED AGAIN AT two hours later, when Martin decided to play Good Cop and let me use the facilities, then gave me some coffee and a box of donuts from Tim Hortons. That didn't get him anywhere with me, though, so he took the leftovers and exited again.

Once more someone returned, this time after I'd napped and then bitched for over an hour to an empty room—it was three in the morning, and a female security guard took me to the ladies room again. She uncuffed me but waited in the washroom outside my stall and really, nothing irritates me more than someone listening to me pee. I got used to it when I had a toddler running around but this was something else altogether. She allowed me to wash my hands and barely dry them before the cuffs were on again and I was being escorted back to the Room of Blank Walls and Doom. Six more hours followed in which I alternated between singing show tunes and napping with my head on the table, cradled by my arms, before the door opened again.

This time Martin stood there, holding the door open, face expressionless as a guard entered the room.

"Are you escorting me personally to prison now, Martin?" I made a move to rise but the guard stopped next to me and released the cuffs. Which was...interesting. I looked at Martin in question but he didn't meet my eyes.

My wrists were ringed in red and the odd indent where I'd leaned on the metal, and I rubbed them to regain feeling. My bandaged forearm ached—I needed to change the dressing soon and pop more painkillers, as no help had been offered me during my confinement. I rose, stepping past the guard—who made no move to follow—and toward my brother.

I strongly suspected they might actually be letting me go.

I half-expected to see West outside the hall, ready to reprimand me for having to bail me out again. Instead I stepped into the corridor and found Laurel waiting to my right.

She'd cleaned up, put on a fresh suit, and wore thin, wire-framed glasses and a pair of crocodile-print, sling-back pumps. A briefcase hung at her side by a shoulder strap, a folder was clutched in one hand, and the look of a businesswoman on a mission was somehow more terrifying than the dragons had been.

"You're free to go," Martin said behind me. "For now."

I batted my eyelashes innocently over my shoulder at him. "Thanks so much for the hospitality." My steps sped until I was next to Laurel, and we continued down the hall without speaking until we reached the door at the far end. "Are you pretending to be my lawyer?" I whispered.

"That was my intention but it didn't work," she replied in an equally low voice. "Whoever got you out wasn't me."

Interesting. "West?" Perhaps he'd helped manufacture a delay as he didn't trust me to stall. I looked around but didn't see Thomas or Pulaski either.

She shook her head. "I have no idea where he is."

I was able to pick up my bag and personal effects on our way out. I had no doubt it had been thoroughly inspected and I hoped they enjoyed their look at my new yoga pants and excess caving goodies. I got several looks as I exited the security area but no one tried to stop me; Laurel and I left the airport without incident. She had a car waiting on the third level of the parking structure. Despite the fact that it was sheltered, a chill fall wind worked its way through the space; I had on a T-shirt, jeans, and my hiking boots, but no jacket and shivered until we were both settled in the car.

"They're probably expecting me to lead them to wherever I stashed the ring," I said.

Laurel slid her key into the ignition. "Where *did* you put it?"

I rifled through my pack and pulled out the plastic gift shop bag from the front pocket. Wedged into one of the ring holders like it had always been there was a brass ring with a fake setting. I pinched the receipt between my forefinger and thumb, and angled it in her direction. "Receipt lists two rings purchased. After seeing the fake one on my finger, this one was overlooked."

"You are scary smart, you know." She shook her head as she pulled out of the lot.

I stuffed the real Seal back in my bag. "A compliment. Really, did we bring back Pod-Laurel?"

She cast me a wry smile. "And a smart ass. Mr. Ashford is expecting you—heading there first?"

Yes. No. I don't know. "Are you going there now?"

"Oh no, after all that, I put in my two weeks and then took my last fourteen vacation days."

"Can't say I blame you in the least."

"So? Can I drop you somewhere?"

I wavered, then nodded. "Yeah, but home. I'm a day late—I'll get cleaned up first, let my kid know I'm not dead, then I'll drop the Seal off at his office."

Unless West gets there first. He might already be waiting—he might take the ring and my paycheck from me. But I'd hold it over him and demand some answers before I decided either way.

28
HOME SWEET...?

———— ◆ ————

LAUREL PULLED UP IN FRONT of my house and I had my door open before she'd even hit the brakes. I didn't invite her in and I didn't think she'd accept either, just called my thanks for the ride and hightailed it out of there. We'd already spent far too long in one another's company to last a very long time, I figured, even if I suspected she'd make an excellent getaway driver given her performance escaping camp the other night.

My pack swung in my hand, ponytail swished against my back, and my bare arms prickled with gooseflesh as I padded up the driveway and past my car parked to the side. A flat cardboard package waited on the porch to the side with a UPS note on the top; I lifted it, didn't see a return address, so tucked it under my arm and continued on. Though I hadn't had nearly enough rest yet, I forgot my aching muscles and jogged up to the front, fumbled with my keys, and burst in the door.

"I'm back!" I pressed the door shut behind me, dropped my pack and the box with it, and didn't bother to take off my boots. The warmth of home enveloped me, place smelling vaguely of cinnamon from a scented candle. The hall and house within were both dark, and the floor creaked under my heavy boots as I walked forward. "Pru?"

No one had indicated whether they'd called her or not. I *hoped* Martin would have the sense to do so—he did the last time he had me arrested. Maybe she went to wait for me at the airport, taking a cab since my car was still here? As I made my rounds through the house, I pulled out my cell phone. No reply from the text I'd sent her on the way home, but I didn't think anything of it at the time—it was just a heads-up. No message, either, so I dialed her number.

It went to voicemail.

The house was quiet and tidy, beds made and dishes done. Em would be in school—

Or would she? She was suspended.

Three days, Pru had said. Jetlag and the overnight visit in customs jail hell had me confused. I thumped for the kitchen again and glanced over the calendar on the fridge—it was the dry-erase kind, and Em and I put it together at the start of every month. A blue arrow dragged from Saturday through the week to indicate my absence, red dots seemed to denote the three days Em was suspended, and black Xs crossed off the days of the month that had passed—every night we checked off that day and had for years. It was why she understood the concept of days and months well before her peers in nursery school.

Saturday was crossed. Sunday wasn't.

I blinked a few times, tried to do the math and failed, so pulled out my cell phone to double check the date—it said Monday morning, 10:07am. School?

I went to the landline where a light blinked, indicating a message; I lifted the receiver, punched in the password, and waited.

"Ms. Talbot, this is completely unacceptable," Eloise Jennings' voice came through clearly, a sour note to her tone. "Your checks bounce, your daughter is *suspended*, and now you don't even have the decency to call when she's late—"

I skipped the rest of the message, checked for others, then replayed the first to catch the time; Jennings had called twenty minutes ago.

But that wasn't anything out of the ordinary—Pru was late getting her to school last week. *Except the car's here—*

Shut up, brain. I dialed Norwood School next and a secretary answered three rings in.

"Did Emaleth Talbot make it to class yet?" I asked before she could finish her greeting.

The click of keys sounded in the background. "No," came her nasally voice. "We have her absent without parental notif—"

I hung up.

Where in the hell was my daughter?

I walked back through the house, my footfalls heavy and purposeful. Once again I stopped at Em's room and peered around inside. Giles was curled on her pillow, purring while he slept. Her book bag leaned against the dresser. If the bed was made, and the calendar hadn't crossed Sunday off...maybe they hadn't made it home last night from somewhere? Shit, what if something happened and Pru needed to go the hospital?

I tried South General, got nothing.

I'm not panicking. I am NOT panicking.

My trembling fingers as I went through my contact list told another story, as did the pounding of my pulse in my temples. I was lightheaded and leaned against the wall, holding the phone to my ear as it auto-dialed.

"Liv?" Denny answered.

"Is she there?"

"What?"

"Em. Is she with you?"

"No, why—"

I hung up, tried Pru's cell phone again, and got nothing. Denny called but I ignored him and tried the rec center where they had a therapy pool, just in case she'd taken her with her and...somehow forgotten about school. Maybe she didn't realize the suspension was over. Maybe...

But the receptionist there hadn't seen them that morning either.

I was officially panicking.

I ran back through the house for the kitchen where emergency numbers waited on the fridge, barely noticing when my shoulder banged the doorjamb, boot treads squeaking as I turned a sharp corner. I blinked furiously, determined not to cry, determined to breathe though my heartrate spiked. No way could I freak out—they were fine. Had to be.

The phone rang in my hand as I skidded to a stop in a puddle of water from the leaky fridge. Pru's number flashed on the screen and I barely allowed myself a breath of relief before I answered. "Jesus, where the hell did you guys—"

"They're otherwise occupied, Miss Talbot."

That voice. I knew that voice. My lips trembled around the words. "Mr. Ashford."

"Yes. Out of customs now, I see."

I sucked in a breath. "Where's my daughter?"

"She's under my care along with her guardian. You're late with my ring."

"I was arrested at the airport—and I wouldn't've been if not for *your* mercenaries turning on me—"

"An unfortunate incident, yes. Documentation from Mr. Fabrini and Ms. James has corroborated it."

"Then you know it's not my—"

"Your fault. Of course it isn't. But now that you're home, safe and sound, I expect delivery of my parcel."

Shit. *Shit.* Absolutely no sign of West... "They confiscated it when I landed."

"I sincerely hope that's not the case. Why don't we meet in an hour and you can give it to me then."

I gripped the phone so tightly my knuckles were going white, lightheadedness threatening to take over me again. I leaned on the counter heavily, slumping on my elbow. "How do I know they're still alive?"

Ashford's booming laugh sounded over the line, throbbing against my ear hard, the sound unsettling enough to twist my gut. "I'm no common thug—of course they're alive. Your daughter's in my drawing room playing on the piano forte; her guardian is resting on the couch in there. Didn't sleep much—she's quite worn out."

"You son of a bitch, she's *sick*. She needs her medication and—"

"Then I suppose you'd best hurry. Bring the Seal to Kent House. One hour. I hope traffic is in your favor."

The bastard hung up the phone.

29
BARGAINING

———— ◆ ————

I STARED AT MY CELL for minutes longer—they ticked by until the screen darkened and still I couldn't move, couldn't think, couldn't breathe. I bit savagely at my lip and my vision blurred, tears rising and I couldn't blink them back.

"Fuck!" The phone left my grip without me thinking as I pitched it across the kitchen. It clattered down the hall toward the living room. Water sloshed under my feet as I stalked after it; the drywall was dented with dust on the floor, and cell phone was cracked but it worked. I blinked some more, sucking breaths in rapidly, and dialed Martin.

"Ready to come clean, Liv?" he said in a cocky voice as he answered.

"Who the fuck is he?" I growled.

A pause. "Liv?"

"Who the *fuck* is Moses Ashford! Why do you want this ring? Why does *he* want this ring?"

"Calm down," he said in an irritatingly soothing voice that only made me want to throw the phone again. "Why don't you—"

"He has my daughter and my best friend. Now *tell me* what the hell I'm dealing with."

"I...I can't, Liv—"

"Jesus Christ—"

"But if you bring me the ring—"

I hung up on him.

Next I cycled through my numbers until I found a recent addition and called Dawson. Five rings had me in an even worse panic before he finally picked up.

"Please tell me you have something more on Ashford."

"Um...no?"

I sank against the wall and crumpled until my ass thumped on the floor.

"Livi?"

Wiping at my eyes did no good. I drew my knees up to my chest and leaned one arm over them. "West told me not to give Ashford the ring. My brother tells me not to give Ashford the ring. Mr. Rolph used his dying breath to tell me to listen to West. But Ashford has my daughter and my best friend and I have no idea what he'll do to them if I don't give him this ring in an hour."

Dawson was silent as a minute ticked by. "Holy shit."

I sniffled. "No, just the usual kind."

"I don't have anything but then I haven't been looking. What about asking Laurel?"

Where her loyalty to Ashford ended and to me began, I couldn't say and didn't want to test. "I don't think we've bonded quite *that* much, and I don't have her number either."

"Police?"

"And tell them I broke several laws that will land me in prison until well after my daughter graduates university, including risking extradition back to Ethiopia?" I had no doubt Ashford would ensure I went down for this—he had all that data from Dawson anyway, video proof of what I'd done.

"Oh. Right. Did West say what to do when you got back here?"

"He said to stall and that he'd come get it from me." I sat up a little straighter; my eyes were drier and some of the panic had abated. "Do you have a number for him?"

"No, he just intercepted my calls. I can look?"

"I'd appreciate it."

"No prob, I'll call you back. Can't be *that* many Dale Wests, right?" He sighed. "Yeah, don't answer that."

A small smile fought my lips as I hung up and stared at the phone. Stupid West—somehow he'd managed to fuck up so many things...

Thomas and Pulaski. "...he and Pulaski are under my orders not to let you from their sight. Again."

I scrambled up and pounded back through the house to the front where I threw open the door and stormed outside. The day was gray and quiet, air damp and threatening rain. I glanced from side to side, seeing nothing but the usual cars on the street, no sign of people but a few on a porch having beers and cigarettes two houses away.

And fuck it—I might as well embrace Crazy Woman status. "Thomas! Pulaski!" I stalked down the driveway, gaze darting everywhere at once. The world was a gray blur as I swung around wildly. "You followed me, right? Where the hell are you? Thomas! Pulaski!"

"Jesus," a voice muttered behind me.

I spun to see both men around the side of the house, glancing back and forth as if the neighbors could put down their smokes long enough to notice. My feet were moving before I could think to tell them to until I was face to face with both; they'd dressed casually but still came across as not quite right in the neighborhood. Thomas still stood like a broad-shouldered tower and Pulaski was his bulldog companion.

"Where's West?" I asked.

They glanced at one another. "We don't know," Thomas said.

"You need to call him."

"I tried earlier." Pulaski shrugged. "No answer. He's got a bunch of numbers and I only have one. Usually he contacts us—"

My lips parted to argue, to scream, to rant, but I shut them again. What was the point? "You know what? Fuck it. West tells me he'll come get the ring, but he's nowhere to be found. So fuck him up the ass with a chainsaw—I am *done*." I stormed back for the house, the heavy footfalls behind me signaling both men followed.

"Miss Talbot—" Pulaski started.

I spun to face him when I reached the door, ponytail whipping hair in my face. "Ashford has my kid. If West wants the Seal, he can take it from him—I'm not his pet and I don't have to do what he says."

"Talbot—"

I went inside and slammed the door, snapping closed the deadbolt immediately and taking a heaving breath. If they could find West, I remained certain they would after that. If they couldn't, well, too bad for him.

I pushed off the door, my feet heavy and dragging, and went for my pack on the deacon bench. My keys sat in a lump there as well on the cardboard box that had been by the door. My cell phone rang incessantly—Denny was still trying to ring me back—so I set it on vibrate and tossed it on the bench.

The package gave me pause. I twisted my front door key around and ran it along the tape, scarcely breathing. The date on the tag said it arrived last night. It could be anything but the last box I'd received...

The last one had been from Ashford.

Please don't be bad, please don't be bad... I could too easily imagine a hand or some horrible warning waiting for me, but curiosity wouldn't merely let the box be. I lifted the tape, the noise loud in the silent hallway, and peeled it away until I could fold back the lid.

Inside was a yellow Post It with *Replacements. —DW.* scrawled in rough, black Sharpie letters.

I set aside the note, jerked back the brown paper and Styrofoam peanuts inside until I saw the contents.

My gaze moved as I stood straight, staring back at the hallway toward my room. I couldn't rush to Ashford's—I had to be prepared. That he'd gone to the trouble to immediately take Emaleth and Pru without giving me a chance to bring him the ring...

He knew. If not exactly what was going on, that something was. Maybe he thought Martin said something to me, maybe he knew West intended to double cross him.

Regardless, I had to get ready.

———————◆———————

MY BANGED-UP CAR LIKELY looked out of place along the old city streets where Kent House lay, but my mind swirled and I didn't give a damn.

I'd downed a bottle of water and eaten an Egg McMuffin on my way to the nice branch of the city. Dumping grease and processed crap on my stomach probably wasn't the best idea but I was exhausted and weak—the calories and protein might help. As long as I didn't vomit it all up.

Rain spit from thick clouds above, not a lot but enough to leave fat flecks of water on the windshield. I pulled up in front of Kent House behind a black Lincoln Town Car on an otherwise empty street and slipped out, not bothering to lock the doors and with the keys tucked in the visor. I highly doubted anyone was going to steal my POS while I was gone and keeping the keys here lessened the risk I'd drop them somewhere on my way. This would go well—I knew it would, it *had to*, but I had no idea what I was dealing with, and an exit strategy is always necessary in that instance.

I wore simple, straight-legged black pants and a burgundy coat that came to my knees; a fitted black shirt beneath was plain, and my hair hung in a long ponytail. I wouldn't draw attention to myself, I didn't think—I'd even left my beat up boots at home and went with simple black ones appropriate for fall weather with just enough of a heel that I looked dressed up. Nothing to alarm anyone, least of all Ashford. Totally professional and calm.

Kent House sat between other houses with little property of its own, quieter than when I'd seen it last, almost as if the manor was dozing. The black iron gate out front was shut but unlatched, and I closed it after stepping through. My steps clicked on the vintage interlock path through a small garden, straight for the wide steps leading to the front door. Nothing greeted me but a damp wind, lifting my hair and fluttering my coat.

I stepped up the stairs and opened the door without knocking.

The interior was not just silent but still, nothing stirring as I walked in the foyer and looked around. I let the door close behind me and it clicked, sealing me in. The foyer seemed far vaster without so many people milling about, the wide staircase dwarfing me. Polished granite floor gleamed in the overly bright light, my own reflection bouncing back at me. I glanced from side to side, eying the wide archways leading to other halls and rooms. Ashford hadn't said specifically where he'd be—the conference room upstairs, perhaps, might be a contender.

I walked up the stairs with slow, steady steps, tense from head to toe and listening carefully for any signs of life. Various art pieces stared back at me on the walls, from classical to contemporary, some with actual eyes to track my movements, others abstract splashes of color that still seemed to watch.

At the top of the grand staircase, I took a corridor that veered left, past more open concept rooms. The click of my boots on the floor announced my approach to anyone who might be listening—there would be no stealth this time. I strangely missed the caves because at least I knew what to expect, whether from the shadows in normal chambers to the cavern with the mother dragon. And monsters, I understood.

It was people I had trouble with.

A closed door waited at the end of the hall, just as it had over a week ago when I first came to meet Ashford, but no elderly gentleman waited to let me in. I doubted anyone was handing out wine, either. I reached for the handle, pressed down and pushed, then let the door swing open while I readied to draw a weapon.

The conference room wasn't much different from how I'd last seen it; lights inlaid in the ceiling were on, glowing over the massive round table. Blinds at the back remained closed, hiding the dark day outside as if this was the only place that existed in the world.

My gaze snagged on Pru immediately. She sat in a chair to the right of the table facing the door, holding very still with her back rigid and shoulders squared. Her wide, dark eyes were on me and I scanned her for any sign of injury but found nothing obvious; she wore track pants and a T-shirt, thick dark hair in a loose ponytail, as if they'd caught her in the evening before bed. No bruises, no cuts, just a steady terror in her expression.

Ashford stood behind her, his hands on her shoulders—dangerously close to her neck, in my opinion, like he could reach for her throat and snap her spine before I could move. His expression in contrast to hers was collected and controlled, eyes half-lidded as if he was comfortable enough to take a nap. He wore a tieless, impeccably pressed black suit, dark hair combed straight back. Armani-wearing businessman head to toe—well-dressed kidnapper.

I did not see any sign of my daughter.

I stopped a few feet inside the room and waited for him to speak as the door swung shut behind me. Besides the exit at my back there were two other doors, one on either side of the room at the very back, and I had no idea where they led. The windows I supposed counted as exits, too, but the floors were extra large here—we were the equivalent to three stories up, I'd say, and not something I wanted to risk us jumping.

"Within the hour," Ashford said without blinking. "Excellent timing."

"Where's my daughter?"

"Where's my ring?"

I wasn't going to play games. No stalling, no negotiating—there was no point. I pulled the thin chain around my neck, plucked the ring from under my shirt, and gave it a yank; the chain snapped and fell, forgotten at my feet. I gazed down at the ring for a moment, then cast it on the table. It rolled and rattled, coming to a stop midway down—a good four feet from Ashford so he'd have to let Pru go to get it.

He looked at me and it was abundantly clear he understood my intent, but didn't argue. Instead he regarded me for ten seconds longer, then let go of Prudence.

She flinched like she'd been expecting something worse but held my gaze fiercely; as he walked away, rounding the table, some of the worry in me eased. My friend wasn't stupid; she watched for my lead, no doubt, expecting I'd have some sort of plan or at least knew what I was up against.

Oh, she was about to be *very* disappointed if this went badly because I was totally pantsing it.

Ashford paused and reached across the table, grasped the Seal, and lifted it for inspection. My chest seized, breath stopped, and I turned my toes to angle toward Pru—I'd have to grab her quickly.

Ashford's thick dark brows pulled tight as he turned the Seal over. "Did you have much trouble locating it?"

"Well...you know...couple people died, but what are you gonna do."

He didn't seem to be listening to me and my attempt at lightening the mood wasn't helping me feel better.

We have to get the fuck out of here... Two feet to the door behind me; Pru was four feet away.

"Where's my daughter..." My breath caught as he slipped the ring on his right index finger.

Tension rippled through the room and even Pru was watching.

"Tell me something, Miss Talbot." He looked over the ring, white light above cutting over the brass. His gaze lifted to meet mine, brows still pulled tight, odd light reflecting in his eyes. "Did you really think this counterfeit was going to fool me?"

30
BLUFF CALLED

———— ◆ ————

THERE WAS PRETTY MUCH NO acceptable answer I could give to that question.

Ashford pulled the ring off again and I could scarcely draw a breath, trying to watch him while keeping Pru in my peripheral vision.

"Where's the Seal?" His voice was low, deceptively steady.

"That *is* the Seal," I said simply.

He tightened his grip around the ring until his knuckles went white.

My shoulder shifted back, one foot inched to put me at an angle; I could pull a weapon or run if he so much as blinked funny at me.

"Do you have any concept of true captivity, Miss Talbot?" he asked calmly, his voice a stark contrast to the rage buzzing in the air around him.

"Well, I've had to watch *Dora the Explorer* for four hours straight on sick days—"

"Three thousand years of confinement is akin to death. *Where* is the Seal?"

Goddamn it, West... "That's what I took from the cave. Check Dawson's video—"

The ring bounced hard on the table as he threw it, rolled and spun out of sight. "It's garbage. Useless."

Stall, stall—how the fuck am I supposed to stall? I hoped Pru was ready to run. "Maybe you're not using it right?"

He gave me a dark look and said nothing.

"I don't—"

"Do. Not. Lie."

Heat descended on the room, sweat slicking my skin under my coat and beading across my brow. For a moment I thought it was me, struggling to drag muggy air into my lungs, the atmosphere picking up a murky, swampy feel from my own fear, but sweat rolled down Ashford's forehead as well.

A clump of black hair fell as he tipped his head down, leaving where it was carefully slicked back and cutting across his forehead. "You have made a very, very big mistake, Miss Talbot."

I do not doubt that one bit.

Time slowed for an instant and then he *moved*; his closed fist slammed down on the tabletop and flames erupted.

For a moment I blinked, orange and yellow dancing, crackling, flames rising where his hand connected with the polished wood. Blackness singed, fire spread, and I snapped out of it, moving. My lips parted to shout at Pru as my hands flicked to my sides, reaching for my new pair of two-tone USP Match pistols.

I'd cleared them from their hip holsters, raised them, and already flames leapt high, obscuring Ashford from view. A great darkness rose behind him, black smoke stretching from his back, reaching toward the ceiling.

Wings.

The place was burning—I had guns out but no idea what to shoot, what to do, my brain slow to react because there was a fire in Kent House and *I didn't know where the fuck my daughter was.*

Fire twisted past me, a ball of it shooting inches from my head, so close I felt the heat, the singing of my hair as it passed. I dropped, falling to a crouch behind the table, shooting blindly at him though it did no good. I burned through half of the eighteen rounds in each gun before dropping my arms again.

Pru was at my side, choking from the rising smoke with her hand up over her face, blinking furiously as water leaked from her eyes.

I leaned over. "Run for the door—I'll cover you." Getting Pru sent out was the first task—she could haul ass but was likely tired and the fire was disorienting. She'd need time.

Next was combing the place for Em—I'd crawl through the fire on my hands and knees if I had to.

The ceiling had caught fire, flames eating through paint and plaster and blackening wood above. A glance under the table and I could no longer see where Ashford stood—*if* Ashford stood—and soon there wouldn't be a room left.

A low, steady growl thrummed the floor below me, noise rising over the hiss and crackle of fire. Chills rolled through me, flooding my system with more fear.

We have to get out.

I have to find Em.

First, Pru. "Run!" I nudged her, half rose, fired randomly in the direction Ashford had been standing. I squinted against the brightness, coughed as smoke filled my lungs—I couldn't make anything out, and if it wasn't for the table in front of me, I'd have no point of reference for where we stood.

I moved back, stumbled—the guns were useless, nothing to aim at, and I slipped them back into their holsters. Smoke rose above us as we crawled toward the door. The same growl was rising, shaking the floor beneath me, and the room seemed to take a collective breath in, stillness settling even among the fire.

Whatever was next was going to be bad, I knew it.

Pru hissed as she reached up and fumbled with the knob then the door swung wide. I pushed her ahead of me out into the hall, still on our hands and knees—no flames had reached this far but it wouldn't be long before the entire place went down. Smoke rolled out after us and flames licked my boots, the hem of my long coat. A deep cough burst from my chest again and my eyes still watered.

The rumbling below us went still; what should have been a relief made my stomach bottom out and I tensed from head to toe. I resisted the urge to look over my shoulder. "What room is she—"

Something thumped the floor again, closer this time; I barely looked up when hands were jerking me to my feet. I blinked into the face of Thomas.

Past him was West.

I hadn't time to sputter accusations or rant—he pushed the door closed, got Pru on her feet, and locked his hand on her shoulder. "Move!"

Jesus Christ, he's going to push her on her face. "She can't, she—"

He didn't spare me a glance, just lifted her easily, one arm under her back the other under knees like she weighed nothing, and started down the stairs.

She'd be safe—of little else concerning West could I be sure.

Now I had to find Em.

I glanced at the row of closed doors and started for the first one when Thomas grabbed me around the waist and started after West.

The breath I'd felt the room taking suddenly expelled.

Fire and smoke blasted the door and it burst, chunks of wood flying, hinges swinging. Warm air hit my face and I turned my head to the side, burying my eyes against Thomas's shoulder. A bellow hit the air, digging into my brain, something inhuman and terrifying. More flames shot out, grasping and eating away at the corridor as it receded.

Em.

Immediately I twisted, landed an elbow in his ribs, screamed at him—he dragged me farther, ignoring my fighting, absorbing the hits and maybe being twice the size of me he really didn't feel anything. Down the hall, farther away from the rooms that could—

"Put me down! Em! Em!" I hollered until my throat hurt, scratched raw and weak from smoke inhalation.

We were on the stairs, starting downward; something cracked in the distance, perhaps the building starting to collapse.

Panic burst more adrenaline in my veins and I didn't see, didn't heard, didn't feel, turning part animal as I fought and screamed.

"She's not here!"

I twisted, met Pru's gaze as she looked over West's shoulder, bobbing as he ran down the stairs with her.

Not here.

Pru shook her head, like she knew what I was asking without speaking.

Not here.

Where the fuck is she?

I couldn't linger, couldn't worry—could only trust Pru, trust that if Emaleth was somewhere in this building she'd die trying to find her as well. My fight against Thomas ceased and he seemed to sense it, too; when we reached the bottom of the stairs, he left me on my own feet and let me stumble after West.

We skipped the front door, instead cutting through one of the archways. "Hey, my car's parked—"

"Not there anymore," West threw over his shoulder.

Thomas's hand hit my lower back, urging me along. Fire licked at the stairs already, growing at an unnatural pace. Instincts warred, wanting to push me on my own path, but West had Pru still so I kept up.

He headed straight for the conservatory we'd first met in, where glass walls and ceiling exposed the near-black storm clouds above and the cold, wet, drab day waiting outside. No door that I could see—he was running straight for one of the glass walls.

West's pace slowed and he met my gaze over Pru's head.

I bolted forward, raising my guns, squeezing the triggers one after the other until I'd peppered a dozen holes in one sheet of glass. Spidery cracks wove along the pane. West twisted, shoulder first, brought his arm up to cover Pru's head, and ran through. Glass shattered with a high-pitched tinkling, and then crunched underfoot.

I stepped out after him, jagged shards in the frame scraping my pants and catching my coat, and I holstered the guns again. Heavy rain fell, beating cold over my battered skin and welcome after the heat. Muddy grass was slippery underfoot and I braced to keep from falling.

Blinking against rain, I glanced around; we stood in a garden where tree branches went spindly under missing leaves and flowers had withered. West still carried Pru and trekked ahead, along the side of the house. A waist-high black iron fence ran around the property; his steps sped and three feet away he leapt. Pru tensed, ducked, but he cleared the fence easily and landed safely on the other side.

I ran hard but couldn't make such a jump. Instead I grasped the edge of the fence and vaulted over. Thomas followed and we chased after West as he turned down a narrow path next to the neighboring brownstone.

"Any sign?" he called over his shoulder.

"No," Thomas said before I could.

I glanced at Kent House where smoke billowed and flames ate at the old manor and the priceless art within.

I could've given him the real ring but without Em here, would this have ended any differently?

I shoved thoughts of it from my head and struggled to keep up. Adrenaline kept at bay the flare of pain from any injuries but I expected once I had time to assess them, I'd be in for a whole lot of hurt. We beat down the cobblestone path and I recognized my car waiting there, on an entirely different street from where I'd parked it. I wasn't surprised to get up close and see Pulaski past the rain rolling down the driver's side window.

West didn't put down Pru until he was right outside the rear door, and even then he all but put her in himself. He gripped the back of my head cop-style and got me in next, then Thomas crowded me before West leapt *over* the vehicle to get in the passenger side. Pulaski had the car in motion before the doors were even shut, peeling down the damp street in seconds.

I twisted, difficult to move with Thomas practically sitting on my lap, and glanced back at the burning house. "Where's Em?"

Pru gave a wracking cough beside me. "I don't know. Not here. He left her at the other place."

Shit.

"You didn't give him the Seal?" West sat in the front seat, staring at me with blue eyes under soaked black hair.

I shot him a glare. "You sent a fake with the guns—I *assumed* you had a fucking plan."

"It...didn't involve that," he said mildly.

I could shoot him in the back of the head but I hadn't looked to see if I still had a round in either chamber. I sat back and pulled out each gun to reload in case I needed a few bullets to take him down.

The matching pistols could've been mistaken for my own at first glance—he even installed a Jet Funnel on each for fast reloading—though these were two-toned, the base black and the slide nickel. At least four or five hundred more a pop for that. The Match pistols were worth every penny, though, with a long barrel weighted for accuracy.

Presents or no, I was still pissed off at him.

"Did he call?" West asked, and I glanced up but he was addressing Pulaski.

The bulldog shook his head. "Nope. Will he be here in time to..."

"I can't find him—probably not."

"Shit."

I leaned forward. "Who?"

They ignored me.

For fuck's sake. I went back to worrying about my weapons. I replaced the empty mags with new ones, stowed the old ones away, and waited with the guns crossed on my lap. Pulaski wheeled the vehicle through the city streets, putting more and more space between us and Kent House. Though early afternoon, it might as well have been evening with the blanket of clouds overhead. A handful of people with umbrellas milled through the streets, otherwise it was all cars sloshing through rising puddles.

I turned to Pru now that adrenaline had settled, my heart slowed to normal and my brain working again. "Are you okay?"

She brushed tangled dark curls from her damp forehead. Tears shone in her eyes and she sucked in a breath—she got that look like an emotional break was imminent. "Yes. Though I could use a nap."

"Where did he have you?"

"Some kind of house?" She shook her head. "We were blindfolded for the drive. In a room with no windows overnight."

Ashford had said *his* drawing room—it must be his house somewhere. "And Em's okay?"

"She was when they took me this morning." Her dark eyes remained with mine, bottom lip quivering. "He thinks when you were arrested yesterday, you agreed to help the police. We were insurance in case you double crossed him."

I met West's gaze immediately; he held it for a moment, a heavy weight to his expression, before he looked at Pru. "Did he mention me?"

"I don't know who the hell you even *are*," Pru snapped.

"Dale West," I said. "Ashford's enforcer. And thorn in his side, I gather."

She shook her head. "Not that I recall but he wasn't...chatty." She crossed her arms, shoulders twitching in a shiver in her damp T-shirt, and glanced out the window.

"He's gotta know something," Pulaski said, eyes still on the road.

"I know." West drummed his fingers on the dash. "But until I know how much..."

No one spoke, apparently some silent communication passing between them.

"Okay, what next?" I turned my attention to West and leaned forward. "Where does he have her? When do we get there?"

He turned back to face the windshield where wipers squeaked and sloshed through rain. "You're going home."

My hands tightened on my new guns. "*Excuse me?*"

"You're *compromised.* He doesn't trust you and now he's pissed. I imagine he'll call you tonight to extort the ring—"

"He *has* my *kid*," I bit out. "Like hell I'm just going to go home and—"

"And you don't have a fucking clue what you're dealing with."

"And whose fault is that? Who has decided to keep me in the dark? *Who are you?*"

He said nothing.

"I should've just given him the fucking ring in the first place."

"*That* is why you're not going." He gestured ahead as we neared a set of lights and spoke next to Pulaski in a low voice. "Up here is fine."

Oh no, oh no fucking *way* was he ditching me. As the car pulled over and West moved to get out, I darted forward, right gun raised. Thomas latched onto me immediately, one large hand locking onto my shoulder, but couldn't reach my extended arm or the pistol in my hand.

West paused, half turned to face me with his hand on the door handle, not even acknowledging the barrel I had pointed at his forehead.

"Liv," Pru said softly, but no amount of pleading was going to quell me.

My arm trembled, finger unsteady as it wrapped around the trigger. Emotion welled, threatening to break me apart, and my chest shook in a suppressed sob. The lines were blurring, Work Me and Mom Me no longer separate identities, and I knew— probably as well as West knew—that I would do anything in that moment that Ashford wanted, anything at all, if it meant he'd give me Emaleth back unharmed.

"What *is* he and where does he have her?" My voice dropped low, barely audible over the tapping of rain on the car roof and windows.

West's grip tightened on the door handle then he relented with a sigh. "He's an *afreet*."

I blinked at him.

"A type of djinn." As if I should've known what he was talking about.

"Genie in a bottle. Seriously?"

Another sigh and he shifted, muscles tense and ready to dart out of the vehicle. "You're in the middle of something you shouldn't be. And it's my fault. But for now, all you need to know is that he can't be killed. Your guns don't work. Hitting him won't work. Decapitating him won't work. And the Seal of Solomon is the only leverage over him we have."

We? I strongly doubted he meant him and me.

"Keep the ring while I try to get a hold of the person who can wield it. There's a chance Ashford doesn't yet realize I'm involved so *I* will get your daughter back and come up with Plan B. *You* will go home and wait, Olivia."

My extended arm was starting to ache but I didn't put the gun down. If anyone looked in the windows, past the rain, they'd think it some bizarre carjacking. "If you don't come back with her, I will tell Ashford absolutely everything I know about you double crossing him. Whatever is going on, this is *your* fight, not mine, West."

His gaze flickered to Pulaski, still behind the wheel. "Put her in her house and don't let her leave."

"Are we authorized to tell her," Pulaski glanced at Thomas, then to West again, "like, anything?"

"Just..." I expected the next words from West's mouth to be expletives but instead he went calm and cool. "Tell her whatever you need to if it keeps her from leaving." He opened the door, completely disregarding the threat I still aimed at him, and climbed out, then slammed the door closed so hard the car shook.

I didn't take the shot and suspected I'd come to regret it.

31
FULL HOUSE

———◆———

THE CAR WAS SILENT AND I was wedged between Pru and
Thomas so couldn't've made a run for it if I'd wanted to. Pulaski
drove through—and out of—New Bristol, and I put away my
guns rather than risk shooting anyone and causing an accident.
When he reached the quiet, rundown suburb I sort of called
home, I leaned forward and squinted past the windshield wipers;
a vehicle sat in the driveway and a man stood leaning against the
side of it in a heavy dark coat, disregarding the rain that plastered
brown hair over his head.

Pulaski pulled up next to him my driveway, exchanging a
look with Thomas in the rearview mirror

"It's fine," I said.

Pru popped open her door so she could climb out. Denny
must've recognized us despite the grim day and pouring rain as
he reached in to give her a hand without hesitation.

I followed Prudence out of the car, coming face to face
with Chase Denham. Under the mask of heavy rain, I still made
out his angry expression.

"Where's Em? What the hell is going on?" He reached for me but I backpedaled and thumped into the car at my back.

Thomas and Pulaski were out and surrounding us in seconds, no weapons drawn but that couldn't be far off. I didn't live in a great neighborhood but random gunfire in my driveway *would* be noticed.

"Inside," I said and waited a beat for the others to move first. It was Prudence who took the lead, and when Denny kept his grip on her forearm, she let him lead her. Pru wasn't an invalid by any means but the abduction, lack of sleep, and missing her meds could leave her exhausted, and exhaustion brought its own set of challenges. I kept up behind them, Thomas and Pulaski at my heels. Pru didn't have her key so I moved ahead and let everyone inside.

For a moment I had at *least* something to do—someone to mother, someone to take care of, and I let myself latch onto that because otherwise I'd dwell and worry and go entirely mad, and then be useless to Em wherever she was. I disregarded my boots and trekked down the hall, around into the kitchen, and immediately got the kettle going.

"Get changed and get settled," I called over my shoulder as I busied about. Mug. A calming mix of chamomile and other herbs. Teaspoon set to the side. Honey. I hadn't offered something to the others but didn't care—Pru was my focus. "I'll bring you some tea and—"

"Liv."

I turned to see Pru in the doorway alone, still in her damp, rumpled track pants and T-shirt, eyes brimming with tears.

"I'm sorry I couldn't help," she whispered. "I'm sorry she—"

I crossed the kitchen in three long strides, boots slapping against linoleum and puddles of water from the fridge, and grabbed her in a hug. For a moment I slipped, my own eyes watering, chest aching, and I drew a sniffling, ragged breath through my nose. "I should've had you wake her up, I should've spoke to her—I thought it was best if she slept but she didn't know...I let her go without letting her know—"

"She knows. It's okay." Pru patted my back.

"But—"

"But we'll find her," Pru promised, and I realized this wasn't me comforting her, wasn't me reassuring and being the mother hen. No, *I* needed the reassurance—I needed someone to promise me everything was going to be okay, and Pru was good at that.

While I wouldn't break, wouldn't lose it completely, I sagged for a moment and let myself flail in the terror that this all would end badly and there was nothing I could do about it.

I only allowed myself a moment before I pulled back and wiped furiously at my eyes. "I'm getting you some tea, so why don't you go lie down—"

"I'm not doing anything until we get Em back. You're not alone in this and you're going to let me help."

I slumped against the counter at my back and looked away. "If I don't go full blown control freak on this sitch, I'm going to break."

"You're not going to break. You're going to put on your big girl panties, figure out what's going on, and come up with a plan, and everything's going to be okay."

I nearly smiled. "Fight now, cry later."

She nodded. "Now, *you* go get changed while I take a pill and make us tea. No matter what the Brute Squad says about staying, we're finding her."

"I want bourbon."

"Bourbon for you, tea for me, then."

Another sniffle and this time I did smile. "I love you."

"I love you too. And I love Em. So let's get moving."

I didn't argue but passed her as she continued on into the kitchen to take care of the tea and find her meds. Pulaski and Thomas stood in the front hall at attention, as if waiting further orders, with Denny between them.

"He can stay," I said, then gestured over my shoulder. "There's a back sliding door between the living room and laundry room, if one of you wants to watch it while the other takes point here. No other exits."

"We know," Pulaski said, his face flushing. As if I hadn't already realized they'd thoroughly checked out my house. He moved to take the back door and Denny followed, though his focus was on me.

And I couldn't take it. Not for a second. His worry would pile onto my own and I'd be useless, so I avoided his gaze and stomped down the dark hall and into my room at the end. Rain pattered against the windows, a steady thump and sending dappled shadows across my bed and floor.

I stripped off my coat; it was soaked and the rough hem suggested it had been singed in the fire, ruined. Next went my boots, my gun holster and weapons, then my straight legged slacks. A jagged cut ran up my ankle and across part of my calf, two inches of it barely a scratch and a deeper puncture higher up. Pressure from my fingertip produced flaring pain and a well of blood—must've been from the broken glass in the window frame. Not deep enough to require stitches, I disregarded it—it was no worse than my forearm where the bullet had grazed, and that was bound up tightly and not causing problems. West's handiwork had held but then I hadn't needed to push myself and risk further injury.

Yet.

Steps approached and belatedly I realized I hadn't closed the door. Just as I turned to do so, I paused as Denny appeared in the threshold.

"Don't start," I whispered.

"What the hell is going on, Olivia?"

I avoided his gaze and stalked across the room, just in my fitted black tee and underwear. Denny had seen far more of me seven years ago and other than some muscle, scars from work, and pregnancy stretch marks, not much had changed. Instead of getting worked up over it, I moved instead for the dresser and jerked the top drawer open.

"Liv!"

My hand froze, locked around a pair of black yoga pants, but I couldn't look at him—just listened, tense to the point I was almost tremoring.

"Where is she?"

I hated the way his voice seemed to break, like the edges snapped off and cut me as well. I sucked in a breath, tried to calm myself, and went back to dragging out a pair of pants to wear. "I don't know."

"What happened?"

I shook my head.

"Liv, you look like someone beat the shit out of you."

"It's just a job thing."

"That's not what normal people look like when they come home from work."

Well, I'm not fucking normal, now am I? My balance was off and I leaned against the dresser as I dragged the pants on; the edge of the drawer dug into one of my many bruises and I winced. "I stole the Seal of Solomon from a cave in Ethiopia for my employer, who is apparently a bad guy"—*and not human at that*—"and despite the fact that I broke several laws both domestic and international in getting it home, he didn't entirely believe I'd keep up my end of the contract."

"*What?*"

Where Denny fell on the scale of Pulse deniers to Pulse believers, I didn't know and had no desire to test. My pants on, I jerked the elastic from my tangled hair and shook the mane out, then grasped my brush, a bottle of spray leave-in conditioner, my guns and holster, and started for the door.

His hands came down on my shoulders before I could push past him. Even with my hands engaged, I could slip away easily, but instead held still. Reluctantly I lifted my gaze to meet his.

Wet dark brown curls were mussed and fell across his forehead, around his ears; his brown suede coat was black with rain and possibly wrecked after standing outside waiting for us for however long he'd been there. He was likely cold and uncomfortable, still in shoes, jeans soaked, but he showed none of it, just concern in his dark eyes.

"Where's my daughter? What the hell did you get into?"

I stiffened. "She is *not* yours, Chase. How many fucking times do I have to say that for you to get it through your head?"

"Liv—" The pain in his eyes nearly broke me further, that same sad look Em had the other night when I snapped at her regarding the same subject, but I shoved guilt aside and shrugged his hands off my shoulders.

"No. The reality is, *yes*, I fucked up—*yes*, Em is in trouble. And you are welcome to stay here and help us try to get her back but do not try to guilt me further. I *allow* you contact with her, but you are not her father and you have absolutely zero authority in this situation. And if you even *dream* of sending the police or CAS after me for negligence when this was nothing of the sort—"

"Christ, I wouldn't—"

"—you will be out of our lives for good. Now are you going to stay and help, or do I need my two bodyguards out there to make things a bit clearer for you?"

He blew a breath past his lips. A raindrop rolled from his hair down his brow, along his cheek, and he made no move to swipe at it. The silence was thick and heavy, punctuated by the incessant beat of rain on the windows. "Jesus," he whispered, a mix of sadness and shock to his tone, and gave the slightest shake of his head. "When'd you get so damn hard?"

"The day I gave birth." I pushed past him and padded down the hall, grabbed a towel from the shelf just inside the bathroom on the way, and continued on. My gaze darted briefly to the open door to Em's room. Giles had moved to the end of the bed, one leg extended so he could gracelessly clean it, oblivious to the rising anxiety of the rest of us. Maybe he knew she'd be back safely soon.

I envied that cat more than a little.

32
HELP

———— ◆ ————

PRUDENCE HAD HER LAPTOP SET up on the end table next to the old couch where she sat with a cup of tea; a glass of bourbon on the rocks sat on the coffee table for me. I tossed her the towel for her hair, set down everything I'd been carrying, and opted for the bourbon first. Ice clinked against my teeth as I downed it in one go, then set the glass back on the wet coaster and sat across from Pru.

Denny hung in my peripheral vision by the doorway, watching us though I pointedly ignored him; Pru, for once, followed my lead. Eventually his steps faded down the hall and I heard the rustle of his coat and shoes as he removed them.

"Towels in the bathroom, help yourself to the kitchen," I called, then turned my attention to Pru. "Did you find out anything about him?"

"Nothing anyone was willing to tell me." She set her tea cup down and pulled over the laptop. "Any direction you can point me in?"

Not that I could immediately think of. I leaned forward, elbows on my thighs and shoulders turned inward. I was tired and achy, and if I sat back in the comfortable chair-and-a-half, I'd probably not get up again. "Dawson couldn't find anything either, just property records in town." *And maybe he'd be worth asking.* I rose with my guns and holsters in hand, and went in search of my pack by the front door.

Thomas still waited there, tall and intimidating—I dared anyone to try to pass him. I eyed him as I hung up the guns and then slipped my backpack strap off the hook by the door. "I was kind of kidding about taking point—you can come in and sit down if you want. Get dry. Have a drink. You must be tired, chasing me around and getting shot and stuff."

His expression didn't change but he fidgeted slightly. In black jeans, a heavy coat, and boots, he didn't look terribly comfortable and was likely soaked to the bone in rainwater.

"Seriously," I gestured over my shoulder to the living room, "I'm not going anywhere, since I don't actually *know* where I'm supposed to be going. And West said you were authorized to tell me *some* stuff."

"I'm not—"

"Supposed to let me *leave*. But the cat's out of the bag regarding Ashford since he grew wings and set everything on fire, and whatever West's game is will probably follow. Maybe you can convince me your boss has everything under control and I won't have to leave?"

"I can't tell you where she is. I'm...I'm sorry, but I wouldn't *know* what to tell you. We don't work in the...the area West does. He called us in to help with the caves, that's it. We haven't been briefed on much regarding...Ashford."

Briefed? Interesting choice of words. "I'm not asking you to give us a location. But I will want to know everything you know about who took my daughter. Humor me."

He gave the door behind him a cautious look, shucked off his coat, then stepped forward and followed me down the hall, back to the living room, even pausing when I stopped to grab the bottle of bourbon. While he wouldn't sit, he hung in the doorway in the spot Denny had previously occupied, while my ex perched on the arm of the couch and didn't look at anyone.

I settled once more in my chair. Though the room was warm and dry, a chill had wrapped around my bones, and I drew the chenille blanket from the back of the chair and settled it on my lap before pouring myself another bourbon. The alcohol burned like liquid fire, warming my veins and somewhat easing the rapid beat of my heart.

"Okay." I set down my empty glass and pulled my cell phone from the pack at my feet. "Dawson ran tech and did a lot of research on everyone from my team. He mentioned property Ashford owned. Maybe...maybe we can narrow it down." I met Pru's gaze as my phone dialed. "You'd at least know the size, right? Something about the interior?"

"It was...big," she said. "Very."

"His home?"

"Probably."

"Hey, Liv," Dawson answered. "Did you find them?"

His voice brought a measure of comfort beyond even the bourbon—he'd been there when everything in Ethiopia went south and pulled through, which I appreciated. I put the call on speakerphone and set my cell on the coffee table. "Yes and no. I wish this was a social call, but..."

"Uh oh."

You said it. I debated pouring another drink, but I wanted a clear head for this. "So you remember I got arrested in customs."

"Yeah."

"Ashford took that as a sign that I defected. West had me try to trick him with a fake ring and it went really, really badly. Like, burning building badly."

"Jesus."

"Actually, a genie, apparently, but we'll get to that in a second. I got Pru back but he still has my little girl and I don't know where."

"Got ya. Pru's the hot friend?"

Pru pressed her lips together, fighting a chuckle.

"Yes, and Dawson? You're on speakerphone."

Silence. "Ah. Um...hi, Livi's hot friend."

Prudence cleared her throat. "Nice to meet you, Dawson."

"Okay, you said...genie?"

I glanced back at Thomas, who nodded. "Yes. Actually, djinn. West specifically said *afreet.*"

"After the dragons I think I'm just gonna go with it and not ask questions."

"That's probably best. I don't suppose you know how to contact Laurel?" If anyone knew at least where Ashford was and maybe *what* he was, it would be her. It wasn't like anything worse could happen by talking to her.

"She *was* staying here at the hotel but I haven't talked to her since last night. I tried earlier for you but no answer."

I sighed. "She told me this morning she'd already resigned."

"Yeah, I think she was leaving town. My flight back to Austin leaves in six hours and it's not like we're BFFs."

Fuck. "If you can keep trying to ring her, I'd appreciate it."

"Will do. Next, you want Ashford's property records?"

"That would be lovely."

Thomas caught my eye. "This *really* isn't a good idea."

"By the way," I spoke to Dawson while looking at Thomas, "West left two of his people here to babysit. I'm not supposed to be pursuing this. So Pru's going to give you some contact information and you two can coordinate over Skype instead." I rose and handed the phone to Pru, then went to Thomas and gestured for him to follow.

We rounded the corner where Pulaski waited by the back door, looking out on a grim, rainy day.

"You both know as soon as I have a location I'm going to leave," I said in a low voice, not waiting for them to respond. "And that's just going to piss off West that you let me get away. *Help me*, here."

"We don't know—" Pulaski started.

"You said you were *briefed*." My gaze flickered back and forth between them, eye level to look at Pulaski and up to the point it was almost a strain to gauge Thomas. "And that I'm caught in the middle of something here. Who do you work for?"

Pulaski shot his partner a look.

"She's not stupid," Thomas said. "West should've told her to start with."

"We're not authorized—"

"We are *so* authorized—"

"But not to tell her *that*, just—"

"But *that* is the thing that might get her to stay—"

Jesus, they were like an old married couple. "Tell me *what*, boys?"

"Oh, oh, oh, *wait* a second," Dawson called from the other room. "Hold on. You're with that agency, PTI, right?"

Thomas and Pulaski exchanged looks.

"I'll take that silence as a yes," Dawson said.

I rearranged the letters a few times in case I missed something but nope, still clueless. "You're what now? PTI?"

When they didn't answer, I spun and headed back. Pru had him on cam and apparently the audio picked up my conversation. "What the fuck?"

"Pulse Threat...Investigation?" he said. "Or Intelligence? One of those."

I glanced over my shoulder at the two men who'd followed; neither confirmed nor denied, and Pulaski had developed a tic in his jaw. "And they...investigate Pulse threats, I take it?"

"They're like the CIA," Dawson responded. "With a dose of the FBI. But yeah, for Pulse-related stuff."

Which meant anything supernatural, I guessed. "American?"

"World. Small numbers, though."

Interesting. Once more I studied the two PTI members in my living room. "West works for them? He's undercover investigating this...djinn, Ashford?"

No answer.

"He's probably like a NOC," Dawson said. "Right? It makes *so* much sense—West has gotta be an intelligence operative undercover. Oh my god, is he your handler? And you're assets he recruited?"

Dawson was getting far too geeked out over this and losing the focus, so I attempted to steer the conversation around again. "Is your organization sending a team in to get my daughter or is your boss merely winging it?"

"Ashford," Pulaski relented at last, "hopefully doesn't *know* who he is."

"Except he changed the plan," Thomas pointed out.

Pulaski waved him off. "Yeah, but that could mean anything—didn't mean he didn't trust West. His cover might not be blown."

"Yeah, but—"

"You two, I don't know what the fuck you're talking about." I waited but they both went silent, so once again I worked on filling in the blanks. "Mr. Rolph," I said as realization dawned. "West recommended him—he was PTI too..." *Which would explain why Dawson couldn't find any info on him.* "So he's also part of this intelligence agency. He was supposed to get the ring for your organization. Did Ashford hire me for extra help or because he didn't trust West's recommendation?"

Pulaski blew out a heavy breath. "We haven't figured it out. Maybe. Maybe not. But West won't blow his cover yet—he spent three years getting this deep."

"Ashford and West are playing a game of chicken with my daughter's life."

The guys looked at one another in a way that was *not* easing my blood pressure. So I was definitely on my own, then.

"Ashford owns..." Pru frowned at her computer. "Like an eighth of the property in all of New Bristol. There's a *lot* to sift through. What was the address on the contract you signed?"

Shit, like I could remember. I stalked over to the filing cabinet by the computer desk and rifled past disorganized bills and tax returns until I found Ashford's contract. The address on the letterhead was from an office downtown, definitely not his home. "No go."

"At least that's one to cross off?" Dawson offered.

Not making me feel any better. We didn't have *time* to check out all these things. I glanced at the landline, expecting it to ring any time with another threat and demand regarding the Seal. I'd give it to him now, in a heartbeat. I should've to begin with.

"This Seal..." I cast my gaze at the fuzz. "When I gave Ashford the fake one, he put it on. I'm assuming it's not to become Dr. Doolittle."

"It controls djinn," Thomas said. "It controls *everything*, pretty much, even Pulse-born. Everything except humans."

Pulaski clutched his head in his hands. "Oh my god, *stop talking*."

Thomas elbowed him. "Shut up. Might as well."

"West's gonna kill us."

Jesus, *I* was gonna kill them soon. "So he puts on the ring, he controls—"

"A lot," Thomas said. "So none of us can get near him. Humans can too easily be killed and anything Pulse-born—with non-human DNA—can be controlled as soon as he puts that ring on."

And Mr. Rolph had been rather concerned when I asked about using the ring. "So can't I just put it on and *force* him to—"

"Not unless you want to be fried from the inside out," Pulaski said with a sigh, apparently deciding there was no keeping mum on this. He was probably right—only truth would potentially dissuade me.

"I was wearing it, though—Tucker wore it."

"You have to *want* to use it," he said. "It hears your want and if you pay the price, its power is yours. But if *you* actually try to use the Seal, it'll kill you. It takes magic juice to power without injury, or someone from Sulaiman ibn Da'ud's line."

Magic juice... "Djinn power, then?"

"Yep. Purebred at that."

"And Ashford's not just any djinn," Thomas said. "This is Musa ibn Sakhr."

I resisted the urge to bang my head on the coffee table. "Look, *I don't speak djinn names*."

"Son of Sakhr," Dawson spoke up from the laptop. "He's like a *royal* djinn, Liv."

I was glad *someone* was googling during my crisis. "Okay. This is sounding worse and worse." Ashford was going to use the one thing that could control him to control everyone else, and although my daughter was still my focus, I didn't like that way the more horrors kept piling up here. "And precisely how dangerous is he going to be once he gets this ring? End of the world bad?"

"Not directly, no," Thomas said. "No plagues or rivers of blood. But *afreet* are nasty fuckers. Djinn in general aren't much different from people—good, bad, and in between. *Afreet* are of the bad."

"He won't end the world," Pulaski took over. "But Ashford's stuck here. They don't stick them in bottles, but the Seal could confine them to places. He's been here awhile."

Three thousand years of confinement is akin to death. Yeah, that was awhile. "If he gets the ring, he can leave," I said.

"And he'll be able to do whatever the hell he wants without a damn thing to stop him," Thomas said. "He will kill you, your daughter, your friends, just for defying him. No laws. No punishments. PTI can't stop him. Conventional weapons can't hurt him."

Information that would've been helpful to me *yesterday*. At least I was seeing the big picture here, though I didn't like it at *all*. I was starting to suspect my brother might be more involved with this than I realized, but doubted they'd tell me much more outside of what I already knew about Ashford and West.

"You say conventional," I pressed. "Non-conventional, then? What does that entail?" *Please say a rocket launcher—maybe I can get one of those.*

"Magic," Thomas said simply.

I blinked. "Magic? Any kind, or—"

"Susceptible to djinn control," he started.

"*If*," Pulaski broke in with a meaningful look, "used by a djinn equal to or greater than him in power."

And since I wasn't currently up to date on where to locate a Local Djinn Directory, I was shit out of luck. So I had no plan. Nothing workable, at least; it wasn't like this was a problem I could solve by jumping in its mouth and driving a sword through its brain.

Unless I find Ashford, give him the Seal, and hope for mercy.

"I appreciate you telling me these things," I said to the two agents. "It's given me a lot to think over. I just hope West can touch base soon."

Both men seemed to relax, which was my intent: shoulders dropped, expressions softened, like this whole time they'd been expecting me to punch them.

"Please, go ahead and make yourselves at home." I gestured to the laundry room which was little more than a closet. "Dry your things, help yourself to food, pull up a chair." When

I felt they accepted this, I turned to head back to my chair to sit and stew.

Denny's hand wrapped around my wrist and halted me as he leaned over to speak next to my ear. "What about your dad? For narrowing the location down?"

Of course Denny knew me and knew I wouldn't lay down arms that easily. My father was worth a shot, I supposed. I nodded, scooped my cell phone from the coffee table, and left the living room with a nod to the PTI guys. "Going to take a shower," I said and they didn't object, instead focused on their damp clothes and the dryer.

In the bathroom, I shut the door behind me and perched on the edge of the tub, staring at the phone as the minutes ticked by. I didn't actually *have* my father's number—he'd changed it at least once, if not more, since he'd disowned me so many years ago. It was Martin I texted, informing it was an emergency and I needed Dad's number *now*.

Ten minutes later he sent it, questioning what was going on.

I ignored him.

My stomach in knots, I dialed my father. Martin could've sent me straight to his assistant or his lawyer or any other number of people, but it was Dad's voice that answered four rings in.

"Yes?"

I swallowed a thick lump in my throat, feeling transported back to when I was a freaked out newly turned eighteen-year-old, in the bathroom with a pregnancy test, thinking about telling my father. But that wasn't me anymore—the worst had happened, he was *capable* of the worst, and I had to keep my head on for Em. "Don't hang up."

Silence. At least he *didn't* hang up on me, though, which was why I opened with that instead of a regular greeting.

"Something's happened. There's a local man named Moses Ashford—he took her. Took Emaleth."

More silence. Not promising.

"I don't know where she is. I know he owns property all over but I don't have time to narrow it down. You know damn near everyone important around here—I just need to know where his house is so I can find her." When he didn't respond, I chanced, "Dad?"

"And this concerns me, *why?*"

Shit, shit, shit... My voice fell to a whisper. "I need help."

"You have *willfully* gotten yourself into trouble your whole goddamn life, Olivia, and I stopped bailing you out years ago."

I clenched the phone, my stomach bottoming out. "This isn't about me, it's about your six-year-old granddaughter."

"Wherever you go, chaos follows. It always has."

"Please—"

"Did you not think of this from the start? Instead of picking the safe route you always had to be so brazen, so *right*, so willing to cut your own path. *You* put your child in danger. *You* let this happen. It is *your* mess to fix."

"Daddy..." My lips trembled around the word. "Please. I'm sorry. I'll do whatever you want, *I'm sorry*, I just... Please, I'll never bother you again, I'll never—"

"There's no such thing as that with you, Olivia, and I'm done with it."

My father ended the call.

33
DICK ASSIST

———◆———

I SLIPPED FROM THE EDGE of the tub and sat in a heap on the cold bathroom linoleum, unsuccessfully fighting tears.

At the end of the day, I felt like a child. A stupid little girl who just wanted Daddy's approval, who expected him to sweep in and save the day. Over and over, no matter how angry I got, I expected him to eventually forgive me—to ask for *my* forgiveness. In the back of my mind was a picture of my father swinging Emaleth up in his arms, out on picnics, sitting around a Christmas tree. And as stupid as those thoughts had always been, they withered further now until they were unrecognizable.

Maybe I hadn't been clear enough. Maybe he didn't know how dangerous Ashford was, maybe he thought it was a front for some kidnapping scheme and I was going to ask for money. But what he thought or knew didn't matter.

He was going to let her die.

I bowed my head, my chest shaking with sobs, tried to keep my lips sealed shut—if I kept the noise in, if I pretended I wasn't crying, maybe I'd stop. Maybe I'd believe myself.

There was still a chance, of course. A chance that West would get her back—that everything would be okay. He might have a plan he hadn't let us in on yet. But West's orders were clearly to remain undercover and get whatever dirt he was searching for on Ashford. Keep the ring from him at all costs. *Not* a rescue mission. How could he get Em without exposing himself? Surely Ashford would notice a child missing after his enforcer showed up.

If either of them were still alive.

I rubbed at my eyes—no, I wasn't going to think like that. I had to pick myself up and keep going forward. If I tried and failed, I'd live with myself more than if I didn't bother at all and instead trusted a stranger to solve this for me.

There had to be someone. I could try Martin again, maybe. Perhaps he could narrow things down. Perhaps Pulaski and Thomas could get authorization from their superiors to tell me something. Perhaps I could call and offer a deal with Ashford, assuming his cell phone hadn't been destroyed in the fire. There had to be *someone*, too, that Pru or I knew who had contacts. Someone well-connected like my father, someone local, someone...

I blinked until my vision cleared and lifted my phone again, cycling through the numbers until I found the one I wanted, glad I hadn't deleted it. I dialed and waited, hoping—

"Olivia," he answered right away.

I winced. "Dick."

A pause. "Richard."

Right. "Richard, I'm so sorry for not touching base with you sooner; I was out of the country."

"Your friend mentioned that. She said you were sick with malaria."

"Turns out I got better—I think it was just food poisoning. I wish this was a social call, too, but I just got back and I could use some help."

"Did they arrest you again?"

So he knew about that too. I tried not to cringe—it was, after all, basically the reason why I was calling him. "Thankfully, no. I'm trying to find someone. The guy who hired me—he's reneged on paying me and I'd like to drop by for a visit but I don't have his address."

"Oh, sure thing. What's his name?"

"Moses Ashford."

"Moses...Ashford..." Keys clicked in the background. "He owns a lot of property."

"So I've heard. I'm looking for a house, though. A rather large one."

"It might take some time."

Not like I had any other leads. "The sooner the better, but I understand." Before he could try talking to me about dinner or flowers or whatever else he wanted to pester me about, I continued. "I really appreciate it, Richard. I'll be home all evening—long trip, so I'm off to take a nap, but text me when you have something."

"Sure, Olivia—"

I hung up before that could go any further and sat with the phone in my hands, staring at the LCD screen.

Someone rapped softly on the door and I swiped at my eyes. "I'll be there in a few."

"Liv?"

Denny.

Before I could object further, he cracked open the door. I saw his face peek around before he saw me, his eyes moving across the small bathroom and then shifting downward to where I was crumpled on the floor. He slipped inside and eased the door shut.

I dragged my fingers under my eyes and blinked furiously. "Yeah, so that didn't go well."

He eased onto the floor, folding his long legs to fit in the narrow space between the bathroom cabinet and tub with me. "Did he hang up?"

"Worse." I set the phone aside and hugged my knees, avoiding his eyes.

"Want me to try?"

I smiled vaguely. "He always liked you." Hell, Daddy *loved* Chase. He used to brag to his friends, *Such a nice boy*. But Denny calling him for this would probably just remind him even more of why he was pissed at me. Remind him I hadn't been a good girl and married my high school boyfriend—remind him that I didn't even know who Emaleth's father was, the night of her conception like so many others where I was ridiculously drunk and partying hard.

Denny would deny up and down that he was anything but Em's biological father, but my dad knew better.

I sniffled and shook my head. "He's a dead end with this one. But I called another guy—he'll hopefully get back to me with an address tonight."

"And then?" He leaned back, unwound some squares of toilet paper from the roll, and handed them to me; my eyes were leaking again, damn it, and I accepted the offer and tried to dry them.

"Then I have to find a way out of the house. And get my keys back from Pulaski. And leave without two"—*not fully human*—"bodyguards knowing."

Keys jangled as Denny reached into the pocket of his still-damp jeans and retrieved them, and he offered the ring to me. "We take my SUV."

We.

He still thought we were in this together.

I glanced up at him then, his brown eyes warm and forgiving. Always so forgiving. I accepted the keys.

His fingers lingered against mine for a moment before releasing the ring. "We'll need a distraction."

I whirled the keys around while I pondered it. "Pru. She can fake some kind of attack, send everyone scrambling for help."

"Out in the kitchen, out of view."

I nodded. "And we can slip out the back."

"As soon as you get the address."

It was *something*, at least. An okay plan.

I looked again at sweet, loyal Denny. He loved Em so much—he was exactly the father to her that I wished I had myself. And I wished I was a different person—wished he was what I wanted, what I needed. Wished I could lose myself in him. That I loved him.

But I wasn't a different person and I couldn't fake what was there. Still, I'd forever be grateful for the place he had in our lives.

I hoped he'd forgive me when I left him behind.

———————— ◆ ————————

THE DREARY AFTERNOON TURNED INTO a dreary evening.

I'd returned to the living room and didn't say anything about what I'd been doing, but my eyes were red from crying so the boys didn't push regarding the lack of shower noises while I'd been gone. I sat and fought tangles in my hair, then worked it into a long French braid to hang down my back and out of my face. Had more bourbon. Talked idly with Dawson and Pru about royal *afreet* djinn, which as everyone had warned sounded pretty fucking unkillable. Prudence talked me into dinner and at least the peanut butter sandwich I wolfed down didn't make me feel ill.

At 7:18, Dick Moss texted me with an address.

I stared at the message for about a minute and a half, fingers trembling around my phone, before I keyed in my thanks. He responded that he'd call but he was in a meeting and would talk to me later, and when I assured him there was no rush, I meant it—despite my gratitude. This stranger had come through over my father, and that tempered any previous irritation I had with him. But I truly could *not* talk then anyway.

I had to move.

Thomas and Pulaski were in the kitchen eating pizza. I sent a text to Denny across the room.

It's time.

His phone pinged and he answered it, then glanced at me.

I sent a similar message to Dawson to pass to Pru—no idea where her cell phone was now—except this time I included the address to Ashford's place: in case I didn't come back, she'd have to send the police somewhere and would need it, but I could trust she wouldn't follow herself, unlike my ex. I followed it up with, *Tell Pru don't give it to Chase.* A few moments later, she looked me, then Denny, then nodded.

We were good to go, then.

Pru rose and started for the kitchen, calling loudly over her shoulder, "Anyone want something?"

Denny was already angling toward the back door. "We're good, thanks."

I rose. Waited.

Something crashed in the kitchen and I bolted around the corner, making a show of being concerned; Thomas had Pru's arm as she struggled to stand, looking weak and faint.

"My meds," she gasped. "I'm so tired, and I forgot to take them—"

"I'll get them," I offered lightly, backing up.

Pulaski's brows dropped into a deeper frown as he looked at me, immediately suspecting something was fishy. I started to say something, then my eyes purposely looked toward the back door, which Denny was already opening. My brows shot up, lips parted in surprise, and Pulaski took the bait, bowling past me to stop him.

I didn't *want* to throw him under the bus, of course. But I also didn't want to worry about him while I was at Ashford's, and a secondary distraction was the only way I'd get past the "guards" here.

I backpedaled in a hurry.

I ghosted down the hall, straight for the front door. My gun harness waited there, loaded and ready; I slipped it over my shoulder, tossed a long black coat overtop, pinched my boots under my arm, and silently eased the front door open. Denny was shouting at Pulaski at the back of the house and Thomas hadn't left Pru yet. A glance over my shoulder revealed I hadn't been caught, so I slipped outside and silently pulled the door closed behind me.

The rain had eased a little but the pavement was cold and wet, and I sloshed through puddles as I raced for Denny's black Cadillac Escalade. Pulaski still had my own car keys—he could follow, even if they didn't have another vehicle stowed elsewhere. Once I popped open the door of the Escalade and stuffed my things inside, I pulled the knife from its sheath tied to my gun holster and punctured the two nearest tires of my own car. It would be money I didn't have to fix later, but fuck it—I'd walk wherever I needed to go. The important thing was that they didn't catch up to stop me.

I cast the knife on the passenger seat, pushed the key in the ignition, and stepped on the accelerator in bare feet as I peeled out of the driveway. If they heard me, if they ran out the door to check on me, I didn't know, didn't see—my eyes were focused on the road ahead, gleaming in orange streetlight, and my destination on the outskirts of the city. The Seal of Solomon was, once again, tucked in my bra, and I was more than prepared to hand it to Ashford and beg for our lives if I had to.

I'm coming, Em.

34
FREEDOM

———— ◆ ————

ASHFORD'S ESTATE WAS A FULL-blown villa.

The sprawling, three floor mansion branched out with various wings up front, sitting up a slightly inclined driveway I could see from the road that approached it. Garden lights shone up over white fresco and the textured roofs looked terracotta. Black gates lay open at the start of the driveway, no one out there to warn visitors away.

He was most likely expecting me.

The rain had completely stopped after a half hour of driving, though the tires spun through puddles on the way to the villa. I'd taken back roads to get there, then pulled over to the shoulder to slip on my boots, gun holster, and jacket before continuing on again, so I was ready to go. The driveway led straight for the house, past a dark, mowed lawn and artfully sculpted bushes. The place was very...proper. Very put together. Very formal, which shouldn't've surprised me regarding Ashford, but I expected more of a villain lair, not a house I'd feel totally at home in. Of course, I'd known my share of privileged monsters and wealthy bad guys; I supposed I was merely used to a different sort of evil, like the kind who usually voted Conservative.

I parked Denny's Escalade in front of the house and climbed out with trepidation.

Though I braced, no one darted out to meet or attack me. My gaze tracked the house—there were windows to climb through, no doubt multiple doors, but the main entrance lay ahead, lit and inviting. If he was expecting me to somehow find him, there was no sense in being stealthy.

I climbed up the handful of wide, shallow steps, my footfalls quick and tapping on the cobblestone. Though my long coat covered my guns, I kept my hands at my side ready to draw. Potted plants sat tall, ominous on either side of the massive front doors. The knocker on each door was the face of a lion, and I skipped grasping the ring in their mouths, instead going straight for the handle.

The door I tried opened easily. It swung wide and I stared, looking for guards or something.

But it wasn't within I had to worry about; a hand grabbed my forearm outside.

I swung around, broke the hold immediately, and followed up with a strike to my attacker's nose.

Pulaski staggered back, cupping his face against the mess of blood my hammerfist had caused and mumbled something quite uncomplimentary. Thomas was at my other side.

Great.

"So you *don't* know where Ashford lives?" I asked coolly, eyeing them and tensing for a fight should they try to grab me again.

"We don't. Didn't." Thomas had his hands splayed. "But we were tapped into your phone messages and had a car around the block."

"And took the main roads," Pulaski added, voice muffled behind his hands.

Son of a bitch. "I will shoot you both before I let you take me anywhere."

They exchanged glances. Finally Thomas turned to me with a sigh. "Backup? It's best if we stay out of view anyway."

That, I could work with. I nodded. "Stay the hell behind me. Like, don't enter a room until after I've been through it or I've signaled you—I don't want him knowing I have help."

"What's the signal?" Pulaski asked, his sleeve soaking up the blood from his nostrils now.

"Probably me screaming. Em's gotta be the focus—if you can, grab her and run like hell." I turned back to the open front door, took a breath, and forced a step inside before I could talk myself into going in another direction, with the weight of two agents at my back.

The foyer was open concept, floor marble, and two wide white staircases forty feet ahead curved and marched upward. Between them was a massive white arch and long burgundy runner than traced a path into a room beyond. Light flickered from sconces and the chandelier above; past the archway ahead flashed flames in darkness, likely—hopefully—from a fireplace and not Ashford playing pyro again.

Ashford had said—and Pru confirmed—that he'd had Em in his drawing room. Halls branched left and right, and with just the front of the villa as an example, I could be searching for hours, even with help from the others. And he could've moved her. Briefly I abandoned the plan to run room to room, hoping to get out before being caught, and instead marched forward. Carpet muffled my steps as I passed the staircases, though the fluttering of my pulse in my ears would've drowned it out anyway.

Gooseflesh prickled my skin under my jacket, my heart sped. I glanced from side to side as I walked, but nothing moved around me, the place eerily still. The villa brought to mind Kadhim cave system, vast and foreboding; if dragons had popped out, I wouldn't've blinked at all. True to their word, Pulaski and Thomas kept well behind, following my lead. I figured that would last about as long until West found out and yelled at them, but for now I didn't object to having them at my back.

I stepped through the archway, down another short corridor. Beyond, a massive room opened up, making it a good eighty feet long, half that wide, and ceiling going up three stories. Mirrored fireplaces on either side of me flickered flames against the darkness; otherwise only sconces and candles lit the expansive room.

Furniture was relegated to the walls, antique divans, end tables, and potted plants aplenty; all were behind columns and shadowed. While the front of the villa was contemporary and bright, this was old world and lush, with dark wood and burgundy curtains over massive windows. Over tapestry-flanked fireplaces sat decorative scimitars in scabbards. Stairs ran along the back, curving like the ones in the foyer and leading to a mezzanine level that rounded the room, dark closed doors beyond.

Movement caught my attention and I stopped to watch; Ashford walked along the second level on my left, strolling calmly with his hands knotted behind his back, head slightly bowed. His suit was again black, pressed, and probably not the one he'd been wearing while Kent House burned. He turned at the back of the room, went down steps to a middle landing, then down the stairs that led to the ground floor, and started forward. No hint of injury from the fire marred him; as he lifted his head and stared straight ahead at me, I saw nothing that even suggested burns.

Ashford stopped across the room from me, holding my stare. I didn't flinch, didn't breathe, and certainly didn't reach for my guns—not yet. No, I waited. He hadn't looked over my shoulders, so with any luck the PTI agents were keeping well out of sight.

"You have that look of knowledge now, Miss Talbot," Ashford said. "It's in your eyes. It's aged you."

My face was also scraped and black and blue which no doubt tacked on a few years, but I caught his drift. "Yet I don't think I'm as old as you, Musa."

"I have not used that name in a very, very long time."

I'll bet.

"Now do we need to have a repeat of our earlier discussion?"

I swallowed and hoped like hell I could actually drag some confident-sounding words out. "No. No games. I just want my daughter—you can have the Seal, I'm not a part of this."

"Then hand it over unless you'd prefer I pluck it from your corpse."

If he was truly sure I wore it currently, I figured he'd murder me on the spot without a doubt. What stayed his hand was likely the possibility of it being missing and my death cutting off his chance to find it.

I pushed. "Let me see Emaleth is okay first."

"Very well." He unclasped his hands, let his right hang at his side while his left lifted slightly, gesturing.

To my right, two figures stepped out of the shadows. Em was in her pink unicorn pajamas, probably what she'd been wearing when they grabbed her and Pru at night. Her eyes were wide, long brown hair hung disheveled, but she looked unharmed.

She wouldn't remain that way for long; the silver face of a long-bladed knife was inches from her throat, though at least out of her line of vision. I followed the hand that held it, up the arm in a dark shirt, past broad shoulders to a face I was quite familiar with.

West's eyes were dark in the low light, steady, face expressionless as he threatened my daughter. My chest heaved, rage rising at the sight, and it took everything in me not to give in and pull out my guns and put a hole in his fucking head on the spot.

He was an operative, they *claimed*. Undercover. One of the good guys. He'd tried to keep me from giving the Seal to Ashford at every turn, and the man before me was admittedly a bad guy, so that put a check in West's favor. *He does his best given how he was raised, but he doesn't see the world as you or I do,* Mr. Rolph had said. West didn't have mere issues, he had *subscriptions*.

And being a white hat didn't mean being virtuous; I wouldn't trust Emaleth's life in his hands for a second.

"The Seal," Ashford said calmly.

My gaze flickered to him for a moment, then back to West. Buttons gave the slightest shake of his head—it could barely be considered a movement, but his eyes widened as well. *No.* No, don't give Ashford the Seal. No, *trust* that despite the position he had my baby girl in, West wouldn't harm her.

Like if I just did everything I was supposed to for him, we could walk out of here alive.

I glanced down at Em. No, I'd take my motherfucking chances with the madman on my own. I'd leapt in the mouth of a dragon three days ago; surely I could take a guy in Armani.

I slowly raised my hand and pulled out the small black satchel tucked under my shirt, between my bra and skin. The ring slid out easily, pinched between my index finger and thumb, and I let the satchel fall. I'd removed the fake pieces with acetone just as West had suggested and there was no trace of the glue now, just the shining face of brass and gemstones.

"Do hold up your end of the bargain now." Ashford sounded *weary*, of all things. Not remotely homicidal, just as tired as his apparent age suggested. Three thousand years trapped here, supposedly, which raised more questions I wasn't ready to consider yet. I didn't care, damn it, not about the Pulse, not about this other world—I just wanted my kid back.

"Give me my daughter first and I'll toss it to you. It's not like I have anyone from the Solomonic Dynasty here. I can't use it to hurt—"

"That ring is my *freedom*."

He took a few slow, steady steps forward; I eased back on instinct.

"This isn't the Disney version, Miss Talbot. We don't sing a song and ride away on a carpet at the end. Thousands of years of confinement is something you can't even comprehend and you *will* hand me my freedom or I will take it."

I squeezed the ring and it flared hotly between my fingertips in warning.

My gaze darted between Ashford and West. This was between them, not me. Not my fight. A deep breath wasn't helping; my heart pounded at a jackhammer pace, thumping hard against my ribcage like it wanted out. The agents still hadn't entered—perhaps they waited just outside, perhaps they were finding another way to watch the room. Regardless, though the distraction would be nice, I still preferred it seeming as if I was alone.

For a final time, I met West's eyes, and he continued to give me the warning stare without actually moving. But he had to know how this would go—had to if he had received any kind of briefing on me, or done any kind of research, which he seemed to have done.

Resolved, I looked at Ashford, rolled my shoulder back, and tossed the ring toward him.

35
CURSE OF THE PULSE-BORN

———— ♦ ————

THE RING FLEW IN A wide arc, spinning mid-air. Ashford's eyes tracked it. So did West's.

I drew both guns at once; my focus was on the smaller target to my left, pointed at the Seal, while my right aimed at West. There was no hesitation as I squeezed both triggers.

One bullet pinged the ring, spun it far to the left and tossed it somewhere in the shadows, because I have one hell of an aim with my pistols.

The second popped West; he jerked back, blood spraying dark across the floor, and the knife clattered at his feet.

I didn't wait to see where the ring landed, where I'd hit West—nothing. Instead I holstered my guns and beat across the floor for Em.

She stood shaking for a moment, trembling like she was about to fall apart and hyperventilate, then she scrambled away from West and raced toward me barefoot, tears freely falling, her tangled hair trailing behind her. She didn't get far as I was already there, crouching, ready as she jumped and landed hard in my arms. I staggered back on my heels but held her tight.

Though she sobbed in my ear, I steeled my heart to it—I didn't have time to break down. Her knees dug into my hips, arms tightened around my neck until I could scarcely breathe but I didn't care, didn't tell her to let up—I was too happy to have her in my arms again.

"You need to run to the door, baby," I said against her hair. "Run real fast."

"Mommy—"

"I'll be right behind you." *But I need to cover our exit.* "Don't look back, just *run.*"

She reluctantly let me go and the moment her feet touched down, I urged her forward. I rose again on weary legs and looked back at West.

I'd hit his chest, the side opposite his heart. The 9mm hole wasn't big but the tear in his shirt leaked blood. He blinked up at me and shifted, once again showing a resilience few were capable of even though I'd weakened him.

I cocked a brow. "Coming with us, Buttons?"

He grumbled something and didn't move; I refused to wait, instead turning to run.

Em raced ahead, through the archway for the hall, and squealed as someone swooped down and grabbed her.

I had both guns aimed, fingers on the triggers, but it was Thomas who scooped her up. She peered back at me with frightened eyes but I gestured for the exit. "He'll help, just keep going."

She didn't fight him, just went with it as Thomas started in the opposite direction.

I hadn't gone three steps when Thomas cried out and collapsed.

I paused, started to turn, when something whispered through the air. Color flashed in my peripheral vision and I had barely the time to dodge when a ball of fire whirled past me. I hit the carpet, skidded with the guns painfully in my hands, and glanced up. The fire collided with the potted fern ahead and knocked the plant over, pieces of ceramic and dirt spitting across the floor among tiny flames.

I glanced over my shoulder, hair cutting across my eyes. Ashford stood off to the side, the Seal of Solomon on his index finger and glinting in the light. Blackness rose above him, starting behind his shoulders and unfurling—wings of black smoke, twisting and snapping as if with a sentience of their own. Fire played under his skin, as if his flesh went translucent to expose the red, orange, and yellow that combined to make him.

I lifted my guns and aimed them at his head. They couldn't kill him, no, but maybe they'd hurt like hell in the meantime.

But it was the sudden yelp at my back that froze me from head to toe.

I slowly turned to see Thomas with my daughter, his fingers gripping her shoulder so tightly she winced, and dragging her into the room. Pulaski appeared through the doorway and followed, his steps slow and body rigid. Fire flickered red in their eyes and both looked helplessly at me.

Shit.

"Miss Talbot."

Ashford drew my attention again, my body shifting, guns aimed straight at his smug forehead.

"Thank you for my ring. And Pulse-born to test it on."

And that was what they'd warned, no? They send humans, Ashford would kill them immediately; anyone else might be stronger but could be controlled by the ring if he got it.

Motherfucker. "Just let us go."

"You know..." He walked slowly, eying me, those horrible black wings twisting behind him. His flesh had returned to normal but I had no doubt the smokeless flames I saw beneath his skin moments ago remained in some capacity. "It's too bad—I had high hopes for you. You could've gone far under my employment but at your first chance, you betrayed me."

"You kidnapped my kid."

"Yes, but someone compelled you to double cross me before that. Isn't that right, West?"

West had gone back to a prone figure on the floor, as if I'd shot him dead. Of course, Ashford had to know he was faking, even if he didn't acknowledge it.

Unless he actually is *bleeding to death. Which would be my luck.*

"I'm not a fan of betrayal, Olivia. So how about we watch your offspring torn limb from limb before it's your turn."

I swung around again as Ashford gestured to Pulaski and Thomas.

"Subdue her," he said.

Thomas cast Em at his partner and started toward me, eyes still glowing, hands clenching into fists. "I'm...s...sorry," he managed to get out and I believed him—believed he had no desire to hurt me or Em, that it would kill him to do so.

But I also believed he didn't have a choice.

I squeezed off multiple rounds, guns popping, bullets peppering his torso, but he kept moving—whatever kept him from dying when hit by Tucker days ago didn't slow him down now either. Pain shone in his eyes but he'd been compelled not to care. Two feet away he knocked my arms to the side and I eased off the triggers with too great a danger of hitting Em. Thomas towered over me over by a foot, a wall of solid muscle.

His fist came toward me; I dodged, whipped my gun across the side of his face. Bloody spittle flew but didn't stop him. Another punch and I went ahead and dropped my guns, raised my hands, redirected and countered with a strike to his throat.

One foot stepped back but that was the only reaction I got. He came at me fast and a powerhouse punch struck my jaw, snapping my head to the side so suddenly I thought my neck could've broken. I staggered back, blinked, tasted blood as it welled against my stinging cheek and over my tongue. He followed through with another punch but my feet kicked in, taking me another two steps back so the hit glanced by my face. I reached, grabbed his shoulder, jerked, thrust him past me and bolted toward Em.

An arm wrapped around me from behind in a bear hug. My arms were trapped with little space but I got my right hand behind me, grabbed his groin and twisted.

Thomas huffed against my ear, started to double over, but didn't let me go—didn't matter what I did, what pain he went through, he couldn't fight Ashford's control. His other hand clasped my braid close enough to my scalp to control me and wrenched my head back until my neck was awkwardly bent and a pained yelp left my lips.

Emaleth was held six feet away and there was nothing I could do.

She looked at me with huge, frightened eyes, sputtering sobs, as Pulaski held her shoulder in one hand and arm in the other. He watched me too, the flicker of flames in his eyes. He shook from head to toe, face red and sweating. His lips were clenched together as if he fought the hold Ashford had on him.

No no no... I struggled, twisted. Screamed until I was hoarse. I wanted to tell her to close her eyes, that Mommy was here, that everything would be okay but I couldn't get the words out, couldn't even think as I launched into full panic mode.

A growl permeated the haze around my head, cutting through the confusion; movement to my right drew my attention as a large white tiger leapt. Ashford turned just as the beast landed on him and the *afreet* went down, skidding across the floor.

Thomas's grip on me loosened and I kept wiggling, gaining more space so I could slam my elbow into his ribs, stomp back on his foot, twist until I could slip from his arms. I jerked my foot behind his ankle and threw my shoulder into his chest to knock him down, then ran for Em.

My daughter, to her credit, had it engrained in her from the time she could walk that if anyone ever grabbed her, she had to get away, and in this instance I was glad; she didn't stand there passively as Ashford's hold slipped and Pulaski slackened, but twisted and punched at his lower half until she slipped away. She stumbled a few feet back and looked at me.

"Run!" I shrilled and she hesitated for barely a second before she listened, bolting away from Pulaski and from the room. She didn't look back and I hoped like hell she wouldn't stop for anything.

For a moment I nearly followed. But Ashford remained, the Seal in his possession, and if he defeated West, he'd come after us next. So I turned back to face the room.

West flew off of Ashford, struck the ground, skidded and then righted himself, climbing to his four feet and growling again. For a brief moment, he snarled at Thomas and Pulaski, who perhaps spoke tiger as they backed up and ran. His white coat was streaked with red and blood dripped on the floor, whether from his gunshot wound or tussle with Ashford, I didn't know.

Ashford began to rise, his lips curling and exposing his teeth. "'And beasts are bound to obey him.'" The air charged hotly, the Seal of Solomon on his finger flaring bright.

Oh shit, so I'm going to have to fight off West, too—

West stepped forward.

My breath caught.

The *afreet*'s eyes narrowed, flashing dangerously. Sweat beaded on his forehead but still the tiger strode forward, whatever control the ring promised not touching West.

Ashford tilted his head to the side, taking a step back. "What are you?"

What is he?

Slowly my gaze shifted to West again.

The tiger growled and ran, eating ground in seconds, powerful paws thumping. Muscles tensed and bunched as he leapt for the djinn.

Ashford swept his arm to the side, striking the tiger midair and knocking him back—shit, so maybe whatever the hell West was, they were still evenly matched. West scrambled again, took a swipe with one heavy paw, claws bared.

I scanned the room, saw my guns, and discarded the idea of grabbing them. There had to be something—

My gaze swept to the fireplace again.

I ran, casting a look at Ashford, though he was preoccupied and didn't notice me; when I was sure he'd all but forgotten my presence, I picked up my speed and narrowed my focus. The fireplace was massive, so I dragged over a divan from beside it and climbed on the edge. My fingers clasped the scabbard displayed on the wall and I pulled.

It held tight.

I rose on my tiptoes, swaying as my balance threatened to fail me, and grasped the hilt with both hands. A yank nearly sent me tumbling but the scimitar slid from its sheath, humming, firelight gleaming on the metal. The scimitar's weight was less than I expected, easy enough to handle, though I had exactly zero experience with swords.

I hopped off the divan and glanced back at Ashford just as fire swept across the floor in an arc straight for West. He dodged but flames singed and I could feel the heat even fifteen feet away.

For a moment the tiger's gaze struck me; whether or not he knew what I planned, I couldn't say, but Ashford saw the look too. The djinn glanced over his shoulder, his black brows deep in a frown and hair cutting across his brow. His jacket and pants were torn, whether he bled I couldn't tell. But his gaze traveled the scimitar in my hand.

Oh fuuuu—

Fire reamed toward me and I dove, missing it by inches. My coat flapped behind me, catching the flames, fabric crackling. I hit the ground, rolled, smothering the fire, then scrambled up and raced again just as West slammed into Ashford with a roar.

Tiger and djinn hit the ground again, West's aggression heightened further as he snapped, clawed, and did his damnedest to keep Ashford down and busy. I didn't waste the chance but ran, closing the distance rapidly with the scimitar at my side. My gaze narrowed on the Seal of Solomon sitting on his right index finger.

As his arm extended on the floor beneath the weight of West's paw, I swung the scimitar above my head and then let the blade drop.

36
'TIL YOU BURN...

———— ♦ ————

THE POLISHED EDGE OF THE sword sliced through skin and bone, severing Ashford's hand from his body.

He howled, thrashed. I backed up but West didn't, digging claws into his chest and *tearing*. Ashford's remaining hand grasped the tiger's neck and jerked him off, slammed him with a heavy thump against the floor. West struggled to rise but slumped, blinking.

Bleeding heavily from the stump, Ashford managed to rise, glaring at me. Those black wings unfurled again and this close I heard them, screaming and howling, faces twisting in the smoke. My stomach flipped and I took a step back as Ashford stood straight. My right foot sank back and I brought the scimitar up between us. Like I had a fucking *clue* how to wield it, but still.

Ashford lunged. I braced. But no hit came, no formal attack; instead his hand locked on the scimitar's blade. Heat flared out to brush my fingers and I dropped it on instinct. Metal hissed and bent under his touch, then he released the blade. The damaged, useless sword hit the floor between us.

Motherfucker. I gazed up at him wide-eyed, praying Em had made it out of the house and wasn't waiting in a corner for me.

I leaned back, started to turn, to run. His remaining hand jerked out again, clasped my throat, lifted me. I kicked wildly as his fingers tightened, tried to gain hold of the situation—jerked his pinky until it broke, but he didn't flinch, didn't acknowledge me, just hate edging his eyes. I had no doubt that once he put me down for good, he'd put the Seal on his other hand and make the others hunt my daughter no matter where she was, if he didn't do it himself.

A blur of movement and we fell, Ashford on me, heavy weight slamming into us as West pounced on his back. When the djinn twisted and slammed an elbow into West, I scrambled back. My heels dragged against the carpet and I was sweating under my tangled jacket but didn't have time to remove it. Ashford backhanded West and flames leapt again; the tiger dodged but not in time and let out a yelp of pain as fire cut across his shoulder, singing fur and blistering skin.

He's not going to stop. Shit. I could grab another sword, maybe take his head off? They said it wouldn't kill him, but would that even *slow* him?

Another flame leapt for West, still in tiger form.

I twisted onto my stomach and scrambled forward on my hands and knees, Ashford's missing hand and ring in sight. I clasped the bloody appendage, bone and meat peeking through, bile rising in my throat, and jerked the Seal off. Light hit the brass and it was warm to the touch; the stones on it blinked and sparked.

Bad idea, bad idea, bad—

I slipped the ring on.

I braced, though nothing happened. Of course, nothing had happened back in Ethiopia, either.

You have to want *to use it.*

Oh, I wanted it.

My gaze shot to Ashford; I turned, sitting, the idea of standing to face him too much for me to contemplate, and I clenched my hand into a fist. I watched him reach for West, grasp the tiger by the scruff of his neck, and slam him against the ground again—remembered the feel of his hand on my throat, the moment when he looked at my daughter with detached cruelty and directed innocent men under his control to kill her in the most painful way possible.

Anger, hate—it twisted in me, tearing through my veins, rushing to where the ring sat on my middle finger.

It hears your want and if you pay the price, its power is yours.

Em was somewhere outside of the building—if I didn't stop Ashford now, he'd kill me and go after her. Whatever price it required—even my own life—I'd pay it.

I panted, sucking in breaths though not fast enough to ease the ache in my lungs, my parted lips trembling. Heat rushed through my body, a painful tingle shooting down my forearm, wrist, and straight into my finger.

If you actually try to use the Seal, it'll kill you. It takes magic juice to power...fried from the inside out...

Ah, fuck it.

I pushed everything into the ring, forced my mind to empty and then focus on a single point: on Ashford stopping.

Pain blasted me and even as I unclenched my fist, it didn't abate, flesh beneath the ring sizzling. I screamed a wet, impotent cry but didn't let up, didn't turn my gaze.

Ashford froze.

Straightened.

Looked at me.

He started to take a step toward me but I *pushed* back, screaming again from the agony. No endorphins kicked in, nothing stopped the pain—not even the painkillers I'd taken for my bullet wound dulled it. Sweat beaded on my forehead, fell. Soaked my hair. All the air I breathed in was warm, scorching my throat and lungs. I was too exhausted, doubt filling me as I realized this was too much for me, and I slumped on my back. I couldn't hold him—couldn't keep him there.

They were right—I was about to boil from the inside.

My flesh blistered and sizzled under the ring, around it, and white hot spots played over my eyes. But I didn't give in on the desire to close them, to rest, to let go. Instead I kept pushing at Ashford until he raised his remaining hand and pressed it to his chest. His eyes widened, black smoke wings shuddered.

Only magic will do him in? Equal strength?

I could make that work.

Propped up on my elbows, struggling to keep my head up, heartbeat a blur like a hummingbird's wings, I thrust the Seal's power at him one final time until I saw the sparks fly from his fingers: pure red, smokeless flames spitting. Black spread across his skin, branching out farther and farther, twisting his flesh into singed flakes that trembled and faded.

It would spread from there. When his torso was ash, head tilted back as his own magic ate him whole, I slumped back, shaking and crying. Ashford crumpled into flakes in my peripheral vision and fire around the room ceased.

I released my hold on the Seal but the pain, motherfucker, *the pain* held on. It was too hot, too hot, too much, sweat drenching me as my body tried to cool, my temples flaring with the steady aching beat, my left hand in so much pain it was nearly numb.

Then West was sitting over me. Human form. His skin was streaked with soot in places, cuts and bruises. The bullet hole remained in his chest, high on the right, just below his collarbone and as he shifted over me, blistered white skin on his side was exposed.

"Stay with me," he said in a low voice. He tore the jacket— literally—from my body and my skin cooled, sweat drying instantly.

I gasped. Couldn't lift my left hand. Couldn't do much of *anything* but lie there while West reached for my arm. I knew what he was doing, knew it would hurt, but didn't have the energy left to brace for it or even beg him not too—instead I gave the barest of nods.

He pulled the ring off.

I screamed, arched, tried to flail but couldn't move. Tears leaked, rolled down my temples. I managed a glance over to see my mangled finger. It was still intact, at least, but the skin below my knuckle was white and blistered in the shape of the Seal's band, and the flesh around it varying shades of pink and red, signifying burns.

I slumped and he let my hand go. West was panting as well, his expression pained. Black hair was soaked with sweat and if I looked close enough, I could see blood around his lips still from

SKYLA DAWN CAMERON

where his tiger mouth full of teeth sank into Ashford again and again. He was sitting but leaned heavily on one hand beside me, still gazing down. And I still couldn't fathom moving, pain near unbearable.

"I forgot my cell phone," I said, my voice dry and monotone, as I stared at the ceiling. It almost seemed to be staring back and I strongly suspected I might pass out soon. "Maybe Ashford has a landline so you can get...the police or your department or something."

"Pulaski and Thomas are already on it." His voice was more weary than numb like mine and he rubbed at his face, as if that might wake him up.

Huh, maybe they did speak tiger. "Okay. I think I'll just lie here."

"Good idea." He didn't move either.

At least we were in agreement.

And then a pale voice said, "Mommy?"

I tried to sit up though my head spun, and barely got my shoulders off the ground when I saw Em running toward me. I hadn't the brain power to chastise her for not leaving the building, just accepted her when she dove down and flopped against me. Her arms wrapped around my neck and she sobbed into my hair. My left hand was still useless but I raised the right and held her tight to me.

"You're a fucking idiot, Olivia," West said beside me, shaking head as he eyed my left hand then pierced me with another stare.

I released Em for a moment to grasp half of my torn coat, and threw it over his bare lap. "And you are once again *naked*, Mr. West."

I let my shoulders sink on the carpet, patted Emaleth again, and heaved out a great breath.

West flopped on his back next to me with a groan as well.

Neither of us spoke or moved; there was just Emaleth's slowly subsiding sobs and the crackle of fire breaking the silence of the room.

Epilogue
Breathe Again

———◆———

THE STEADY TICK OF MY car's blinker punctuated the silence.

"You *need* to go to school." I drummed my fingers on the steering wheel while we waited at the lights, and cast Emaleth a warning look.

She gazed up at me, batting her sad, long-lashed eyes. "Please?"

This was ridiculous. She hadn't been to school in two *weeks*. I'd called and given the excuse that I fell ill after being in Ethiopia and decided it best to keep her home in case she was contagious. Practically speaking, it gave time for my lighter injuries to heal so I could leave the house without a whole lot of questions. My gaze flickered to my left middle finger, where a tender, healing wound remained—without gloves, an ugly mark would be a pretty obvious scar for my remaining life. The stitched up bullet gash on my right forearm was just as obvious but at least I wore long sleeves to cover it and West did an excellent job, or so I was told by the doctor who removed the stitches.

The real reason we skipped school, though, was that I wanted two weeks to lounge on the couch all day with my daughter in my arms. The novelty of that wore off with her after the first three hours but she tolerated me hovering so long as I kept handing her freshly baked cookies and left her in charge of television programming.

We talked. A lot. About everything. And I tried not to push her to do it, but that's my kid for you. Still wasn't sure she got it from me, but the way she picked herself up after trauma had to come from somewhere. I had her on a waiting list to see a therapist. For now it was me and Pru until I found someone who would take her long term on a sliding scale.

The light changed to green and the cars ahead of us moved. I could all but see her in my peripheral vision, sticking her lip out at me.

"I have to go back to the scary house," I warned her. "It might give you nightmares."

She cocked her brow skeptically. Okay, she *definitely* got that from me.

Last minute, I flicked off the blinker and went straight; the car behind me honked but I gave him the finger and kept going.

"Fine," I said. "But you're going *immediately* afterward. Understand?"

Em nodded, grinned, and sat back in her seat.

Little vixen.

We were headed for Ashford's villa. There was still the matter of payment, and apparently dead djinn had trouble coughing up cash, contract or no. Dale West—an intelligence *operative*, and I would never stop shaking my head over *that*— was to meet me there. Plus I had something to deliver and I was quite eager to be rid of it.

I drove us outside the city to where the villa waited, and in the bright morning light, it was a normal, stunning house. Interior would need some work, or at least that one big room would—blood in the carpets was a real bitch, and it had a bunch of fire damage. But the sprawling mansion with its well-kept gardens stood proud in the October sunshine, almost inviting as we drove toward it.

I glanced at Emaleth frequently but she showed no signs of being scared. Pulaski and Thomas had nearly killed her, and yet she accepted when the latter carried her out of the villa when an ambulance came and carted me out on a stretcher. Tough stuff, that little girl.

White gravel spit under my tires and flicked against the underside of the car. There were three other vehicles parked out front—none I recognized, but then agents could be milling around the djinn's house and I wouldn't be surprised.

I parked near the front and looked at Em again. "If you're coming in, you need to stay in sight *but* keep out of the conversation. Okay?"

She nodded and gave me her most innocent look, which suggested a whole lot of trouble was brewing. And I'd been so sappy lately, my Scary Mom Eyes did *nothing* to frighten her anymore.

As I released my seatbelt and pocketed my keys, my cell phone jingled. I half-expected Martin—he'd been calling and texting last night with lots of mentions of *urgency* and how I *had to* call him back *immediately*. But I ignored him because he's my brother and that's just how I played things, especially considering he still refused to tell me anything regarding what he knew about the situation I'd found myself in.

Instead the name and number surprised me. I climbed out of the vehicle and answered. "D...Richard. Hi." I'd ducked three of his calls during the past couple of weeks, which was surprisingly few, and I probably owed answering him at last.

"Hey, Olivia," he said in a warm voice. "Feeling better?"

Em slammed her car door, shoved her hands in her blazer pockets, and kicked at stones beneath her feet. If I didn't get moving, she'd get bored and god knows what would happen from there.

"Much, actually I'm about to head into a meeting."

"Ah, glad I caught you, though. You, me, dinner this week."

My lips parted to say no. He'd helped me find Em, yes. I appreciated that. But I wasn't sure I wanted dinner with the man—definitely didn't want to lead him on.

But then besides an overly eager streak, what had he actually done? Nothing. He wasn't a bad guy, that I could see. And...and maybe it would be fun. I'd nearly died. Nearly lost my daughter. And I could use a nice evening out after confining myself to the house for so long.

"Sure," I said at last. "Sure, Richard."

He took in a sharp breath, as if he honestly hadn't been expecting that, and I grinned absently. "Excellent. Thursday at eight?"

"Sounds great."

"I'll make reservations."

"I look forward to it." I ended the call and stared at the phone for a moment, then shook my head. It could backfire, but what the hell?

Emaleth was watching me as I rounded the car. "That's your Date Face."

I frowned at her. "My what?"

"Pru said. Date Face. The face you get when you're going out with a boy."

Pru and I would be having a talk later. I strolled past Emaleth and swept up the stairs. "I have no idea what you're talking about, Miss Talbot."

Gravel crunched underfoot as she chased after me.

I knocked on the front door but no one answered, so I tried the handle; it was open. We stepped inside and I braced for a shiver, but it didn't come. The villa foyer was bright and happy, relaxed during day. I glanced back and forth but still didn't see anyone.

Em shuffled in behind me and I shut the door. She peered around as well, then reached up and laced her fingers with mine. I gave her hand a squeeze and started forward, past the stairs and into a place I remembered all too well.

The huge, split level room where everything had gone down two weeks ago was quiet during daylight as well. No flames in the fireplace. Carpet singed and stained. But white light shone through the windows along every wall, almost giving it a cathedral feel.

Halfway into the room and movement caught my attention; I turned to see West standing in the shadows off to the side.

Em and I exchanged a look and she hesitantly released my hand, then padded ten feet away to poke at the empty fireplace.

I returned my attention to Dale West as he walked across the room to meet me. He looked no worse for wear, though admittedly I had no idea how someone part tiger would heal from the injuries he'd sustained. His "operative" clothes looked no different from normal ones, which I supposed was the point: jeans, a black T-shirt, and thick brown coat. A Cheshire grin was in place, which reminded me why I'd spent so much time wanting to shoot him.

West stopped in front of me. "How are you?"

"Playing at being a stay at home mom, so wonderful right now. You?"

"I've been undercover for three years and all they gave me was a three week vacation."

"I'd take that up with the union."

"I would if we had one. So?" He raised a brow in question.

I reached into my jacket pocket and withdrew the small box I'd put the Seal in. I'd temporarily kept it while his department got their shit together and sorted things regarding Musa ibn Sakhr, djinn prince—or at least officially. Unofficially, I told him I'd sell the fucking thing on the black market if no one paid me soon.

For a moment I hesitated, staring at the box. I'd said I'd sell it but, honestly, I wanted to be done with it. I'd always wear a scar from the thing and the longer it was in my possession, the more bothered I got. I handed the box to West without another glance.

He opened it, peered at the ring for a moment, then his gaze shifted up to meet mine. "The real one?"

"You're the only faker in the room, *Agent* West."

"Ouch."

A figure started across the room to join us—one I recognized.

"Moti?" I said.

Moti, one of the original members of our Ethiopia team—who had the sense to haul ass *out* when things got bad—smiled broadly at me. "*Attam jirta?*"

"*Nagaa*," I replied. West gave me a look but I offered no explanation—I'd simply desired to learn some Oromo and I was *so* goddamn bored over the past two weeks at home, it was my first area of study.

Though Moti stopped next to me, it was West he faced; the operative handed him the box. Moti opened the lid and peered at the Seal for a moment, something passing in the air I sensed but didn't quite understand.

"He wasn't just a local guide or caver," I said, recalling his argument with West after our initial rescue.

"He's one of the last known survivors of King Solomon's bloodline," West said.

So he could wield the Seal's power. And the conversation in the car while leaving Kent House as it burned—that's why they were stalling, trying to get a hold of him. "That means trouble for any *afreet* like Ashford who wants to misbehave, which is great, but what about the...Pulse-born, I think Thomas said?"

West winced. "Was there anything they *didn't* tell you?"

There was a lot but I didn't give him details. "Anyone like that would be susceptible. It's not the *afreet* I worry about, but them."

"He's on the PTI ethics council, so you don't need to be concerned."

That's supposing the council can be trusted. But I didn't say that aloud. Instead I returned Moti's nod when he gave me one, then he backed up and swiftly left the room.

"This is why we couldn't risk him," West continued. "Not in the cave when I saw how bad it was. And he was put in a safehouse when he left Ethiopia—I hadn't had time to reach him."

My thumb rubbed over my finger where the ring had singed my flesh. "They wouldn't send him here to just end the Ashford thing faster."

"No. Deemed 'too risky.'"

Whether to Moti's life or West's cover being blown, I didn't know. Or ask. I suspected I wouldn't like the answer. "Mr. Rolph was one of—"

"Yes," he said quietly, though he didn't need to.

A somewhat uncomfortable silence stretched.

"I suppose you want to know about payment," he said at last.

My stomach twisted unexpectedly and though I kept up my grin, it threatened to falter. "I'm not getting any, am I?"

"It's not the PTI policy to pay for this kind of thing. Expenses associated, yes, those would be reimbursed, but—"

"But *Ashford* already covered that. Right." *Motherfucker. MotherFUCKER.* I sighed. Clenched and unclenched my jaw. I knew I shouldn't still be wanting to shoot him—this part wasn't his fault, after all—but I might've if I'd brought my guns.

Or replacement guns, which I got to keep. They were expensive. I wasn't really *out* any money, honestly, and at least I had the fifty grand down payment from Ashford kicking around. Some of it was gone for rent and bills, new tires, taxes, and I was about to drop a rather substantial tuition check at Em's school.

Now I'd have to stretch that cash *far* and experience warned me how hard that was to do.

"I could possibly offer another solution, though," West said.

I didn't trust his smile one bit. "What?"

He started walking and I followed, down the center of the room with slow, steady steps. He glanced over the walls and sunlight hit his black hair. "Ashford's assets were all seized by us. You know how bureaucracy moves, too goddamn slow to be much use. It'll be many years before it works through the system and something's done with it."

"What are you saying?"

West stopped, turned to face me, and shrugged. Still smiling. "Want a villa?"

I let out the most unladylike snort imaginable. "You gotta be fucking kidding me."

"I could potentially ensure PTI would look the other way. The accounting department is very busy as it is. And it's the kind of house you're more accustomed to. You'd be paying bills, of course, so I'd think really hard about how much heat to use in winter..."

I shook my head and looked away. He was crazy. Fucking nuts. I'd come a long way and while I *wanted* this kind of home, I didn't *need* it now. I didn't. *Didn't.*

You don't need this, Olivia. But why didn't I believe myself?

That answer was simple, of course: every day I got up on my own, every time I got ready and headed out on a job, and every goddamn moment I looked at my daughter, I just wanted someone to swoop in and fix it all. I'd never grown up to leave the nest like normal kids: I'd been kicked out, tossed into adulthood, and had none of that learning stage in between. Although I had basically chosen my path, sometimes I got so damn tired I just wanted something of what I used to have *back.*

My gaze kept snagging the architecture. And of all the thoughts, it was Em running down halls as long as our current house that stuck in my mind, giggling and twirling, having the life she *should* have.

But again I shook my head. "I can't afford to live in a place like this. Even if the damn property tax was covered. Heat in the winter, air conditioning in the summer. Gas just to *get* here. And Pru's not going to be walking through here every day with—" I stopped abruptly. Her disorder wasn't a secret, but the less he knew about our lives, the better in my opinion.

"It has a pool," he offered. "Heated. You friend wouldn't need to travel for exercise."

So he knew about her MS. I shouldn't've been surprised.

"Besides," West continued, and he looked at me like he thought I'd already said yes and this was merely a formality. "This would make a good base of operations. Ashford lived here for a very, very long time. His library would be invaluable and you'd have space for help."

Now he'd lost me. "Help?"

A tilt of his head to the side and shapes moved to the left. I glanced over to see both Dawson and Laurel off to the side.

Laurel had her usual suit, this one in dove gray, with a pair of wired framed glasses and elegant black satin kitten heels. But her smile had warmth to it—warmth I believed, like she was happy to see me. And Dawson of course wore a big grin which was absolutely infectious. He waved; I returned the gesture before looking at West.

Yep, he already assumed he'd won.

"I can't afford a staff," I objected.

"Both could receive cuts of what you make."

Which brought us to the main issue, though. "Except I don't know if I'm staying in this line of work. I'm...very used to breaking limbs and nearly getting shot. But this..." My smile faded and I suppressed a shiver. "This was something else. He went after my child and my best friend."

West said nothing, likely because he couldn't. He held my gaze, of course, as I doubted he had it in him to look away from anyone, but there was no arguing with that.

And I pushed. "And he went after my family because of *you*. You and the PTI. He suspected you, he called your bluff, and I got tossed in the middle of it. I don't *want* anything from you guys. Ever."

"So what are you going to do? Waitress again?"

He really *had* done his research. My cheeks heated. "If it means I'm alive to see my kid grow up, yeah."

West nodded and he seemed to ponder it. "If you really think you can give it up..."

I didn't think I could. I certainly knew much of me didn't *want* to. But it was too soon to make decisions, the horrible things that occurred in this room too fresh in my memory. "Besides, as much as I want...*this*," I gestured around us, "I want to get it on my own terms. I'm not taking handouts from people anymore—I'll *earn* my way in this world, West."

Earning meant no one would ever be able to *take* from me again.

Which was another point he couldn't argue with, and to his credit, he didn't try. Instead he simply nodded, kept his mouth shut, and that seemed to quell my urge to shoot him.

I flicked my hand at Em and she thumped across the floor to my side, as if she'd been watching for my gesture. Probably trying to eavesdrop, too. She clasped my right hand and I led her toward Dawson and Laurel.

"That's the naked man, right?" she whispered *far* too loudly—all children only seem capable of embarrassing stage whispers, it seemed.

"Yes, and he's clothed now, so remember—"

"Don't tell Miss Jennings," she parroted with a frown, tugging on my hand and swinging my arm back and forth. "I *know*."

Hopefully his nudity wouldn't show up in a "How I Spent My Fall Vacation" class report this week.

Dawson and Laurel began walking with us toward the exit. I glanced back once at West to see he remained in the center of the room—the center of the sunlight, at that—watching us go. It took force to look away from him and focus ahead.

"So you declined?" Dawson asked.

Bastard had already apprised them of it. "Yep. Sorry. Did he bring you both out here just thinking I'd say yes?"

"No, we had to debrief," Laurel said.

Dawson sighed. "And debrief some more. And sign confidentiality agreements. West scares me."

"They sent some boring suits to my place last week for my debriefing and paper signing," I said. "Thankfully I avoided him in that instance."

"I can't believe he's PTI," Laurel said with the shake of her head.

"Am I the only one who didn't know they even existed?" I asked.

"A lot of Pulse conspiracy and underground networks have mentioned them," Dawson said. "But they're not mainstream. But yeah..." He slipped through the doorway into the foyer ahead of us. "All this time he was one of the good guys."

Laurel cleared her throat, and something about it chilled my veins.

"What?" I asked as I glanced at her.

"It's just..." She looked back and I did the same, but West still wasn't following. Regardless, she lowered her voice as we walked through the foyer. "I know the kinds of things he did as part of this job. None of that was an exaggeration. You don't hire a good guy to go undercover for someone like Ashford."

I sucked in a breath, my stomach twisting again.

She wasn't wrong. If you want someone to lie and betray, you don't send in a Boy Scout. You send someone with no moral qualms about getting the job done. And I was quite glad I hadn't accepted anything from the PTI—with any luck, this would be the end of my association with them. West...West intrigued me. But when he held that knife to my daughter, undercover or not, I couldn't be sure he wouldn't've used it if mission called for it.

And I had a problem with that.

We stepped outside the villa and down the front stairs. Emaleth continually tugged on my hand, being drawn back to me as she started toward damn near everything she saw. Em didn't see big houses like this as my brother and his boyfriend came to my place over the holidays—everything was new, interesting, and waiting to be explored.

It would be nice to offer that to her, but...not yet.

One of the cars was gone—probably Moti's. Laurel went toward an SUV and Dawson started for the passenger side.

"I'll give you a call when I land," he said with a bright smile.

It was too bad he was going home—*him*, I'd definitely keep around. Ah, hell, maybe Laurel too—she was still here, not even blinking at West's suggestion, so maybe the treasure hunting bug had bitten her somehow after all. I stepped off the bottom stair, let go of Em, and went straight over to give Dawson a hug. He returned it, squeezing me hard enough to break a rib and lifting me briefly off my feet, but I could only chuckle.

"We'll chat soon," I promised.

"You bet." He climbed in the passenger seat.

Laurel was about to head into the front when I threw my arms around her and gave her a hug as well. She let out a sudden awkward squeak, patted my back, and all but froze like she didn't know what to do.

Which of course just made me hug her a beat longer.

"Maybe vet future employers a little better next time," I suggested.

"Definitely. Try not to get arrested for a while." She popped open the door and slipped inside.

"No promises." I stepped back and watched the car speed off; beneath the sound was footsteps on the stairs and I wasn't surprised to see West there.

He paused on the bottom step, tracked the retreating car with his eyes, then looked at me. "I don't get a hug?"

For fuck's sake... "Em, go get in the car."

She did so without argument, even shutting the door so any conversation would be muffled on her end.

I stepped slowly toward him and he made me go the entire distance, not offering to make a single move toward me. Just a grin. The cat waiting to snatch up a mouse. I didn't know where the trap was or when I'd see it, but I was sure I'd be snapped in half eventually.

Though I climbed the bottom step to face him, I kept my hands in my pockets. "There's something that's been bothering me."

"Can't imagine what."

I chewed at the inside of my mouth. Scrutinizing the expression of a trained, professional liar was pretty much impossible. "The Pulse happened four years ago. But if you've been undercover for three...that means your organization is at least three years old. I've done a lot of committee work and I used to date a politician's son—government-like departments, councils, and committees do not form overnight, and do not gain *any* sort of organization in one year or less. Or even ten. Care to explain if there's some factor in this equation I'm missing since my math isn't adding up?"

He remained locked on my eyes and if any of this had made him nervous, he of course didn't show it. "The trouble, Olivia, is that you're assuming the Pulse four years ago was the first."

A chill crawled up my spine, my heart hammering wildly. Like the blinders were shifting, a new world was opening—one I tried desperately to clamp back down again, despite my natural curiosity, because I wasn't ready for all this.

And because I didn't think he'd tell me more about it anyway.

I bit back questions, closed the six inches between us, but still didn't remove my hands from my pockets for an embrace. Instead I leaned forward, on my toes, and pressed my lips to his jaw in a brief peck.

Just as he shifted to look down at me, I pulled back and stood flat on my heels again, my heart thudding like I'd run a marathon.

A moment of silence struck and wind stirred my loose hair, cutting strands across my face. "Goodbye, Mr. West."

Still, I couldn't read his expression. Nor did I bother trying. Instead I pulled my keys from my pocket and continued on to my car where Em waited.

"So is it going to be another no to dancing?" he called after me.

I pursed my lips, fighting a grin as I climbed in the car. "Not gonna happen, Buttons."

———— ◆ ————

AFTER DROPPING OFF THE TUITION check at the front desk, Emaleth and I rushed down the hall toward Miss Jennings' first grade class.

"I'll pick you up as usual." My heels clicked on the tile floor at a steady clip, Em's hand in mine. "After homework, maybe we can get pizza."

She said nothing, but the closer we got to the classroom door, the more she dragged her feet.

At last I paused a meter from the door where her teacher and classmates were in the middle of a lesson, spun, and knelt in front of her. "What is it?"

Her big eyes seemed lighter than usual, and fat tears brimmed around the edges. "I don't like school."

"No one likes school, baby girl."

"But they're *mean* to me." She nearly tipped into a wail and I winced.

"Who is? The other kids?"

She nodded.

This wasn't the time or place for this discussion, and I truly blamed myself—I'd kept her home for so long, of course she didn't want to go back. And the words were ready on my lips, the usual spiel about going in anyway, and putting up with it, and...

And it all rang hollow in my head—I couldn't say it. Because my daughter was genuinely upset and I didn't want to be one of those parents who patted her on the head and sent her on her way, pretending what she was feeling wasn't valid. She'd been through things. Bad things. Things a six-year-old shouldn't have to. And I wasn't going to stuff her feelings under the proverbial rug, like my father would've.

I pressed my knees down on the tile to steady myself as I knew I might be crouched there for a few minutes and took her shoulders in my hands. "Kids *are* mean, sweetheart. Kids always have been and always will be. They say bad things to hurt your feelings, and they make fun of others, and I know it sucks. Kids will be mean now, and they'll be mean when you're a teenager. And one day," I spared a glance at Miss Jennings, where I could see her standing at the front of the room talking, no smile passing her lips, "they'll grow up and be mean adults."

Her bottom lip was trembling now.

"*But*," I continued, "here's what I want you to remember: they're just trying their best. They have parents who weren't very nice to them, or ignored them, or didn't talk to them. They don't know how to *not* be mean. When they say horrible things, and act stupid, it's not because of you, it's because of them. And at the end of the day, their best isn't half as good as your worst.

"You're a Ferrari, baby. And those mean kids? They're not. They're not built for speed. They can't go as fast as you, can't make the same turns, and aren't flashy and awesome. It's not their fault you're smart and sensitive and fabulous—that you're going faster than them. So they'll try to slow you down, but no matter what—and no matter how badly you want to punch someone in the face—you have to remember you're better than that, and you can't let them get to you."

Her tears had stopped but she still sort of looked at me like I'd lost my mind. "A Ferrari?"

"Yep."

"Denny has a racing game with a Ferrari."

"So you know what I mean. You know how some of the cars don't go as fast while others do? That's you, babe. *You* are a motherfucking Ferrari." Her eyebrows damn near shot into her hairline, but some words are necessary for emphasis. "You are. Say it: *I* am a Ferrari."

Em took a breath. "*I* am a Ferrari."

"Good girl. And you don't slow down for anyone. Are you ready to head back out on the road now? Work hard, speed past those other cars?"

She nodded and when I opened my arms to her, she flew into them. I gave her a tight hug, enjoying it for a moment—for now, I could tell her she was awesome and she'd believe me. Eventually, she wouldn't. Eventually she'd be like every other little girl and have to find worth on her own. But for now I was Mommy, parent and deity in equal measure, and if I said she was a badass car, she'd believe me.

At last I let her go and stood. She gave me a nod and we walked up to the classroom door. This time I knocked as I was trying to set a good example.

Miss Jennings sharply turned our way, stared for a moment, then gestured for us to come in.

I took a breath, tried not to feel like *I* was the child in trouble, and then opened the door. A gentle nudge sent Em in ahead of me, knapsack thumping against her back. "Sorry we're late," I said. "I had to—"

Jennings gave me a dismissive wave. "It's fine." Immediately she looked away, focusing once more on the class.

Em gave me a sad look, then kept going.

I softly closed the door behind her, stepped back, but still watched. I should leave. She'd be fine, I knew. But my stomach twisted nervously and I couldn't walk away. Not until she was settled and looking okay with things.

Emaleth took her seat, second row, third from the window. Miss Jennings turned toward the blackboard, jotting down notes like it was high school lit and not the ABCs they should be learning.

A kid behind Em poked her back with her pencil.

Two little girls snickered. I clenched my hands into fists—what the hell was this shit? I glanced at Miss Jennings, but if she noticed, she didn't acknowledge the disturbance.

Again, the kid poked my daughter.

Em jumped and I strongly suspected the horrible brat used the pointed end of the pencil. My daughter turned back to glare at her and the girl made a face, saying something I had no doubt was snarky.

My protective instincts were overwhelming, suffocating as I stood there—how could her teacher *not* notice? These kids

SKYLA DAWN CAMERON

were in first grade, for Christ's sake. Beginning of the year. This shit should be nipped in the bud.

I was reaching out to knock again when Emaleth suddenly stood and spun, her face painted crimson.

"You will leave me alone because I'm a motherfucking Ferrari!" Her voice carried straight through the door to me.

Oh...fuck.

Miss Jennings slapped a yardstick across the desk and Em jumped, swung around, her eyes wide and face still red. I caught a sharp reprimand and mention of the principal's office.

This was bullshit. I opened the door before Em had taken one step.

"Ms. Talbot—"

I cut the teacher a look that silenced her on the spot. "Save it. Because you know what? This is a shit school, you're a shit teacher, and my kid is too good to be here. She's a motherfucking Ferrari! So you can bite me and my stripper ass." I snapped my fingers and glanced at Em. "Get your stuff. Now."

Emaleth didn't waste time and the sound of her collecting her book bag was the only noise in the otherwise silent classroom. Even Miss Jennings stared, shocked to silence.

I should've dropped the f-bomb during our last parent/teacher meeting.

Em scurried past me and I slammed the door behind her. My pace toward the front of the building was just shy of a sprint and she struggled to keep up.

Truthfully, I wanted to get out before they called security.

"You said bad words in front of the teacher," she said in a hushed voice.

"Yeah, well. You did it first."

We paused by the office, where the receptionist held a telephone receiver to her ear and looked at me like I'd turned into a *drakon.* I plucked the check off her desk where she hadn't filed it yet, tore it into eleventy-million pieces, then tossed it on her desk.

"Have a great motherfucking day," I called, and hoofed it straight outside with Em behind me.

I kind of felt like ice cream.

———— ♦ ————

EM MANAGED TO DRIP SOME of her chocolate sundae on her white school shirt, which meant I probably wasn't going to be able to sell it even secondhand to the poor parents like me who tried to send their kids to Norwood. Oh well. I'd let her tie-dye it and write "School Sux" or something on the back. She carried her sundae in one hand, Pru's with a lid on it in the other, and I had a banana split in a container myself. I took care of closing the car doors, and then letting us into the house when we got home.

"Pru, Pru, Pru!" Em shouted, skipping taking off her shoes to run into the living room where Prudence waited. "We brought ice cream!"

"Um..." drifted out. I kicked off my boots and followed, finding Pru sitting on the couch with her laptop and a frown. "What?"

"We staged a rebellion." I set my ice cream on the coffee table and slipped off my jacket. "I'm open to suggestions regarding one of your hippy schools, if you want."

Prudence blinked at me. Oh, I couldn't *wait* to give her this full story.

Em handed off the ice cream, stripped off her blazer, and sat in front of the coffee table to finish eating. "It was *awesome.*"

Pru shook her head. "Looking forward to hearing it. Did you get paid?"

"No." Plastic crackled as I pulled the lid off my ice cream. "West offered me a villa."

Em blinked at me. "What's a villa?"

I stuffed a scoop of banana and vanilla ice cream in my mouth and mumbled around it. "Eat your damn ice cream before I send you back to school."

"She also got *Date Face,*" Emaleth said in a conspiratorial whisper.

"West?" Pru guessed.

I shook my head and swallowed enough ice cream that I thought my brain was going to freeze. "Moss. Don't judge. I know he's..."

"You said McStalkerpants."

"Yeah, but...the thing I want you to realize..." I sighed dramatically. "He's really tall, Pru."

She grinned and poked her spoon around the ice cream. "You're terrible. By the way, Martin called."

"Again?" I groaned and stared longingly the approximately five thousand calories of ice cream I really felt like I earned and needed.

"He said it's urgent."

Ugh. Well... I glanced at the phone. I was in a mood. A pretty decent one, since I hadn't started panicking yet. Dumped the oppressive school, scored a date, was offered—and turned down—a goddamn villa. *Everything's coming up Livi.* "Fine. I'll call him."

I grabbed the phone and left the pair of them as Em tried to commandeer the television. Pru could handle her but would cave, I knew, because we both loved that little girl and enjoyed spoiling her. I carted the phone to my room where I could both change into comfy clothes and keep Em from hearing any *more* expletives, which tended to pop up when I talked to my brother.

His number was the last to call, so I cycled to it and hit dial. While it rang, I dug yoga pants and a T-shirt out, and started stripping out of my dress slacks.

"Hello?" Martin answered just as I was hopping on one foot, trying to get my pants off.

I lost my balance so plopped onto the end of the bed to finish. "You rang. I have a date with ice cream, though, so—"

"We need to talk."

"We *are* talking." I cast the pants behind, pinched the phone between my shoulder and ear, and reached for my yoga pants.

"I mean in person."

"Martin, the last time we spoke, you had me arrested—"

"This is serious—"

"And you have thirty seconds. Ice cream melts." I got my left foot into my pants, started with the right—

"Dad's dead."

I froze.

Silence ticked on, Martin's steady breathing on the other end, but I didn't really hear it—nothing was registering. The yoga pants dropped from my grip, crumpling on the floor.

"Livi?"

The phone was loose in my hands and I couldn't make my fingers work to hold onto it any tighter. I blinked at the dresser ahead of me and try as I may, I couldn't get my brain jumpstarted.

"Livi?" Martin repeated.

I still stared.

"Liv?"

ACKNOWLEDGEMENTS

———— ♦ ————

I'VE BEEN WORKING ON LIVI Talbot's adventures since 2012 and there are numerous people I'd like to thank.

First, to the early readers of this book, Melissa Hayden and Danielle Kendall—West's sister-wives—for their constant enthusiasm and support. They love these characters and this world like I do, and they encouraged me every step of the way.

Shelley Kinsman read and offered critiques on an early draft, not only strengthening the manuscript but giving me the confidence to publish it—I value her opinion tremendously, and she didn't hate the book so I knew it couldn't be that bad.

Lilith Saintcrow for blurbing the book and believing Livi (and me). There are insufficient words for how much her support has meant to me.

My platonic murder wife, Dina James, permitted me use of the Ferrari metaphor. I hope I did it justice and thank her again for telling me I was a Ferrari when I needed it. She is also "Dr. Dina", whom I run things by every time I do something horrible to my characters. When the zombie apocalypse comes, at least I might know how to stitch up a wound.

Agnes at the Church-key Pub (formerly The Stinking Rose) brought me nachos and drinks while I labored over this book for months—best place to write, hands-down, and best writer fuel.

My mum loved this book from the moment she read it three years ago, and I'm pleased to finally hand her a polished, published copy of it.

Aunt Judy also read a copy three years ago, and sent the print book back to me with a note about how much she enjoyed it, and how she was looking forward to *Odin's Spear*. It still hurts to think about how she never got to read the rest of Livi's adventures—every time I finish a zero draft of something, my first urge is to send it to her. I miss you, Aunt Judy.

Finally, many thanks to my Patrons of Snark. You have done so much for me with your monthly support. I hope you enjoy this book and the many more to come.

AUTHOR'S NOTE

———————◆———————

THANK YOU FOR PURCHASING AND reading *Solomon's Seal*.

Livi popped up in my head April 2012. The series I was currently writing, though I loved it, wasn't selling, and I wanted to try something a little more high concept. *Tomb Raider* meets *Gilmore Girls* seemed to fit the bill.

What I wasn't prepared for was the sheer amount of research it would take, nor how taxing it was mentally to write outside of my comfort zone. Add onto that the character of Dale West, who continually holds all the cards and doesn't tell me what's going on until the very end, and it seems to take me at least a year to write and polish each book. But I love them—the characters are among my favorites, and some days a writer just needs to settle into a world with a heroine who would jump in a dragon's mouth.

Besides the character of Livi, who is near and dear to my heart, two others mean a great deal to me.

Her best friend Pru came about, first, because I was tired of seeing urban fantasy heroines with no female friends (which I am guilty of writing as well)—I wanted a book where women are friends, not rivals, and create their own family. Second, Pru exists because I wanted to see a disabled character in an urban fantasy novel who a. didn't magically get better, and b. wasn't given super human abilities because of it. Multiple sclerosis is a terrible, scary disorder that my very close friend battles every day, and I frequently participate in the MS Walk to raise money for research. If you have some extra pennies, please consider donating them to your local Multiple Sclerosis Society. Although Pru has the same disorder as my friend, she is in absolutely no way based on her (she is, in fact, the opposite of my friend). As the books progress, her disease will progress, though I'm hoping together we will find a real world cure that I can steal for fiction before long.

And then, of course...there is West.

Before I started writing him, I knew next to nothing about North Korea. I didn't even know he was *from* the north until halfway through the book when he whispered it in my ear. Suddenly he made a lot more sense, particularly the more I read about the country.

There are a handful of books translated into English written by North Korean defectors who survived the "labour camps" and their horrendous conditions. NK uses an archaic "three generations" rule, meaning if you're caught trying to escape, speaking against the government, or any number of "offences", you and up to three generations of your family will be shipped off to the camp. Children born in the camp remain there, often worked to death and severely abused. West came from a camp for irredeemables, where he was born and would've died had he not escaped, considered part of the *joktae kyechung* or "hostile" caste. I've written a novella prequel partially from his POV as well as some of *Solomon's Seal*, and both gave me nightmares just learning all he went through. He's always present in my head much the way the character of Zara Lain (from *Demons of Oblivion*) is.

In the west, we've turned North Korea into a joke, laughing at the eccentricities of the country's leaders without fully acknowledging the horror the average citizen goes through. I encourage readers to expand their understanding of what the people endure there by looking into some of the biographies of defectors. There are a couple of organizations out there working to resettle NK refugees who are always in need of help.

So here's the sitch with the Livi Talbot series: I know the arcs of each book and I'm gonna need ten of them to tell this complete story. That's a lot of books, and several of them have cliffhangers, and a lot of things can happen between books one and ten. I have been through cancelling two series now (*River Wolfe* and *Demons of Oblivion*) due to low sales and illegal distribution. Since becoming chronically ill, my stress level dictates what I do and do not publish, so I'm committing to publishing two sequels to *Solomon's Seal*, no matter what, to see how they do.

"How they do" is fairly subjective. I don't have a sales threshold, it's more a question of, "Do people like these books?" and "Are they paying for them or stealing them?" I can't afford to keep up a series that isn't selling enough for me to pay at least some of my bills. There are so many exciting things coming up in this series (I am dying for people to read the fourth, *Shiva's Bow*), so I'm hopeful it'll run for a while.

Again, thank you for reading. If urban fantasy is your thing and you haven't checked it out yet, the five-book *Demons of Oblivion* series is now complete, and I have YA paranormal books beginning with *River*.

Look for Livi Talbot's adventures to continue with *Odin's Spear*, tentatively scheduled for first quarter 2017, and hopefully *Zheng's Tomb* later in the year!

ABOUT THE AUTHOR

Skyla Dawn Cameron has been writing approximately forever.

Her early storytelling days were spent acting out strange horror/fairy tales with the help of her many dolls, and little has changed except that she now keeps those stories on paper.

Skyla is a fifth generation crazy cat lady who lives in southern Ontario, where she writes full time, works as a freelance designer, stabs people with double pointed knitting needles, is an avid gamer, and watches Buffy reruns. If she ever becomes a grownup, she wants to run her own Irish pub, as well as become world dictator.

You can dip into some madness online by visiting her website at **www.skyladawncameron.com** to sign up for her newsletter, see what she's working on, and drop her an email. When she's not writing or being glared at by cats, she's probably on Twitter. You should ping **@skyladawn** and tell her to get back to work.

To support her work directly and get sneak peeks at upcoming books as well as exclusive content, please visit **www.patreon.com/skyladawncameron**.

ODIN'S SPEAR

A LIVI TALBOT NOVEL

ALL'S FAIR IN SIBLING RIVALRY AND WAR.

After nearly losing her family and her life, Olivia Talbot is trying to leave the world of supernatural artifact hunting behind. But an adrenaline junkie unsuited for a 9 to 5 job can't hide herself forever, especially when deadly operative Dale West comes knocking with off-book work for his covert organization.

It'll be "easy", West says—just a trip to the museum. But a deranged former solider is seeking to reunite the pieces of Gungnir—spear of the Norse god Odin—which is capable of starting war, and this job is much bigger than anyone has let on.

Followed by the dogged son of a tabloid mogul, competing with her archeologist older brother, and still struggling to trust West against her better judgement, Livi will venture into an ancient underwater city in the Mediterranean to stop the dawn of a new war. But the spear of a god has plans for them all, and power not even she might be able to withstand.

Made in the USA
Las Vegas, NV
11 February 2022

43712775R00204